THE WAY TO A MAN'S HEART

MARY ELLIS

HARVEST HOUSE PUBLISHERS

EUGENE, OREGON

Cover photos © and design by Garborg Design Works, Savage, Minnesota

This is a work of fiction. Names, characters, places, and incidents are products of the author's imagination or are used fictitiously. Any resemblance to actual persons, living or dead, or to events or locales, is entirely coincidental.

THE WAY TO A MAN'S HEART
Copyright © 2010 by Mary Ellis
Published by Harvest House Publishers
Eugene, Oregon 97402
www.harvesthousepublishers.com

Library of Congress Cataloging-in-Publication Data

Ellis, Mary
The way to a man's heart / Mary Ellis.
    p. cm.—(The Miller Family series ; bk. 3)
ISBN 978-0-7369-2734-5 (pbk.)
1. Amish—Fiction. 2. Holmes County (Ohio)—Fiction. I. Title.
PS3626.E36W38 2010
813'.6—dc22

                                                    2009053684

Printed in the United States of America

10 11 12 13 14 15 16 17 18 / RDM-NI / 10 9 8 7 6 5 4 3

Acknowledgments

Thanks to Carol Lee and Owen Shevlin, who welcomed me into their home and opened doors for me in the Amish community.

A special thank-you to Roseanne, Joanna, Kathryn, and Esther, members of the Old Older Amish community, for their delicious recipes and allowing me to sample their handiwork.

Thanks also to Rosa and Kim Blake for answering plenty of questions about horses.

Thanks to my wonderful agent, Mary Sue Seymour, who had faith in me from the beginning, and to my lovely proofreader, Mrs. Joycelyn Sullivan.

Finally, thanks to my editor, Kim Moore, and the wonderful staff at Harvest House Publishers.

And thanks be to God—all things in this world are by His hand.

ONE

April

As Leah untied the gelding and climbed into the buggy, she caught the heady scent of honeysuckle—her favorite flower and one of the few that didn't cause a fit of sneezing. She inhaled deeply to savor the fragrance of the perfect spring day. The cloudless blue sky, plenty of sunshine, and not even a trace of humidity added to her good mood. Eighteen-year-old Leah Miller was a successful business-woman—people came from all around the county to buy her pies. They could purchase a slice in the basement cafeteria of the auction barn or a whole pie in the ground floor grocery store.

For the past four years she had tweaked her recipes until every one of them was a crowd-pleaser. The cafeteria manager had her baking popu-lar standbys such as Dutch Apple, peach, and coconut cream while still inventing new concoctions to try out on the clientele. Maybe the red current pie and the pineapple cream didn't exactly have folk begging for seconds, but Leah knew she had found her calling in life. Her sis-ter, Emma, and Aunt Hannah had their smelly, wool-producing sheep, and *mamm* enjoyed sewing on her good days, but Leah's place was in the kitchen. Ten bushels of beets to blanch and can, along with twenty baskets of apples to peel, core, and mince into applesauce? No problem. She would make short work of the task, no matter how large.

And the farther she stayed away from dander-ridden critters or pollen-laden meadows the better. Now that her mother took new medications for her arthritis, the two of them could handle the household tasks—which was a good thing, as Emma had married James more than two years ago and moved to his family's farm in Charm.

With her love of baking and the drive to succeed, it hadn't taken long for Leah to replace her coffee can of cash with an account at the bank. With her own savings passbook, commercial-grade baking pans, and a reputation for the best-tasting pies in the Mount Hope auction barn, life was good. It was so satisfying she often had to remind herself not to grow too proud or bigheaded.

As Leah left the cafeteria with her payment tucked in her purse, she noticed that a "road closed" detour sign had been put up on the route she usually took home. The highway patrol often closed stretches of road when oversized farming machinery was being moved to new locations. But with weather as nice as this, she didn't even lift an eyebrow. Slapping the reins against the horse's back, she turned down the township road running diagonally from town that would eventually take her the roundabout way home. Leah was mentally listing the chores she needed to do before supper when the sound of heavy construction grabbed her attention.

"Whoa," she called to Jack. As she focused on the commotion she began to cough and sneeze. Bulldozers had raised a thick cloud of dust in a partially paved parking lot. Backhoes were loading debris into dump trucks, while workers in hard hats scurried around picking up tools and loading sawhorses into pickups. They appeared to have finished for the day and were cleaning up the site.

"The old train cars," she murmured to the family buggy horse. The gelding picked up his ears but offered no comment. Leah was also struck speechless. She stared at the once ramshackle passenger car and rusty caboose she'd admired nearly four years ago. Leah had entertained such lofty dreams back then but had soon forgotten her impractical notions. She had been so busy with household chores and pie baking that she'd forgotten about the abandoned train cars at the edge of town.

But someone else had recognized potential among the knee-high weeds and broken bottles. A person with vision—and deep pockets—had turned the rundown relic into a vision of bright enamel paint, new wooden shutters, and flower boxes of red geraniums and white petunias. The window glass had been replaced and lacy curtains fluttered in the breeze. A trellis of climbing morning glories flanked the entryway, while a neon-lit sign proclaimed the obvious: Diner.

It was as though they had read my mind...but I certainly would've picked a more imaginative name.

A snort from Jack broke her concentration. He wanted the bucket of oats waiting at home, but Leah needed to see more of the work in progress. She parked at the edge of the property and tied the reins to a fencepost. As she stared at the restaurant, anticipation coursed through her veins as if the establishment were hers. After the last workers left the lot, honking horns and hollering goodbyes, Leah inched closer until she stood in front of the shiny front door. Unfortunately, the train cars had been elevated with concrete piers, making peeking into windows impossible.

She noticed only two vehicles remained in the parking lot as she crept around to the back of the train. No fancy shutters or pretty flowers decorated this side, but a large shipping container had been left underneath one window. Without a moment's hesitation, Leah climbed onto the crate and peered into the passenger car, willing herself not to sneeze from the dust.

Two women in long pastel dresses and small white prayer *kapps* stood facing each other. Leah knew from their style of dress that they were Mennonite. Both looked to be in their early thirties and neither woman was smiling.

"No, April," said the taller of the two. "I told you yesterday I couldn't stay late today. Paul wants his supper on time for a change, and I won't have him watching the kids after school. That's my job." She lifted her chin defiantly.

"But, May, we're supposed to open in three days. I can't unpack and wash everything by myself. I still need to write up my food order and start shopping. How can I bring supplies into such chaos?" Her hand gestured at the overflowing boxes of dishes and glassware on the floor. Desperation to the point of hysteria edged her words. "You promised to help me when I signed the lease."

May released a sigh commensurate with bearing the weight of the world. "I have helped you every single day but the Lord's day. My house is a mess, the laundry sits in piles, I still don't have all my garden seeds planted, and Paul is tired of his dinner being late."

"Paul's tired?" April wailed. "I haven't slept more than four hours a night since the remodeling began. My vegetable patch is still buried beneath a groundcover of weeds and last year's leaves. And my husband barely speaks to me." Her voice rose as shrill as a hawk's cry.

Leah knew better than to eavesdrop on their argument, but if she climbed down now she might be discovered. The women had moved closer to the open window as they faced off like circling barnyard roosters. She tried not to breathe deeply as dust settled in the parking lot.

"This was your bright idea, not mine!" May snapped. "I said I would lend a hand and I have, but I made no lifetime commitment to your pipe dream. I doubt very much that Amish and Mennonite people will be flocking here in droves. Most folk pack a cooler when they come to town on business to save money. And if you price your menu too cheaply, you'll lose every cent of the money Dad loaned for start-up capital."

The shorter woman crossed her arms over her wrinkled dress. "Then I would think you'd be more willing to protect his investment."

"I have painted and caulked, scraped and sanded. I've sewn curtains and donated hours of my time. I helped you lift and carry in those heavy booths till my back nearly broke. And I've encouraged you, April, despite my opinion you were biting off more than you could chew." A hint of sympathy crept into her voice.

Time seemed to suspend as Leah felt a wave of heat radiating from the diner's interior.

"I know you have and I am truly grateful. If I live to be a hundred years old, I'll still be in your debt, but can't you stay a few more weeks till I'm up and running? Maybe until the word spreads that I'm open for business?" April placed a tentative hand on her sister's arm.

Even Leah, knowing nothing about these women beyond this conversation, knew asking for a few more "weeks" was a bad idea.

Any compassion in May's face drained away. As though plucking a piece of lint from her skirt, she removed April's hand. "You will never change, not as long as people keep enabling you. I will stay a couple more days to help you open, but that's it. After that, you'll not get another minute of my time. You must sink or swim on your own. And if you go belly-up, maybe Dad will stop bankrolling your hair-brained schemes and throwing away his money." She looked as though she might say more, but at that moment Leah's luck ran out.

Without warning the slat-board packing crate gave way with a splintering crash. Leah tried to grab the windowsill but she toppled backward, landing on her backside in the weeds without an ounce of dignity.

"Oh, great." May's voice carried through the open window. "Sounds like a family of rats has moved in before your first customer arrives. I'm going home!" The sound of her words faded until the front door slammed with finality.

As Leah clumsily rose to her feet and brushed off her clothes, she heard a squeaky screen being raised above her head. "Are you okay? What are you doing out there?" A woman's head appeared in the opening.

Two honest, direct questions, yet Leah was stymied. "Ah, well," she stammered and then opted for the truth. "I spotted this rundown train years ago and noticed something going on today. I was curious so I decided to peek inside, not knowing anybody was still here." She shook the remaining dead leaves from her skirt. "I thought everyone had gone home. I'm sorry. I didn't mean to spy on you." Shame brought a rush of color into her face.

The woman's perplexed expression changed into a grin. "No harm done. My sister and I argue all the time. Business as usual. Come inside and have a look. See if you like what I've done." She glanced down at the broken crate. "Only don't trip over anything. I'm not insured yet." She lowered the screen and closed the window.

Leah had no choice but to walk around the train, feeling sheepish.

In a moment the front door was flung open. "Come in. Don't be shy. I'm April Lambright and this is my diner. Well, it's mine along with the bank and my landlord, but the business is all mine." Her dazzling smile turned her rather plain features pretty.

Leah stepped inside to cluttered disarray. Booths had been installed, but only half the tables had been set on their pedestals. Boxes, crates, and shopping bags were everywhere, while the light fixtures hung at odd angles on their electrical cords. An eight-burner commercial stove blocked the doorway to the caboose. Piles of construction debris made walking anywhere hazardous. But Leah Miller fell in love with the place. A new terra-cotta tile floor had been installed, the walls were painted sunny yellow, and an old-fashioned counter lined one side of the train car with bright red upholstered stools. When the restoration was complete, it would look modern and yet nostalgic at the same time.

"Oh, my goodness," she whispered in awe.

"Is that a good 'oh, my goodness' or a bad?" April asked, studying her curiously. "And do you have a name, young lady?"

Leah snapped back from her perusal. "Definitely a good, ma'am. And I'm Leah Miller from Winesburg. Pleased to meet you."

"Since I spotted your buggy parked outside, I didn't suppose you were from Cincinnati." She laughed with good humor. "Are you Old Order?"

Leah felt her cheeks flush. *"Jah,* I'm Old Order. My *daed* is a deacon in our district." She bent down to stack some spilled canned goods. "I always thought this place would make a great restaurant. When I was fourteen, I wanted to buy it myself." She met April's gaze, waiting to be laughed at. That was the reaction she'd usually received.

However, the woman merely nodded. "Do you like to cook? And bake? Most Amish gals do. I'm Mennonite if you haven't figured that out. And that woman who stormed out of here is my sister May."

"I love cooking! I bake most of the pies and pastries for the cafeteria in Mount Hope. They order at least a dozen every week." Leah hoped that didn't sound too prideful, but it was the truth.

April's eyes grew round as saucers. *"You* bake those pies? Even the Chocolate Mousse Cream and the Dutch Apple-Walnut?" She stared at Leah as though waiting for a denial.

"Yes, ma'am. I made up both of those recipes. Have you tried them?"

"Many times, and my skirts fit tighter because of you, but stop calling me ma'am. I'm April. Ma'am makes me feel ancient, and I'm only twenty-eight. How old are you, Leah Miller?"

"Eighteen," she answered as a dozen ideas darted through her head like minnows in a shallow stream. Even though the interior of the diner was growing oppressively hot and her scalp itched beneath her *kapp,* Leah stared at the restaurant owner with fascination.

April seemed to be pondering a conundrum because her forehead scrunched into creases and folds. "As you probably overheard, May has been my reluctant assistant, and she's putting in her resignation after opening day." She shook her head sorrowfully. "Can't say I blame her. If I had known how much work and how expensive it would be to turn this dump into a diner, I never would have signed the lease and borrowed so much money. She's right—I bit off more than I can chew." She lowered herself to a step stool and cradled her chin with her hands. "I can't get this place shipshape by myself, and I already paid for a newspaper ad advertising my grand opening."

Leah spoke without hesitation. "I would be happy to help you set things up until you can find a replacement. I'll check with my mother, but I'm sure she can spare me for a few days."

April jumped to her feet. "That is wonderful! But what about you?"

"What about me?"

"Why don't I hire you to replace my sister? I know lots of Amish girls work before they get married. Believe me, May's pies can't hold a candle to yours." She blushed and then said, "But please don't ever repeat that."

"Hire me to do what? Clean up the place at closing time?" Leah thought she might faint on the spot.

Maybe because of the train's stuffy interior or all the dusty boxes, but Leah suddenly felt dizzy and lightheaded. The room began to tilt to the left. "April, could we step outside? It's hard to breathe with the windows closed."

"Of course. You look white as snow." April grabbed Leah's arm and led her down the steps.

Outside, Leah inhaled and exhaled several deep breaths. "Oh, that's better."

"I'd like to hire you as my assistant," April continued. "To do whatever needs doing—cooking, manning the lunch counter, and cleaning up when we're done. We would split duties down the middle." Her smile was so wide it revealed a gold-capped back molar.

In the fresh air and sunshine, Leah's head cleared as her excitement grew with leaps and bounds. "*Jah,* I'd love to work here very much! It would be my dream come true, but I can't accept the offer until I talk to my parents."

The owner shrugged. "No problem. If you decide to join me, let me know either tomorrow or the day after. Then we can set up a schedule for you."

"I won't work on the Sabbath," Leah said.

"Of course not. We're closed on Sundays."

"And no Mondays, because my *mamm* can't manage the laundry without me because of her arthritis."

"We'll be closed that day too, since not many people come to town on Mondays. Anyway, I have my own chores at home with a husband and kids to look after." April rocked back on her heels, deep in thought. "How about you work Wednesdays through Saturdays here at the diner? Then you'll be off on Sunday and Monday. I can manage Tuesdays here by myself—all the action is in Farmerstown at the livestock sale. On Tuesdays, I'll pay you to stay home baking the bread, pies, cakes, and cookies we'll need for the week. We will open at seven for breakfast and close after lunch—no supper. Our people usually start for home by three o'clock, and the *Englischers* can eat at the big tourist spot up the road."

Leah felt as though she might levitate off the floor. Impetuously, she threw her arms around April and squeezed, not considering proper boss/employee behavior. "*Danki,* that sounds perfect! I'll be back as soon as my parents give their permission." She released the hug.

April patted Leah's shoulder, laughing. "My, goodness. You're certainly more enthusiastic than my sister has been."

"April and May? What happened to June?" Leah asked.

"She lives in Baltic with her husband and five children. We have a brother named August too. We assume Mom spent too much time staring at the wall calendar while carrying us."

Leah wrapped her arms around herself. She knew she was going to like this woman. "We don't have a phone, so if it's all right with you, I'll just show up if they say I can." She took a step backward, eager to be on her way home.

April offered her hand to shake. "Just showing up sounds fine with me, Leah. I still remember that slice of Dutch Apple-Walnut pie I tasted, and that must have been more than a year ago. I'm glad you were nosy enough to peek in my window. Today is my lucky day."

Blushing, Leah shook the outstretched hand and murmured a

quick goodbye. She ran to her buggy and almost broke the reins trying to get them off the post. She couldn't wait to put the task of asking her parents behind her.

It was a good thing Jack knew all possible routes home because Leah's mind was already swimming with favorite recipes, lists of ingredients, and how to approach her father with the opportunity of a lifetime.

~

Matthew Miller thought there was nothing quite like the first warm day in April, with sunshine so bright it hurt your eyes, a cool breeze tickling the back of your neck, and birds singing from the treetops to bring music to your ears. Clover in the pasture was coming up thick and green for his favorite friends. Black flies would soon hatch to annoy man and beast alike, but today there wasn't a single thing to swat at. Matthew could certainly get used to days like these after the overcast skies of March. His teacher had once read a poem to the class about spring, but never being much of a bookworm he'd forgotten all but the pleasant memory. At nineteen, Matthew was living exactly the life he had planned.

His sixteen-year-old *bruder,* Henry, had finished school and possessed few aspirations other than farming. Henry loved to plow and disk even the hardest soil. He would plant seeds during downpours, round up cattle in a blizzard, and could pick sweet corn until his fingers seemed worn down to the knuckles. After chores he would curl up in the hammock with a glass of cider and a book about pirates or Civil War generals whenever Pa wasn't looking. That boy loved to read.

Matthew's vocation and great joy in life was four-legged and bushy-tailed, with long dark eyelashes and grass-stained teeth. From miniature ponies to Belgian draft horses, he loved anything equine. He'd once seen Clydesdales in a TV beer commercial at the home of their

English neighbors. He had been so mesmerized that Mr. Lee copied the commercial into a black machine, and Matthew had watched it over and over that summer as he helped Mr. Lee paint his house.

Now he didn't have to sneak around watching somebody's TV to see all the different breeds. His job at Macintosh Farms gave him access to the Arabians, saddlebreds, and Tennessee walkers of rich *Englischers*. He worked with racing quarter horses; Kentucky-born thoroughbreds; and standardbreds, the harness-racing trotters. Amish folk often bought this breed for their buggies once their racetrack days were finished. Four years ago Mr. Macintosh had hired Matthew on the spot after a short demonstration of his handling and bareback riding. Mr. Mac said he had the "gift"—an ability to get inside a horse's head and get it to do your bidding without breaking its spirit. Matthew didn't know much about that. He just knew the day he was promoted from exercise boy to assistant trainer had been the happiest day of his life.

And it would likely remain his happiest day forever because he couldn't seem to summon enough courage to take Martha Hostetler home from a Sunday singing. His big sister said if he weren't careful he would end up an old man with females named Quicksilver, Quiche, and Juniper for his sole company. Emma was probably right, but what girl would want to court someone with freckles and spiky red hair?

At least he now did more important things at work than muck out stalls, clean water troughs, and measure grain into feed buckets. He trained horses on the lunge rope, exercised some around the track, and assisted with foalings. It was such joy to watch God's hand at work. So wobbly and weak at birth, the colt would quickly gain a thousand pounds of strength and energy within the first two years. He used to fantasize about becoming a jockey and riding a thoroughbred in a real, all-out race. But because he weighed one hundred seventy pounds, some owners didn't want him astride even for training.

"Hey, Matty!" A voice pierced his reverie. "Stop daydreaming and give me a hand."

"I'll finish filling the stanchions and be right there," Matthew called to Jeff Andrews, the trainer he apprenticed under.

At least the guy no longer referred to him as "Amish Boy." It had been a long road to earn his respect. Andrews had few friends at Macintosh Farms but many admirers. He knew his stuff. But when Matthew changed a few balky riding horses into mounts tame enough for kids, Andrews had dropped the moniker and started calling him Matty. *Now if he would just stop knocking my hat off,* Matthew thought as he worked.

Such behavior only happened when Mr. Mac wasn't nearby. The stable owner respected Amish people and tolerated no foul language, beer drinking, or rowdy behavior anywhere on his property. Jeff Andrews was slowly coming around, so Matthew secured the gate behind him and hurried to catch up. The trainer had headed into the quarter horse barn, one of his special places.

"What should I do?" he asked when he reached Andrews' side.

"The couple that owns the yearling in stall twelve is driving up from Columbus tomorrow to see how things are progressing." Jeff spoke softly and not with his usual loud bluster. "Things are going right fine, but that colt might have pulled a muscle yesterday in the ring. Nothing to worry about, but I don't want them getting upset." He lifted the latch and they entered the stall. The yearling picked up his head to study them. "The guy's wife is a bit high-strung. You know how women can get worked up over even a fly bite."

Matthew nodded his head in agreement. "*Jah,* my sister Emma is like that. She wants to call the vet each time one of her sheep has a runny nose."

Jeff met his eye. "And your family lets her? That can get mighty expensive." He gently scratched the colt behind his ears to settle him down.

"Nah, my pa sends for Aunt Hannah, who comes over with a stack of sheep books. They'll keep reading until they figure out what's wrong and how to fix it. We almost never need to call Dr. Longo."

Jeff nodded sagely. "Always best not to get too emotional. I like horses plenty, but this is business. I imagine it's the same way with sheep and cows." The colt licked the trainer's hand. His pink tongue looked comically too large for his mouth. "Women become attached. They want to treat every critter like a new puppy."

"That's for sure." Matthew said, but in reality, other than Emma with her sheep, he knew little about females with animals. His *mamm* and younger sister stayed as far away from them as possible. Leah's eyes grew puffy and her nose plugged up if she even walked into the barn.

"Okay, now. You keep rubbing his ears to keep him quiet. I want to tape up these forelegs to make sure he ain't limping when those Columbus people get here. That and a good night's sleep will make him good as new."

Matthew readily obliged. This quarter horse was one of his favorites. He'd just started learning about bloodlines, but this colt's ancestry must be impressive judging by his characteristics. While he stroked the neck, the trainer wrapped the legs—not too tight to impede circulation, and not too loose to be easily shaken off.

"There, that oughta do it." Jeff stood and brushed wood shavings off his palms. "Thanks for your help, boy." He offered Matt a rare smile and slapped him on the shoulder. "Why don't you go find Mr. Mac and tell him we're ready for the owners' visit?"

"Sure thing." Matthew closed the stall door behind him and strode toward the front entrance of the long barn. He'd almost reached the doorway when he remembered the new leather gloves he'd set on the ledge. His *daed* always warned he would never save money if he didn't stop losing things. Turning around, he walked back to the stall quietly, hoping Jeff wouldn't witness his forgetfulness. *No sense giving him something else to tease about now that we're starting to get along.*

As Matthew picked up his gloves, he spotted Andrews down on

his knees beside the colt. He was murmuring gentle words to keep the horse calm. Why hadn't Jeff finished his ministrations while he was there to help? With growing unease, Matthew watched the trainer pull a hypodermic needle from his pocket, remove the cap, and inject a syringe of fluid into the colt's flank.

Andrews wasn't supposed to administer medications. He wasn't a vet or even a licensed technician. Rich folk tended to be nervous about their animals just like that Columbus wife. With an odd feeling, Matthew crept back from the stall until he could turn around and then he hurried from the barn. He went looking for Mr. Macintosh as his uneasy feeling swelled into something downright troubling.

～

Julia knew something was up the moment she spotted their buggy racing up the lane. Leah never drove fast; she didn't trust horses enough to let them go faster than a trot. Drying her hands on a towel, Julia hurried onto the porch with a mother's growing anxiety whenever something wasn't normal with a *kinner*.

"Whoa!" Leah hollered. Driveway stones scattered in all directions.

Simon walked out of the barn, frowning at the gravel displaced into the lawn. "What's the big hurry, daughter? You hear about Mason jars on sale over in Walnut Creek?" He grabbed hold of Jack's bridle as Leah jumped down from the buggy.

"Better than that, *daed!*" she exclaimed. "Wait until you hear."

Even from the porch Julia could see that Leah's cheeks were flushed with excitement. This was the daughter who seldom worked herself up about anything, unlike Emma, who could be laughing one minute and sobbing the next.

"Henry!" Simon bellowed. "Come rub down this horse and then turn him out in the pasture. Your *schwestern* has news that apparently can't wait till supper."

Henry appeared with his usual calm demeanor, took the reins, and began releasing the horse from the traces. He offered his older sister only a casual glance.

Leah marched toward the house. "*Mamm*! I'm so glad you're home. I have great news to tell."

"Where else would I be?" Julia asked, lowering herself onto the porch swing. "It's practically suppertime." She patted the seat beside her.

"I'm too excited to sit," Leah said, shaking her head. "Hurry, *daed*!"

Simon stared at her as he lumbered up the steps, breathing heavily. "Were you stung by a hornet? What's the matter with you?"

"No hornet bites today. Remember that old train car on the railroad siding at the edge of town? Emma and I saw it years ago. This Mennonite lady—her name's April—tried my apple pie once and said she'd never tasted better. She's opening up a diner mainly for Plain folk, but her sister doesn't have time to help and so she quit. April let me inside to take a look around. It's beautiful." Leah finally paused to take a breath as she paced from one end of the porch to the other.

Julia and Simon stared at their child in utter confusion. She was looking back at them as though all this should make perfect sense.

Leah slapped her forehead. "I left out the most important part— she offered *me* a job! She wants me to take her sister's place." It would be impossible for her to look happier.

Her parents remained silent.

"That is, if you say it's all right," she added quickly. "It would only be four days a week. Well, five, but only four days away from home." Apprehension began to replace enthusiasm as her news failed to generate the anticipated reaction.

"Sit down, Leah," Julia demanded. "Stop prancing around and tell us the whole story from the beginning."

"Oh, boy, what are we in for now?" Simon muttered, lowering himself to the steps.

Leah complied, and after two deep breaths she gave her parents a full account of her trip to Mount Hope to deliver pies. When she had finished, covering every possible objection with a practical solution, Julia and Simon had no choice but to give her their blessing.

After all, how much trouble could a girl get into four mornings a week in a small town like Winesburg?

Two

The new diner in town did not open in three days as the newspaper advertisement promised or in four or even five. But it wasn't from lack of trying. April and her first employee had showed up the very next day bright eyed and eager, and later returned to their homes weary but undaunted. The two women scrubbed and unpacked and organized. They prepared endless lists and printed menus by hand on colorful poster board. And they shopped for meat at the local butcher's, fresh produce at farmers' markets, and paper products from the dollar store. Leah was amazed how much you had to buy just to prepare simple dishes for regular folk. When every square inch of storage space had been filled with staples, condiments, and canned goods, April ordered a storage barn to be delivered to the back lot. They hung fruits and vegetables from the ceiling in wicker baskets on spring-loaded pulleys. The cooking caboose was crowded but cheery due to a large skylight installed during the remodeling.

They filled new salt and pepper shakers, pump-type catsup bottles, and chrome napkin holders. They lined up varieties of bottled juice and soft drinks on the narrow shelf near the ceiling so they could merely point instead of reciting the list of options dozens of times per day. By the Sabbath, they were tired but ready. Leah was grateful it wasn't a preaching Sunday, and her *mamm* let her sleep an extra hour before she needed to come down to fix breakfast.

Julia wasn't quite as agreeable come Tuesday morning—Leah's assigned baking day. Because April had forgotten to advance Leah a stipend for supplies, she was forced to raid the household pantry for sugar, flour, and eggs. But instead of depleting their stock of home-canned fruit, Leah took the buggy to Wilmot, where an *Englischer* sold produce from the back of his panel truck. She bought every quart of strawberries he had hauled up from Florida. They were firm and sweet, probably because the first fruit of the season always tasted the best. Ohio strawberries wouldn't be ready for another four weeks.

When Leah arrived early Wednesday morning with several straw-berry pies, muffins, and enough sliced and sugared berries to spoon over shortcake and French toast, April clapped her hands with delight.

"Goodness, Leah. We'll have the first strawberry festival in Ohio and beat the rush. I'm going to cut a giant strawberry out of red poster board and attach it to our 'Open for Business' sign down by the road." She flicked the switch and the giant word "Diner" sprang to life in glowing neon.

Leah grinned the entire time she cut the first pie into eight uni-form servings and whipped up a batch of egg salad. Her spirits contin-ued to soar despite the fact the breakfast hour came and went without a single customer.

April stayed busy too, labeling the contents of every package in the chest freezer while whistling an odd tune. "Don't mind me. I always whistle whenever I get nervous. Can't help myself." She glanced at Leah. "What'll we do if nobody shows up and all those pretty ber-ries turn to mush?"

Leah pulled back the lace window curtain. "You can stop whis-tling. Our first customer just pulled in."

The two restaurateurs fussed over the elderly English farmer, despite the fact he only ordered a cup of coffee and knocked dirt off his boots onto their new doormat. He had as much caked mud on his boots as was on his truck's wheel flaps.

"What happened last week?" he barked after his first sip of coffee. "I know folk stopped by to git some lunch and it was locked up tighter than a drum." His eyes were ringed with deep, permanent squint lines.

"I sort of bit off more than I could chew." The dimple in April's left cheek deepened.

The farmer laughed. "Done that myself a time or two. Maybe I'll try a slice of that pie. Is it any good?"

Leah refilled his coffee cup. "I don't know if it is or not. I haven't sampled this batch yet," she said shyly.

April nudged her over as she placed the pie in front of him. "It's fabulous. She's the one who baked it, but she's too modest to say so."

Leah hid in the kitchen dicing celery and onions until their customer finished eating, paid the check, and left a dollar tip. There was no way could she watch him eat, even though she'd been cooking for her family since she was twelve years old.

"He bought two slices!" April exclaimed as soon as he left. "He told me he'd never tasted any better!"

"Maybe he's never eaten strawberry pie before," Leah said, feeling a swell of pride.

"And maybe you're the best cook in the county and the best thing that ever happened to me!" April grabbed both of Leah's hands and started jumping up and down like a child. Leah had never seen a Plain, God-fearing woman behave like that, but before long she was bobbing and swaying too...just to be polite. Their foolishness was short lived, however. Soon the bell over the front door jangled and two women with their grandchildren came in hungry for hamburgers. Leah set down menus and glasses of water. After a quick scan, one woman asked, "Don't you have French fries?" Her tone sounded as though they lacked a roof overhead.

Leah felt herself start to perspire. "Let me get the owner, ma'am," she murmured and fled like a scared rabbit.

April appeared carrying a complimentary bowl of bread-and-butter pickles and radish rosettes. She had overheard the exchange. "Trust me, ladies, once you taste my homemade potato salad and my grilled, not fried, burgers served with sliced beefsteak tomatoes, you'll forget all about fast-food standbys." She smiled gloriously. "My caboose kitchen is too small to do any deep frying. Everything in the place would smell like grease within a few days. Besides, cold salads are healthier and more refreshing now that the warm weather is here."

Both ladies nodded with approval and accepted April's suggestions for their order. Afterward, they not only bought a dozen muffins to take home, they promised to tell their friends about the new restaurant and left a five-dollar tip. Leah was astounded how smoothly April had handled the situation.

"When you're working with a limited menu, you make them want what you have," said April, helping to clear the table. "It's all in the power of suggestion. Most people leaf through those ten-page menus some restaurants have and feel nothing but confusion."

Later two teenagers on bicycles came in for Cokes and chips off the metal rack. Opening day might not have been the grand gala one hoped for in Cleveland or Columbus, but April was pleased when she switched off the neon sign and flipped the door sign to "Closed."

"We're off to a good start," she declared. "I'm exhausted. How about you?"

Leah slipped her apron over her head and tucked it into her totebag. "Actually I feel fine," she answered. "Which is a good thing, because I had better get home to start cooking dinner. My *mamm* made me promise I wouldn't let home responsibilities slip if I started working here."

"Off you go, then. I'll just lock up and be on my way too." April shoved her toward the door.

"Wait, what about the tips I collected?" Leah did a quick tally of the bills and coins. "It looks like seven dollars. Should we split it down the middle?"

"Absolutely not. You keep that in return for the baking ingredients you used."

"*Danki*, April. See you tomorrow." Truth was, all those fresh strawberries had cost more than twenty dollars, not counting the staples from the pantry. But Leah didn't want to make a fuss on such an auspicious occasion. She would replenish her family's household ingredients out of her first paycheck and consider the price of the fruit an investment in her career.

Over the next two weeks, word quickly spread through the county about the new home-style diner. April and Leah tweaked the menu several times and settled on the basics for breakfast—ham, eggs, bacon, sausage, oatmeal, and one daily special—French toast, waffles, or pancakes topped with whatever fruit was in season. One day they would fix the special sweet, with either chocolate, caramel, or praline sauce, whipped cream, and chopped walnuts. They also offered a fruit-and-cottage cheese plate and yogurt for the English gals, who always seemed to be on a diet.

Lunch was simple but hearty: deli sandwiches with side dishes such as macaroni salad, sliced beets and pickled eggs, or chow chow. Tossed salads and chips were always available for those with city tastes. In the cool months, they planned to add kettle baked beans, soups, stews, and chili. All youthful customers received an ice cream bar, cookie, or cup of mandarin oranges as a treat.

Each day their business grew until every table was usually full from when they opened the red front door until closing time at three. They often had to turn off the lights at three-thirty or customers would stay and nurse their coffee all afternoon. Leah had chores waiting at home—cooking, cleaning, and laundry. Blessedly, Henry had taken over the henhouse duties, for which Leah was especially grateful. Scrubbing out a henhouse had to be the most onerous task on earth. Even gathering eggs sometimes proved difficult when an irritable hen was fussy and uncooperative.

Leah often noticed April watching her while she flipped pancakes on the griddle or delivered plates to a table. But the woman was always smiling, so Leah relaxed into waiting on customers and making small talk with those at the counter. Slowly, some of her shyness—nonexistent among family and friends—began to ebb.

That is, until their first Amish customers strode in one Wednesday afternoon. They were two young men, both handsome. They entered the diner, tipped their hat brims, and asked if they could sit anywhere. Leah just stared mutely, as though they were speaking Japanese.

Fortunately, April pointed them to a booth and brought water and menus, allowing her employee to retreat to the caboose. While the men perused the daily specials, April took them beverages and then banged through the swinging kitchen door. "What's wrong with you, Leah?" she asked, her grin showing off her gold back tooth. "Surely you've seen Amish people before?"

Leah backed up against the chest freezer. In a kitchen this small there was no place to hide.

"*Jah,* I've seen them, but I don't know those two. They're not from my district. Why don't you wait on them while I mix up another batch of tuna salad? It's really selling well today." She tried to step around her boss.

April held up her palm like a crossing guard. "No way. You didn't know any of the English folk during the past two weeks and you still managed to be cordial. Don't pay any attention to the fact that they are Amish."

Leah couldn't help rolling her eyes. "The problem isn't that they're Amish." She parried to the left, but April blocked her escape with her hands on her hips, elbows out. Leah sighed. "The problem is that they are...men, young men. I'm nervous, that's all."

"That's all?" April asked. "Aren't you eighteen?"

Leah nodded.

"And you haven't started courting yet?"

This time Leah shook her head. She was beginning to feel like her *bruder*'s trained pony.

"I was married by your age!"

"Not everyone is in an all fired-up hurry. My life is quite pleasant just the way it is." Leah lifted her chin higher.

"Oh, Leah." April studied her carefully. "Pleasant, you say? Old grannies rocking on porch swings should have pleasant lives, not somebody eighteen years old. You go out there and take their order." She nudged her toward the door, pushing an order pad into Leah's hand. "Go talk about the likelihood of rain later in the week. I know that's your favorite topic with elderly customers. Let's see if young ones appreciate your weather forecasts just as much. I'll take care of the tuna salad."

Ready or not, April shoved Leah through the swinging door. The motion drew the attention of all the patrons present, including the Amish fellows. Leah had no choice but to walk to their table. As she did so, she saw one elbow the other and say something behind his upraised menu. She cleared her throat and asked, "What'll you have to drink?"

The dark-haired man laughed while the other pointed his index finger at their Cokes. He had light brown hair, cut shorter than usual, and hazel eyes. The fact that he looked even handsomer up close did nothing to calm her nerves.

"Oh, I see you've got drinks. Have you spotted something you like?" She poised the tip of her pen on the pad.

The dark-haired one's gaze trailed from the hem of her apron to the top of her *kapp*. "*Jah,* you could say that." He burst out laughing as though the joke were funny.

"*Mir leid* about him," said the other apologetically. "It's his first time off the farm in weeks." He took off his hat and set it on the seat. "My name is Daniel and that *dummkopp* is Steven." He offered both a nice smile and his hand.

Leah shook his hand like a quick priming of an old-fashioned pump. "Leah Miller, nice to meet you. What do you want for lunch?" She glanced at the other tables to give them the impression that she was busy.

Daniel replied without an ounce of urgency, "What's good today, Leah Miller? What do you recommend?" He appeared to be studying the very short menu as though he had all the time in the world.

She was uncomfortable with their easygoing banter and yearned to answer *I recommend that you two hightail it out to your buggy and git!* But she knew April wouldn't appreciate that, so instead she said, "You can't go wrong with the ham-and-cheese with a side of coleslaw."

Steven met her eye, looking contrite. "Sounds great. I'll have that, Miss Miller."

Daniel handed over his menu. "Double that order. I have a feeling we'll be back often enough to try just about everything."

She picked up the menus and practically ran to the kitchen. Her cheeks felt flushed, her palms were damp, and her forehead had started to perspire. Those two Plain boys had made her very nervous. She couldn't relax until they had finished their sandwiches, paid the bill, and left.

Each had left her a twenty-five percent tip.

And the one named Steven mumbled an apology on his way out. Daniel tipped his hat for the third time and said, "Hope to see you again real soon, Miss Leah Miller."

April had found the whole scene rather amusing. She warned Leah at quitting time that she had better get used to receiving attention from Amish folk.

Leah wasn't sure what that had meant at the time, but oddly enough the woman's prediction proved correct. As the novelty of a new restaurant wore off among the *Englischers* and many returned to the sumptuous buffet up the road, word had spread within the local Amish and Mennonite communities.

Soon all the booths and spots at the counter were again filled.

April began talking about ordering outdoor picnic tables for over-flow customers.

~

Emma Miller Davis paced from one end of the flower garden at Hollyhock Farm to the other and then back again. She checked the contents of her picnic hamper and her purse several times. The ice in her cooler was already starting to melt. Yet her husband of almost two years still hadn't brought their buggy around. She dug in her purse for her phone to check the time. "Goodness gracious!" she exclaimed and marched toward the barn. They were going to be late for preaching service...again.

The love of her life, James Davis III, couldn't seem to get used to how long it took to get places in a horse and buggy. He'd turned New Order three years ago as part of his commitment to living Amish before they married. He had finished his schooling at Ohio State Agricultural College in Wooster that summer, sold his shiny truck to his brother Kevin, and taken up Plain ways soon after. His best friend, Sam Yoder, had helped him make the transition as certain details weren't covered in books on the Amish lifestyle. Sam had been raised New Order. His wife, Sarah Hostetler, had been raised Old Order same as Emma. But the transition for the two brides, longtime childhood friends, had been a walk in a new mown meadow by comparison.

James had been English. He was still discovering little things he could no longer do the familiar way since turning Amish. But he said it had all been worth it to marry Emma Miller of Winesburg.

Now Mrs. Emma Davis of Charm felt the hair on the back of her neck rise as she pushed open the barn door, searching for her *ehemann*. She found him in the main walkway, trying to untangle a knotted double harness. His black felt hat was tipped back on his head, while his bluntly cut hair framed his face like a golden mane. However, his expression was utter bewilderment...until he spotted her.

"Ah, my sweet Emma. Some fool got this thing all tangled and then hung it on the peg like that." One corner of his mouth pulled into a half smile.

She set down her cooler and hamper on a bench and went to help. "That fool would be you, dear one. Remember when we came home from Sam and Sarah's? You took it off wrong and were too tired to straighten it out."

His cheeks turned a deep scarlet. "*Jah,* I remember now. I spent the day at his farm digging new postholes with a rusty auger. I was beat by bedtime."

Emma took the harness and with nimble fingers began to straighten out the knotted leather. She clucked her tongue with disapproval. "You keep forgetting that it takes ninety minutes to go ten miles. We will be admonished by the brethren if we keep showing up late."

He leaned over to brush a kiss across her *kapp.* "Ah, Emma, they know we're newlyweds. They'll give us some leeway."

She pulled the last straps loose and pushed the harness up against his chest. "We've been married almost two years, Jamie. We're not newlyweds anymore. You must get used to the idea that you can't wait until the last minute to leave." She heard the sternness in her voice and immediately felt ashamed. He was trying so hard. Perhaps she should learn to be more patient, especially as he was head of the household. A wife shouldn't chastise a husband...at least, not very often.

Emma stretched up on tiptoes to kiss his cheek. "I'm going to refill the ice in the cooler while you bring the buggy around. When we get there, we'll be there. The Lord knows we love Him in our hearts...our tardy hearts."

As she walked back to James' childhood home, Emma stewed about more than sneaking into preaching services during the first sermon. Her mother-in-law still treated her like a guest—a favored summer visitor who was vacationing from another country—and not like the wife of her son.

His mom still invited James to social events at her English church. And she often still looked surprised when he came downstairs for breakfast wearing his solid plain clothes—as though he were play-acting for a historical exhibition that soon would end.

It had been almost three years since James had been baptized and committed his life both to Christ and to a simpler lifestyle. Did Barbara Davis resent Emma? It didn't seem so, but how hard it must be for her to accept the fact that her son had left the world she and her husband had raised him in.

Emma crept quietly into the kitchen, but she found Mrs. Davis sitting at the table sipping coffee. Her Sunday school materials were spread out for last-minute review.

"Hello," she said. "You two are still here?"

"*Jah,* we are." Emma's answer was succinct and unnecessary. An uncomfortable silence spun out in the tidy room while Emma filled the cooler from the automatic ice dispenser. She hoped she didn't sound curt, but she didn't want to criticize her husband by mentioning their tardiness.

Her husband. A warm sensation filled her every time she remembered his tender proposal, his conversion to Amish life, and their joyous wedding. James had worn his old Levis for weeks with solid dark shirts, suspenders, and either a black felt or straw hat along with his work boots. After Emma had laid several new pairs of pants she'd sewn herself around their bedroom, he'd finally taken the hint. James had held one up, complemented her sewing, and then said, "But I'll look exactly the same as everybody else."

Emma had snaked her arm around his waist. "That's the point...not to set yourself apart or above anyone else. You will be known to God by what's in here." She'd placed her hand on the spot above his heart.

"You'll still be able to find me in a crowd, right? Like when you wander off on auction day?" He sounded only half joking.

"Without a doubt, I will always find you."

"All right, then." He threw the pants over his shoulder and headed off to change. That day, ten pairs of good Levis had gone into the charity bag, and he never went back to English clothes again.

When Emma walked back outside into the yard, James pulled up with their new standardbred horse properly hitched. "Your carriage awaits," he said, offering his hand for assistance.

"A one-seat buggy is too small to be considered a carriage," she said, settling herself beside him. "Carriages are even bigger than two-seat surries."

"I know, but I just like saying it."

Fortunately, a three-hour service meant that plenty of church still remained when Emma and James slipped in and found seats in the back. Only a few pairs of eyes turned in their direction, and only the retired local schoolteacher looked peeved. James smiled and tipped his hat to her.

He still listened to learn-to-speak-German lessons on a small CD player with earphones while he farmed, so it would be a while before James understood everything said during the service. The Amish read a High German Bible but spoke a colloquial *Deutsch*. Their language must be heard to be learned and could not be studied from any book. The New Order singing was faster and more upbeat than Old Order. Although the service was in German, the ministers occasionally threw in some English.

The only real difference Emma had noticed was that a members' meeting followed the service before lunch was eaten. They would discuss upcoming community and outreach projects to hospitals and prisons. Their church was even sending a group to Haiti to rebuild schools destroyed by an earthquake. Because Old Order Amish didn't do missionary work, Emma hoped she wouldn't be asked to travel to a foreign land. Cleveland and Lancaster County, Pennsylvania, were far enough away for her tastes.

Soon the congregation spilled outdoors into the bright May sunshine. Tables had been set up under the elms for a potluck lunch while the hosts dragged out large coolers of soft drinks. Pitchers of lemonade and iced tea were already waiting in the shade.

James rubbed his palms together in anticipation. "Let's get the hamper, Emma, and put our stuff on the table. I am starving." He took her arm as they headed toward their buggy.

Emma waited until they were away from the crowd before she whispered into his ear, "Leave the hamper and cooler, Jamie, and please hitch up the horse. I'm taking that food to my *mamm's.*"

"Your *mamm's*?" he squawked. "It'll take us two hours to get to your parents'. Everybody in our district is here and the food is ready to eat."

She thought she heard his stomach growl to emphasize his point. "Please, Jamie? Can't we go see my family this afternoon? It's been weeks and I miss them so much." She wrung her hands together.

He met her gaze and smiled. "Okay, Emma. Someday I'll be able to say no to you, hopefully by the time I'm fifty. But today isn't the day, so let's go visit your folks." He handed her up into the buggy. "It's been a while since your *daed* grilled me on my *Deutsch* lessons."

After hitching up their ornery horse, they started the long drive to Winesburg. Emma had plenty of time to mull over the fact that she'd told only half the truth. The real reason she didn't want to stay for the afternoon socialization was that her new district intimidated her. Did they have to be so vocal, so loud about their faith? Testifying about personal struggles and shouting "amen" was hard to get used to. Emma much preferred a quieter session with God without creating so much fuss.

～

Matthew had never been so happy to see his sister as that Sunday when the Davis buggy pulled up the Miller driveway. He had missed Emma plenty since she'd married and moved to her husband's family farm. But if Emma were there, James would be too. And he needed to talk to an *Englischer,* or rather, a former *Englischer.*

In the week since he'd seen Jeff Andrews doing something suspicious at work, he couldn't think about much else. Andrews treated him the same as always—brusque but civil. He had no idea his actions had been observed. What else was the guy up to behind Mr. Mac's back? Matthew had heard some talk in the bunkhouse, where the hired help took their meals, but he hadn't paid much attention. He'd figured those kinds of shady dealings happened near the big horse racing centers in Kentucky and New York, but not in Holmes County, Ohio. And certainly not on a farm where he worked.

"Hi, Emma," he called. She was walking his way with arms outstretched.

"*Guder nachmittag,* Matthew," she said, wrapping him in a warm hug.

He felt his face turn red enough to blend his freckles together.

"Have you lost weight? Maybe you've grown taller. I hope you're not working too hard between your chores here and at Mr. Mac's farm." She finally released her embrace. "I've brought a noodle casserole. You'd better eat some or my feelings will be hurt." Emma rattled on, kissed his cheek, and then headed toward the house to find *mamm.* She didn't wait to hear any replies.

James Davis had been studying the reunion. "I'll bet now that she's married you can get a word in edgewise around the house." He stuck out his hand. "Good to see you, Matty."

Matthew shook heartily. "When Emma moved out, Leah took up the slack in the talking department. She always has a story to tell about that diner she works at."

"Speaking of food, has your family eaten yet? I'm starving! Emma gave me only one peach to tide me over."

"*Jah,* we've eaten, but Ma always keeps things warm. She figured you two would show up today, but I have no idea how."

They walked toward the house, talking like old friends. Matthew couldn't get over the change in James. Each time he saw him he looked a bit more Plain. Even his deep suntan was gone since now he kept his hat on while working outdoors. Only his accent gave him away. He would probably never sound Amish even when he mastered their mixed language. But that was no big thing. The guy loved Emma enough to leave his worldly conveniences behind, and that meant a lot to Matthew. He didn't care if he never understood a word his brother-in-law spoke in German. He just hoped he could find someone to love that much some day. But in the meantime he had more important fish to fry.

He waited until James had eaten plenty of fried chicken, steamed greens, noodle casserole, and cheesy potatoes. Then Matthew said, "Say, Jamie, let's walk out to the barn. There's something I'd like to show you."

"Sure," James readily agreed. "These women will be jaw-boning for hours."

True enough, Leah was rapid-firing tales from her new job while *mamm* slipped in news and gossip from the district when Leah came up for air. Emma kept up with both lines of conversation effortlessly, throwing in appropriate comments and asking questions of each. The three seemed to be competing in a talk-a-thon.

"They won't even notice we're gone," James said as they left the kitchen.

Matthew waited until they reached the fence line to speak. "I need some advice, Jamie. I saw something at work I didn't much like, but I'm not anxious to cause a stink and get fired. Jobs aren't easy to find in this county, and jobs working with horses are plumb impossible."

He glanced over at James. He'd pulled up a weed to chew but wasn't about to interrupt.

"I saw the trainer that I apprentice under inject something into a colt's leg. I figured it had to be steroids—maybe to reduce some swelling. The colt pulled a muscle during a workout. The trainer ain't supposed to be giving injections, but I think he didn't want the owners to see their expensive horse limping when they came to visit."

James scratched at his chin. His beard was well trimmed and growing longer all the time. "He could do more harm than good if he doesn't inject it exactly into the correct spot. That's why a vet or vet technician usually administers shots. What are you going to do?

Could you talk to him privately? He'll lose his trainer's license if word gets out."

"He and I aren't exactly pals. I doubt he would appreciate me bringing up the subject." Matthew watched two hawks circling the pasture. "I don't rightly know what to do."

James rested one boot on the bottom fence rail. "You gotta do what's right...eventually. But I wouldn't be hasty. Don't stir up a hornet's nest over what might be nothing."

"Thanks. It helps to tell somebody. It's been eating away at me."

But, truthfully, he was no closer to knowing what to do than he was a week ago.

THREE

L eah felt ninety years old one Tuesday morning in May, but she didn't dare catch an extra forty winks of sleep. Yesterday she'd finished the family laundry almost single-handedly and had baked for both her family and the restaurant. At noon, April would pick her up in her truck for a whirlwind lesson on shopping for a diner. They planned to visit a local butcher, produce vendor, and stop for lunch at the buffet to see what the competition was doing. Leah swallowed two aspirin, rubbed lotion into her reddened hands, and hurried downstairs.

Julia had breakfast almost ready. *"Guder mariye,"* she said. "I'll bet you slept well last night." She set a bowl of scrambled eggs and plate of bacon on the table.

"I would've helped you, *mamm.* You should've waited." Leah reached for a piece of toast.

"I'm not helpless. I can still cook breakfast for my family...unless you only eat fancy recipes these days." Julia winked at her across the table.

"Nothing's very fancy in our diner. The kitchen's too small. I can't wait until *daed* brings you to town to try it out."

"He said he'll wait for you to work out the kinks on unsuspecting folk and then we'll stop in."

Leah and her mother shared a hearty laugh. "This afternoon I'm going shopping with April. Is that all right?"

"*Jah*, but don't make a habit of going off every Tuesday. That wasn't what we agreed upon."

"Don't worry. She's just giving me an idea of how she runs things." Leah sipped her coffee and enjoyed a meal cooked by someone else for a change. After washing the breakfast dishes, she had enough time to sweep the floor, iron some shirts and dresses, and bake two Dutch apple pies.

When April picked her up promptly at noon, Leah's education in restaurant supply began in earnest. They visited a poultry farm and a beef processor but placed only small orders because their freezer space was limited. In both cases April signed her name to a paper instead of giving cash or writing a check.

"Why did they let you leave without paying?" Leah asked in a whisper.

"I've set up accounts here," April explained while they loaded the meat into ice chests. "It's how the world does business. It's so much easier."

"How did you learn all this?"

"I took a course on business administration and another on restaurant management at the community college. I loved going to school, but my husband said a couple classes should be enough."

Leah nodded. She had loved school too and had wished an Amish education didn't stop after the eighth grade. But like her *daed* said, "Just because you stop going to school doesn't mean you have to stop learning." She would get quite an education at the diner.

"It's been almost four weeks that you've worked for me. How do you like the job so far?" April asked once they were back on the county road.

"I love it!" Leah answered without hesitation. "At first I didn't like all that chitchatting with the customers, but I'm getting used to it. Everybody sure wants to talk, don't they?"

April laughed. "Yeah, they do. Farming is a solitary occupation, so when they come to town they want company. And the Amish young men like talking to you, but that has nothing to do with them being surrounded by draft horses all day."

Leah pursed her lips. "Well, what does it have to do with?" She wasn't sure she liked where the conversation was headed.

"I know Old Order doesn't spend much time looking at themselves in mirrors, but you do have a hand mirror, don't you?"

Leah turned on the seat and frowned. "Of course I do."

April glanced at her from the corner of her eye and then refocused on the road. "You're very pretty, Leah. Why else do you think all these young men keep stopping in?"

Leah crossed her arms and stared out the window. Spring was in glorious full bloom. Every tree had opened with thousands of tender green leaves. "I thought they enjoyed our cooking. You said folk like my pies."

"Yes, that's part of it."

"My sister, Emma, is the pretty one. I planned to have a career in case I don't find somebody to marry." She stole a glance at her boss.

"There's nothing wrong with being pretty as long as it doesn't go to your head. And I don't think you should worry about not finding a husband."

"Where are we going now?" Leah was eager to change the subject. They turned down a township road not far from the one on which she lived.

"We're going right here." April pulled down a tree-lined lane that led to a tidy white farmhouse and smaller *dawdi haus*. The absence of power lines indicated Old Order, while a windmill to pump water to the house from the well meant they weren't the more conservative Swartzentrubers.

"What are we buying?" Huge fenced pastures, rolling as far as one could see, plus a very long one-story barn indicated a dairy operation.

"Cheese," April replied. "The woman who lives here makes the best cheese. At least she used to. She's getting up there in years, but she made a yogurt-cultured cheese that's wonderful to bake with."

Leah's interest was piqued. "I think I sampled some once at a work frolic."

When they climbed out of the truck, April peered around and then instructed, "You go to the dairy barn. I'll check up at the house and back garden. This time of year she could be anywhere."

Leah wandered down the well-worn path to the barn. Inhaling deeply, she breathed in the honeysuckle growing along the trellis. She kept her distance from the rest of the blossoms. Because the door stood ajar, Leah figured this was where the elderly lady might be and walked in boldly. "Hello?" She cupped her hands around her mouth and hollered, "Is anybody here?"

"*Jah*, what's all the yelling about?" A tall, dark-haired young man stood up with a scrub brush in one hand. He wasn't more than ten feet away, but he had been hidden from view by a half wall.

They locked gazes and stared at one another until Leah glanced away, blushing. "Beg your pardon. I was looking for an older woman. That's why I was speaking loudly."

He scratched at his clean-shaven chin. "Do you shout at all old people or just at my *mammi*?" Dimples deepened in his olive-toned complexion.

With nearly black hair, he had a Mediterranean appearance, or how she pictured people living in the Holy Land might look. *Except for his clear blue eyes.* They grabbed her attention and held on to it like thistle burrs on cotton socks. She couldn't turn away. "I believe she's the first *mammi* I've ever yelled at. I thought she might be hard of hearing."

The man set his brush on the wall and then wiped his hands on a towel. "Oh, no, not at all. She has uncannily good hearing. Don't try to whisper something behind her back or it will never stay a secret."

Leah giggled unwittingly. "I'll keep that in mind. What are you doing?" She glanced around but saw no livestock.

"I'm scrubbing down the equipment with bleach—sterilizing it so it'll be ready for the next milking."

Leah again peered around. "But where are your cows?"

"They're out in the pasture eating grass like good cows are supposed to. Do you live in town or something? Maybe over the grocery store or behind the grain elevator?"

Leah blushed to the roots of her hair. Truthfully, she had no idea why she was asking such inane questions, but the mysterious man with piercing blue eyes had caught her off guard. "No, I live on a farm," she said, rubbing her forehead, "but I keep mainly to the house due to my allergies."

"*Jah,* that makes sense." He walked around the half wall until he stood only five feet away. She had to tilt her head to look up at him, and she noticed that he had big hands and very broad shoulders. She couldn't stop herself from staring.

He stared back with one eyebrow lifted questioningly. "What are you doing, miss? Why are you searching for my grandmother?" He slipped his hands beneath his suspenders.

"Oh, sorry. I was looking for her to buy some kind of oddball cheese. April—that's my boss—said it's a variety of artsy cheese. She bought it from her a while back. My boss went up to the house and sent me in this direction." The tickle in Leah's nasal passages that she'd been fighting back had grown unbearable. Suddenly she released an explosive "Ah choo!"

"*Gesundheit*! My *mammi* never sets foot inside a barn unless it's something mighty urgent."

Leah felt her nose start to run in an unladylike fashion while her eyes began to itch. The animal dander in the air had found its mark. She sneezed again while her eyes watered as though she were crying over a sad story.

"Let's step out into fresh air." He practically dragged her outside as she held a handkerchief over her nose.

They walked away from the barn toward the pasture fence. Leah tried to focus through blurry vision. *"Danki,"* she murmured, sucking air into her lungs. "Much better out here."

"Well...there they are," he said in lazy fashion.

"Who?" Leah asked, glancing left and right.

"My cows, of course. Two hundred head of them, doing exactly what I had predicted."

Leah focused on where he pointed, even though occupants of pastures seldom held much interest. There—grazing, frisking, wandering aimlessly, or lying in the shade—were more Holstein cows than she'd ever seen before on an Amish farm. She counted at least three dozen calves. "My goodness. Aren't you Old Older, same as me? Do you milk all those cows by hand?"

He appeared to be biting the inside of his cheek. "No, I have equipment powered by a diesel generator. We run generators for the milking apparatus but don't use them for anything else."

"What about keeping the milk cold?"

He leaned both forearms on the fence rail. With his sleeves rolled up from cleaning chores, Leah could see his arms were tanned and muscular.

"We have one gas-powered cooling tank for the milk we turn into yogurt cheese. But it would cost too much in diesel fuel to provide refrigeration for grade-A milk certification. We sell our milk to cheese producers same as most Amish except for what my *mamm* uses to make specialty cheeses." He studied her from the corner of his eye.

"Jah, that's why we stopped here today." Leah tucked her handkerchief back up her sleeve; the sneezing fit had subsided.

Just then April and another woman appeared around the corner of the barn. "There you are!" April called, sounding relieved. "I feared you'd fallen into a milk tank or worse."

Leah felt guilty for no reason and thought she should explain. "I couldn't find the lady you wanted, but I found her grandson." She pointed him out so there would be no confusion.

The grandson tipped his hat and walked by Leah's side as they approached the two women. "She found me fair and square, but I really wasn't trying to hide," he said.

Everyone but Leah laughed. *Is it possible to say anything today that doesn't make me sound like a ninny?*

"This is my *mamm*, Joanna Byler. She is the one who makes the oddball cheeses now that *mammi* has retired."

"Oddball?" Mrs. Byler demanded. "There's nothing oddball about my cheese." She smiled but placed both hands on her hips.

Leah's mouth went dry. "I meant artistic, ma'am. Didn't mean no offense."

Joanna's brows knitted together over the bridge of her nose. "Artistic? Like one of those painters who wear funny hats and dab paint on an easel?"

April furrowed her forehead. "You'll have to excuse her. Leah's newly hired and just learning the terminology of the business."

"No harm done." Mrs. Byler turned and headed toward the house. "Let's load your truck from the walk-in refrigerator in the cellar. I've got a Van Gogh of a cheddar I think you might like. Or maybe it's a Salvador Dali."

"Please come help, Leah," April called over her shoulder.

"I'll help too. And, by the way, my name's Jonah. I'm glad your boss let your name slip since you didn't seem willing to tell me." He stuck out his hand as they walked.

For a moment Leah stared and then gave it a quick shake. She had shaken more hands during the past four weeks than in all her life previously put together. "Leah Miller," she murmured, "but I wish you hadn't said oddball cheese to your *mamm*."

"But that's what you called it, Miss Miller."

"I know I did, but only because I'd forgotten the right word." She was growing exasperated.

"Artisan?" he asked. "That's what the advertisement calls it." He remained cool with a voice as silky as water flowing over smooth rocks.

"*Jah*, that's it. Why use such a fancy word?"

"My grandmother says English people like big words, so you could charge an extra dollar per pound by giving it a fancy name."

Leah stopped on the path even though her boss and the cheese-maker had disappeared from sight. "That doesn't sound like a nice thing to do."

"I said you *could* charge it, not that we do. Are you saying my *mammi's* not a nice person?" He cocked his head to the side.

"Hush," she begged, "before you get me fired. I really like this job. I'm sure she is the nicest woman in Holmes County." Leah felt as though she were baling out a leaky rowboat. "Could you please go back to whatever you were doing before I interrupted you?"

"I thought I would help load the cheese order." His blue eyes twinkled with mischief.

"No, I'll do that. If you help anymore, I'll be looking for another job. Please?"

"All right, but only because you said 'please,' Leah Miller." He turned and walked away.

Leah watched until he disappeared inside the barn. *How does one develop such a calm demeanor?* She certainly didn't posses one as she ran all the way to the house. She was breathless by the time she found the door to the walkout basement.

April and Mrs. Byler were already carrying out boxes of cheese. "There you are," April said. "We feared you'd gotten lost again. Why don't you just close the door behind us? We have this handled."

She did as instructed, but Leah didn't stop perspiring during the entire drive back to the diner, despite the truck's air-conditioning being on full blast.

~

Emma wouldn't get used to the Davis family kitchen if she lived there another ten years. So many unnecessary gadgets and appliances.

Her mother-in-law owned a food processor, a bread machine, and a coffee grinder. Emma could chop up a head of cabbage for coleslaw in less time than it took to clean the processor. The bread machine was just plain silly unless your hands were too crippled to knead the dough, like her *mamm*'s. Her own hands were strong and flexible. And the coffee grinder? Whole beans cost more than coffee already ground up and sold in a can. Why would people pay more for extra work when she couldn't tell any difference in the taste?

Barbara Davis was very patient and kind to Emma, but she preferred to run her own kitchen...unless she was assigned extra hours at the hospital where she worked as a nurse. Then she would merrily announce at breakfast, "It's Emma's turn to cook tonight. We're in for a treat!" But Mrs. Davis usually had a pot of something she'd prepared over the weekend and then frozen. Emma's specialty had become heating things up, tossing salads, and steaming vegetables. She had no competition in the kitchen from James' sister. Lily had little interest in cooking, even when she was home from vet school on break.

Emma loved being married because she loved her husband so much. If he could give up his English clothes and truck, she could adjust to living with his parents until he saved enough to build their own house. Mr. Davis had paid a surveyor to stake off ten acres of farmland for their wedding gift. Some day she would have her own home, and it would contain a minimum of electrical appliances.

One gadget allowed in New Order districts that she did like was a cell phone. With a farm as large as Hollyhock, you couldn't very well holler out the window when it was time to eat. James had bought her a matching phone for her birthday. As long as she remembered to put it in the cradle to charge overnight, it truly was a blessing. Unfortunately, she forgot to charge it most of the time.

With Barbara Davis at work, it fell to Emma to fix lunch for James and his dad. She boiled eggs and potatoes for cold potato salad and decided on turkey sandwiches under the shady elms. The men preferred to stay outdoors until day's end, when they could shuck off dirty coveralls and leave work boots in the mudroom.

After Emma made the salad, she boiled a kettle of water for iced tea and started fixing their sandwiches. She thought tea tasted better made the old-fashioned way rather than as sun tea. When the sandwiches were finished, she walked outside to look for her husband. She spotted him on his tractor moving hay bales into the pasture containing Black Angus steers. She hiked up to the fence and waved her arms in the air to get his attention.

"Hey, Emma!" he shouted, lifting his straw hat like a rodeo rider. "I'll just be another ten minutes."

Emma climbed onto the fence rail to enjoy the view. Hollyhock Farm was a busy, thriving business with workers scurrying in all directions. Horses, sheep, beef cattle, a variety of crops, an orchard, and even a berry patch made this a far more diversified operation than most English farms. Only during two winter months were things quiet—after the final harvest and before spring birthing. Yet even then planning and budgeting took up any idle time.

James parked his tractor near the pasture gate and strode toward her. "Couldn't stand to be away from me that long?" He planted a kiss squarely on her mouth.

"Stop that before someone sees us," scolded a blushing Emma. "You are still so bold."

"I noticed you waited till the kiss was over to yell at me." He slipped his arm around her shoulder.

"Never you mind. Are you ready for lunch?"

"I've been hungry for an hour. How about under those trees?"

"That's what I thought. Why don't you find your *daed*, and I'll carry it outside on a tray."

"You've gotta deal." He tugged one of her *kapp* strings and then headed toward the farm office at the back of the indoor arena.

Emma offered a silent prayer of thanks to God for His grace. Seldom did falling in love with an *Englischer* turn out so well. She grinned all the way up the porch steps, right up until she pulled open the back door.

A horrible acrid smell struck her like a blow. She reeled back, filled with dread. It wasn't wood smoke like she'd smelled the night of the barn fire, but something metallic and toxic. Covering her mouth with her handkerchief, she ran into the kitchen, where smoke and noxious fumes had filled the room. She began coughing and choking while her eyes stung and ran with tears.

In an instant, she knew what had happened. Before leaving the kitchen to call James, she had set their lunch plates on the stove—the plastic plate liners directly atop the electric cooktop. The plastic had melted, and solidified into a mess of red-and-yellow goo. "Oh, no," she cried and quickly turned off the burners. She tried to open every kitchen window but began to gag from the smell.

"Emma, come on out of there!" James demanded from the doorway.

She ran to him and sobbed. "I ruined your *mamm*'s kitchen! She'll never speak to me after this. I'm so sorry."

They stepped onto the porch, leaving the door open. "Are you all right?" he asked, scanning her from head to toe. "What happened?"

"I forgot to turn the burners off and they were still hot. I set our plates down to move them off the counter. I am the world's stupidest person."

He pulled her head down to his shoulder and hugged tightly. "No, dear heart. You're not, not even close. Think of all the people living in jungles and backwoods that nobody knows about."

"Oh, James!" She smacked him lightly on the chest. "Is the stove ruined? Should I buy your *mamm* another from my wool money?"

"No, I'll scrape off the plastic later. It might need new electric coils, but like my gram says, never cry over melted plastic."

Emma dabbed at her eyes. "I'll bet she never said that," she murmured, but she felt a little better. Being within his embrace tended to do that.

"She would have, given the chance." James placed a string of kisses across her forehead. "I'm going out tomorrow to buy a propane stove. We'll install it in the mudroom, and then we'll move it to our own house someday. I should have thought of that long ago."

"Danki," she whispered. Her tears were no longer because of smoke.

And he was a man of his word. Emma never had to cook on an electric stove again.

～

Leah rocked slowly back and forth in the porch swing, the first time she'd been able to relax all day. Supper dishes were washed and dried. The week's baking was finished and hidden away until tomorrow, safe from goats, insects, or her brothers' insatiable appetites. Her tiredness was the good kind—born of hard work that she loved. She no longer suffered the tedium of one day blending into the next, with nothing to look forward to but a work frolic months away or a visit from Emma. Her job divided her week into four days of excitement, two days of catch-up and preparation, and one day to thank the Lord for leading her to that dusty parking lot.

Though the year's longest day was still a month away, plenty of daylight remained. When she rose to get some lemonade, she spotted her best friend coming around the barn. Rachel Hostetler lived across the street from Aunt Hannah, whose farm adjoined the Millers' along the back property line. A well-trodden trail through meadow, wood-lot, and around the beaver pond connected the two families. Considering all the wild creatures and bugs that lived in that bog, besides a cornucopia of weeds, Leah never set foot on that path. She would walk the road or hitch up the buggy even if it took twice as long.

"Hey, Leah," Rachel said as she climbed the porch steps. The girl stood barely five feet tall and was well rounded with apple-red cheeks and pretty green eyes. She was almost always smiling. "Since you've

been too busy to see old friends, I've come to see you. I chanced crossing paths with coyotes along the way, but it's a lovely evening." She
plopped down on the swing and then scooted back until her feet
didn't touch the floor.

"I appreciate your risking your life. I'm happy to see you," Leah
said. "How about some lemonade?"

"Good idea. I'm parched dry." Rachel set her flashlight down on
the table, slipped off the swing, and followed her inside.

While Leah filled glasses, Rachel rattled off an update of Hostetler
news. Leah stored it away like a squirrel with nuts so she could pass
it along to her mother.

Once back on the swing, away from eavesdropping siblings, Rachel
changed the subject. "Tell me about your new job at the diner. Martha says all the menfolk love the place and can't stay away. And it's not
because of your Blackberry Cheesecake pie, either."

Leah shook her head. "Since your sister has such a vivid imagination, she should write novels in her spare time and not sell eggs and
produce from a farm stand."

"She would have to write under the covers with a flashlight. *Daed*
says she has too many romantic notions the way it is." The girls enjoyed
a good laugh until Rachel returned to her subject. "So you're saying
the customers aren't all men?"

"Not all of them, no. Women stop in, especially English women."

"Ah ha! Martha was right for a change."

"Don't make a big deal out of it. My boss runs a fair-priced diner
with good food. Most Amish gals pack their lunch if they'll be gone
for the day. They're too practical to stop in a restaurant unless it's for
a special occasion."

"Ah ha!" Rachel repeated. The emphasis and tone indicated disbelief.

"Will you please stop saying that?" Leah hadn't seen her friend in
a while and didn't want to argue. "I met some new people today who
live two roads over. They have a huge dairy farm and make all these

fancy cheeses. The son—his name's Jonah—has a diesel generator to run the milking equipment so he can keep a herd of over two hundred head. If diesel fuel weren't so expensive, he'd be able to sell his milk grade A. Instead they make a yogurt cheese that I'm dying to try in cheesecake. You know, that would cut down on the calories," she murmured more to herself. "Jonah says his *mamm* also makes artisan cheeses in her processing room." Leah paused long enough to sip her drink. "I can't wait to try this aged cheddar we bought. The next time I see—"

Leah allowed her sentence to hang in midair. Her best friend was staring at her strangely.

"I can see why you changed the subject from what's cooking at the diner," Rachel said.

"What do you mean?" Leah finished her lemonade with an undignified slurp of ice cubes.

"I mean, who would want to discuss meatloaf and mashed potatoes when one could talk about this Jonah person?" Rachel finished her drink noisily too.

"Be careful. You're starting to sound like Martha. And that's not a good thing." Leah gazed at a spiderweb on the trellis, the hanging basket of fuchsia, and then the distant hills bathed in golden light—anywhere but at Rachel. "I'm just curious about cheese-making, that's all. I happen to enjoy a slice every day on my sandwich."

Rachel's laughter sounded more like the bray from *dawdi*'s old mule. "If you were really curious about cheese-making, you would get in line with all the *Englischers* and take a factory tour in Walnut Creek. I think you're a lot more interested in Jonah. And I can't wait to see him and figure out why."

FOUR

The next morning Leah spent the buggy ride to work rehashing the conversation with Rachel in her head. How could she be such a goose? With all the things she'd wanted to share about her new job, she had filled up the time rambling about a dairy farmer two roads away. Even so, she was curious about certain things. *Where did he come from?* If he was Old Order, why hadn't she seen him at preaching services? Maybe he'd been shunned so long ago he was just an outcast on his grandparents' farm, never socializing with decent people.

Whoever he was didn't matter. Leah didn't want to get riled up over any man. Her sister had lived for years on an emotional roller coaster before marrying James. Leah didn't even want a *Rumschpringe* after watching Emma fret over one problem after another. Leah had a job, a real job, that did not consist of chasing after sheep all day. But she also didn't have a minute to spare, considering the breakfast customers who were already pulling into the parking lot when she arrived.

"*Guder mariye,*" two voices called out.

Leah jumped down to find Daniel and Steven walking toward her. "Let me unhitch your horse for you," Daniel said with a tip of his hat brim.

"The diner doesn't open for another thirty minutes," she said, reaching for her purse.

Daniel took the reins from her while Steven released the horse from the harness. "We know," Daniel said, "but we thought we'd be your first customers. It's auction day."

"*Jah*, I remember. *Danki* for tending to my horse. Please put him in the shady pen around back." April's husband had fenced off an area of the backyard for Leah's horse during the workday

"I've got a brush in my buggy. I'll rub him down until you open for business." Steven seemed to be trying to make up for his rude behavior the other day.

When she stepped inside the air-conditioned diner, April was already mixing batter for pancakes while bacon and sausage sizzled in the frying pan. "Those boys arrived fifteen minutes ago," she said. "Might as well take them some coffee but no food until we open." Her white prayer *kapp* was already askew and baking powder smudged her nose.

"Do you think it's wise to encourage them?" Leah asked, slipping an apron over her head.

"Yes, I do. A restaurant lives or dies by its regular customers, so don't be so inflexible." April flipped the bacon without spattering the grease.

Properly chastised, Leah carried out two cups of coffee as soon as it finished brewing.

"You read my mind, Miss Miller," said Steven, taking a long sip.

"It was a very short story, no?" Daniel teased, picking up his mug. "This was very nice of you, *danki*." He seemed intent on blocking her path back into the diner.

"You'll have to thank Mrs. Lambright. It was her idea. Now if you'll excuse me, I'll help her open up." She stepped around him and marched up the steps like a soldier.

"We're counting the minutes till the sign lights up," Steven called and then they both laughed.

Leah rolled her eyes, but felt a small thrill. She wasn't used to this sort of interest.

April is right—those two do seem to possess an attraction for me. Probably like mosquitoes to a bug zapper.

Once back inside, she became so busy that she forgot to turn the sign on. Creamers and shakers needed filling. Strawberries had to be washed and sliced. And then April assigned her to the griddle to start pancakes. When a tap on the window drew her attention, Leah ran to unlock the door. Several others had arrived besides the two early birds.

"Thank goodness," Daniel said. "We couldn't wait another minute." The men carried in their mugs and took their usual booth. "Is it pancakes, waffles, or French toast today?" he asked with eyes as round as an owl's.

"Pancakes," she said, fighting back a grin.

"My favorite," said Steven. "Give me the special."

"You say that no matter which one it is," Leah said without looking up.

"I'll have it too," added Daniel. "Did I mention you look especially pretty today?"

"No need to mention things like that." She wrote two specials on her pad and then went for the coffeepot.

Soon the diner filled up with people headed to the auction, so for an hour neither woman knew which end was up. When the breakfast crowd cleared out, Leah wiped down the counter with spray cleaner. Someone was sitting in the last booth she hadn't noticed before. His nose was buried in a newspaper but the top of his head revealed hair as black as a crow's.

Upon recognition, Leah felt a shiver of excitement. Carrying over the coffeepot, she smoothed her wrinkled apron along the way. "Hello," she said merrily. "I didn't think I'd see you again so soon."

Jonah Byler set down his paper and glanced up. All of Leah's aplomb vanished when she looked into those robin's egg blue eyes. "Hi, Leah. I wanted to see where you worked...to see what kind of a diner needed oddball, artistic cheeses." His deep dimples reappeared.

"Do you think you might be able to forget those two words?" She tipped the pot to refill his cup. Unfortunately, a moment or two passed before she realized the pot was empty.

He pushed away his oatmeal bowl. "I'll never bring it up again if you get me some fresh coffee."

Leah set the carafe down. "How exactly did you find out where I worked? I never mentioned it." The mysterious man grew ever more so.

He leaned forward and whispered, "I was very clever." He glanced around to make sure no one was listening to them.

Leah felt a ripple of nervous energy snake up her spine.

"On my way to the barn, I read 'The Diner, County Road 505, Winesburg, Ohio' on the side of your boss' pickup." He laughed and returned to his newspaper.

With cheeks aflame, Leah stormed into the kitchen. "World's biggest ninny," she muttered.

"What was that?" April asked when the door swung closed.

"I'm just talking to myself," Leah said, beginning to load the dishwasher.

"Since there's a lull before the lunch rush, talk to me instead." April set down her rolling pin.

Leah put in the last plates and turned around, hoping her face wasn't still cherry red. *Am I about to be fired for my inflexibility?*

Her boss drew in a breath and appeared to be collecting thoughts. "Things are going much better than I dreamed they would. After that rocky first week, business picked up and has stayed brisk ever since. And I owe it all to you, Leah."

This wasn't what she'd expected. After a moment's pause, Leah said, "Folks love your cooking, April. It's not just my pies they're coming in for. Your French toast is lighter and fluffier than mine."

"Yes, the town was ripe for another eating establishment and my low prices bring in the locals, but many people come back because of you. A restaurant must be more than great food that is fairly priced.

You must make people feel welcome and appreciated so they'll stop in over and over. Your weather reports have become a major hit. That one elderly *Englischer* stops in all the time for coffee, pie, and to find out if it will rain."

Leah chuckled, grateful that April hadn't mentioned the Amish fellows stopping in. Her *daed* would make her quit if he found out they came in to flirt. "I finally got the hang of this chitchatting thing."

"Yes, you have. We make a nice team together, sharing the chores equally. You're not afraid to work hard, and that's why I'm offering you a full partnership."

Not even a cube shifted in the automatic icemaker to break the silence.

Then Leah gathered her wits so she wouldn't stammer. "I don't rightly know what to say, April. I've only worked here four weeks. You've invested your father's money to get started. I can't very well barge in after you've put your savings on the line." As soon as the words were out, Leah realized April would know the full extent of her eavesdropping. But it was better she found out now.

April didn't bat an eyelash. "Yeah, my savings and a loan from Dad, but we could probably work something out if you're interested in partnering with me." She tucked her hands into her apron pockets.

Interested in a partnership? In these adorable train cars I fell in love with four years ago? The restaurant where I can try out new pie recipes to my heart's delight? Leah didn't think about checking with her parents or sleeping on the decision or praying for the answer—something that had never failed her in the past. She nodded her head briskly. "*Jah,* I'm interested. I'd love to be your partner!"

April clapped her hands. "That's wonderful. We make such a great team together, Leah." She poured two glasses of orange juice.

"But what about the financial end? How's that going to work? Don't partners put up money or something? I heard my *bruder* say some Clevelander wanted to buy into Macintosh Farms, but Mr. Mac said 'no thanks.'"

April cocked her head. "Do you have money to invest, Leah? Do you want to buy in and do things right, legally speaking?"

"Well, sure. I have money saved from selling pies to the auction cafeteria for the past four years. I don't want people to think I'm some mooch, worming my way in." She felt buoyed by the adult responsibility.

"I don't think anybody would think that about you. But just the same, it's probably a good idea if you invest since I still need to pay the man for those picnic tables." April handed her a juice glass. "I never thought this place would take off like it has. I'll be able to pay my father back and you can replace your savings in no time at all. Let's toast to our deal the way they do on TV." She clinked Leah's glass with hers and drank the juice down all at once. "To our partnership!"

Leah had never seen anything like that on TV. The only show she had watched was a baseball game at Mrs. Lee's until she had dozed off. But she smiled and drank down the juice. "To our partnership!" Leah repeated, hoping her savings would be sufficient. She had no idea what diner partnerships cost these days. "I have three thousand dollars, and I'm willing to invest twenty-five hundred," she blurted out. "Is that enough?"

April's head bobbed backward. "You saved three thousand dollars from selling pies to the cafeteria?"

"*Jah,* and to the grocery store at the street level."

"That will be a fine investment." April put their glasses in the sink and then pulled a bowl of tuna salad from the refrigerator. "I'd better fix a few sandwiches since they're the daily special."

"I'll slice fruit for fruit salad. That always does well on hot days." Leah turned her cleaver on a watermelon with fervor.

"There's one more thing," April said, not taking her focus off the tuna salad.

"What's that?"

"I decided during the drive in today to change the name of the place, providing you were interested in the partnership. The Diner sounds dreary, the more I thought about it."

Leah set down the knife. "Change it to what?"

April grinned. "How about Leah's Home Cooking? It has a wonderful ring to it. And since Amish people are flocking here to see you and partake of your wonderful pies, I thought it would be perfect!"

Leah felt as though she might faint. Every girlhood dream was coming true. God was granting her grace she hadn't even asked for. It was as if He knew her hopes and wishes, which of course He did. She blushed with embarrassment. "Don't you think your husband and *daed* would prefer to see your name above the door? After all, it's still your place and your idea. I came in as an afterthought."

"Not at all," April said. "They want whatever will make this restaurant successful, and the new name is a giant step in that direction."

A tiny voice in Leah's head cautioned *Slow down. Don't get too full of yourself.*

But she paid no attention to it. Leah's Home Cooking danced through her head like a nursery rhyme as she sliced up a cantaloupe.

"I'm going to order a new sign after closing. This is so exciting!" April squeezed her shoulders in an impromptu hug. "But now I better check to see if any lunch customers have arrived. I thought I heard the bell above the door."

It was then that Leah remembered her last customer—reading his newspaper, awaiting more coffee. She nearly chopped off a finger. "I'll check, April. I need to refill coffee carafes anyway." She fled through the kitchen door at a run.

But she was too late. The booth of the dark-haired man—the subject of porch swing chatter with Rachel—was empty. He'd left a neatly folded newspaper and a thirty-five-cent tip. Thirty-five cents… Leah didn't think her service worthy of even that amount.

She'd been a full partner for less than five minutes and she was already chasing customers away.

~

April watched Leah climb up into her buggy, shake the reins over the horse's back, and start for home. The girl hadn't stopped smiling since the break between breakfast and lunch. She'd hummed a tune while scrubbing frying pans and whistled while mopping the floor—two chores that had seldom inspired song in the past.

Switching the "Open" placard to "Closed" in the door, she pulled the phone book from under the counter. She would order the new sign before she lost her nerve. Her husband had warned her about adding anything else to their credit card, but hadn't she promised her partner? Because every booth and stool at the counter was usually occupied, April was confident they would have plenty of profits to pay the bill. After all, it would be weeks before it came in the mail, and a couple more before the payment's due date.

She must stop worrying so much. This was her dream too, same as young Leah's. One needed to take chances in life, especially to get ahead in this world. April called the sign-maker and ordered Leah's Home Cooking with black lettering on a white background—and the man promised delivery by Independence Day. With a final check around the diner, April turned down the AC and switched off the lights. As she walked toward her truck, she noticed it was no longer the sole vehicle in the parking lot.

"Mrs. Lambright," a voice called and a man got out of his sedan.

Her heart thudded against her chest wall as she recognized the landlord.

"Mr. Jenkins, what brings you to Winesburg? We just closed for the day."

"I'm not here to eat. I'm here because I've left a couple messages on your answering machine and you've neglected to return my calls." He slicked a hand through thinning hair in dire need of shampoo.

"I'm sorry about that. My husband checks the machine and sometimes erases any messages he thinks are from solicitors." April hiked her purse higher on her shoulder and shifted her weight to the other hip.

Jenkins looked at the diner and around the yard. "How's business?" he asked, his tone harsh and unfriendly.

"We're off to a good start. Of course, another train car would've been nice. We're limited to the number of people we can serve for lunch."

He met her gaze with brown eyes almost hidden within the folds of surrounding skin. His face had the deep-set wrinkles of someone who never wore sunglasses. When he focused on the five wooden picnic tables, he frowned. "Those look brand new."

"They are. We needed more seating for overflow customers, at least during the nice weather months."

He pulled on his chin. "How is it, Mrs. Lambright, that you can afford five brand-new picnic tables but can't afford to pay me the rent money on time? This property and those train cars are mine. You're just renting them. You only own the business license." He swatted at a bug on his neck.

April's spine stiffened. "We have a two-year lease with option to purchase. I've put my life savings into the restoration of those train cars. When you bought them, they were close to being unsalvageable."

"Everything is salvageable, at least to a scrap recycler. And the terms of our lease state that you make regular monthly payments. Not just send a check when you get the notion." He scratched the spot of the bug bite.

April decided a different tack was in order. "I apologize, Mr. Jenkins. I know we signed an agreement, and I fully intend to hold up my end. I just took on a partner, one with cash to invest. You'll have my rent check in the mail by the weekend."

"I'd be happy to take that check right now and save you a stamp. Seeing that I made the trip from Akron and all."

She pulled her purse off her shoulder and rummaged around

inside. "Oh, dear, it looks like I left my checkbook at home today. I hurried out in a rush." She offered a tiny smile.

"Mm-hmm," he said without an ounce of conviction. He studied her for a moment before giving his chin one last pull. "I'll expect that check by the weekend. And I've taken the liberty to tuck some pre-addressed envelopes under your wiper blades. I'd like you to use one each month and see that your payment reaches me on time."

He glared once more before turning and shuffling back to his car.

April remained rooted until Whip Jenkins left, raising a cloud of dust. Then she marched to her pickup and plucked the stack of envelopes from the windshield. She tucked them inside her purse, along with bills from the butcher, the produce vendor, and the carpenter who had made the picnic tables.

She needed to get home and check the answering machine herself tonight. But she wouldn't let a visit from her impatient landlord dampen her spirits.

Leah Miller had agreed to become her partner. She got along fine with that lovely young woman. Together they would turn the diner into a highly profitable enterprise.

And she prayed for that all the way home.

~

James Davis came to the dinner table that night not in the best of moods. The horse he bought for his buggy still remained balky, despite everything he'd tried. Riding a horse and driving a horse were two very different skills, and although he was accomplished with the former, the latter remained a total disaster. He'd had no success training any of the family's Morgans or Arabians to pull the buggy, hence the purchase of the typical Amish standardbred. His luck had only marginally improved.

"What's for supper, *fraa*?" he called as he washed up for dinner.

Emma met him in the mudroom with a cold drink and a warm smile. "I've reheated a pot of stew, steamed some broccoli, and tossed a salad of garden vegetables. I've been working my fingers to the bone." She pressed the back of her hand to her forehead. "I'm faint with fatigue," she teased with great drama.

He pulled her into a hug. "Oh, that's right. Mom's working late at the hospital and men's Bible study is tonight for Dad. Does that mean we have the house to ourselves—a quiet dinner for two?"

"Not exactly," she whispered, bobbing her head toward the doorway.

"Hey, bro!" His brother Kevin called from the other room. "I'm back."

"Home from college already? Funny, you don't look any smarter." James walked into the kitchen and embraced his younger brother rather awkwardly.

"Maybe the smart stuff comes next semester. But for now, finals are done and I'm a free man till August." The two men sat down at the table while Emma carried over the stew and salad. After Kevin's update on the travails of his previous semester, James filled him in on Hollyhock Farm news.

"I didn't see your truck in the yard. Where did you park?" James asked.

"Around the side of the house under the willow. Didn't want the sun to fade the paint or anything." Kevin exchanged a look with Emma before ducking his head into the refrigerator. "Things look great around here," he said. "Your conversion to New Order certainly hasn't hurt productivity. If anything I think the place looks better."

"Staying home to help Dad run things has helped," James agreed.

"You mean not spending your time taking agricultural courses in Wooster?"

"That, and the minor adjustment of not having a truck at my disposal. I get a lot more done." He squeezed Emma's hand affectionately.

They bowed their heads to pray before the meal, and then Emma scooped stew into three bowls while James divided up the salad.

"Your truck is running great, and I appreciate the bargain-basement price you sold it for." Kevin began to eat heartily.

"I wish I could say the same thing about the new buggy horse I bought. That standardbred is willful, stubborn, and not too smart. If that gelding were a car, we'd call it a lemon."

"I told you who would help you with that, Jamie," said Emma. "But you're letting your pride stand in the way." She set her salad fork down.

James' mouth dropped open. It wasn't like Emma to speak critically, especially not in front of people. He didn't appreciate a dressing down in front of his brother.

"I need to learn to control the horse myself, Emma. Your brother, as talented as he is, won't make me a better handler."

"But that's just it. He could teach you some of his tricks, show you his methods. He's helped his friends before with balky horses—men born and raised Amish."

Kevin glanced up from his dinner. "Sounds like a good idea. At least it's worth a try."

James pulled on his beard. "The problem is that Matt lives in Winesburg and I'm down here in Charm with a buggy for transportation."

"I'm not doing anything tonight. Why don't I drive you up there? I haven't seen your brother-in-law since your wedding."

Emma's face lit up. Before James could reply, she asked, "Could we, Jamie? I'd love to show *mamm* some of the new wool shawls I've made on the loom. I created the pattern myself."

So it was decided. The three Davises finished supper, loaded the dishwasher—an appliance Emma rarely used—and headed to Winesburg, a thirty-minute trip by car. During the entire drive James tried to remember a Scripture his father used to quote when he got "too big for his britches." But he couldn't recall it and his annoyance with Emma grew like a seedling in the sun.

Is this what happens when you get married? The wife who once thought you capable of just about anything starts picking at minor insufficiencies without a thought of who is listening? It wasn't as though he didn't know a thing or two about horses. Hollyhock Farm had bred, raised, and trained prize-winning show horses and provided countless people with quality riding mounts. Now his reputation was on the line because he bought the world's surliest buggy horse? Fortunately, his brother kept up a steady stream of banter about the Ohio State football team so he didn't have to engage in small talk.

Once they arrived at Emma's parents' home, James breathed a sigh of relief. The peaceful serenity of the Miller farm amazed him. Hollyhock was a beehive of constant activity, but here the pace was slower and calmer. Yet the Millers still managed to get chores done without livestock going hungry or the petunia bed drying up. He hoped for this atmosphere for his own home, where he and Emma would raise a family in an Amish household without the constant reminders of his former English world.

Emma kissed his cheek. "*Danki*, Jamie. You won't be sorry you sought my *bruder*'s advice. Everyone has a special gift from God. Matthew's is horses." She quickly ran off toward the house, so she didn't witness him clenching down on his back molars or notice the steam coming from his nostrils.

"Come on, little brother," he said a moment later. "Let's go find the horse whisperer. I apparently have plenty to learn."

An hour later, James Davis had been duly humbled.

Matthew Miller demonstrated incredible expertise with his driving horses. In his patient, quiet manner he not only got the beast to do his bidding, but he taught James without the least bit of condescension. And he had used a horse belonging to a friend for the demonstration, not one of his own.

So nothing would bruise my ego or typical male pride. Emma was right, he thought, feeling ashamed.

Matthew gave him plenty of pointers and then suggested that he ride back with them to Hollyhock Farms. Because tomorrow was his day off, he could spend time coaching James and his gelding. Kevin readily agreed to drive Matt back to Winesburg in time for afternoon chores.

Emma was joyous for extra time with a family member.

Kevin was happy to do anything not connected with college or textbooks.

And James? He would pick a large bouquet of flowers for his wife when they got home and maybe throw in a foot rub.

Proverbs 29:23, which he couldn't recall during the drive to the Miller farm, popped into his head on the way back. *Pride ends in humiliation, while humility brings honor.*

He would try to do better.

But it sure wasn't easy learning how to live all over again.

FIVE

June

The diner was booming. Just as the regular customers tired of fresh strawberry waffles and pancakes, local blueberries were ready to pick. Although neither restaurateur had time enough to visit pick-your-own farms, the berries were plentiful and fairly priced at the local market. April still didn't have sufficient cash flow to advance a weekly stipend for baking supplies, but she paid Leah's wages on time and insisted she keep all tips, no matter who had served the table. Leah wasn't about to quibble over dollars and cents now that she had handed over twenty-five hundred dollars and been made a full partner.

Wednesday was an auction day; Daniel and Steven always stopped in for breakfast before heading there.

"*Guder mariye*, Leah," Daniel called as they entered. Steven repeated the greeting when Leah brought over mugs of coffee.

Leah noticed that a third young man had joined them. "Hello," she said. "Welcome to Leah's Home Cooking."

He blushed profusely and stammered, "How do, miss, my name's John." He then buried his head behind the menu, not easily accomplished with a single sheet of paper.

"He's shy, Miss Miller," Daniel said. "Doesn't get much chance to come to town, being that he's the only son on a very large farm." With that explanation John lowered the menu and smiled tentatively.

"Hmm," she murmured, glancing at customers arriving and several waiting by the cash register. "How about three specials of the day—blueberry pancakes?"

"Done!" Daniel said. He grabbed the other menus to hand to her. "Did I ever tell you my trade?" He leaned slightly forward while Leah scribbled down the order.

"No, I don't think so." The bell jingled, signaling the arrival of more customers. She turned her focus back to the men.

"I'm a blacksmith. I apprenticed under my *daed,* and he's the best in the county. We repair lots of farm equipment and make tools. Besides that I'm a farrier, in case you ever need shoes."

She leveled him a look over her tablet. "In case *I* need shoes? Do I look like a horse?" The other two men howled with laughter. "I need to get this order in if you want to make the auction on time." She hurried off without listening to red-faced Daniel's blustering excuses.

Every seat at the counter was filled and most of the booths too.

Ten minutes later, when she brought their breakfasts to the table, Steven said, "I'm a furniture maker at the large Amish oak showroom on the state route. I started as a carpenter and I've advanced to full master craftsman." He gazed up into her face.

She had no clue how to respond, and all the eye contact was making her nervous. After an uncomfortable pause she asked, "Do any of you want maple syrup?"

After three negative nods, Leah went to her other customers. During the short lull between breakfast and lunch she found April slicing cucumbers and tomatoes.

"Men can be so strange," Leah said with a weary sigh. "Those two Amish boys brought one of their friends, and each decided to tell me his life story. My busiest time of day, and they wanted to explain what they did for a living. Why did they think I needed to know all that?"

April lifted her brows quizzically and peered at her. "You're joking, right?"

"About what?" Leah asked, artfully topping the lettuce on side salads with radish and carrot curls along with purple cabbage.

"You really don't know why Amish boys would try to impress you with their achievements or standing in the community?"

Leah stopped making salads and turned toward her boss as realization germinated in her head. "Oh, no," she moaned. "You don't think they're out to court me, do you? And vying for attention by trying to impress me?" She scowled at the blatant shamefulness of the whole idea.

April laughed. "That's pretty much how I see it. What's the matter with you? Most girls would be flattered by *three* men flirting with her." She returned to making a sweet-and-sour cucumber salad with a shake of her head.

Leah thought for a minute. A part of her did enjoy their flirting. It surely was more interesting to talk to young men, all handsome at that, than listen to elderly counter customers rehash the good old days before Amish culture became a tourist attraction. But still, it made her feel guilty too, as though she were behaving boldly or in a manner her *daed* wouldn't approve of.

"I am a little flattered, but it also makes me feel like a critter on display at the auction barn before the bidding starts. And I sure don't like that!"

April patted her arm on her way to the swinging doors. "You have an unusual way with words as well as with pies. But you're right about men...they can be strange at times. I'm going to wipe down the tables and counter again so we'll be ready."

"That reminds me. Is it all right if I leave early today? Say, right at three o'clock? I'm working up a couple new pie recipes and I'd like to talk to Mrs. Byler about her cream cheeses."

"Sure thing. Give Joanna my best regards. Oh, and say hello to Jonah for me too." She winked with great exaggeration.

"I'll do the lion's share of the cleanup tomorrow." The door swung closed behind April, so Leah's reply echoed in an empty room. She was glad she was alone, because just the mention of Jonah Byler's name caused her face to flush and her palms to sweat. That man had some strange powers she didn't appreciate one bit.

The afternoon flew by with plenty of business on the warm summer day. Many chose to carry their lunch out to the picnic tables, despite having to come inside for drink refills. One overdressed *Englischer* in a wide-brimmed hat and high heels asked if tableside service was available at the outdoor seating. When Leah momentarily gaped at her, the woman smiled and changed her preference to the next available booth. Another woman sitting at the counter asked for the potato salad recipe. Without looking up from refilling coffee cups, Leah rattled off, "Redskin potatoes, don't overcook; sweet red onion; chopped boiled eggs, no yokes; diced celery; sour cream not mayo; salt and pepper to taste."

When Leah finally made eye contact with the customer, the woman looked taken aback. *So much for improving my people skills.*

~

Promptly at three o'clock Leah hitched up her buggy and headed to the largest Amish dairy farm in the area. She'd washed her face before leaving and changed her *kapp*. She'd also brushed her teeth and sprayed on a little of Emma's forgotten peach body mist. Yet despite her efforts, she was totally unprepared when Jonah, instead of Mrs. Byler, answered her knock at the door.

"Jonah, I...I thought you'd be in the barn. I was expecting your *mamm*," she said, breathlessly.

"Hello, Leah. Nice to see you. I am allowed out of the barn sometimes, especially for good behavior." His voice was exasperatingly soft and gentle, without a hint of the nervousness she possessed.

"I'm glad to hear you've been well behaved and haven't gotten anyone fired recently." She crossed her arms over her pinafore.

When he leaned his shoulder against the frame, his bulk almost filled the entire doorway. "I have been exceptional, but I take it you didn't come to see me?"

"No, I've come to talk to Joanna about cheese, and I'll probably buy some too. Since I've run into you instead, there is something on my mind." She forced herself to look at him, despite his unnerving effect on her.

"Want to sit outside?" He pointed toward a bench near the vegetable garden, where a weeping willow tree provided cool shade.

After a moment's hesitation, she agreed. It wasn't comfortable craning her neck like this. Once seated—she tall and straight, he slouched and relaxed—Leah wasted no time with preliminary chitchat. "The other day, why did you leave the diner in such an all-fired hurry?"

He set his hat on the bench and slicked a hand through his hair. It looked freshly washed and silky.

"My bowl of oatmeal was finished, you'd forgotten my request for more coffee, and I got tired of waiting for you to come back."

"I wanted to apologize for that. April needed to talk to me about something important and it took longer than expected. I plumb forgot about your coffee."

"Did she fire you for insulting my grandmother?"

"No, she didn't." Leah refused to be baited.

"Did she scold you for neglecting one of her regular customers?"

"No, she said I've been good for business and she offered me a full partnership."

His face bloomed into a grin. "She didn't!" He laughed, a husky sound from deep in his throat.

"She did." Leah folded her hands primly in her lap, fighting back a smile.

"Good for you, Leah! Congratulations. Tell Mrs. Lambright I wish her the best of luck with that." He looked toward the house and rose to his feet. "Ah, there's my *mamm*. I'd better get back to work."

Leah spotted Joanna carrying a basket of laundry to the clothesline. "Please wait," she said. "There's something else I wanted to ask."

He was two steps away when he stopped and turned.

"If you're Old Order like us, and I know this road is part of our district, why is it you never come to preaching services?"

He studied her before answering. "Why are you so curious, Leah Miller?"

"That's just how I am." But her courage began to wane. If he had been shunned for something terrible, he probably didn't want to talk about it. "Of course, if you'd rather not say, I understand. I don't mean to be rude...again."

Jonah came back to the bench. "It's not a mystery, so don't worry. My *mamm* and I moved here a few months ago after my *daed* died. We came from Hancock, Wisconsin. Have you ever been there?"

Leah shook her head but remained silent.

"Pretty place, really, but my *mamm* wanted to live with her parents They're getting up in years. So she sold the farm and we moved." He looked at her with eyes filled with sorrow. "I didn't have much say in the matter and *dawdi* needed my help, so I left my friends and everything I knew and came here. I'll start attending preaching services soon. My grandmother has been bugging me about that. Up until recently I've been traveling back to Wisconsin on the bus to help my uncle. He hurt his back and hasn't been able to hire any help. He bought our old farm and combined it with his. When his sons are older, he'll have all the help he needs, and there will be an extra house when one of my cousins marries." He stood again, looking over his shoulder at his mother. "You'd better speak to her while she's hanging clothes, and I need to get set up for afternoon milking."

Leah rose too. "I'm sorry that I pried, Jonah."

All vestiges of sorrow vanished from his face. "You can make it up to me with a free cup of coffee. Then we'll call it even." He marched off without a backward glance.

As Leah watched him leave, she had to rack her brain for why she'd come to see Joanna Byler in the first place. She had imagined some big scandal, while Jonah had simply been helping his uncle with his now larger farm responsibilities.

First, poor service, now asking nosy questions...she certainly wasn't impressing this young man with her good Christian character.

Leah found Mrs. Byler on the back porch folding laundry she had taken off the line. The woman helpfully explained the cheeses she produced and how each might be used in cooking and baking.

"I'd like to see the cheesecake recipe you're working up," said Mrs. Byler. "Come inside so I can grab my reading glasses."

Leah followed her into a large, tidy room smelling faintly of cinnamon. While Joanna studied the recipe, Leah studied the kitchen, even though it wasn't much different from theirs.

After a minute Joanna said, "Mmm, this sounds yummy. Are you going to use fresh peaches?"

"*Jah*, I want it light and fluffy during the hot summer months. Then I'll adjust the recipe for the winter and use either bananas or canned peaches and substitute a heavier, richer cheese."

"Oh, my. I have just the perfect thing. Stay right there." Joanna disappeared down the cellar steps.

Leah happily complied, because from where she stood she could see Jonah in the yard. He was hitching a team of draft horses to the hay wagon. His shirt sleeves were rolled up, and even from this distance she could see the strength and power in his arms and shoulders.

And then she felt a flutter in her stomach she couldn't quite describe and one that she didn't quite like. Maybe she was coming down with the flu or had eaten something well past its prime. Leah hated to think she was becoming like her sister—affected by the mere proximity of a handsome man—because Jonah Byler certainly fit that description.

~

Matthew worked a pair of Quarter horses in the ring for most of the morning. He was making good progress with the two-year-olds, and they would soon be ready for the racing circuit. Mr. Mac and the owners were pleased with him. Even Jeff Andrews, who was listed as trainer of record and still oversaw his work, grunted out an occasional compliment.

He enjoyed his job. The pay was good; in fact, he'd been promised another raise at the end of the month. If his savings account continued to grow at its current rate, he'd soon be able to start seriously courting. But he refused to pursue any woman without the means to build their own home. As much as he loved his *daed,* he'd rather not subject a bride to living with the deacon. He still remembered the first few months after Aunt Hannah moved in with them. Wool flew in all directions until those two finally made their peace. Now they got along fine, but it hadn't always been that way. He would rather start off married life with a few less obstacles.

Unfortunately, his courage around women was not growing as fast as his bank account. It was so much easier to deal with horses. He could look into a mare's big brown eyes and know exactly what she was thinking. Not so with females of the human variety. What were they constantly whispering about after preaching services? And they never seemed to run out of things to talk about the way he did with his friends. He would probably save a king's ransom before summoning enough courage to ask out a certain girl.

At least he was making progress at Sunday singings. He not only had said hello to Martha Hostetler, but goodbye as well. And he thought he'd seen her glancing in his direction once or twice between songs. He planned to sit across from her next Sunday and ask about her vegetable stand on the county road. Emma advised him to find common ground and then get the gal talking about herself. Because he'd once sold eggs at a roadside stand, this was the best common ground he could think of.

As he led the two twin fillies back to their stalls, he saw Jeff Andrews returning from the indoor arena with the yearling colt Matthew admired—the same colt Andrews had injected with medication.

Feeling a tightness deep in his chest, Matthew noticed that the horse was still limping. As soon as he put his horses away, he approached the head trainer. "I see that colt's still a little gimpy," he said in a conversational tone as he knocked dust off his trousers with his work gloves.

Andrews' head snapped around. "He's fine," he said, "barely limping at all. Much better than last week."

Matthew approached until he was very near, so as not to be overheard by other stable help. "Do you think so? I think he's limping just as badly after a workout. Maybe you should have the vet take a look at that foreleg."

Andrews leaned so close Matthew could smell cigarettes and coffee on his breath. "Do you think so, boy? I'm curious as to who died and left you boss?"

Matt took a step back. "Nobody. I just thought you'd want an objective opinion from someone not working the horse on a daily basis."

Andrews led the colt into the stall and began wiping him down with a towel. Matt followed right behind and then planted himself in the doorway.

"Objective, huh? Well, Matty my boy, don't get yourself all worked up about this yearling. He ain't yours and you've got nothing to worry about anyway." He threw the towel down in the shavings and began rubbing down his coat with a soft brush. "I'll put liniment on that leg, tape it up, and then give him my miracle potion. He'll be good as new." The trainer patted the colt's hind flank.

Matthew shut the stall door with one muddy boot. "Does that miracle cure come in a hypodermic needle? You got no business injecting steroids without the owner's permission. Besides, Mr. Mac wants a vet or licensed tech to give injections because of all the liability."

Andrews reared back as though the colt had kicked him. His expression morphed from shock to outrage to anxiety in a matter of seconds. He grabbed Matthew's shirt in one meaty fist. "Who told you about me giving him a shot?"

Matthew glared at his boss. "Let go of my shirt before it rips."

Andrews glared back but released his hold.

"Nobody told me about it. I saw you with my own eyes a couple weeks ago. I had to come back to his stall to get my gloves."

The trainer's face regained some composure. "Who did you tell about this, Miller?"

"Nobody. I had hoped it was a one-time episode, but now I'm not so sure."

Andrews' features returned to their normal glower. "This ain't none of your business. You just do what I tell you and keep your nose clean." He jabbed a finger into the apprentice's chest.

Matthew grabbed hold of the man's finger and pushed it away. "Don't do that." He gritted out the words, even though he was ill equipped for the confrontation. Plain folk usually removed themselves from conflicts like this, especially with an *Englischer.* "You told me I needed to watch to learn the business. But I didn't think I would see you doing something illegal."

"That shot was no illegal drug. I gave this yearling what anybody else would've given him." He stroked the horse's neck.

"You're not licensed to give shots. You should've called the vet."

"Then the vet would've called the owner, and they'd hightail it up here in a tizzy, especially that man's wife. She would want to take the colt home and put it in a crib next to her bed." He spit something disgusting into a baby food jar he kept in his pocket.

Matthew tried to hide his contempt. "It's her horse, so she has a right to let it sleep anywhere she chooses." He ran a hand down the colt's silky mane.

This wasn't the response Andrews had expected for his bad joke. "Are you soft like her? Because this is a job, a career, not a 4-H project. You've got plenty of potential, Matty, lots more than those slackers Mr. Mac always seems to hire. But you better listen to me, boy, and learn how the real world operates. I'll call the vet for the colt if that leg isn't better in a few days. But in the meantime, you just keep your big mouth shut." He jabbed his forefinger one last time into Matt's chest and then stomped off, leaving the stall gate open behind him.

Matthew glanced back at the yearling. The horse took a tentative step forward and started rubbing his head on Matt's arm. Somehow that gesture made the young trainer feel a whole lot better.

~

Emma slapped at a deerfly that seemed determined to ruin an otherwise perfect morning. Those pesky bugs could try the patience of a saint. But when she straightened her spine to inspect the neat rows of her vegetable garden, Emma liked what she saw. The green beans were almost ready to pick. Green onions, radishes, and carrots had been planted in stages, so they would add color to salads for weeks to come. Her cabbages were round and plump, while five varieties of peppers, including a new habanero, promised plenty of late-summer spice. She had been cutting romaine lettuce and fresh spinach every day as she waited for the iceberg lettuce to form firm heads. Maybe they wouldn't grow to the size of their West Coast counterparts, with California's endless sunshine, but hers could be picked at the peak of sweetness instead of early for shipment.

Emma surveyed her garden with pride. It was not only a joy to behold but provided healthy nutrition for the cost of seeds—worth every slug and mealy bug she'd picked off by hand. As she absently swatted her cheek once more, the sound of crunching gravel diverted her attention from the deerfly.

A large pickup had pulled up the drive. Loud, raucous music poured from the open windows. When the doors flew open and two young men and an equal number of big-haired girls climbed out, Emma knew they weren't here about riding lessons. Wiping her dirty hands on her apron, she left her small patch of paradise, careful not to step on the cantaloupe runners.

As Emma approached the foursome, the blonde whispered

something behind her hand to the brown-haired girl. The brunette grinned at whatever had been said.

"May I help you?" she asked, closing the distance between them.

"Ah...yeah," said one young man. "We're looking for Jamie. We're old friends of his from high school." He was wearing tight blue jeans and a tank top that left more chest exposed than covered. Emma saw little point to a shirt like that.

"He's cutting hay in the south fields," she said. "I'll send someone to get him."

"Are you his wife?" the blonde asked. "Someone told me he got married a couple years ago." She smiled pleasantly, but Emma couldn't stop gawking at her clothes. She was wearing the shortest skirt imaginable, and the hem of her cotton top didn't come close to the skirt's waistband. A wide expanse of her tummy and back showed. Emma felt a sting of embarrassment for the girl.

"*Jah,* I'm Emma Davis." She stood like a statue, not sure if she should shake hands or what. Considering the state of her hands at the moment, she chose to brush them across her apron instead.

"I'm Kim, and this is Corrine, Mark, and Josh," said the blonde without sufficient clothing.

The two men nodded while the one named Corrine smiled. "Kim was Jamie's date for our high school prom," she said. Her skirt was equally short, but her top was so long it looked as though she wore no skirt at all.

"Is that right?" Emma asked, with little inflection. "Jamie will be happy to see you all, I'm sure. Why don't you wait on the porch? I'll be right back."

The four friends walked toward the house while Emma headed to the farm office, feeling discombobulated. It would've been nice to bathe and put on a fresh dress before meeting her husband's old pals.

In the office the foreman called James on his cell phone and asked him to come to the house. Once she knew he was on his way, Emma walked slowly back to the group, trying to calm her fluttery nerves. *Why the visit after five years of being out of school?* Climbing the porch steps, she smiled as pleasantly as possible. "Would anyone like something to drink?" she asked.

The taller of the two men said, "Sure, I could use a cold one."

"Yeah, me too, if it wouldn't be too much trouble," said the other man.

Emma gazed from one to the other. "A cold one what? Iced tea? Lemonade? Coke?"

The girls snickered; the men looked stricken.

"A cold beer, if you don't mind," answered the first man.

Emma blinked. "We have no beer in the house, warm or cold."

"We'll all have Cokes, Emma," said Kim quickly. "That sounds great."

"Coming right up," Emma murmured.

Inside the kitchen she fumed. *Cold beer at two o'clock in the afternoon?* What a ridiculous idea. What did they plan to get done later? And one of them would be getting behind the wheel of the truck. The more she thought about it, the more irritated she grew, but she kept her features expressionless as she carried the tray of soft drinks outside.

Blessedly, James came marching across the lawn with his face beaming. "Hi, everybody, long time no see." He hugged all four old friends, including the two women.

Emma felt the ugly emotion of jealousy rear its head.

"Oh, my gosh, Jamie, look at you! You look just like an actor in a History Channel movie," Kim said, holding him at arm's length. "It's really true, then. We had heard you turned Amish, but I wouldn't believe it until I saw for myself. Congratulations, if that's the proper thing to say."

Five of the six people laughed. James stepped back from Kim and put his arm around Emma's shoulders. "*Jah,* I turned Amish three years ago, right after I finished at OSU's Agricultural College. We got hitched the following year."

Emma watched Kim's face while James explained. Her smile melted like a snow cone in the sun.

"You've been married for two years already?" Kim asked.

"We have," he said, tightening his hold on her shoulders.

"How old is your kid?"

James shook his head. "No children yet. We hope for a baby someday, but so far we haven't been blessed."

Kim stared at Emma. "I'm surprised...surprised by everything coming out of your mouth, Jamie Davis." She picked up her Coke and drank down half of it before stopping.

"How's your family?" asked Mark, giving Kim an odd look.

"Fine, everyone's good," said James. "Dad is still not ready to retire. He likes working too much to stop. Mom's nursing in Canton. Lily's at vet school, my older brother is an associate pastor in Wooster, and my little brother is home from college. That's everybody."

"Did you finish at OSU?" asked Josh.

"Yeah, I fit everything I needed into two years. I couldn't wait to be done with school."

"You and me both, old buddy," said Mark. "My folks insisted that I get my MBA when I graduated from Bowling Green with an undergrad degree. They said it would improve my job prospects. So I didn't finish until last month, and I don't want to open another textbook for the rest of my life." All of the males laughed at this.

"So what do you do here?" asked Corrine, glancing around.

"I help my dad run his business and I farm."

"Using those giant horses I see in the fields?"

James smiled easily. "No, we're New Order. We use tractors and other mechanized equipment."

"Oh, that's good." Corrine looked quickly at Emma. "I mean...it's faster and easier with a tractor than with horses, isn't it?"

But James wasn't the least bit uncomfortable. "It sure is. I get as much done as I did before."

"I see you still have your truck," said Kim. "I saw it parked near the barn."

"It's Kevin's truck now. I sold it to him."

Emma heard the timer go off on the stove, signaling that her muffins were done. "If you will excuse me, I have to tend to something in the house." She slipped out from under her husband's arm and hurried inside.

She didn't want to spend another minute on the porch in her untidy dress while James' former prom date stole surreptitious glances at her.

Why are his friends looking him up after five years? This was Holmes County. They probably saw plenty of Amish people every day.

Maybe it was her imagination, but Kim seemed to possess more interest than normal for someone supposed to be "just a friend."

SIX

Leah trotted the horse all the way home from Mrs. Byler's that day. She hurried to fix supper, tried to hurry her family through the meal, and rushed to clean up the kitchen. She couldn't wait to try the new cheese in the recipe she was inventing. And the results were better than expectations.

Peach Parfait Supreme was light and creamy, sweet yet tangy, with firm ripe peaches that melted on your tongue and left only a delicious memory. It was a slice of summertime—perfect alone or topped with vanilla ice cream or frozen yogurt. She had baked up two pies that night with some Georgia peaches purchased from the fruit seller in Wilmot. Her family had raved and devoured the first pie that night. April had gushed over her sample slice the next day and then took the remainder of the second pie home to her family. On Leah's next baking day, she made an even half dozen. The recipe would only improve once Ohio peaches were ready to pick.

Now today was Thursday, and if Jonah Byler didn't stop by the diner soon, there would be no pie for him to try and report back to his mother. She should have baked one extra to set aside for Mrs. Byler.

She shouldn't have let Daniel, Steven, and John have second helpings during the inaugural week of Peach Parfait Supreme. She was sure they only did so to get on her good side.

And she shouldn't let all their attention puff her up like a crowing barnyard rooster. It was only pie. But everyone who tried it seemed to truly like it.

Later during the lunch rush, the bell over the door jangled to announce another customer. Leah didn't even turn her head as she delivered a full tray of plates to a booth. Everyone seemed to have a special request that day: *More pickles, please. Could you grill my burger a little more? I'd prefer the dressing on the side instead of already on the salad.* And every place at the counter had remained occupied since breakfast. Daniel and his friends took up three stools and didn't seem to be in much of a hurry. They dawdled over cheeseburgers and chips while offering updates from their blacksmith shop, furniture factory, and farm, respectively. Leah was too busy to pay much attention, but she nodded and added a few comments to be polite.

Half an hour later, she crossed paths with April while carrying a tray of dirty dishes to the dishwasher. "I'm surprised you didn't want to wait on Jonah yourself," April said.

"What?" Leah squawked. "He's here? When did he sneak in? Where is he sitting?"

April faced her. "That's four questions in one breath. If I didn't know better, I'd say you rather like the guy."

"Liking has nothing to do with it," Leah said, tucking a stray lock under her *kapp*. "I just want him to try my creation and report back to Joanna." She pulled off her soiled apron and slipped on a fresh one in under three seconds.

"You'd better hurry. Last time I checked there's only one piece left. And he's sitting in his regular spot."

Leah swallowed hard, feeling as though the radio had announced tornados were headed their way. She charged through the swinging door and headed straight for the refrigerated display carousel. The last piece of Peach Parfait Supreme sat forlornly under plastic wrap.

In the few moments it took to reach the pie a customer's voice sang out. "Say, Leah, I'll take another slice of your new recipe. It wasn't bad at all."

Leah pivoted. The speaker was the elderly *Englischer* who had been their very first customer. The buttons on his work coveralls were already straining from his exceptional appetite.

Leah looked past him toward the last booth. Sure enough, Jonah Byler was poring over *The Daily Budget*. "Mr. Rhodes," she whispered. "I was saving the last piece for somebody. Would you mind terribly if I gave it to him?"

Rhodes swiveled on his stool in the direction Leah had been looking. He wheezed with laughter. "Sure thing. I was young once. At least my wife tells me we were. Can't remember much about it."

She smiled. "Thank you, Mr. Rhodes. How about some Dutch Apple Crumb on the house instead?"

"Done!" Rhodes looked pleased with the bargain. Leah served up his pie and then hurried toward Jonah's booth with the dessert special before someone else wanted it.

She set the plate down on his table with a clatter. "Hello, Jonah. Nice of you to drop by."

"What's that?" he asked, barely glancing away from his newspaper.

"My Peach Parfait Supreme—the new recipe I made with the specialty cheese I bought from your *mamm*." She felt giddy with anticipation.

"Sure, I remember, but I'm really full, Leah. April heaped up my sandwich with ham and cheese like she was trying to fatten me up. Extra macaroni salad too." He flashed a smile over the newspaper. "I'll try it another time. Really, I can't eat another bite."

She felt deflated, as though he had actually poked a hole in her. "Jonah, please, just sample a forkful and I'll wrap up the rest for you to take home. I would like your mother to try it. I practically had to wrestle this piece away from another customer."

"Someone requested this slice of pie, but instead you brought it to a person who hadn't ordered it?" His tone of voice was maddeningly soft and conversational.

"Pretty much. I wanted *you* to try it."

"All right. I'll taste a bite once the sandwich settles a little." He glanced at her before returning his focus to the newspaper.

Leah's level of annoyance ratcheted up a notch. "Jonah Byler, would you please put the paper down and pay attention to me?" As soon as she said the words, she felt vain and bold, but it was too late to recall her hasty words.

He folded *The Daily Budget* in half, set it aside, and focused his sea blue eyes on her. "You don't need my attention, Miss Miller," he said calmly. "You've been getting compliments from plumb near everybody else all morning." He nodded in the direction of the counter. Her three regular Amish customers were sneaking peeks at them over their shoulders.

Leah prayed for the floor of the train car to give way beneath her feet. "Sorry. You're right," she mumbled. "I'm acting like a child. You would think I'd found the cure for a deadly disease or something." Her cheeks flamed with embarrassment while the back of her throat burned. She picked up the plate of dessert but Jonah grabbed her hand.

"Please leave it. I do want to try it, and I'm sure my mother will be curious."

The touch of his fingers was more than she could bear. She pulled her hand back as though stung by a bee. "I'll get you a small box." She walked to the kitchen with legs turned to rubber and then delivered a Styrofoam container on her way to another table. Fortunately, April then sent her to the kitchen to start more coffee and iced tea.

Shame from her foolish, prideful behavior washed over her like a dense fog. The more she thought about her actions, the worse she felt. Tonight she would pray long and hard to be delivered from herself. Her job was changing her, and not for the better.

"Leah?" April called from the doorway. "Jonah needs you at the cash register."

Leah looked up from measuring loose tea. "Could you please ring up his bill? I'm in the middle of something."

"No, I can't. He wants to speak to you." She let the door swing shut to circumvent further argument.

Seeing no recourse, Leah trudged to the small counter by the door. Jonah stood waiting with his trusty newspaper folded beneath his arm. The pie box was nowhere in sight.

"May I help you?" she asked. "Where's your bill?"

"I already paid April. I wanted you for two other reasons." He waited a few seconds until she finally met his gaze. "First, I ate a bite of pie and then another, and pretty soon the piece was gone. You'll have to bake more and see that my *mamm* gets some from the next batch. It was very good." His grin filled his entire face.

"*Danki,*" she said weakly without a fraction of her earlier enthusiasm. "What was the other thing?"

"This," Jonah said, tapping a notice in the paper with his finger. "This Saturday is the summer draft horse sale in Mount Hope. They'll be auctioning off all kinds of Belgians, Percherons, and crossbreeds. It's the second biggest horse sale of the year."

Leah waited patiently but had no comment on the subject.

"Were you planning to attend?" he asked.

"Absolutely not." She wrinkled her nose. "Horses make me sneeze and my eyes water—at least their dander does. You saw what happened when I was in your barn. I try to stay away from large numbers of farm animals. Why do you ask?"

"I need to pick up a pair of work horses, maybe four if the price is right. *Dawdi's* team is almost as old as he is," he joked. "But I'm not a good judge of horseflesh. My knowledge is confined to dairy cows." Again he waited for a reply that didn't come.

Jonah, who apparently wasn't daunted by anything, forged ahead. "April tells me your *bruder*, Matthew, knows his stuff when it comes to things equine."

Leah nodded, feeling her palms start to sweat. *Is Jonah about to ask me to attend the auction with him?* "*Jah,* that's true. Matthew has been riding bareback since he was five years old and can get a horse to do anything but wash dishes. He works over at Macintosh Farms as a trainer."

"That's what I hear. So do you think he will go to Saturday's sale?" He shifted his weight to the other leg and leaned on the counter. The movement brought his face that much closer to hers.

"If he doesn't have to work, he'll be there. He'd rather be near horses than just about any person he knows."

"Since I've never met him and you say he's not the most sociable sort of fellow, do you think you might tag along to introduce us? And ask him to help me find the right pair? I don't want to buy a couple of nags to match the pair *dawdi* already has." He tipped back his straw hat. "I'd be much obliged, and you wouldn't have to give me that free cup of coffee you owe me."

Leah closed her eyes for a second. "You probably think I'm an awful person, or at least the most forgetful one you've ever met. Truth is, from the time I arrive I'm so busy I forget everything else other than cooking and serving customers." She smoothed her damp palms down her apron, hoping nothing would prompt shaking hands. "The other day a customer asked what color my eyes were, and I had to think about it before answering."

She forced a giggle, but his laughter filled the diner and drew the attention of several patrons. "Your eyes are the richest shade of brown—dark and warm, like polished walnut."

"*Jah,* well, I gave him a short answer compared to all that."

"What do you say, Leah? Will you put up with your allergies on Saturday and introduce me to your *bruder?*"

Strangely, the whole diner had turned graveyard quiet after his question. "I have to work on Saturday," she said in a tiny voice as that notion occurred to her. She tried unsuccessfully to ignore the butterflies taking flight in her stomach.

"Maybe if you ask real nice, April will let you leave after the breakfast rush. She seems to like you for some reason. The auctioneers sell farm equipment and carriages first and don't sell horses until the afternoon."

"I tend to grow on people," she said.

"I'm finding that out." His smile revealed perfectly straight teeth.

The quiet in the normally noisy diner grew deafening. Leah backed away from the cash register. "Could you wait here for a minute? I'll go ask her right now."

She pushed open the swinging door with more force than necessary and nearly smashed her boss against the wall.

"Sorry, I didn't realize you were there," Leah said. "You weren't listening in on my conversation with Jonah, were you?"

"Well, I was curious why the guy had adjusted his hat three times while waiting for you. Besides, I learned eavesdropping from you."

Leah blushed. "*Jah,* I remember. Well...what do you say? Can I have time off to attend the horse sale?"

"Hmm...let me think a moment," April said, laying an index finger across her cheek.

"Please? I know Saturdays are busy but maybe your sister can help out this one time."

"I'm teasing you!" April threw her arms around Leah's neck. "Of course you can go. You've worked so hard for weeks. You're even baking on your day off. I'm so happy Jonah asked you out."

Leah's head snapped back. "He didn't ask me out. He asked me to go to a stinky horse sale so he can meet my *bruder.*" She straightened her *kapp,* which was knocked askew from the hug.

April cocked her head to one side. "Yeah, right. Anyway, I'm pleased as punch you said yes."

Leah walked to the large coffeemaker. "Please don't make a big deal out of this. Jonah Byler thinks I'm rude and incompetent. I need to take him this coffee to try to make up for my forgetfulness." She filled a Styrofoam cup, added the cream and sugar she knew he favored, and snapped on a lid. On the way out she whispered, "*Danki,* April. I owe you one."

"Just don't spill that coffee on him, and I'll take the one you owe out in pie."

Jonah was standing where she'd left him with his heavy-lidded and dreamy eyes. She set the cup on the counter to make sure their fingers didn't touch. His effect on her was unnerving.

"She said *jah*." The words sounded hoarse but recognizable. Clearing her throat, she said, "I'll ask Matthew to pick me up here at the diner on his way to the sale." She pushed the to-go cup toward him. "This is on the house for your ride home."

Jonah picked up the coffee and headed for the door. "I look forward to the auction even more than my next slice of Peach Parfait Supreme."

How can he do that? How can he say the most outrageous things as calmly as asking for the time of day?

∼

When Matthew arrived home from work that day he was hot, hungry, and tired. Cooling off in the pond took care of the first problem, and his dinner warming in the oven would take care of the second, but sleep would have to wait until after evening chores. He'd been expecting to find *mamm* in the kitchen, but Leah sat at the table instead, sipping tea.

"*Guder nachmittag*," she said. "Your supper's ready. I'll get your cucumbers and pickled beets from the fridge."

"*Danki*. I'm hungry enough to eat a bear." He slid into his chair and tucked his napkin into his collar. When his sister set a plate of fried chicken down before him, he began to gobble his meal without his table manners as he was the only one eating.

Surprisingly, his *schwestern* sat back down with him. "You don't have to stay while I eat, Leah. I promise I won't choke to death on a chicken bone." He dabbed his mouth with his napkin.

"I need to talk to you. That's why I waited."

"No, I will not gather eggs for you. You can't give all your chores to Henry and me just because you've got a job."

Leah pulled a face. "Henry already gathered the eggs. This has nothing to do with the henhouse."

"What then?" he asked between forkfuls of mashed potatoes and chicken.

"May I go with you to the summer draft horse sale on Saturday? That is, if you're planning on going." She looked him straight in the eye.

He nearly choked on a piece of chicken after all. He set down his fork. "Am I hearing things? You want to go to the Mount Hope auction?"

She nodded.

"Leah, only horses will be there. And flies. And you know how your allergies flare up when you're around all that animal dander."

"My boss is bringing me over-the-counter antihistamines tomorrow. She said if I take two every four hours I should be able to tolerate the beasts."

Matthew ate some cucumber salad. "The big question is why would you want to? Your buggy horse is well trained and gentle as a lamb. You won't find anything better than your gelding. 'Sides, they'll be selling working draft horses that day, not buggy horses."

Leah rolled her eyes. "I'm not looking to buy a horse. Will you please let me finish?"

"Sure, but while you're finishing could you pour me something to drink?"

Leah went to the fridge while saying, "I have a new business acquaintance from Wisconsin who needs a pair of draft horses. He heard from April that you know a thing or two about horses and so he would like your advice on which to bid on." She set down a glass of lemonade in front of him.

Matthew continued to watch her over his chicken leg. "And..." he prompted.

"And what?" she asked.

"Why would *you* go to the auction if your business acquaintance wants to buy a team?"

"He doesn't know you. There will probably be dozens of people there. How would he pick you out in the crowd?"

Matthew finished the bowl of mashed potatoes. "Most likely there will be hundreds of people there, but you could always give him an exact time and location to meet me. I'd be happy to help the guy find the best stock for his money." This was very unlike his sister. Leah didn't have a devious bone in her body, but she was behaving strangely.

"I want to go because he asked me to come too," she said simply.

He was tired after dancing around the head trainer all day, so he chose not to pursue this further. "Okay, Leah, if I can get time off work, I'll pick you up at eleven o'clock at the diner. It's on my way to the auction anyway."

"Danki," she said, kissing the top of his head before running up the stairs.

The gesture was also unlike Leah, causing more curiosity on his part regarding this "business acquaintance."

But that question would have to wait until Saturday.

～

Reluctantly, Jeff Andrews gave him the day off when Matthew asked him on Friday. On Saturday morning he hurried through chores and then helped Henry with his before jumping into the shower. He had just enough time to pick up Leah before the horse sale. He liked to carefully inspect the stock prior to the bidding to form his own opinions.

Leah ran down the diner steps the moment he pulled into the parking lot. She looked different somehow. "That isn't the same dress you had on this morning, is it?" he asked as she climbed into the buggy.

"No, I changed after the breakfast rush." She smoothed down her skirt and began rubbing lotion onto her hands.

"Why would you put on a nice dress to come to an auction? It's just dusty old barns, dusty bleachers to watch the promenade, and dusty parking lots. I think you have the wrong idea of what this will be like."

She slanted him a glance. "I know exactly what it will be like."

"Okay, then tell me about your business acquaintance—the key to this mystery. He has to be the reason you're coming to a horse sale."

"I don't know what you're talking about." She stared off at the passing scenery.

"Come on, Leah. I'm not stupid. You can tell me if you like this guy. I won't run and tell *daed*."

She pursed her lips. "There's not much to tell. I think I like him, but it's too soon to say for sure."

"That figures! My younger sister is going to start courting before I do." He shook the reins and the gelding picked up his pace.

"Nothing is stopping you. You could always work up your courage and ask Martha if you could take her home from a singing." Leah made a clucking sound exactly like a hen.

He laughed in spite of himself. "I am a chicken. But who told you I have my eye on Martha Hostetler?"

She swatted his arm. "Nobody did, but I have seen you staring at her at preaching services."

He felt color rise up his neck into his face. "I'm that obvious? Do you think she's noticed?"

"I'm pretty sure she has."

He thought his case of mortification might be fatal. "Oh, great. I've probably scared her off."

"I don't think so. The few times you weren't staring at her, I noticed her watching you." Leah pinched his forearm.

Matthew felt momentarily dizzy. "Don't tease me, Leah. That's not right."

"I'm not. I'm perfectly serious. Why wouldn't Martha be interested in you? You're handsome and nice, most of the time, and you're a hard worker."

He looked at his sister from the corner of his eye to make sure she wasn't joking. She seemed earnest. "So you think I should ask to take her home sometime?"

"*Jah,* before someone else does. She's not going to wait for you forever, Matthew Miller."

He chewed on that thought for the short ride into Mount Hope. They joined a long queue of buggies entering the tie-up area beyond the auction barns. While Matthew watched the horses being paraded around the grounds in hopes of catching the eye of buyers, Leah almost fell out of the buggy craning her neck. She appeared to be searching the crowd for her business associate.

And something told Matthew this acquaintance, looking to replace the family team, wouldn't be the elderly *dawdi*-type.

~

"My goodness. There he is." Leah raised her hand in a little wave. She'd seen Jonah mainly because he was a head taller than everyone else. He was wearing black trousers and his black felt hat, but at least his shirt wasn't Sunday best. She hadn't been the only one to overdress for the occasion.

When he spotted them, he began pushing his way through the crowd. Matthew had been right about the large number of attendees at the summer auction.

"Hi, Leah," Jonah said when he reached them. "That is a very nice dress. I don't think I've seen that one before."

"You haven't," she said abruptly. "Jonah, this is my *bruder* Matthew. He'll help you pick out some decent teams to bid on. You can ask him as many questions as you like."

Jonah turned toward her *bruder*. "Hi, I'm Jonah Byler."

"Matthew Miller, as you heard. Please to meet ya." The two men shook hands. "Let's go get programs. That'll tell us what's up for sale today and what kind of lineage the horses come from. It'll also explain what kind of trainin' each horse has had, if it's young, and how it has been worked if it's not."

"Sounds like a good place to start," Jonah said. "I don't suppose they'd be nice enough to indicate at what price the bidding will start."

Matthew scratched his chin. "That would be nice, wouldn't it? But what would really be helpful is an idea how high the bidding will go. So we're not waiting around till midnight for horses we can't afford anyway."

The two men laughed like old friends.

Leah interrupted them with, "Until midnight? This horse sale might go that late?" She didn't think she had enough antihistamines to last until the wee hours.

They turned toward her—Jonah looked indulgent, but her *bruder* already looked peeved. "*Jah,* it usually goes well past midnight. There are a lot of horses to sell. What did you expect, Leah? It would be over in a couple hours and then we'd all go for coffee and pie?"

Leah fumed inside. "Well…*jah.*"

Both men laughed again. "Don't worry yourself," said Jonah. "Maybe the pair that catches my eye will be one of the first sold."

"Don't count on it," said Matthew. "They love to get rid of the duds early on to newbies who don't know any better." To his sister he said, "When you get tired, you can rest in the buggy. I threw one of *mamm*'s old quilts in there for you." Matthew stretched on tiptoes to scan the grounds. "Let's go register and get programs. I'll take a buyer's number too in case I see something I can't resist bidding on. Follow me, Jonah. Keep up, Leah. Don't get separated from us in the crowd." He began walking toward the office, where people milled in groups outside the door.

"You can hang on to my arm if you like," Jonah whispered to her. "This is a lot more commotion than I expected."

"I'll be fine," she said, keeping her sweating palms by her side. She started to follow Matthew and stepped right into the path of a pony pulling a sulky. The seller was showing off the pony's easy handling to potential bidders.

Jonah yanked her out of harm's way just in time, and none too gently.

"Please, Leah, look in all directions. If you get trampled to death while helping me buy a horse, I don't know what I'd tell my *mamm*." His eyes twinkled with high spirits.

"Okay, I'll be careful, if for no reason other than that." This time she kept up with him, practically treading on his heels while they registered for the auction.

After perusing the program in the shade for what seemed like an inordinate amount of time, Matthew announced, "All right. I see you've marked a few to check out and so have I. Let's start in the first barn and see what they've got. You might spot some others you'll want to bid on."

As they strode toward the barn, Leah fell in step behind them. Because the horseflesh prancing past held little interest for her, she studied Jonah instead. He was not only taller but must weigh at least forty pounds more than Matthew. However, he wasn't remotely plump. Judging by his arms and his back and shoulder muscles, he must get plenty of physical exercise in the dairy business. *Maybe to spare his* dawdi*'s ancient team, he attaches the hitch to himself and drags the plow through the fields.* The mental picture caused her to laugh aloud.

Matt and Jonah stopped chatting to stare at her. "Did you see something amusing in one of the stalls, Miss Miller?" Jonah asked in his soft, hypnotic voice. "Or maybe one of the mares told you a joke while we were distracted."

"Or maybe you're losing your mind?" asked Matt, snickering.

Leah ignored her *bruder*, but she found Jonah's use of her formal name unnerving. She met his gaze. "No. I was daydreaming and a funny story came to mind. One I'd rather not share."

The dimples deepened in his cheeks. "Step up here and take a look at this Morgan-Shire crossbreed. Notice the strength in those broad shoulders and back and those powerful legs. God took the best features from both breeds and put them together in this horse. This gelding is beautiful, don't you agree?" He took her arm and nearly dragged her to the stall.

She stepped up on the bottom rail and assessed the beast. He wasn't anywhere near as large as *daed*'s Percherons, but he did look sturdy. As though the animal knew she was evaluating him, he lifted his head and arched his neck. He gazed at her with one mesmerizing black eye.

"Ah-choo!" She sneezed, and the horse shook his long mane in protest.

"*Jah*, I almost forgot your allergies." Jonah drew her back from the stall.

A second sneeze was followed by a third. "Can I have a drink from your water bottle, Jonah?" she asked. "I'd better take two more pills."

"Sure, but be careful. Don't take too many. Let's get you some fresh air."

Leah thought she saw her *bruder* rolling his eyes, but she wasn't sure. She didn't want to be troublesome. The three walked to a bench near the smaller grandstands. A crowd was growing in anticipation of a new training harness about to be demonstrated. "You two go back in and check out horses. I'm going to sit right here and watch this show. It looks interesting."

After a minor amount of argument, they left her at the bleachers, where she viewed a rather *uninteresting* demonstration. When the men returned from the stalls, they all headed to the main grandstand, where they watched horses pull every conceivable implement to demonstrate their prowess. Leah did her best to remain enthralled.

"Where will these horses be auctioned?" she asked after what seemed like hours.

"We're going there now," Matthew answered, giving her another roll of his eyes. Inside the auction barn, packed with mostly Amish buyers, the bidding had begun.

"Since the horses Matthew and I are interested in have high bidding numbers, why don't we have some lunch?" Jonah asked. "It'll be a while before they're auctioned."

"Oh, great idea!" she said before Matthew could object.

"You just want to check out the competition."

Leah ignored her sibling as they crossed the street.

"She has no competition, at least not in the dessert department," Jonah said.

Leah smiled, hoping he was right. As it turned out, lunch at the buffet restaurant became the high point of her day. Usually the restaurant was filled with tourists, but today the crowd was at least half Plain folk.

Although everything they ate was delicious, Jonah continued to rave about Leah's Home Cooking. Matthew, without a shred of interest in talking about food, changed the subject to horses. Jonah, who seemed determined to discuss a topic Leah could participate in, kept changing it back. A rather bizarre three-way conversation ensued as Leah tried to mediate.

Although she felt grateful for Jonah's compliments, she couldn't wait for lunch to be over. The antihistamines, heat, and larger-than-normal meal made her drowsy. As they crossed the street and headed back to the auction arena, Leah couldn't keep her eyes open.

"Are you all right?" Jonah asked, taking her arm.

"I'm fine. I just ate too much lunch. I think I'll sit in the buggy for a while."

"I'll walk you there," he said.

"I'll find us seats in the arena," said Matthew, shaking his head as he walked away.

Leah steadied herself on his arm. "Thank goodness we parked in the shade," she murmured once they found their buggy among the others.

"Will you be okay by yourself?" Jonah asked, almost lifting her up the steps.

"I will be fine. Don't worry about me." She stifled a yawn behind her palm.

"If you need anything, send one of the boys assigned to feed and water the horses to find me."

She smiled sleepily. "Go buy yourself a horse or two, Jonah. And don't pick out any duds, okay?"

He winked one of his magnificent azure eyes and strode off. "I'll check on you later," he called.

She didn't know whether he'd checked on her or not, because Leah curled up on *mamm*'s old quilt in the back of the surrey and fell asleep. She slept for hours, barely rousing when Matthew climbed in to head for home. But when he shook her awake in front of their house, she was holding Jonah's coat. It had been folded and tucked under her head for a pillow.

He was a man of his word after all.

SEVEN

James lightly kicked the flanks of his gelding and galloped up the face of the hill while a worker drove cows toward him from the other side. They were moving a herd of Black Angus steers from this pasture, through a gate, and into higher, denser grassland. Television shows about ranches out West made the task look much easier than it was. The stubborn cattle didn't realize they had already chewed this area down and would find much tastier grass on the other side.

Sometimes old adages rang true.

Waving his hat like a rodeo rider, he doubled back to keep a few calves up with the rest. The sooner they relocated the herd, the sooner he could call it a day. He couldn't wait to shower, change, and spend the entire evening with his wife.

Emma wouldn't discuss the afternoon his old high school friends dropped by for a visit. "No sense in rehashing a pack of nonsense," she had declared, but she hadn't let him out of the doghouse, either. He shouldn't have hugged his friends, especially not the female variety. Amish folk maintained more distance and weren't as demonstrative as *Englischers,* and he'd forgotten himself. But when he'd seen Kim again, he knew he had made the right decision in his conversion to Amish life. Not only did he love Emma with every fiber of his being, but Kim's very short skirt and flirtatiousness showed disrespect for herself and for the choice he'd made. He'd expected more from an old friend.

However, Emma's hurt feelings had been his fault. He could have prevented her from feeling left out. Tonight, while his mom worked late and Dad went to Bible study, he would mend fences. And that thought lifted his spirits as he drove the last of the steers through the pasture gate and up the ridge.

James stopped in his mom's garden to pick a bouquet. Every woman loved flowers, and Emma was no exception. He was wondering if his sister had chocolate hidden somewhere when his dad spoke behind him. He almost jumped out of his boots.

"Come out of there, Jamie. I reckon you have enough flowers for a diplomatic funeral."

"I got carried away. I want to surprise Emma at dinner tonight." He walked toward his dad, careful where he stepped between the rows.

"You'll have to give them to her quickly, son. I need you to ride to Zanesville with me. We'll eat at the new steakhouse that just opened up." Jim Davis snaked a hand through his graying but still thick hair.

"Steakhouse? But Emma's fixing pork chops for supper—my favorite." He caught up with his dad halfway to the house. "Isn't this your Bible study night?" he asked, hoping his eagerness to be alone with his bride wasn't too obvious.

James Sr. stopped in his tracks. "I'm not going to the meeting. I need to pacify an irate client instead—for something that you were supposed to take care of." His tone of voice conveyed anger and disappointment.

"Wait!" Jamie demanded. "What do you mean? I don't know anybody in Zanesville."

His dad released a weary sigh. "I asked you to meet with that buyer from Columbus. He was looking to take every quarter horse yearling we've got for sale at a premium price, based on his earlier assessment and their certification. Because he's a busy man, he didn't want to make another trip to Charm." He scuffed his boot heel in the path and seemed to be choosing his words carefully. "I asked *you* to talk to him, but you sent Larry instead. He doesn't know half what you do about the breed. Mr. Young asked questions Larry couldn't answer." He stopped kicking dirt and met his son's gaze.

Jamie's words caught in his throat as the memory of the appointment came flooding back. His father hadn't looked this mad since the day Jamie and Kevin had spray-painted a huge football insignia on the barn.

"Mr. Young called me all bent out of shape," James Sr. continued. "He asked if his business wasn't important enough for an owner to spare the time. He felt insulted, and I can't say I blame him." Jamie's dad stared off at the setting sun, just above the western treetops. "I told him a family emergency had come up and that was why Larry had been sent. You know I don't like telling falsehoods, Jamie. It doesn't sit right with me. So tonight we're taking Mr. Young and his wife out to dinner. We'll answer any questions he might have about the horses, and you will apologize to the man." A note of finality hung in the air. The matter wasn't up for further discussion.

Not that Jamie wanted to argue.

He hadn't liked sending someone to do his job, knowing a situation could arise exactly like this. He'd felt guilty, even though Larry had reported that the meeting had gone well.

"I'm sorry, Dad. I thought Mr. Young would come here, but he picked a meeting place too far away to reach by horse-and-buggy." He swept his hat from his head. "I tried to find somebody to drive me down, but nobody was available except Larry. I guess I should've firmed up my plans sooner." The more he talked, the lamer his excuses sounded. And the more ashamed he felt.

"So why didn't Larry drive you?" his dad asked, his words filled with incredulity. "Why did he go alone? He trains pleasure horses for stables, not racehorses."

Jamie chose not to mention that the solo appointment had been Larry's idea. Bored with his current position, Larry sought the better pay and excitement on the racing circuit. He had assured Jamie he had done his homework.

"Larry's been studying up on quarters and hopes to start working with them, but I take full responsibility. I should have gone with him to the meeting, but at the last minute Emma said she wasn't feeling well." His words drifted low until they were barely audible.

His dad shook his head. "You're not a newlywed, son. And you're not a kid anymore, either. The best thing you can do for your family is to make this farm profitable. We need to maintain our reputation. In this day and age, you'll be lucky if you don't inherit a pile of bills and liens on the place. You're only as good as your word in this business."

Jamie clenched down on his back teeth. He hated to be scolded like a boy, and he hated it even more when his dad talked about death and inheritances. But he kept his focus on the gravel and his ego in check because every word of the chastisement was justified. "I'll get my folder of notes on quarter horse yearlings and then shower for the dinner meeting." He turned to walk away, but his father's hand on his shoulder kept him where he was.

"You told me when you joined the New Order church that you could still be my right-hand man." His father's eyes were ringed with dark circles of fatigue. "You said turning Amish wouldn't affect your ability to do the job…that you would adjust to the limitations of horse-and-buggy. Well, I don't see that happening. You seemed content to work your fields, tend to the livestock, including Emma's sheep, and then sit on the porch sipping lemonade with your wife. You don't go to town even when you have someone to drive you." Dad released his sleeve. "I need to know I can count on you, son. I want to hand over more responsibility, not be checking up on you like some slacker from the county labor pool."

The two men held each other's gaze for a long moment. "I'll meet you out here in twenty minutes." Then James Sr. marched off, leaving Jamie feeling ashamed, annoyed, and a little confused about what he wanted in life.

～

Tuesday morning dawned sunny and clear—a perfect day weather-wise for Leah's first bus trip to Cleveland. A group of friends on *Rumschpringe* had planned to attend an Indians ball game. Leah was no big fan of baseball, unlike most Amish youths. She also had little interest in *Rumschpringe* outings. She was content to work at the diner during her running-around years before joining the church and getting married. April had promised to teach her to drive in the parking lot, and that was enough excitement for her.

But with so many young people going to the game, there was a good chance Jonah Byler would be among them. And that's why she was willing to watch grown men swing bats at little white balls. She hadn't seen him in more than a week, not since the horse sale, which certainly hadn't turned out as planned. Due to the antihistamines, she had slept through the entire auction, and she never saw the four horses Jonah bid on and purchased. And he hadn't been back to the diner since, not even to claim the coat he'd tucked under her head. She'd washed and ironed it with utmost care, but it'd been catching dust in the kitchen closet all week.

When Rachel stopped over with the news about the bus trip, Leah had expected her *mamm* to say no. Instead, after reading the flyer, she'd announced, "It would do you good to spend time away from the kitchen." Of course, Julia still had plenty of "dos and don'ts" while mother and daughter waited for the bus to come: *Don't go to the restroom by yourself. Don't eat too much junk food. Don't try to catch a fly ball with your bare hands.*

The last warning had been the strangest. Leah couldn't imagine why she would want to catch a baseball. When the bus rumbled down the road and stopped at their drive, Leah kissed Julia goodbye and climbed aboard for a day of fun.

"Hi, Leah!"

"Hullo, Leah."

"*Guder mariye,* Miss Miller." Three animated voices sang out as she reached the top of the steps.

"*Guder mariye,*" she greeted, recognizing Steven, Daniel, and John. As she walked down the aisle, anxiety crept up her spine. Every smiling face she passed was male. *Am I the only girl who opted for the trip?*

"Back here, Leah," called a familiar voice.

She exhaled with relief when she spotted Rachel in a small knot of girls in the back. Joy radiated from their faces as they chattered like crows on a telephone wire.

"Can you believe it?" Rachel whispered when Leah took the seat beside her. "I counted four boys to each girl here!" Her brown eyes glittered with excitement.

"You can have my extra three, so that'll give you seven total, okay?" Leah whispered, joining in the playfulness.

"Don't let my sister overhear you. She's chaperoning today." Rachel's cheeks turned pink as she swatted Leah's hand. "You're a mischief-maker, Leah Miller. Do you see your favorite cheese-maker?" Her head bobbed left and right.

"His mother makes the cheese; he runs the dairy farm. And no, I don't see him yet." Leah decided to have a good time with or without Jonah. *This is the day the Lord has made. And I am thankful for it.*

As the landscape changed from rural to suburban, and finally to the commercial sprawl of the city, Leah soon forgot about the cheese-maker and enjoyed the scenery. Vehicles sped past the bus on both sides, while the amount of traffic going to or coming from Cleveland astounded her. But nothing could compare to the sheer pandemonium surrounding the ballpark. Once they left the bus, they joined a tide of people flowing toward the stadium. Other than themselves, everyone had on bright red-and-blue matching clothes. Many people were wearing earphones, most wore ball caps, and every person was either eating, drinking, or talking loudly—or all three at once.

"Don't be frightened," Daniel said, appearing by her side. "I'm here to protect you."

"Danki," she murmured, feeling more amazement than fear.

"Who'll protect her from you?" hollered Steven as they passed through the turnstile.

A woman taking tickets smiled at her. "Enjoy the game, hon," she said, not looking twice at their Plain clothes.

"Everybody is so happy here," Leah said to Rachel, who had finally squeezed up to her side. John and Steven were close on their heels.

"You can't help but be in a good mood at a ball game," said Rachel.

"Check your troubles at the door!" John had squeezed in between them and looped an arm around both their shoulders.

"Where's your straw hat?" Leah asked. His head of curly dark hair was bare.

"I left it on the bus. Look what I bought, Leah. Got one for you too." He dug into a plastic bag, extracted two Indians caps, and handed her one.

"Oh, no. I could never wear such a thing." She shook her head, sending her *kapp* strings flying.

"Sure you can, just during the game. After all, it's our *Rumschpringe.*" He turned his cap backward like some of the *Englischers* had done.

"Try it on, Leah," encouraged Rachel.

Leah examined the hat while the chaperones looked for their section. It had a nice long bill that would shield her face from the sun. "Okay," she agreed, "but only over my *kapp*. And only if I can wear mine frontward since I forgot sunglasses."

Once they reached their seats, her excitement ratcheted higher. Thousands of people had filled the stadium—smiling, waving, singing, and clapping their hands. The cheering escalated to an earsplitting roar as the team members ran onto the field. A few moments later everyone rose to their feet for the national anthem. After that was finished and people were seated again, Leah requested a bag of peanuts from a vendor and it sailed through the air to her as though it were a fly ball. *This is so much better than watching the game on TV at Mrs. Lee's.* Although she couldn't follow what the batter was doing, an enormous screen frequently replayed the action for everyone to see. Her head swiveled back and forth between home plate and the giant screen until her neck grew stiff.

"That was called a strike," Daniel said in her ear. He was sitting directly behind her. "The ball was right over home plate in the strike zone." He made an indecipherable motion with his hands.

"She understands the game," Steven snapped. He'd plunked down in the seat on her right. "She's not stupid."

"No, I'm not," she said. "But I don't know why those men in the field keep changing their minds about where to stand. They move to a different spot with each batter."

"That's easy," Steven said, with an entirely different tone than the one used for Daniel. "Some batters are known for hitting fastballs— hard hits that put the players back toward the wall. Others try to sneak a bunt or a short hit near third base, so the infielders come in closer to the plate." Steven proceeded to describe other variables in positioning, but Leah's mind and gaze had started to wander. She spotted Rachel and the other girls surrounded on all sides by males. *How did this happen when we had planned to sit together?*

The boys had finagled it! The realization sent a jolt of current up her spine. She'd never felt attractive until this spring, and she had to admit she liked it.

Without warning, everyone erupted into jubilation. The couple in front of her spilled their soft drinks. "Home run!" Steven shouted, pulling her to her feet. "With the bases loaded—a grand slam!"

She clapped her hands and whistled through her teeth—a rare talent her father said a girl was better off forgetting. Exploding fireworks filled the sky with a dozen loud booms that would rattle windowpanes for blocks. "A home run," she repeated with newfound appreciation for the event. Then she sat back down and folded her hands in her lap. It wouldn't do to look overly competitive. Fans of the other team could be sitting nearby.

"This is for you, Leah. My treat." John, looking less bashful than usual, handed her a giant soft pretzel and a soft drink. He had leaned over two people to do so.

"*Danki* very much," she said, taking a bite. "Your next three pieces of Peach Parfait Supreme are on the house." The mood of the afternoon had altered her acute business sense.

Before the end of the inning, Daniel returned to his seat with two foot-long hot dogs. "Try this, Leah. It has relish and stadium mustard." He passed one over her shoulder.

"Oh, goodness, that's just how I like 'em." Just to be polite, she ate the entire hot dog, an accomplishment that greatly pleased Daniel.

The sun, marking a path across the sky, found its way under her cap brim. The heat, the excitement, and the cuisine were starting to wear her down, but she couldn't ever remember having so much fun.

"Another homer," Steven shouted, "with men on second and third." He pulled her to her feet to join the fracas. She tried to clap but spilled Coke down her dress instead. She took the spilled soda in stride. Tomorrow she could always wash her dress, but it wasn't often she saw the home team take the lead in the ninth.

Much too soon the game was over; the Indians cinched the win in the top of the ninth inning. The crowd roared, fireworks exploded, and Leah, tired but jubilant, joined the others heading for an exit. Steven reappeared at her side. "Here you go, Leah. I bought some nachos. I hope you like jalapenos." He still looked full of energy.

She took one glance at the soggy tortilla chips with melted cheese already congealing and felt her stomach take a tumble. "No, *danki*. You go ahead and enjoy. I'm a little full."

Steven didn't recognize a polite refusal when he heard one. "Just try a couple. I ate a whole plate of them during the fifth inning. They're really good." He held them under her nose in an attempt to entice. The jalapenos seemed to multiply in number. She shook her head, and was about to stand firm when they were interrupted.

"If she doesn't want any, she doesn't want any," Daniel said, coming up from behind them. "Don't be a pest."

Steven's face turned as red as his ball cap. "Who's being a pest? You're the one butting his nose in where it don't belong. Leah's only trying to be polite."

Things might have gone differently if their group hadn't spilled into the throng in the main concourse. People, eager to reach their cars, jostled and nudged the line along. Unaccustomed to large crowds like this, Leah felt the tension around her escalate.

"She doesn't want any nachos," Daniel insisted. He reached out to grab the plate away, but in the midst of pushing and shoving the nachos ended up splattered across Steven's shirt.

Then things happened so fast Leah wasn't sure what took place. A fist shot out that connected with Daniel's nose with an audible thud. Then a returning punch landed smack in Steven's solar plexus, doubling him over and causing him to gasp for air.

"Leah!" a female voice yelled. Sarah Yoder, Rachel's married older sister, pulled her out of harm's way.

"That's enough!" bellowed Sam Yoder, Sarah's husband. "You two should be ashamed of yourselves." He yanked Steven upright none too gently, while he shot Daniel an expression that could have curdled cream.

Apparently they were ashamed, because the fight ended as quickly as it began. But the damage had been done; they had attracted plenty of gawking from passersby.

Leah's face burned with shame.

Yet a small thrill inched up her spine too. *Those men were fighting over me.* As distasteful as fistfights were, Leah felt flattered that their tiff was over her.

Flattered, yet embarrassed…and a little queasy.

Sarah and Sam Yoder, who'd come along with another married

couple as chaperones, looked mad as hornets. Daniel, with spots of blood on his shirt from his nose, and Steven, with melted cheese down the front of his clothes, looked mortified.

Would word of the altercation get back to the bishop? Most assuredly it would. And Leah had been at the center of the disagreement. She suddenly didn't feel buoyed by the attention anymore. How did it look to *Englischers* when all they heard about Amish folk was their peaceful, gentle nature? Leah realized the seriousness of Daniel's and Steven's actions during the walk back to the bus. Sarah Yoder was frowning. Sam looked furious. And Rachel looked frightened, along with most of the others as they exchanged glances with Leah and the two brawlers.

In addition to humiliation and anxiety, irritation jumped into her stew of emotions. *Did I ask those boys to fuss so much over me? Have I ever encouraged their attention and frequent visits to the diner?*

She certainly hadn't wanted all the snacks they'd bought as her stomach roiled in protest. The bus ride back to Holmes County would be no Sunday picnic. She would soon be in trouble with her parents and maybe the bishop when gossip reached his ears. With so much to contemplate, she slumped down in the seat next to Rachel.

"Don't worry. My sister will calm down by the time we get home," Rachel whispered. "And this will soon blow over." But her pale face indicated that even she didn't believe her optimistic words.

Leah snatched the ball cap from her head and scrunched it into her purse. Closing her eyes, she planned how to explain the mess to her parents. Fortunately, when the bus dropped her off at home, her *daed* had already gone to bed.

Julia sat at the kitchen table sipping tea when Leah pushed open the door. "There you are. How about a cup of fresh mint tea? I just picked the leaves today," she said. With Leah's affirmative nod, Julia continued, "And I made a double batch of your favorite Spellbinder bars. Can't let you think your *mamm* forgot how to bake now that we have a professional in the house." A smile brightened her tired face.

Leah slipped into a chair at the table. "*Danki*, but can I eat a couple bars for breakfast? It feels as though Curly kicked me in the stomach from all the junk food I ate at the game."

"All right." Julia studied her while stirring a teaspoon of maple syrup into the tea. "What's wrong, daughter? You look worse than from a simple bellyache."

Leah met *mamm*'s gaze and began to relay the entire disgraceful story.

When she had finished, Julia shook her head and clucked her tongue as any mother would. "Sounds like you need to think long and hard about the messages you're sending to the boys of this district. You might not be responsible for that fistfight, but I suggest you reconsider encouraging those hotheads." She paused to sip her drink. "You have one reputation. You need to handle it like a porcelain doll."

Leah didn't fully understand what she meant by messages or the comparison to a breakable knickknack, but she was too tired to ask questions. She wanted to swallow a couple Tums and sleep until noon.

"Take your tea to your room and don't forget your prayers," Julia said. "Ask God for insight for how you might have prevented this unpleasantness. Then go to bed."

Leah counted her blessings all the way up the stairs, not waiting to kneel beside the bed. She'd expected a much worse lecture from her *mamm*. The topic might not be finished once her *daed* heard the story, but at least she didn't have to pray for God's guidance this time. The answer came to her like a lightning bolt. Steven, Daniel, and John would get no further attention from her beyond simple customer courtesy. She would concentrate on cooking and baking—things she enjoyed best anyway.

~

As they say, "No good deed goes unpunished."

Jeff Andrews had given his assistant every onerous stable chore during the ten days after Matthew confronted him. He'd had to muck out stalls, scrub water troughs, and mop the floor in the men's bunkhouse, all because he'd seen Andrews administer an injection.

For all the good it had done. Matthew hadn't seen a vet visit the yearling's stall, and the colt was still limping. But at least the trainer had suspended his workouts to give the leg time to heal. Andrews muttered under his breath every time Matt walked by. Despite his good intentions, things had gone from bad to worse. Last night Matthew had prayed long and hard for the right path to take. On the one hand, he liked the work and jobs for horse trainers were hard to come by. Getting fired would put building a house further into the future, just as courting Martha had become a distinct possibility. On the other hand, he'd forged a special bond with the colt in stall twenty-three. Somebody had to speak up for those who communicated with a shake of their mane or the toss of their head.

By dawn, as the birds raised a ruckus outside his window, he had known the answer. A man got only one chance to do the right thing, but he had to look at himself every morning in the shaving mirror.

"Mr. Macintosh, sir?" Matthew asked, after knocking on the owner's partially closed office door.

"Come in, come in," a voice boomed.

Matthew stepped into his employer's office for the first time. Even when he'd been hired, the interview had been in the smaller stable office. In a side wing off the house, this room had floor-to-ceiling bookcases on three walls while the fourth had windows that overlooked rolling pasturelands. Mr. Mac glanced up from his scattered papers.

"Excuse me, sir," Matthew said. "The foreman said I could find you here." He took a step closer to the huge old-fashioned desk.

"What can I help you with, son? I've been hearing good things from the owners of every horse you work with. What *exactly* do you whisper into their ears?"

Matthew smiled. He liked his nickname once the movie reference had finally been explained to him. "I tell them if they do what they ought, there'll be extra sorghum in their feed."

As Mr. Mac laughed, Matthew shuffled his feet and cleared his throat. He didn't want to waste time with small talk because his courage might evaporate at any moment. "Mr. Mac, I don't enjoy tattling on another man, especially on one who knows his stuff and works mighty hard for you. But I saw something that wasn't right, something that has bothered me ever since." He paused to collect his thoughts.

"Go on, son. Speak your mind." The stable owner studied him curiously.

"A vet needs to look at that colt in stall twenty-three. I think he might have a torn ligament in his foreleg. Andrews injected something meant to reduce swelling, but I think it's more serious than a strain."

His boss stared at him. "Have you talked about this with the other assistant trainers?"

"No, sir. I discussed it with Andrews but no one else. I care about the colt, but I ain't out to ruin a man's reputation."

Mr. Mac pursed his lips together. "I'll mosey on down and take a look at the colt myself. I'll just happen to notice…that way Jeff won't fire you for going over his head, and he would be within his rights. If a vet is warranted, one will be here today. You can be sure about that. But in the future, do your job and learn what you can from Andrews. That guy knows this business inside and out." He pulled down his reading glasses and peered at Matthew over the top of them. "Whereas you, son, still got plenty to learn."

Matthew had a bad taste in his mouth for the remainder of the day. He wasn't sure what he'd expected, but it sure wasn't Mr. Mac turning a blind eye to Andrews' shenanigans.

Those who wink at wrong cause trouble. Proverbs 10:10 was one of his pa's favorite Scriptures.

He just got a firsthand look for himself.

EIGHT

Jamie wished he'd taken a course on time management in college, because being in two places at the same time wasn't easy. Since the successful dinner meeting three nights ago, he'd put in fourteen-hour days to catch up on paperwork and get ahead with chores. His father was pleased but his wife had grown sullen. They had no time alone but plenty of company at every meal. Late in the evening before they went to bed, he would hold her in his arms on the porch swing. Only then would Emma laugh with him as they talked of their future.

But today they were headed to a family wedding in Winesburg. And because he'd recently been so industrious, they would spend the night with his in-laws. Emma had baked and cooked and packed two hampers. The look of joy on her face was worth every mile of the two-hour drive.

"*Mamm, daed,*" she called when she spotted them outside the building where the wedding would take place. She walked as fast as she could without running.

"Hurry up, daughter," Simon hollered. "It's time for the service to start."

"Save me a seat," Jamie called to her. "I'll unhitch the horse and be right there."

News and gossip would have to wait until the three-hour preaching service that included the exchange of wedding vows was over. Then after the wedding dinner, they would have an afternoon of socializing.

When he and Emma finished eating, she hurried off to join a group of young matrons while Jamie spotted his brother-in-law sitting alone in the shade. He headed in that direction. "They're starting a game of horseshoes if you want to join in," Jamie said.

"I'd rather just sit and think. Got plenty on my mind these days." Matthew's words sounded as downcast as his face looked.

"Prefer to be alone to sort it out?"

"Nah, I'd appreciate your company." Matt gazed up with hangdog eyes. "I did the right thing, Jamie. I went to Mr. Mac with what I'd seen. Although he called in a vet, he pretty much told me to mind my own business and do what I'm told."

Jamie sighed and plopped down next to Matt in the grass, despite his Sunday clothes. "Sometimes doing the right thing comes with a price," he said softly.

"That seems to be true for me. The trainer treats me worse than before, if that's possible. Even though Mr. Mac acted like he noticed the colt limping on his own, I think Andrews knows I went over his head."

"People who do bad things always believe other people do too," Jamie said, and then he immediately realized his mistake. "Not that *you* did a bad thing—"

"I'm glad I told Mr. Mac. At least a vet came to treat the horse. I don't care what Andrews thinks about me." Matthew leaned his head back against the tree.

Jamie knew his brother-in-law cared a great deal. It was normal to want to get along at work, but he let it slide. This would be one long row to hoe for Matthew with no easy solution, so he changed the subject. "Say, I wanted to tell you my standardbred buggy horse is minding every one of my signals and commands. You did a world of good with him and with me too. Even my dad can hardly believe he's the same horse."

Matthew's expression brightened considerably. *"Ach,* you're not used to buggy trainin', is all. I didn't really do that much."

"That's not true. Even my friend Sam was impressed with the change in temperament, and he is used to buggy horses. I don't feel right not paying you, Matt. All you got for your trouble was a plate of Emma's fried chicken."

"And fine fried chicken it was. Consider us square." Matt rose to his feet and brushed off his trousers. "I miss Emma's chicken. Nobody does it better, but don't tell Leah I said that."

Jamie decided now was a good time to speak his mind. "You know I meant what I said about Sam Yoder being impressed. Apparently it's not only ex-*Englischers* who run into trouble with balky horses. Have you ever thought about offering your services to Amish folk? Lots of people buy horses at auction and break them instead of training them because they don't know any better. You could advertise the services you're good at in the community. People could turn a bargain nag they bought at auction into something worthwhile."

Matthew was staring at him skeptically, but Jamie also saw wheels turning in his head. Then he said, "I earn a good salary at Macintosh Farms. Nobody will come close to paying me what I earn there." He broke eye contact and gazed off at the fields. "I need to save money to build a house. Lumber and nails aren't getting any cheaper. I would like to get married before I turn seventy."

"True, it would take time to establish a reputation and get the word out, but I think there's money to be made. Lots of Amish are breeding horses to sell and starting riding academies and farm vacations for tourists. They could use your services too. At least give it some thought. You'd be your own boss and wouldn't have to deal with the likes of Jeff Andrews ever again." Jamie stopped and caught his breath. Talking someone into a life-altering decision wasn't a good idea. This was something his young brother-in-law needed to decide for himself.

But the wheels seemed to be turning faster as Matthew stuck out his hand to shake. "*Danki, bruder.* I'll think on it. Now let's go hit the dessert table. I intend to sample everything there."

"I'm right behind you." Jamie shook the outstretched hand and hoped he hadn't overstepped his bounds. Starting a business enterprise wasn't easy. But if Matthew's facial expression and long strides were any indication, at least considering his options had lifted the his spirits.

~

Leah could barely catch her breath during the lull between the breakfast rush and lunch. Besides her normal prep work, she wanted to bake a double batch of brownies to take to the wedding she'd been invited to. Because her family was already there, she would join them on her way home from work. The district hosting the wedding stayed on "slow time." They didn't go on daylight savings or "fast time" the way her district did. But even if she left promptly at three, she would miss dinner. Brownies could be nibbled later on when folk grew hungry from socializing.

Usually a from-scratch kind of cook, today Leah pulled two boxes of Pillsbury brownie mix down from the shelf. They would taste just as good as homemade once she added plenty of chopped walnuts. While blending the batter she noticed an advertisement on the side of the box. The annual baking contest was open for those with new recipes. She read until her gaze landed on the grand prize: "Winners will share in $1,000,000 of prize money." Dropping her spoon into the bowl, Leah grabbed the box to study the rules as her customers' comments about her Peach Parfait Supreme swam through her head.

Didn't one English woman suggest I should enter it in a contest?

Hadn't that elderly farmer declared it was the best pie he'd tasted in eighty years?

The "$1,000,000" seemed to grow larger on the box.

She turned her attention back to her brownie mix when April carried in a tray of dirty plates for the dishwasher, but an idea had been born. She could secretly enter the contest with her favorite recipe. If she didn't place, no one would be the wiser. And if the impossible happened? A portion of that prize money would restore her savings from the diner investment and build up the medical bill account for every Amish community in the U.S. Leah set the pan of brownies in the oven, put the windup timer in her pocket, and went to prepare her tables. But the Pillsbury Bake-Off occupied her thoughts throughout lunch and then all the way to the wedding.

Although the service and dinner were over by the time she arrived, people still milled around the dessert table. She greeted the bride and groom, presented her gift, talked with her parents, and then spent the next hour hiding from Steven and Daniel. The behavior of both of the men who had fought over her was subdued compared to their time in Cleveland. At least, that's how it seemed to Leah as she spied on them from behind a willow tree. Subdued or not, she didn't want to be seen talking to either man.

"Are you stalking someone, Miss Miller? If so, you're not very good at it."

The sound of Jonah's voice nearly caused her heart to stop. She wheeled around to see him looking very handsome in his Sunday best. Her heart struggled to regain its normal rhythm. "More like trying not to be seen. There are a couple customers I'd prefer to avoid." She met his gaze and then glanced away. His eyes could bore holes through concrete.

"What happened? Did you give them food poisoning and now they're threatening to call the authorities?" He approached until they stood only three feet apart.

She shook her head. "I don't know which menu item gave you such a negative impression of my cooking, but no. I have other reasons to discourage an encounter."

Jonah looked in the direction she'd been focused on. A muscle twitched in his jaw, but his tone remained friendly. "Then why not take a walk with me? That might put off any unwanted intruders."

Leah swallowed a lump in her throat, remembering *mamm*'s warning about her reputation. "I don't know. Maybe I should go sit with my family and stop this silliness altogether."

One of his black eyebrows arched while his dimples deepened "You would consider walking with me to be continued silliness? What have I done to deserve that?"

Leah blushed. The fuss at the ballgame wasn't Jonah's fault. "You haven't done anything. I'm the silly one—spying from behind trees." She tried to steady her nerves. "Okay, Jonah. I'll walk with you as long as we stay in the yard with everyone else."

"Let's head to the pond. We can watch the kids swimming and wish we were young again."

Leah mulled this over as they walked side by side in silence. As he'd predicted, some of the younger boys had changed from their good clothes into their worst and were splashing around in the shallow end. Mothers hovered nearby, talking to friends while keeping their *kinner* in sight. Jonah headed to the split-log bench farthest away from the others. They sat down a foot apart to watch summer's favorite pastime.

"Why would you want to be young again?" she asked. "I couldn't wait to be out from under *mamm*'s eye every minute."

Jonah's gaze remained on the swimmers as he spoke. "Life was simple then. I had my chores, but when they were done my time was my own. I had lots of friends from school. We would meet to swim or play baseball or ice-skate. And I had my *daed* back then. We went squirrel hunting in the woods and fishing in the lake near our farm. He taught me useful things, like starting a fire without matches and how to roast corn using only the hot sun."

Silence spun out again between them. Even the laughter from the pond seemed distant. "You still miss your *daed*," Leah said softly, stretching her legs.

"Every day of my life." He raised his chin while a muscle in his neck jumped.

"And Wisconsin too?" Her question hung in the humid air.

"*Jah*, I miss my home. *Dawdi* is real nice, but it's not the same. He was a stranger up until a few months ago. I don't mind working for him; don't get me wrong. I just wish we hadn't had to move."

"We know how to have fun in Holmes County," she said, hoping that didn't sound too defensive. "Once you make friends, things will seem different"

"You're my friend, Leah, and I'm happy to know you. Now, why don't we go get something to eat?"

Leah knew he wanted to change the subject, but she persisted. "If you start coming to preaching services, you'll meet the other young men in our district. And since you play baseball, you can join their next pickup game. Plus we have volleyball parties, hayrides, and cookouts besides Sunday singings. I think you'll find Ohio folk to be just as nice as Wisconsiners."

He looked at her with eyes bluer than the pond's deep water. "I'm sure that's true, but my *mamm* says no social events until I start attending church again."

Leah felt herself relax. "Then it's simple. If you're not traveling back and forth to Hancock anymore, come to preaching on Sunday. It'll be at Amos Miller's on Route 390. Your *dawdi* knows where it is."

"It's not simple at all, sweet girl." He lowered his voice to a harsh whisper. "I'm no hypocrite. I won't show up for service and go through the motions. If a person has lost their faith, a church filled with believers isn't a comfortable place to be."

His demeanor seemed normal, yet he spoke the most shocking words Leah had ever heard. *What does it mean to lose your faith? Does Jonah no longer believe in God? How could the company of other Christians be uncomfortable?*

He stood abruptly and looked down at her. "I'm hungry. I didn't eat earlier with the crowd. You want to get in the chow line with me?"

"You go ahead, Jonah. I want to watch the swimmers some more. I'll see you later."

"I didn't mean to upset you. But you kept asking questions and I didn't want to lie to you."

His soft and gentle words touched her heart. If she could help him she would.

She rose to her feet. "You didn't upset me, but I think they packed the food away except for desserts. Are you staying for the wedding supper? It won't be until this evening, but I know it'll be delicious."

"I wasn't invited." It was a statement of fact, delivered without emotion.

The second wedding meal was strictly for friends of the couple. Because no one knew him in the district, the bride and groom wouldn't have extended an invitation to a stranger. "I was invited," she said. "And you can come as my guest." Her mouth turned dry while he pondered the idea.

"If I leave now, I can probably get enough chores done to come back later." His eyes widened. "All right, Leah. I'll meet you back here at six thirty." He grinned, started to walk away, and then turned back. "Tell me. Which contribution to the dessert table did you bring?"

"The walnut brownies, far to the right."

"*Danki* for letting me know, and for the supper invite." With a wink he headed toward the parking area for buggies.

And she was left to wonder if he meant to sample or avoid her brownies.

~

Leah spent the remainder of the afternoon chatting with girlfriends, her old schoolteacher, and her mother. *Mamm* had spread a quilt under a shady tree, and when they'd talked themselves out, Leah fell asleep in the warm afternoon air. When she awoke she found a note anchored to the quilt with a rock.

Gone home. Have a good time at supper. Don't stay late. Your bruder will drive you home in our buggy. We took yours.

Mamm

Leah was glad Matthew had been invited. He might just get his chance to talk to Martha tonight. She also wouldn't be tempted if Jonah asked to take her home. After the nonsense at the ballgame, she would just as soon not encourage anyone until things cooled down.

Jonah. Leah dug in her handbag for a watch she never wore but kept handy since she'd started working. How long had she been asleep? She hurried toward the house with enough time to wash her face and hands and brush her teeth. Once presentable, she waited for Jonah to arrive on the porch steps, pondering his odd confession. Leah not only prayed several times a day, but she also asked God for guidance too many times to count.

If someone lost their faith, whom did they turn to when they were hurt or scared or confused, especially if that person had no friends?

Considering how nice Jonah looked when he arrived, she figured at least a couple gals would be willing to befriend him before the night was over.

He walked toward her carrying a basket and an armload of gladiolas, irises, and lilies. She rose to greet him, and together they started for the barn where the wedding supper would be held.

"You don't get the big bunch," he said with a sly grin. "It's for the bride, but I did pick this for you." He pulled a small bouquet of wildflowers from behind his back.

"*Danki,* I love them." Leah took the flowers and inhaled, despite knowing wildflowers held little scent. She was grateful that he remembered her allergies and had brought her a bouquet that wouldn't tickle her nose. "What's in the basket?"

"An assortment of cheese spreads and smoked meats for the happy couple. And some Hershey kisses to give them ideas."

Leah opened her mouth to comment on chocolate, but the sight before her rendered her speechless. They had entered the same barn that held the service, but it had been transformed into a wonderland of silver and white. Hundreds of streamers had been strung between the rafters while clusters of helium balloons and vases of flowers adorned each table. White tablecloths and real china had replaced the casual tableware of the noon meal.

"Oh, my goodness," he said.

"You can say that again," she murmured. "Look, there's Matthew and some of my friends. They saved us seats." Leah introduced Jonah to Rachel and Martha Hostetler and to another newly married couple.

While they ate Jonah talked cordially with everyone at the table, allowing Leah time to relax. They dined on tender beef roast with asparagus spears and new potatoes. Now that she cooked for a living, she tried to figure out each seasoning and ingredient used. This was her first wedding supper, and it was far more romantic than she'd imagined. *Will an occasion like this be part of my future?*

Afterward, while people watched the bridal couple open gifts, and Matthew talked to Martha, Leah whispered near Jonah's ear, "You seem to be breaking the ice. Before you know it, you'll have more friends than you can shake a stick at."

He inclined his head very near. "This is for your sake. I don't want you to regret asking a hermit to supper."

She laughed aloud as a mental picture of an old man with a grizzled beard who lived in a cave flitted through her mind. Then again, Jonah never came to the diner with anyone else. Plain folk weren't loners by nature, so Leah grew more curious by the minute. "Do you think we could wander over to the coffeepot and then take a walk outside? I'd like some fresh air." She felt a little shy about leaving, because the couple was still unwrapping gifts, but a better opportunity might not arise.

"Sure," he said and took her elbow as they walked to the coffee urn.

With mugs in hand, they slipped outdoors into the clear, starry night. "What did you mean by the company of believers makes you uncomfortable?" she asked boldly. "Surely you still believe in God."

He didn't answer until they were well away from the barn. "Probably deep down I still do. It's hard not to when you've been raised to believe. But since God has forgotten me, I thought I'd take a vacation from Him too." He took a long swallow of coffee.

Leah was appalled. She glanced quickly around to make sure he hadn't been overheard and then glanced skyward too. Never before had a person spoken so blasphemously in her presence. Yet her second reaction was one of sheer pity. How awful Jonah must feel to be separated from the one true Helper. "Let's sit for a minute," she said, pointing at a bench. "Tell me what happened that made you think like this."

He sat down heavily and squinted into the thin moonlight, as though trying to see something that wasn't there. "When my *daed* got sick, I prayed morning, noon, and night that he would be spared, as did my *mamm* and plenty of others. I worked my tail off at the farm and earned extra money on the side for medical treatments. I didn't mind; I managed everything while *mamm* stayed at the hospital in Kenosha." He tilted his head back and closed his eyes. "When she brought him home, he went straight downhill and died. I didn't even get a chance to say goodbye."

Leah reached out to pat his hand, but Jonah didn't seem to notice. Sorrow had closed around him like heavy fog.

"Afterward, I continued to work from dawn till dark to keep the farm going. And I prayed constantly that we'd be able to stay right where we were. But my *mamm* got it in her head to sell the place and move here. I had to leave everyone I knew and everything I loved behind. So I learned that prayer works fine for some people, but not so good for me." His voice had drifted to a raspy whisper.

A question niggled at Leah, one she had to ask. "Did you leave someone special back in Wisconsin?"

Jonah turned on the bench, but she was thankful darkness hid her anxious face. "I'd started to court a gal, but I didn't know if it was love. We surely didn't know if we wanted to spend our lives together by the time I moved."

"You sound mad at your mother besides God."

He released a humorless laugh. "I begged to stay behind, Leah. I wanted to buy the place and make payments until I'd paid her what it was worth. I didn't care if I had to work sixteen-hour days. But *mamm* insisted I move here to help *dawdi*. I'm a grown man, yet she treated me like a child."

"Are you still angry with her?" Leah heard the childlike tone of her voice.

"No, sweet girl, not anymore. Let's go back inside before your *bruder* wonders where you are." He pulled her to her feet and started to walk back to the barn.

She didn't get a chance to ask if he was still mad at God. But then again, she thought she already knew the answer to that.

～

Matthew breathed a sigh of relief when he saw Leah walking toward him at the end of the evening. He'd hoped she wouldn't accept a ride from the new dairy farmer because he needed his sister's advice. With so many ideas buzzing around his head, he thought it might explode.

"Glad you're coming home with me," he said as Leah stepped up into the buggy.

She glanced around. "Aren't we taking Martha home? Didn't you ask her?" She sounded exasperated.

"Hold your horses. I'm not a man who rushes things." He shook the reins gently and the horse started at a slow gait.

"That's an understatement! Once word gets around she's no longer courting Joseph Kauffman of Berlin, plenty of boys will step up. You'd best not wait too long."

"Leah, I don't need something else to worry about. My plate's already full."

"Just giving you a little sisterly advice." She crossed her arms over her shawl.

He huffed out his breath. "I do want to court Martha. She's the reason I'm working at Macintosh Farms, and trying to save enough to buy the acres off Mr. Lee that he's thinkin' about selling."

"That's *wunderbaar*! You would build your house right across the street?"

"That's my dream, except it looks like I won't be working at that English horse farm much longer."

Leah turned on the seat and demanded. "Why ever not? You make a good salary there. Why quit before you have enough money saved?"

Reluctantly, he sketched out his woeful tale with Jeff Andrews and finished with the encouraging conversation with James Davis.

"Oh, my. I can't believe Mr. Mac wasn't furious with that trainer."

"Me neither. If he seemed miffed with anybody, it was with me." He inhaled a lungful of air while waiting for traffic to clear at the stop sign. "So what do you think?"

Leah shook her head. "About Mr. Mac?"

"No, about Jamie's idea…about me striking out on my own."

She looked bewildered. "Matty, I'm not the best person to ask. I don't know anything about the horse business. I'm having a hard enough time learning about restaurants. All I can say is talk to *daed* and the bishop. They would know if you could make a go of it or not."

Matthew clucked his tongue and the horse picked up the snail-pace, wondering why he hadn't thought of that. Between his pa and the bishop, they knew everyone in the surrounding area. If this idea were feasible they would know. He decided to change the subject. "How are things going with you and Jonah?"

Leah flashed him a glare. "We're not courting if that's what you're asking. And don't start spreading rumors to the contrary."

"Simmer down. I was just making conversation. After all, I saw you two walk outdoors, and before that there was your sudden interest in the Mount Hope horse auction."

Leah seemed to be suffering from acid indigestion. "Jonah Byler is very confusing. Part of me wants to know him better, while this little voice keeps warning 'Beware.' "

Matthew snorted. "How mysterious could a guy be who milks cows for a living?"

Her forehead furrowed into creases while she chewed her lower lip. He decided to let the matter drop. Turning up their driveway, he saw that the barn lights were still on. Good. *Daed* must still be up and he could talk to him.

Leah jumped out as he pulled up in front of the house, *"Gut nacht,"* she called.

Matthew unhitched the horse and led him into the barn. He found Simon rubbing down a mare.

"You're home," Simon stated as Matthew entered the adjacent stall.

"Jah, Leah's already in the house. Weddin' supper was real nice. Good eats." Matthew took a brush and applied it to his gelding's coat with long, smooth strokes.

"All well and good, but I got a bone to pick with you, son."

Matthew tensed as he waited.

"Henry did your chores again today and that ain't right. You came home from work long enough to shower and change clothes and then you left."

"It was my first weddin' supper, Pa. I don't get too many invites." He decided not to mention anything about Martha.

"I don't care if it was your first supper or your fiftieth. I need Henry helping me in the fields, not doing your livestock and barn chores. You said working for that *Englischer* wouldn't affect your home life, but that ain't the case." Simon breathed heavily before continuing. "You will pay your *bruder* for helping you today since the almighty dollar has such great importance to you. And you will not stick your chores on him again without checking with me first. Hebrews 13:5 says: 'Keep your lives free from the love of money and be content with what you have.'"

How his father managed to put so much authority into Scripture amazed Matthew, but he knew he had no defense. He exhaled through his teeth. "I can't argue," he said. "I'll pay Henry my full day's wages." He continued to work tangles from the gelding's mane.

Simon's head snapped up. Apparently he'd been expecting a different response. "All right, son. Finish up and get to bed. Everything else in here is set for the night."

His pa walked off slowly—the years were taking a toll on him. Matthew felt a wave of guilt wash over him for not keeping his promise. Maybe working for himself from home would have advantages money couldn't buy.

NINE

Leah finished mopping the diner floor and headed into the kitchen to clean up in there. It had been April's turn to leave work early for a doctor's appointment. Leah was glad that the last lunch customers hadn't lingered. She would make a couple pies before she went home, primarily to measure each ingredient that went into her Peach Parfait Supreme pie. She didn't usually follow a recipe exactly, but she would need a precise ingredient list and instructions to send to the bake-off people.

Excitement built in her veins like an old-fashioned iron tonic. She thought of ideas for plate presentation that should move her to the head of the herd of bakers. Her favorite was the basket weave pattern: She would draw a crisscross pattern using a tube of peach jam and then dust the plate with cinnamon and brown sugar. The sugar adhered to the jam to create a yummy, pretty design. She often decorated the plates for the daily breakfast special of French toast or pancakes. Softly singing a hymn, she finished her pies and the recipe. Baking couldn't be considered work when it brought her so much joy.

With the pies in the oven, Leah sat down at the small desk by the back door. April kept her checkbook and ledgers there, along with store flyers, shopping lists, and product catalogs. Leah hunted for an attractive card to copy her recipe onto instead of using the back of an envelope. What she found instead made her breath catch in her throat and her stomach tighten. Bills, invoices, and final notices filled the top drawer. She spotted more shoved underneath cookbooks in the side drawers. Leah ruffled through a few letters and then shut the drawer, bewildered.

Snooping wasn't very nice. Yet on the other hand, wasn't she a partner? Shouldn't she know what was going on financially? Reopening the top drawer, she pulled out an especially insistent-looking envelope and peeked inside. She scanned the notice to discover it was from the State of Ohio, Department of Taxation. They wanted remittance for the sales tax collected on restaurant purchases. It was their second request. Leah felt queasy as she carefully shut the drawer.

Come to think of it, she hadn't seen April writing in the ledgers since they got busy during the second week. Wasn't she keeping accurate records of the meals they sold? You can't very well remit taxes if you didn't know how much you owe.

Leah finished cleaning the kitchen while the pies baked, and then she placed them to cool in the pie safe. After she locked up the diner, the drive home provided plenty of time for contemplation. If she told her parents what she'd seen, and if *daed* felt April wasn't running things properly, he would make her quit. There might be a logical explanation for the drawer full of bills. Perhaps April had paid the bills but neglected to file away stubs and throw out envelopes. Even the sales tax request might have crossed paths in the mail with the payment. She was no longer a little girl who ran to her *mamm* with every problem. Instead, she would pray that April caught up with the record-keeping and bill-paying. No business in the world ran wrinkle free during the first year.

When Leah arrived home, she found Rachel pacing the length of the front porch. "Where have you been?" her friend asked the moment Leah reached the house.

"Baking pies after work. What's up?"

"Please say you'll come with me tonight. I'm barrel-racing over at

Yosts' farm and I need supporters. Martha is coming but she refuses to yell loudly."

"That's tonight?" Leah asked, feeling exhausted. Rachel had mentioned the competition, but Leah had forgotten to write down the date.

"*Jah,* it's tonight. Please say yes. I've been practicing every day." Rachel's round face pinched into a frown.

"Of course, as long as *mamm* says it's okay." Leah handed Henry the reins and headed into the house. She silently hoped Julia needed her because she was too tired to go anywhere. But a pot of soup was already simmering on the stove and her *daed* had gone out on deacon business. *Mamm* told her to have a nice time.

Leah changed clothes, climbed into Rachel's buggy, and sat next to Martha. Rachel's racing horse was tethered to the back as they set off. Rachel looked joyous as Leah asked polite questions along the way, despite her opinion that horse-racing was an inappropriate pastime for girls. Once they arrived at the Yosts', Leah's opinion began to change. So many young people had shown up—both male and female—that her fatigue melted into anticipation. Leah soon learned that barrel-racing was primarily a female sport, at least in the Plain world, and that many girls thought horses were delightful creatures to associate with.

Lawn chairs lined the hillside next to the paddock. Leah found a ringside seat to watch the girls practice and warm up their mounts. Martha sat beside her with some friends as the competition began.

Rachel had been correct—Martha clapped during her sister's turn to race around the barrels but didn't raise her voice. Leah however shouted, "Go, Rachel!" "Yay!" and "Great ride!" at regular intervals. After all, wasn't that why she'd been invited? Unfortunately, her yelling attracted attention.

"Hello, Leah," Daniel said, sitting down next to her. "We never would have guessed you would come tonight."

"Hi," she said. "Who do you mean by we?"

"John, Steven, and me." He hooked a thumb toward the gate where the other two were standing. Both cautiously lifted their hands in greeting.

Leah waved back. "You three are speaking to each other? I'm surprised after how you acted in Cleveland."

Daniel's face turned pink as peonies. "We're mighty sorry about that. We got a bawling out from the bishop and had to apologize to Sarah and Sam Yoder." He cracked two of his knuckles. "We're also sorry we embarrassed you. And I'm speaking for all of us."

She glanced back to the gate. Sure enough, the other men looked contrite. "Let's just forget about it, okay? I want to watch my friend race." She focused on the paddock, where men were resetting the barrels into a different course.

"The gals are finished," Daniel said. "They just go once through. Rachel Hostetler took third place. The races are timed, so you find out who won once everybody's done."

"I see. I kind of thought they would all come out and race around together."

Daniel stared at her and then laughed. "You're funny, Leah. The guys will race next—sort of impromptu since so many of us turned out tonight. Just for fun, no prizes." He grinned before striding off to rejoin his friends.

Leah contemplated looking for Rachel when Jonah Byler sat down where Martha had been. His hat was pulled low on his forehead, shading his wonderful eyes.

"What a nice surprise," he said. "I thought horses bored you to sleep like a bear in winter hibernation."

"I told you that was due to the medication," she said, trying not to reveal how pleased she was to see him.

"Really?" He lifted his head. "I thought my company was like a glass of warm milk before bed."

She realized arguing would be futile. "The men are getting ready to race around the barrel course. Don't you want to mount up and join them?"

"Nope. I'd fall off and get my duds dirty. I've never been much of a horseback rider. I'll just sit with you and watch." He tugged his brim lower again and viewed the hubbub.

Leah grew nervous with his close proximity. She never possessed the upper hand with him the way she did with Daniel, John, and Steven. "My friend took third place and won a trophy," she said.

"Rachel? I thought that's why you were screaming and yelling. Tell her I said congratulations if we don't run into her." He refocused on the paddock, apparently content to sit with but not talk to her.

"You know, now that I take something for my allergies, I'm starting to like horses, at least a little."

"Does that mean I'll see you racing around these barrels one day?" He asked without taking his focus from the men climbing onto tall Arabians.

"Absolutely not, but at least I don't call them 'big fly magnets' any more."

Leah saw Jonah's lips pull into a smile but his hat still hid half his face. She wished he would at least notice her new dress. It had been finished last night with *mamm*'s help. Martha had said that the color complemented her complexion. But soon the racing began with far more hooting and hollering than the girls had inspired.

Daniel raced through the course second, performing quite well. He might not be a Matthew Miller, but he handled the horse competently. After racing the circuit, he rode to where Leah sat, reined to a stop, and swept off his hat with a flourish.

"I pictured you waiting at the finish line, Miss Miller, and that spurred me on. My time is the best so far." Daniel settled his hat back on his head.

"You're only the second rider," Jonah said. Leah buried her face in her hands to hide her laughter.

"First place is first place," Daniel replied, undaunted. He dug his boot heels in the side of his horse and galloped off.

The next barrel racer wasn't quite so agile. He knocked two barrels askew and lost his hat in the dust. Leah recognized John when he galloped past. As he raised his hand to wave at her he nearly fell off the horse.

"Looks like your friend Daniel will keep his first place position after that sorry showing." Jonah spoke very softly close to her ear.

"At least he got up there and tried," she said, feeling a frisson of excitement. Jonah knew Daniel's name and he sounded a tad jealous.

Steven entered the paddock next, called to her, and then rode around the barrels as though he were being chased by a swarm of bees. Then he pulled up hard on the reins and stopped suddenly in front of Leah's chair. With a smooth motion, he plucked a long-stemmed daisy from the horse's mane and tossed it to her. Then he galloped off, almost missing the last two barrels.

Jonah laughed. "That little stunt cost him time. If he hadn't given you that flower, he could have bumped Daniel out of first place. He is one great rider." He scratched at his chin. "What do you make of that, Leah?"

She was speechless. People were staring. All three men had made a fuss, and all the while she had been sitting with Jonah Byler. She rose to her feet, clenching her hands into fists to stop them from shaking. "I conclude that men are the most illogical creatures on earth...other than perhaps goats. And I'll never understand their need to compete with each other."

"I can't argue with you there," said Jonah. "We often don't make sense, but at least I'm not getting up on a horse just to toss you a flower. I'll be happy to pick some from Mrs. Yost's garden if you like."

Leah made a sound similar to a dog's growl and marched toward the house. She needed Rachel and Martha—female company—but she didn't see either one of them along the way. And the girls she did pass were staring at her strangely. After washing her hands and face, she decided to search for her brother. If horses were involved, he would be here somewhere.

She expected to find him among those waiting their turn on the barrel course. But he too was nowhere to be found. An unsettling feeling churned in her belly as Leah picked up her skirt and ran to where the buggies were parked. From a distance all the buggies looked the same, but close up each had been personalized to stand out with hardware on hitches and colorful blankets. Rachel's buggy was no longer here, nor was Matthew's.

Just then she spotted Jon Yost, their host, and hurried toward him. "Have you seen my *bruder* Matthew? I can't find his buggy."

"I saw him earlier. He'd been dropped off after work by an *Englischer.* He told me he didn't want to show up the amateurs on the course, and he rode home with Martha and Rachel Hostetler. They left right after Rachel got her trophy." Jon continued hitching up a horse.

"Something wrong, Leah?"

She wheeled around to find Jonah leaning on a buggy wheel. "*Jah,* I rode here with Rachel and Martha, and they seemed to have forgotten me. They've left and I have no way home."

One side of his mouth pulled into a grin, deepening his dimple. "You only live maybe a mile and a half away. It's not like they abandoned you in Kansas."

Leah was too tired to laugh at his humor. She stood with her teeth and hands clenched.

"Don't fret. I'll take you home. Let me thank Jon Yost for the invite and we can leave right now if you like."

Leah nodded and then stepped up into his buggy and closed her eyes. She was curious as to why he had followed her but too exhausted to ask during the brief but tense ride home.

～

Matthew couldn't believe his good fortune. He had not only run into Martha at the Yost farm, but she'd offered to give him a lift home. He hadn't planned on attending the barrel races because they would be over by the time he arrived. But just as he finished his chores, one of the Macintosh workers stopped by to deliver his order of bridles. The man lived on the same road as the Yost family. Matthew accepted a ride to the races without eating dinner. Food could wait, but opportunities like this didn't come often.

Martha had chatted all the way back to the Hostetler farm, relieving his anxiety about tripping over his own tongue. She was not only the prettiest girl in the district but the most thoughtful as well. She'd praised her younger sister's riding and then smiled at him while saying *gut nacht*. After the door closed behind her, he ran home through the bog with only the stars to light his path. If he had fallen into the pond, he doubted he would have noticed. His mind was too filled with dreams and plans and big ideas for the rest of his life.

He knew he was *in lieb* with Martha Hostetler without a shadow of a doubt. He figured something else out on the path between the two farms. When he contemplated explaining his work predicament to her, he was filled with revulsion. It was time to part company with the likes of Jeff Andrews. Money might buy acres of land from Mr. Lee, but it couldn't buy self-respect...or the respect of the sweetest girl in Holmes County.

Breathless but exhilarated, Matthew reached his backyard just as his father walked out of the barn. *Daed*'s expression turned into a frown when he spotted him.

Matthew held up both palms. "Wait before you scold me, Pa. I did my chores before going to the Yosts'. And I'm back early enough to finish up anything else you might want done."

Simon pulled on his beard, which seem to grow grayer with each passing day. "You missed supper, son." He sounded more tired than angry.

"I took a bologna sandwich to eat on the drive over. I got a lift from an *Englischer* I work with."

Simon shook his head and muttered "bologna sandwich" under his breath.

"Could I talk to you a minute?" Matthew asked, walking almost on Simon's heels.

"All right. Let's sit on the porch." Simon walked as stiffly as Emma had right after they removed the casts from her legs after her buggy accident. He lowered himself to the swing while Matt took a green plastic chair.

"I wanted to tell you what's going on at work, and then I'll need your advice."

Simon settled back and began to rock. "Go on."

Matthew poured out his tale, beginning with the day Jeff Andrews noticed the colt limping up until the present, glad that the lamplight through the window didn't illuminate his face. Throughout his explanation, his father didn't interrupt with questions or comments.

Finally, after Matthew explained Mr. Mac's lack of reaction, Simon asked, "What are you going to do, since your boss has turned a blind eye to his employee's shenanigans?"

Matthew almost tipped over in his lawn chair. Normally his pa would bluster and deliver ultimatums right about now. "That's the second thing we need to discuss." He braced his hands on his knees and sucked in a deep breath. "What do you think about me starting my own training business for the Amish? I can help folk who have trouble with balky horses, train their yearlings, and help with new purchases." He paused to collect his thoughts.

"Do you think you could find enough customers to make a living?" Simon leaned forward into the kerosene light. "Most people train their own horses to the buggy or to their farm equipment."

"I don't know; that's why I want your opinion. Between you and the bishop, you would know if there would be a call for what I do. But I do know many folk try to train and aren't very good at it. That's why they're always in the market for new horses. And there are new Amish breeders in the area, plus tourist farms and trail riding stables."

"You've got a point. I hear plenty of complaints about horses not minding signals and commands, especially when the wives are driving. If they were well trained, it shouldn't matter who held the reins."

Matthew forged ahead with his second gift of grace that evening. "Emma's husband was real happy with the job I did at his place. He said his gelding is a whole 'nother horse." He hoped he didn't sound prideful, but this was his only chance to make his case.

"*Jah,* I heard the same from Emma." Simon had retreated back into the shadows, his face unreadable.

"Jamie is the one who put the idea in my head. With everything that has gone on, it might be my best option…if you and the bishop agree." He allowed half a minute to pass before delivering his final argument. *This must be what it's like to be one of those lawyers Englisch-ers hire to fight their battles.* "And I would be home more," Matthew continued. "Folk could drop their animals off for me to train, and I'd only have to call on the big breeders and riding stables."

Simon rose clumsily to his feet. "You've done enough convincing. I'll talk with the bishop and let you know his opinion. I'm going up to bed. You coming?"

"In a little while, Pa. I want to sit and think some more. It's a good night for it." He thought Simon would chafe and send him upstairs like a child, but he was wrong.

"Your *mamm* saved a slice of blackberry pie for you. That and a glass of cold milk might help your thinking."

"*Danki,* I won't be long." Matthew followed him inside and then devoured the pie along with two glasses of milk. He also ate a wedge of cheese, some stale muffins destined for the hogs, and a peach before returning to the porch swing. Although a table of snacks had been set out at the Yost farm, Matthew hadn't eaten. He'd been too busy watching the racing and formulating strategies on how to teach people riding skills. He had never seen so much mishandling. It'd amazed him how some were even able to stay astride. Although several men had urged him to race, he chose not to alienate potential customers to his future enterprise.

Emma could help him make flyers, and James' *bruder* could drive him around to hang them up. Maybe he could get the bishop's permission to install a phone line in the barn, strictly for business purposes. He knew others in the district had such an arrangement.

Before he knew it, he would be taking Martha home in his courting buggy. Leah was right. If he let grass grow under his feet, the girl of his dreams would be snatched up by someone less shy. He would have faith. If God thought his plan was a step in the right direction, he wouldn't fail. He planned to run an honest, fair business, and save his profits to build a two-story house with—

"Matthew Miller! What's the big idea?" Leah's sharp tongue cut through this reverie of a pleasant life with Martha.

Leah stomped up the porch steps and halted before the swing, blocking his escape route. Even in the dim light she looked piqued.

"What are you talkin' about?" he asked.

Both hands were perched on her hips. "I'm talking about you, Rachel, and Martha hightailing it out of there and leaving me stranded!" She tapped the toe of one boot on the porch floor.

He stared at her thundercloud face while puzzle pieces began fitting together. "Settle down, Leah. After Rachel received her trophy we went looking for you. Martha was eager to get home. She has to get up early tomorrow to start canning green beans. She's planning on putting up—"

"Don't get sidetracked. Get on with it."

"Well, we set off to look for you but ran into Jonah Byler instead. He congratulated Rachel on winning third place and talked to us for a few minutes about wishing to learn to ride. He hoped that I would teach…" Matthew noticed Leah's right hand clench into a fist. Although he knew her to be a pacifist, he decided not to take the risk. "Jonah said we shouldn't worry about finding you. He said he was taking you home. That seemed okay to us since you told Rachel you liked him, and he was the reason you went to a draft horse sale…"

Matthew stopped explaining since Leah was no longer listening.

She was staring off into the dark side yard with an odd look on her face. Her expression could be described as surprise, annoyance, and awe rolled into one.

"He told you that?" she asked hoarsely.

"*Jah*, he did." Matthew didn't know what to make of this. "Are you mad at me, Leah? Did we do something wrong?"

"No, nothing wrong." She glanced back at him. "I don't understand Jonah. He wanted to take me home and then barely said two words the whole drive. He seemed peeved about something."

Matthew stood, put his hands on her shoulders, and gently backed Leah up. "As soon as I get a few things straightened out, I'll be happy to help you figure out Jonah. But right now I can barely keep my head above water." He pulled open the screen door. "Let's go inside. Things might make more sense in the morning. I'm sorry if we upset you by leaving you at the Yosts'. It must have been a case of miscommunication."

Leah walked into the house, looking as though the wind had been knocked out of her. "Must have been. *Gut nacht,* Matthew." She headed up the steps while he locked the door and blew out the kerosene lamp.

~

That night Leah remained on her knees in prayer longer than usual. She had more to take care of than rote prayers of forgiveness and thanksgiving. She needed help to understand the new people in her life. Lately Daniel, Steven, John, and now even Jonah behaved in ways no right-minded female ever would.

Finally, when no insight or revelation came to mind, Leah stood and walked to the maple desk under the window. Drawing stationery and a pen from a drawer, she began a long overdue letter to her sister. Emma had endured plenty of missteps and roadblocks while being courted by James Davis, yet she had remained steadfast in her convictions and faith, and in the end, she married her one true love.

Were Miller girls destined to suffer great anguish while other girls courted, fell in love, joined the church, and then married without constant turmoil?

Leah hoped that wasn't the case, but even so she vowed not to follow in Emma's footsteps as she wrote her letter:

Dear Emma,

I hope my letter finds you and Jamie well. It's been quite warm these past few weeks, no? I bought a small battery-powered fan for my room, but I can't use it for long or the batteries go dead. Sometimes when the upstairs is unbearable, I sleep downstairs in mamm's old recuperation room. With the windows open on both sides, a nice breeze blows through, if there's any breeze at all. I'm eager for our next face-to-face visit. I'm afraid the more I'm around menfolk the more confused I become. I find myself running and hiding from boys instead of looking forward to being courted. At least I have the diner to keep my spirits up. Business is good, and I love baking up new recipes.

Maybe I'll just stay single and be a career girl like some Englischers. A cup of this, a pinch of that, a certain amount of time in the oven, and you can count on good results. Not so with people of the male variety. Hurry home soon.

Your loving sister,
Leah

～

The next day Matthew worked his shift at Macintosh Farms as though walking in his sleep. He went through the motions while words and sentences spun through his mind. At three thirty, quitting time, he once again knocked on Mr. Mac's carved oak door.

When the florid-faced owner glanced up from his computer monitor, Matthew said politely, "Excuse me, sir. There's something I need to talk to you about."

TEN

Leah and April bustled through the diner delivering daily specials and cleaning tables at a frantic pace. The diner was filled with *Englischers* who had come down to visit farm markets, look through quaint country shops, and sample rural life. Few Amish had stopped in except for coffee ordered to go. There was a barn raising in the area, and all the Amish within a reasonable distance would be there from sunup until sundown. April had picked Leah up that morning and would drop her off at the farm getting a new barn. She would also deliver pies and a roaster of barbeque beef that Leah's Home Cooking was donating to the cause.

Because local raspberries were in season, a thick layer topped the pancake special along with whipped cream. *Englischers* truly loved their sweets, although seldom did Plain folk decline the topping. The pancakes sold out by the time they had switched over to the lunch menu.

Today all the patrons seemed to have questions for Leah with their orders.

"Where's your horse and buggy?" and "Why no gentlemen admirers today?" came from her elderly regular customer. "How come you don't have buttons on your clothing?" and "Why don't you ever tie your *kapp* ribbons?" came from those experiencing Amish culture for the first time. Leah didn't mind. Curiosity was human nature. She'd been more curious than normal herself lately.

April selected chicken salad with walnuts and grapes for the lunch special, to be served in sandwiches or on a bed of lettuce. When the chicken salad sold out by one thirty, Leah wanted to close up early, but April objected.

"No, we'll stay open until three as usual and feed as many people as we can. That stodgy Mr. Jenkins wants the rent paid by the end of the week or he says he'll change the locks." She abruptly halted her forward motion and turned to look at her partner. "He was just kidding, so don't worry. But we can't afford to turn customers away during our first year. Profits are hard to come by." April hurried off to circumvent further discussion.

Leah was too cowardly to ask questions. But she wondered if April had meant *this* month's rent or last's, or maybe the month before.

The two women cleaned up after closing and then left in April's pickup. Leah remained silent as her mind busily reviewed the previous few weeks. She had noticed more than once April taking cash and making change without actually ringing up the sale in the register. In the past, she'd assumed April would ring it up later when not so busy. Now Leah wasn't so sure. She considered questioning April about their financial condition, but she couldn't muster the courage. Despite Leah's lofty title of partner, April still acted like the boss and treated Leah like what she was...eighteen years old.

Because trucks made better time than buggies, they arrived at the barn raising within twenty minutes. Leah decided to put her worries aside for the lovely June afternoon. After unloading the restaurant's contribution into the food tent, April left while Leah searched for her family. She found *mamm* sitting in a long row of lawn chairs. The women looked like spectators at a sporting event, each of them shaded by the thick brim of their black bonnets.

"Where's your bonnet?" Julia asked as though reading her mind.

"I forgot it this morning," Leah said, twirling one ribbon of her thin white prayer *kapp*.

Julia clucked her tongue. "You'll have to keep to the shade all day. This hot sun will fry your face like an egg."

If her mother knew how many eggs Leah had fried up that morning, she wouldn't make such jokes.

"I'll come sit with you under that big tree," Julia said, rising to her feet.

Leah picked up the lawn chair and carried it to a spot under a huge oak, still within sight of the barn. Soon a hubbub in the rafters caught their attention. Men and boys on ladders, on the ground, and on roof scaffolds scurried like ants around an anthill. "Who is in charge today?"

Julia spread out a quilt for her daughter and then settled back in her chair. "Mr. Klobentz. He tells each crew what to do."

"The same Mr. Klobentz who directed the rebuilding of our barn?" Leah asked, remembering the horrible night of their barn fire four years ago. The acrid smell, the smoke stinging her lungs, the fear that flames would spread to the house, the terrified livestock fleeing for safety—the memory of that night would linger for the rest of her life. The exact cause of the fire had never been determined.

"His son, Marvin," said Julia. "The elder Mr. Klobentz retired, but he's around here someplace, making sure things are done correctly. I'm glad your *daed* and Henry are positioned on the ground, moving piles of lumber to where they are needed. I worry about your *bruder*, crawling around those rafters like a monkey. He doesn't have a monkey's sure-footedness."

Leah focused on the barn and tried to locate Matthew among the workers. Instead she spotted Daniel, Steven, and John, and they seemed to have noticed her too. "Oh, dear," she murmured.

"What's wrong?" Julia asked with growing alarm. She craned her neck and bobbed her head back and forth.

"Nothing, *mamm*. I just remembered something I forgot at the diner." Hopefully, her small white lie would be forgiven, because she didn't want to explain her three frequent customers.

"Speaking of the diner, your *daed* is taking me to lunch there next Wednesday. He has business in town, and we reckon you've worked out the kinks by now." She winked impishly.

Leah grinned. "I'll fix something *extra* special for the daily special. And bake Peach Parfait Supreme and Chocolate Mousse Cream pies. I've received so many compliments on them." Leah settled down on the quilt and stretched out her legs. "Everyone just loves my pies, *mamm.* We have customers who come in for nothing but pie and coffee and then buy a whole pie to take home whenever we have some to spare. Even the Winesburg grocery orders more than I can bake. There aren't enough hours in the day. Now that our peaches are ripe, I won't have to buy them from the produce hauler. And I'll start making plenty of profits."

Leah glanced up to find Julia staring at her. And she wasn't smiling.

"Is that why you work at the restaurant—to grow a big fat head from people's praise and flattery?" Julia asked. "I thought you simply wanted to try working before you settled down and got married. I didn't know you were looking for ways to feel more superior than others." Her soft tone conveyed barbed words that felt like fence wire.

Leah felt heat rush to her face as her palms began to sweat. Never before had anyone spoken to her like this. Perhaps to independent, willful Emma, but never her.

"I'm sorry, *mamm.* I guess I am talking big, but I really do love my work, even without the compliments." Leah bit down on her lower lip as her eyes filled with tears.

Julia shook her head. "The Good Book is filled with stories of those who start out doing good and then run off track the minute they become successful. Read the Old Testament for stories about people whose heads grew too big. Ask the Lord to guide you, and He will." Julia reached over to pat her daughter's hand. "Enough about that. Nobody grows up without making mistakes, I daresay. We adults often fall far short of how the Savior taught us to live too." She glanced back at the barn. "Matthew is coming down the ladder. Why don't you take him a drink? I'm going back to sit with the women."

"All right," Leah said, glad for the diversion. She fetched a paper cup of tea and a bottle of cold water and then found Matthew standing near the barn's foundation. He was wiping his brow with a handkerchief as she approached.

"*Ach*, you're a sight for sore eyes. I'm parched dry." He finished the tea in one long swallow and then opened the bottle of water to sip.

"Hi, Leah!" A voice shouted from overhead.

She shielded her eyes from the glare and peered up at Daniel. The man was waving energetically.

"One of your secret admirers?" asked Matthew.

"What do you mean?" Leah snapped, growing wary.

"I heard you had a swarm of them at the barrel races, all trying to impress you with their bad riding." He held the cold water bottle to his forehead.

"Only a few immature boys acting silly. They sure weren't very secret." She crossed her arms and tried not to look toward the rafters.

"That's what we tend to do at times when we've got our eye on somebody." He drank down half the water. "I once called 'Hi, Martha' loud enough at a singing to be heard in the next county."

"Can we change the subject, please?" she asked. "Why the need for a new barn?" She did her best to ignore the fact John was now waving at her. "I don't see anything singed or charred like we had in our poor yard after the fire."

"Nah, no fire. Their barn was old and full of dry-rot. They decided to take it down before it fell down. I don't reckon the cows would have appreciated that too much. They plan to use some of the dismantled materials for inside partitions, but nothing load-bearing."

"Hullo, Miss Miller!" A voice boomed. "What do you think about—"

As Leah turned her gaze skyward, she heard a sudden shout and then saw Steven sliding down the roof. Along with three other men, he had been lifting sheets of plywood to nail in succession over the roof rafters. If his claw hammer hadn't caught on something during his slide, he might have fallen off the roof completely, a drop of at least twenty-five feet.

"Oh, my goodness!" she exclaimed while Matthew ran to the ladder. By the time he scrambled up to where Steven had been hanging precariously, several other men had already pulled him to safety. Once back on the scaffolding, Leah watched the foreman wag his finger at Steven, but his words were indiscernible down below.

With the accident narrowly averted, one by one the spectators returned their focus to ground level…and several focused on her. Some glared outright as though she were somehow responsible for the close call. For the second time in ten minutes, Leah's face flushed to an angry shade of red. As Steven shakily descended the ladder, she turned on her heels and ran. She had to get away from finger-pointing people, from young men determined to make fools of themselves, and from her own guilty heart. She had encouraged them to a certain extent. She'd laughed at their jokes, blushed at their compliments, and had returned almost as many surreptitious glances as she received.

She didn't stop running until she reached the stand of pines separating the yard from croplands. Once she felt thick pine needles beneath her feet, she sank down into a heap and buried her face in her skirt. Tears were her first response, followed by prayers to be delivered from her own weakness, and finally hope rose from deep within. Would the man she truly favored show up?

Didn't Jonah have a knack for turning up when least expected?

She prayed he'd witnessed her escape from the construction site and then trailed her to see what was wrong. He might offer to drive her home in his buggy, and this time she wouldn't sit mutely like a ninny. She would tell him about Steven's close call and then turn the conversation to him. He could talk about cheese-making or about the different varieties his mother made. Maybe he could suggest new products to try in her baking. And maybe she would find enough courage to ask about his falling away from his faith.

She could offer help or consolation. And she would stop being so hopelessly self-involved.

But Jonah Byler made no afternoon appearance.

After her tears dried on her cheeks, and her red face returned to its normal paleness, Leah shook pine needles from her clothes and crept back to the house. She busied herself by heating things up in the kitchen and carrying them to the chow tent. At least when she was surrounded by food she stood on familiar ground.

～

Julia folded up her lawn chair and Leah's quilt and went back to sit with the other women. She sent her daughter away so she wouldn't keep beating her point into the ground. Leah wasn't at all argumentative, and Julia knew that if she harped too much, Leah would retreat into her shell. A mother needed to maintain communication with a teenage daughter, whether officially on *Rumschpringe* or not.

The women had moved their chairs under the shaded canopy near the lunch tent. The younger matrons were busy refilling food tables because the workers ate in shifts, not all at once. The elder women would be called to help when needed.

From her vantage point she had watched Leah deliver cold drinks to Matthew and remain to chat. With horror she'd seen a young man lose his balance while waving and slide down the plywood. If not for God's mercy and the quick reactions of his crew, he would be on his way to the hospital emergency room instead of catching his breath on the scaffold.

The object of his enthusiasm had been Leah. "Who was that young man who almost fell from the roof?" Julia asked the woman beside her. She only knew her casually because she belonged to a different district.

"His name's Steven Fisher. His family goes to the same services we do. He is a good boy." Her tone held no vacillation.

"He had better mind what he's doing. He could have fallen to the ground," Julia said, rubbing the backs of her hands. It probably would rain tonight, based on her arthritis.

"That's your gal he was waving to, no?"

"*Jah,* that's Leah, my younger daughter. And my boy Matthew, who was standing with her."

"That was my son, John, who was trying to get her attention earlier."

Julia uttered no words, merely a grunt of acknowledgment.

"And his friend Daniel, who was also waving up a fuss." Her comment seemed to hang in the humid summer air as though waiting for Julia to respond.

Julia failed to see how the actions of three boys could be construed as Leah's fault. "*Jah,* they all better keep their minds on what they're doing. A barn raising is no place for shenanigans." Julia hoped the topic was finished.

"At least your gal went running off so the boys could concentrate on their work."

Julia chewed on the inside of her cheek.

"Is she the 'Leah' from Leah's Home Cooking, that new diner in town?"

"*Jah,* but it is April Lambright's business. Leah does most of the cooking and helps serve." For a moment, Julia contemplated moving her chair to the other end of the row, but she knew how rude that would look.

"I never ate there myself, but my son uses any excuse to go to town and stop in. *Leah's meatloaf, Leah's baked fish, Leah's chicken salad—* you'd think the boy never ate those same foods in his own kitchen. And the way he goes on and on about her pies." The woman clucked her tongue in disapproval.

Julia silently counted to five before replying. "I suppose a young man of your son's age loves a change of scenery in town. The diner is still a new attraction—the novelty will wear off in time. My Leah has always loved to cook and bake. She goes the extra mile with her recipes. She surely didn't learn that from me." Julia released her breath through her nostrils, feeling confident her reply had been as Christian as humanly possible.

It was the other woman's turn to grunt. "Has your daughter made up her mind which boy she wants to court yet?"

Julia turned in her chair with her mouth agape. Amish parents rarely discussed their *kinner's* courting. It usually remained a big secret until an engagement was announced. She shut her mouth with a click and then said, "She seldom goes to Sunday singings yet. She's usually too tired after her busy week. I don't think she's courting anybody." Julia hoped her crisp tone would lay the matter to rest.

The woman stretched her neck and arched her back, reminding Julia of a barnyard goose. Then she turned in her chair to meet Julia's gaze. "Some of the women with daughters in my district think your girl should release the fish back to the pond that she doesn't mean to fry up in her skillet."

Julia was rendered speechless while she pondered this odd analogy. Then she said in a low tone, "If you have no further parental advice for me, I'll go see if I'm needed in the lunch tent." She rose to her feet and walked off as her temper flared. Fortunately—or not—no snappy comebacks occurred to her until well away from the meddlesome woman. But it was just as well, because James 1:26 came to mind: "If you claim to be religious but don't control your tongue, you are fooling yourself, and your religion is worthless."

Julia busied herself at the buffet line, stirring roasters and filling plates while figuring out what to do next. She noticed her daughter marching to and fro from the house and could tell by her downcast face all was not well. But one thing was certain: She would discuss this with Simon tonight before bed. It was far better for him to hear the news from his wife than from another father standing around the grain elevator. Julia knew that most men liked to gossip almost as much as women and needed to be reminded of what the Good Book had to say on the matter.

～

Simon barely noticed that his family was very quiet as the gelding took them home from the barn raising. Everyone was exhausted. Henry, at sixteen, did more than his share moving lumber around the construction site. Leah had helped in the food tent after her regular shift at the diner. And Julia? Her arthritis bothered her more than she revealed, despite her medications. Hot humid weather inflamed her already swollen joints. He too was tired but glad he had felt well enough to pitch in. Because the horse knew the way home, he dozed on his sleeping wife's shoulder.

"Where's Matthew?" Henry asked from the backseat. "How come he didn't ride home with us?"

Simon shook off his somnolence. "He's spending the night there. He was asked to remain to finish the interior partitions and hang the barn's windows and doors."

"What about his job?" Leah asked. "Doesn't he have to work at Macintosh Farms tomorrow?"

"No, he quit his job there," said Simon.

"Oh, that's too bad. He loved working with horses all day. And he made good money." Leah leaned forward over the front bench.

"There are more important things in life than a paycheck, daughter. You keep that in mind. Your *bruder* didn't like how the *Englischer* ran things, so he's striking out on his own."

"Oh, dear," she said, settling back on her seat.

"I hope you'll keep your negativity to yourself," Julia snapped. She apparently hadn't been sleeping after all.

Simon seldom heard Julia be short tempered with Leah. It was usually one of the boys who found her last nerve.

"I will," Leah agreed, sounding either chastised or half asleep. "If anybody could make a go of it, it would be him. Everyone thinks he's the best horseman around."

"The bishop said starting his own business is the right course of action, all things considered," said Simon. "Sometimes we must show faith. The bishop will ask the men who stay to finish the barn to help spread the word about his horse training. Word-of-mouth is the best advertisement."

A yawn was Leah's final comment on the subject, which suited Simon fine. Peace and quiet was what he needed, and a good night's sleep in his own comfortable bed. Never before did their humble home look so welcoming as they turned up their driveway.

"See to the horse, Henry. You're a bit younger than me. Check all the water buckets and then come to bed." Leah jumped out and practically sprinted to the house. Simon helped Julia down from the buggy. "I'm glad tomorrow is Saturday. Sleep in, wife; it was a long day. Anything you need to do can wait an extra hour."

"I think I will, but before we go in, I need a word with you."

"Tonight, when we're both so tired? Can't we talk at breakfast?"

She touched his arm lightly. "It won't take long, I promise. And I want to get this off my chest."

"*Ach*, sit down on the porch." He pointed to a straight-backed chair so she could get up easily. "And tell me what won't wait until the morning."

After Julia settled herself she gazed up, her soft brown eyes catching reflected light through the window. "It seems that our shy little girl has bloomed, Simon. And like the honeysuckle bush when filled with blossoms, she has attracted quite a few bees buzzing around the diner."

Simon huffed with impatience. "I'm too tired to figure out metaphors tonight. You had better spell this out to me in simple words."

Julia reached for his hand. "Several young men from the next district over have become smitten with our daughter. They appear to be vying for her attention."

"For Leah?" Simon asked in disbelief. His younger daughter had shown no interest in such things thus far, and he'd been very pleased with that. She hadn't even wished for a *Rumschpringe*.

"*Jah*, our daughter Leah. I heard at quilting that there was a scuffle during the Cleveland baseball outing, but I'd assumed the story had been stretched out of shape."

He studied her weary face as best he could in the dim light. "Go on."

"And then a woman spoke to me this afternoon, the mother of one of the boys who frequent the diner. She has the notion that Leah is encouraging this competition among the young men."

Simon slapped his palm on his leg. "That is the most ridiculous thing I've heard in a long time. She must have been sitting too long in the hot sun." He pushed away from the porch rail and offered his hand. "Let's go inside. You had me worried for a moment that it was something serious."

Julia grasped his hand tightly but didn't get up. "I want you to speak to our daughter, Simon. She's no longer a child, not since she started working. Make sure she understands that a girl's reputation is fragile. And that she shouldn't encourage flattery or male attention to stroke her ego." Julia struggled to her feet, accepting his arm for support.

He felt blindsided by Julia's words. *Are we talking about the same child?* "This sounds like womanfolk talk, *fraa*. Don't you think she should hear this from you?"

"True enough, but I've already spoken to her today about another matter. I thought we could spread out the parental duties."

"Two lectures in the same day—a total equal to the number she has received in the last two years? What is the world coming to?" He helped Julia to the door feeling ninety-five years old.

"Let's contemplate that question after a good night's sleep."

～

The next morning Simon was waiting for his daughter in the kitchen when she arrived downstairs. *"Guder mariye,"* Leah said, slipping on one of her work aprons. "You already started the coffee?"

"I'm not helpless in the kitchen. I know how to make a pot of coffee," he said, sipping the strong brew.

"Do you want me to cook your breakfast before I leave for work?" She glanced around the room with a puzzled expression.

"No, I'll eat with your *mamm* after my morning chores, same as always. Get your coffee, Leah, and sit down."

Leah filled her travel mug and added milk right to the rim. "Can this wait till after work, *daed*? Saturday is our busiest day at the diner. I don't want to be late."

"It cannot. Sit down," he ordered. Apparently, he was down to one child who did his bidding without challenge—Henry.

Leah's complexion paled considerably. "What's wrong?"

"Your *mamm* said there was some fuss over you at that ballgame and a reoccurrence of trouble at the barn raising. Is this true?"

A blush replaced her paleness but her voice remained calm. "I suppose one could say that." She sipped her coffee as though they were discussing someone else.

"I'm asking how *you* would describe it. And if you'd like to get to work before lunchtime, I suggest you start talking."

She snapped on the travel lid and then met his gaze. "Two boys started a fight at the ballgame because one wanted me to eat nachos and the other one didn't. I had no taste for greasy nachos since I'd already eaten too much junk food, but nobody seemed to listen to me. They got themselves in trouble with the chaperones because they punched each other. One ended up with a bloodied nose and the other got the wind knocked out of him." She didn't break eye contact as she recounted the story as though reading aloud from the newspaper.

"And what happened yesterday?" he asked. "Did it involve the same two boys?"

"*Jah* and one more. All three come to the diner quite often for breakfast. While they were working on the roof, they started calling to me and waving. One lost his balance and slipped down the plywood because he wasn't being careful. Luckily for him, members of his crew pulled him back before he fell to the ground." She offered a tentative smile. "I didn't do anything wrong, *daed*. I was taking a cold drink to Matthew like *mamm* said I should."

Why in the world doesn't Julia talk to her about this? I have no expertise in these matters. "You didn't stick around to distract them from their work?"

"No, I walked to the shade trees for a while and then stayed in the food tent until it was time to go home."

"Have any of these boys asked if they might court you?"

Leah's placid demeanor turned stormy. "No, and I hope none of them ever do!"

"Why not?" Simon couldn't believe he was asking such a question, but her vehemence intrigued him. "Have they acted boldly or rudely toward you, or do you think they have no prospects?"

She stared at the vase of larkspur on the table. "They're nice enough, I suppose. One is a blacksmith, one's a furniture maker, and the third is a beef farmer. I just don't want to court any of them."

Simon exhaled a sigh. "All right, Leah. Go on to work, but make sure you're not flirting with them or any other nonsense. And you tell me if they cause more trouble. It's your reputation that will suffer from gossip in the district, not theirs. A girl must protect her good name."

She smiled at him like the sweet, docile child she'd always been. "I will, *danki*." Leah patted his hand, grabbed a peach from the fruit bowl, and hurried out the door.

Simon had an uneasy feeling she had no idea what he was talking about.

ELEVEN

The Last Sunday in June

Emma sat rereading Leah's letter for the third time as she waited for her *ehemann* in the buggy. Jamie had been a little better about leaving on time for preaching services, but today he had slipped back into old habits. No matter. Now she had time to think about her sister's words. Leah's painful confusion was all too familiar. The days when Emma had first started courting Jamie—an *Englischer*—were filled with bittersweet memories. All appeared to be hopeless many times. Emma also understood Leah's newfound joy in the restaurant. When the future looked anything but rosy, it was easy to bury yourself in work, especially if you loved your job. She had her sheep while Leah had her cooking and baking. Both were a source of diversion and comfort during trying times.

At least Leah's pies didn't break down fences and trample *daed*'s corn crop. Remembering her father's blustery face only made her feel lonesome. She wouldn't want to trade places with Leah, despite the fact her own situation was far from idyllic. She'd written back to Leah and given the best advice she could, but it was funny how single women believed everything would be perfect once you got married.

Jamie's family was polite to her but still treated her like an outsider

Even his sister, Lily, hadn't become more relaxed around her since that first afternoon she'd come to Hollyhock Farms with Aunt Hannah. Maybe a woman in veterinary school didn't think she would have anything in common with someone with an eighth grade education.

Emma sighed. That wasn't fair to Lily, who had once told her, "You don't need to go to school to learn. There's a world of education to be found in books." Emma, like Aunt Hannah, loved to read. She knew that she and her sister-in-law hadn't grown close for the simple reason that Lily was seldom home. Ease in a relationship couldn't be had if people rarely saw each other. No, the problem wasn't Lily or even Jamie's mother, although Mrs. Davis still treated her like a child. Emma supposed that happened when a new bride moved into another woman's house.

The problem was herself. Emma longed to have her own home and have time alone with Jamie, at least until *bopplin* started to arrive. There were so many people around—coming in, going out—and always in a hurry. It was hard to live a simple Amish life, even New Order, in an English home.

"Emma!" Jamie's voice finally broke through. "You're busy woolgathering even when you're not with your flock."

She smiled as he climbed into the buggy. His damp hair was combed back under his black hat and he smelled faintly of Ivory soap. He looked so handsome in his Sunday clothes.

"*Guder mariye* again," she said. "Are you finally ready?"

"I had to check over an order." He pulled on his well-trimmed beard, the mark of a married man.

"Working on the Lord's day?" she asked, not hiding her annoyance.

"Not really work. I just had to read a paper my foreman stuck in my face. The order turned out to be fine, no changes necessary. I told him again not to wait until Sunday to tie up loose ends from the week." Jamie shook the reins over the mare's back, and they took off down Hollyhock Lane at a trot.

"I'm glad you reminded him," she added and turned to watch the scenery as the buggy reached the county road.

"Today's the day, my sweet wife." He reached over to pat her knee.

"And what day is that?" She looked at him with one eyebrow raised.

"The day that the James Davis family stays after preaching for lunch and visiting with the other folk." He stared at the road ahead.

Emma felt her heart quicken, her back stiffen, and her stomach tighten all at once. "We couldn't possibly stay after the church service. I didn't fix any food to share." She slouched down on the buggy seat and began fiddling with a *kapp* string. "I can't show up at a gathering empty handed. It just isn't done."

Jamie reached over and pulled the ribbon from her fingers. "Relax, dear heart. We're not showing up empty handed, although I believe there are worse sins in the world than that. I asked my mother to fix a roaster of sausage, peppers, and fried potatoes for us to take. I already put it in the back of the buggy."

She pivoted on the seat. "Then it should be your *mamm* going to this get-together instead of me." She hadn't meant to sound so cross, but her words just spilled out.

His eyes narrowed while his smile melted like snow on a spring day. "I asked her to do this because I knew you'd make another excuse as to why we couldn't socialize within our district. It's high time, Emma. We've been married for two years." His statement didn't invite further discussion. "We don't have to hurry home to tend livestock or visit kin or any of your other excuses."

She pursed her lips together. "All right, Jamie," she said weakly. He was right. People would think something was wrong with them or with their marriage if they didn't start behaving like a normal couple. But for some reason, Emma was afraid of these people. Despite their Plain clothes and the fact that they used horses and buggies, members of New Order talked on the phone, worked with computers, and were far more worldly and knowledgeable than she. She'd wanted to keep Jamie and herself removed from their new community except for worship.

In some ways, she hadn't wanted to share her beloved husband. So she'd made him angry instead. "Your *mamm* must think I'm a terrible wife." She gripped the bottom of her white pinafore with both hands.

He laughed without an ounce of restraint. "No. Actually, she thinks you try hard but are still very shy."

"I can't argue with that," Emma said and returned her focus to the farms they passed. She spent the next forty-five minutes planning her behavior and what topics she would talk about to these almost strangers. She had been worrying and praying about mingling with the ladies without Jamie at her side for more than a year. Now that the day had arrived, she experienced an odd sense of relief. Soon the problem that had loomed large in her mind would be behind her.

Only ten minutes late, James and Emma Davis walked inside the building that was holding the preaching service. When the crowd spilled into the yard three hours later, the Davises didn't flee to their buggy. Instead, Emma found herself surrounded by the friendliest group of women she'd ever met. As was usually the case, her fears had been for naught. She'd drawn conclusions and prejudgments that had been unfair and had caused her months of unnecessary grief. The other women both young and elder made her feel at home in their community.

Oh, Lord, please let me turn to You in all things. I surely would have had an easier time with this if I had.

~

Jonah Byler studied his reflection in his shaving mirror, not liking the man he saw. He felt like a phony, a fraud. He was on his way to a Sunday preaching service without a smidgen of the same convictions as the other believers. The only reason he was going was to please his *mammi,* and because if he didn't his *mamm* wouldn't allow him to attend social gatherings. Thus far he'd only gone to work bees or business-related affairs. But if he was always working somewhere, he'd have no time to get to know Leah Miller. How could he find out if she was the one for him if the diner was their sole meeting place? Plenty of other would-be suitors were always surrounding her there.

Jonah didn't like being a hypocrite, yet he planned to bow his head, recite the prayers, chant the hymns, and do his best to contemplate the minister's message, even though God had turned His back on him. All his prayers for his *daed* to be healed had gone unanswered. His pleas to remain living in Wisconsin in the town that he loved had gone unanswered. Jonah had felt cast off, unworthy to receive the smallest measure of solace. Didn't Matthew 5:4 say, "Blessed are those that mourn, for they shall be comforted?" Jonah knew he'd grown bitter, but he couldn't find the strength to rise above his anger. He would attend church today and pretend to be devout...for Leah's sake. He'd seen the look of shock and anguish on her sweet face when he'd told her of his fall from grace. Gentle and kindhearted Leah was one of God's favored children. Didn't the Beatitudes also say: "Blessed are the pure in heart, for they will see God"?

His own heart felt anything but pure. But maybe if he went through the motions he would regain something, a small bit of what he had lost.

"Jonah? Are you ready? Your *dawdi* wants to leave now." His mother's voice carried up the steps.

"*Jah,* I'll be right down," he called and took one last look at himself in the mirror. Then with gritted teeth he marched out of the house toward the barn.

At least the farm hosting the service wasn't far away. They arrived in less than thirty minutes, yet folk were already filing into the barn. He had no chance to look for familiar faces. He and his *dawdi* found places on a bench close to the front because the back rows had already filled up. His mother and grandmother squeezed in at the end of the third row of the women's side. Jonah slipped a finger inside the tight neck of his white shirt, attempting to loosen the collar. He glanced around at his fellow worshippers, half expecting fingers pointed in his direction, accompanied by "skeptic" or "doubting Thomas" or at least "backslider." But no one hurled invectives his way. He'd garnered only mild curiosity because this was his first service since moving to the district whereas his grandparents were well known in the community.

Jonah began to relax on the bench...until he met the gaze of Leah Miller directly across the room from him. She smiled and mouthed a greeting. He felt the building tilt as though an earthquake had shaken the foundation. He nodded a return greeting as blood rushed into this face.

Jonah Byler never blushed. Perhaps being in the house of the Lord had caused changes to his biological makeup. He couldn't meet Leah's gaze with his face red as a tomato, so he picked up the *Ausbund* to thumb through. He would count bugs trapped against the window glass or the number of rafters overhead before he would look at Leah.

Although the building was very warm, he tried to concentrate on the minister's message, followed by the Scripture readings, several hymns, and finally the second sermon delivered by the bishop. But despite his good intentions, his mind began to wander to a girl with golden brown eyes and reddish brown hair and skin the color of rich buttermilk. But picturing Leah wouldn't help him much in his current predicament. When the three-hour service concluded, he walked outside with his *dawdi*, but the elderly man soon sought the company of his peers. Jonah headed toward a table where cups of lemonade waited in the shade.

"My, my, will wonders never cease?" Leah Miller had crept up behind him. Her question caused his heart to miss a beat.

"Whether or not it's a wonder, here I am, Miss Miller. Are you happy to see me?" He turned to face her.

"I don't know yet. Too soon to tell." She reached for a drink the same time as he. Their fingers touched for a single moment. "I had my eye on that cup of lemonade first," she said.

He picked up the particular cup among many others and handed it to her. "I don't see your bevy of admirers," he said, reaching for another cup of lemonade.

She pulled a face. "And you won't see them here. They live in a different district. Why do they concern you so much? This isn't the first time you have asked about them." She sipped her drink.

Jonah thought and found no suitable answer other than the truth—something she might not want to hear. But he'd be no worse off than he was right now if she turned him down. In his few moments of hesitation, people had walked up to the table and crowded in on all sides. "Will you walk with me to the pond? It's still in sight of your parents and my family. I'd rather have a little privacy."

Leah glanced around before answering. "All right, but it's almost time to eat."

They walked a short distance to the weathered dock, which had been built for fishing or to cool off on a hot summer day.

Jonah took off his hat and slicked a hand through his hair. Feeling Leah's gaze on him, he forged ahead. "I asked about those fellows because one or two or all three are usually hovering every time I come around. I want to know how you feel about them, and if you have settled on one to court."

Her head snapped back as though she hadn't been expecting the question. One or two uncomfortable moments passed before she answered. "I don't wish to be courted by any of them, but I do consider them my friends."

"What about me? Do you consider me your friend?" he asked, stepping closer.

Her forehead furrowed into creases and folds. "*Jah*, I guess I do. And you certainly need friends, don't you, Jonah?" Her dimples deepened with the beginnings of a smile.

"I do, but I can look elsewhere for pals." He didn't wish to joke around. "I'm looking at you as someone I'd like to court. But if you're not interested in me, then I'd appreciate it if you would tell me that right now." He set his hat back on his head and stared out at the cool dark water.

Silence spun out between them and then she giggled. "Goodness, you are direct. Tell me, Jonah, if I say I'm not interested in courting you, will you hurry back to the lunch tables and set your sights on someone else?"

He stared at her. "Nope. If you say you don't like me, I'll walk off this dock into deep water." He hooked a thumb toward the rickety end that was listing to one side.

"On a day like today?" she asked, suppressing a laugh. "The cool water would feel *wunderbaar.*"

"Maybe so, but I grew up in Wisconsin, remember? Our ponds and lakes are so cold I never learned how to swim."

A grin filled her pretty face. "We can't have that, can we?" She tugged his shirtsleeve to pull him back from the edge. "Folk jumping in to pull you to safety? And then sitting around all afternoon in damp clothes?"

"I would make a poor impression on my first visit to church services."

"Does it mean we're no longer friends if I agree to court you? Because the way I figure it, you'd be back down to zero." She clasped her hands behind her back.

He laughed and shook his head. "That's not true. Rachel and Martha Hostetler seemed to like me at the wedding supper as well as your *bruder.* So I would still have three." He bent low, close to her ear. "But I'd really like it if you were my friend and considered being my girl." He straightened up and drew on every ounce of his courage. "Because I think you're awfully pretty, Leah, and nice, and not a bad cook, either." He'd added his last statement to lighten the moment, but it produced the opposite effect.

Now his compliments had become personal, and suddenly Leah resembled a scared rabbit. All frivolity vanished from her face as she crossed her arms over her pinafore. She recalled her father's words and wanted to move forward with caution. "Stop your flattery, Jonah Byler. I agreed to ride home with you after a Sunday singing and maybe get to know you a little better, but you've got no cause to start filling my head with nonsense." She stomped her booted foot and marched off the dock. "I'm getting in line for lunch before it's all gone. Come along or stay where you are. It's up to you."

"I'm coming," he called, hurrying to catch up without a clue why the mood had changed. They walked in silence halfway back, and then she abruptly stopped on the path. "Is this why you came here today, to ask me to court you?" The breeze blew a strand of golden brown hair across her face. She tucked it beneath her *kapp* while watching him intently.

"It is." He liked her so much he decided to tell the honest truth.

"Is it the only reason?"

He shrugged. "My *mamm* said no social occasions unless I start attending church."

"I guess it's a start, isn't it?" she said as they walked back to where a buffet line had formed. But sadness shaded her words, as though she'd been hoping for a different response.

He could have lied to her but he hadn't. *She* was the only reason he'd come today. He'd tried paying attention to the sermons and to the Scripture, but his heart had hardened to the words. Sorrow had put up a wall around him—one that might be able to allow Leah Miller in, but was intended to keep God out.

∼

Although the tourist business was usually thin on Tuesdays, the day turned out anything but quiet for April. This was Leah's day to stay home baking the pies, cakes, muffins, and cookies for the diner for the coming week. She also baked for her family and helped her mother with the ironing. That meant that April waited on tables, cooked, and cleaned up afterward alone. Even with a light crowd, she barely had a chance to draw a deep breath, let alone sit down. She prepared a lunch special of barbecue beef over mashed potatoes or served in a sandwich. The cold salad plate had been no-fuss beets and cucumbers, and the vegetable soup sold out early. Fortunately, only a few customers selected menu items that needed to be cooked to order.

April rang up the bill for a group of ladies on their way to a quilting seminar and exhaled a weary sigh of satisfaction. She would close up the restaurant, pick up her kids from the babysitter, and take them swimming while the afternoon remained hot. Then she heard the bell over the front door jangle as she was turning down the air-conditioning and switching off lights. "We're closed," she hollered through the kitchen door. She listened but heard no follow-up jingling to signal that the customer had left.

"I don't know why folks can't read the sign on the door or check out the posted hours," she muttered to herself.

Slipping her apron over her head, she marched out to see what the tardy customer wanted. Except it wasn't a customer at all. Whip Jenkins sat at the gleaming chrome and Formica counter eating the last of the blackberry pie straight from the tin. He hadn't bothered with a plate and must have helped himself at the silverware drawer. April swallowed down her irritation with his rudeness as she approached her landlord.

"Why, Mr. Jenkins," she said. "You've just saved me a postage stamp." She forced a brittle smile. "I have your rent check in my purse."

"Is that right?" He glanced up and then dug into the second slice as though it were a county fair eating contest. When he finished off the pan with a smack of his lips, he focused his deep-set eyes on her. "And I trust you're talking about a two-month rent check?" He reached for a napkin, swiped at his mouth, and threw the wadded paper down on the counter.

"Yes, sir, this month's rent and last. Thank you for being patient." She tried the phony smile for a second time.

"The truth is, Mrs. Lambright, I'm not really a patient man. For some reason I'm being more so with you than my other deadbeat renters." He stared with eyes colder than spring water in January.

"I'm not a deadbeat, Mr. Jenkins. At least I don't mean to be. I'll pay you every dime of what I owe. It's tough to…manage all the expenses during the first year of business. There's a lot of record-keeping to get used to."

"That's just what I'm talking about. I heard some disturbing rumors around town. Sounds like you owe quite a few people money. I can't be too lenient with you or you'll pay everybody else first and leave me until last." He let his gaze scan over her in a most unpleasant manner. "You're a nice enough lady, but I don't want to get stuck holding the bag. I've got a mortgage on this place and property taxes. Heck, you're paid up now—at least you will be when you hand over that check you've been talking about—but we're at the *end* of June. July rent is due by the tenth of the month. And I want it by then or I'll have to start advertising for a new tenant. I know you're new at this, but times are tough. I gotta look out for myself." He straightened up on the stool. "What'll your customers think if they read in the newspaper that this place is looking for a new renter? Rats will desert a sinking ship every time." He rubbed the stubble on his jaw.

April felt her spine stiffen while some rather mean-spirited thoughts flitted through her mind, but she shook them off. "We have a one-year lease," she said, struggling to keep her tone even.

"And that agreement is based on you keeping up your end of the bargain!"

"I've put a lot of time and my own money in remodeling this place. It was a dump when you bought it."

"All the more reason for you to pay the rent on time."

Neither person spoke for several moments; then he scraped his fork around the edge of the pie tin. "You know…this pie is really good. I hope you do make a go of this restaurant. I've got nothing against you, but I'm a businessman, pure and simple."

April released her pent-up breath slowly, trying to expel anger at the same time. She refused to let him get under her skin on such a fine summer day. Unexpectedly, her eyes filled with tears—an unwarranted response for a *businesswoman*. She picked up the empty pan and his fork and busied herself rewiping the counter.

But he'd seen her display of weakness and turned away. "I noticed on the chalkboard that your lunch special was barbeque beef. I love that stuff on rye bread with sweet pickles. You got any left?" he asked.

April tossed the dishrag into the sink. "There's a quart container; that's all." She narrowed her gaze on him. The tears were gone.

"Well, if you give me that quart of beef and those last two pies in the spinner rack, I'll let you have until the fifteenth of the month, but no longer. After that, I'll be placing that newspaper ad if I don't have your check."

One or two un-Christian responses came to mind, but she swallowed them down like stomach acid. She nodded, pulled the pies from the metal carousel, and placed them in boxes. Then she strode into the kitchen to get his rent check and the container of beef from the refrigerator.

The sooner this repugnant man was on his way, the better.

Then April would drive to the babysitter for her children, praying the entire way to be delivered from the mess she was in.

TWELVE

It didn't take Jonah long to ask Leah out once she agreed to get to know him a little better. She had told him yes on a Sunday and by Tuesday she found a note in her mailbox. He asked her to spend the Fourth of July with him in Millersburg the following Monday. If she were willing, his Mennonite cousin and wife would pick them both up and bring them home after fireworks. Leah began a note of reply within minutes of finding the letter, but then she remembered she should first check with her parents. She assumed there would be no objection, but if the quantity of *mamm*'s questions were any indication, Leah had plenty to worry about.

"An Independence Day celebration?" asked Julia while peeling cucumbers at the sink. "You know Plain folk don't participate in political doings."

"*Jah*," Leah agreed, "but this will be more like a big birthday party for our country with a parade, pie-eating and watermelon seed-spitting contests, good eats, and fireworks at dusk."

Julia looked at her incredulously. "Seeing who can spit a seed the farthest—this is something that interests you?" she asked.

"Sure, plus there will be a stroller parade of *bopplin*," she answered with a cheery smile. Spitting seeds sounded marginally interesting only if Jonah were by her side.

"Who are these cousins of the Bylers? I don't know them."

"They are a much older couple from Wilmot—at least thirty years old. Their two little girls will be coming too." Leah sliced the peeled cucumbers with amazing speed and precision and then swept the pile into a bowl.

"Much older?" Julia asked, peering at Leah over the top of her glasses. "That would make your *daed* and me ancient, no?"

Leah realized her error. "I didn't mean it like that, only that his cousins are reliable folk."

Julia picked up some beets to scrub and trim. "There will be nothing but fair-type food in Millersburg—the same stuff that gave you a bellyache in Cleveland." She wielded the brush against the vegetables as best she could.

Leah gently pulled the brush and beets away to clean. "I'll pick and choose my snacks more carefully this time. I won't mix such bizarre things." She offered her most endearing smile.

"Where did you learn that cat-in-the-cream grin?" Julia asked. "From Emma?"

The exaggerated smile vanished. "Emma didn't teach me to smile. I've known how to do that since I was little." She attacked a particularly muddy beet with gusto.

"Monday is wash day. You surely don't think I can manage by myself, do you?"

"No, *mamm*. They won't pick me up until after one o'clock. I can get three loads of clothes washed and on the line by then. Then I'll finish up the rest the next day while I'm baking for the diner."

"Is this Jonah the boy you were talking to after preaching? Amos Burkholder's grandson?"

"*Jah*, he's the one."

"And he ain't one of those boys making a fuss over you at the restaurant?" Her tone implied what her response might be if Jonah were one of them.

"No. I met him and his *mamm* when April and I were buying cheese at their farm."

"Well, you may go if you don't attend any political rallies or go anywhere near the beer tent, and if you come right home after the fireworks." She leveled Leah a stern look. "And I hope you remembered what your *daed* said about a gal's reputation."

Leah had been expecting the response to be: "I'll talk to your father about this and let you know." So when Julia consented, Leah blurted, "Do you mean I can go?"

"What's the matter? Don't you still want to?" Mother and daughter locked gazes and then both burst out laughing.

"*Jah,* after all that convincing, I just hope I have a good time."

"That's up to you. Now, please put up a pot of water to boil. I stewed a chicken this afternoon, and buttered noodles will go nicely with it."

～

The old adage "A watched clock never moves" applies to wall calendars too. Leah thought Monday would never arrive. Even though the amount of laundry was larger than usual, she did it with a smile. If nothing else, she planned to get to know Jonah well enough that she wouldn't hyperventilate each time he spoke. After all, he was delivering special cheeses to the diner on a regular basis since they had added a fruit-and-cheese plate to their menu.

Leah was waiting on the porch steps rubbing lotion on her hands when Jonah's cousins picked her up at one o'clock. After introductions she sat up front next to Mrs. Woodhall while Jonah climbed into the back with the *kinner.* Conversation proved easy because their nine-year-old daughter was quite a chatterbox. She talked about the jugglers, face-painters, and magicians who would be at the celebration—the latter two subsequently forbade by her parents.

Leah glanced over her shoulder at the little girl but then stopped when she'd felt Jonah's eyes on her like a spotlight beam. Mrs. Woodhall filled the remaining time with questions about the diner. She had heard of Leah's Home Cooking but hadn't yet made the trip to

Winesburg. The young wife was amazed that two women could handle ordering, cooking, cleaning, and keeping up accounts by themselves without male intervention.

Once they parked the van in Millersburg, Jonah and Leah had the day to themselves. The Woodhalls set up lawn chairs on the town square and would remain there in the shade for the duration. "They're having an Abe Lincoln impersonator deliver the Gettysburg Address," said Mrs. Woodhall. "Then we'll watch a veterans' ceremony honoring men and women from five different wars—six if you count Iraq twice."

"What five wars would that be?" asked Leah shyly.

Following Mr. Woodhall's list, Leah realized she'd never heard of "Operation Enduring Freedom."

"Then there will be a variety of music from bluegrass to patriotic to show tunes performed by the high school band," said Mrs. Woodhall as she spread out a blanket for her three-year-old son. Her daughter had already joined a group of sidewalk chalk artists.

"Would you like to walk around Millersburg?" Jonah asked.

"*Jah.* I want to see everything if it's all right with your cousins."

"Of course, off you two go," said Mrs. Woodhall with a wave of her hand.

Jonah and Leah browsed through bookstores, galleries, and antique shops; they wandered through an elegant historic hotel and ate at several food stands. But when she remembered her mother's warning, she fed the rest of her fried elephant ear to the birds. Black crows flew down from atop marble statues for the sweet treat.

Jonah was attentive and charming—if Leah understood the meaning of that word—up until she asked the wrong question. "What did you think about the bishop's sermon, about setting out with the right intentions each day? Perhaps if we did that we wouldn't veer so far from the path."

Jonah's sea blue eyes darkened. "I thought it was a lot of good Sunday talk."

"What do you mean by Sunday talk?"

"It sounds great while you're sitting in the preaching service. But come Monday morning you find it doesn't work so well. Nothing ever changes."

Leah blinked from the sun's glare. "You must have dozed off and missed part of the message. Having good intentions isn't enough. You begin with them, *jah*, but then you must put them into action and assume that things will work out in the end. You start with a certain mind-set, like me serving customers all day without getting my dander up. You make up your mind that's what will happen."

"Do you really think it works that way—the big stuff, the things that matter?" He paused next to a video store and pulled her out of the throng.

In the cool shade of the building, she turned to face him. "If it's God's will, it will work out."

"So it's not up to us at all." Jonah crossed his arms over his chest.

Leah frowned. "Just because we can't determine the details or know His timetable doesn't mean we shouldn't be assertive. We must be patient. God wants His children to be happy, to thrive while they serve Him."

Jonah shook his head. "I envy you, Leah. You have such faith. God must never have told you no."

Her heart tightened within her chest. Jonah's pain was evidently still raw. She wanted so much to choose the right words—those that might be a salve for his wounded spirit. "It's not that I've never been told no, Jonah. God has told me no plenty of times when what I asked for has nothing to do with my purpose." She stepped closer and lifted her chin. "I once prayed for blond hair and freckles across my nose like my sister, and you can see that God ignored that request."

He burst out laughing. Several people passing on the sidewalk glanced in their direction. Leah tentatively reached for Jonah's hand, yearning to offer comfort. "So now I pray for others more often than myself. And I try not to ask for things that would end up a burden... like praying for a hundred customers when our diner won't even hold that many. And I stopped praying for more rain, or less rain, or a mild winter. I decided that God has the easy stuff like the weather and seasons already figured out."

Jonah leaned close and brushed a kiss across her forehead. "*Danki,* Leah. Tonight I will pray to regain some of my lost faith so I don't envy yours so much. Let's go sit a spell with my cousins on the square."

Leah saw her opportunity slipping away. "But that's just it, Jonah. You can't pray to gain faith. You just make up your mind to have it and go from there. God hears the prayers of those who believe, who trust Him with their future. If you're sitting around waiting for your faith to come back, you're wasting precious time."

Jonah's eyes narrowed while he seemed to pull back. "I'll give what you said some thought, but don't beat me over the head, okay?" He nodded toward the street. "Let's get back so they don't start to worry."

She grasped his elbow lightly as they walked back to the town square, but all the while her mind was spinning with ideas.

She decided to make it her business to help Jonah regain what he'd lost.

Because to her, the idea of living apart from God was simply unthinkable.

～

During the past two weeks, Matthew learned to move slowly around the horse that was his first client. And he couldn't imagine a bigger challenge for his initial assignment as an independent trainer. An elderly neighbor had picked up a horse at the Sugar Creek kill pen for a small sum. Because they had no bidders at the recent auction, these horses would be euthanized if no one bought them. Sometimes they were too old or had some medical ailment or had proven too balky to be trained for riding or to pull a buggy. This particular Dutch harness horse fit the latter description. The farmer who'd brought the horse home from Sugar Creek entrusted Matthew with the retraining.

He approached with a brush in one hand and his other palm open and flat. "Easy there," he cooed and slowly reached for the animal's flank. After ten days the gelding now allowed Matthew to groom, lead him around the yard with halter and rope, and would pull the old pony cart as long as it remained empty.

Someone must have broken the animal's spirit with a heavy-handed crop because the horse grew agitated whenever a human approached. Matthew couldn't fathom how anyone could be cruel to a horse—such gentle, loyal, intelligent creatures. He hoped he never witnessed that kind of cruelty, otherwise he might have to suspend his pacifist convictions.

"Are you making progress yet, son?" Simon's words startled Matthew and the gelding equally.

"Stay back, *daed*," he instructed. "Don't enter the stall until he settles down. He's still mighty skittish around folk." He calmed the gelding with soft words and a gentle touch.

"How long will you work on Ben's gelding?" Simon asked from behind the stall wall.

"As long as it takes. He said to send word when he's trained to the buggy. Then I'll probably have to spend a week training Mr. Hartman when I'm done here."

Simon chuckled. "Not many folk have your talent or patience. But this could take the rest of summer. How will you figure out how much to charge Ben? This could turn out to be the most expensive 'free' horse Hartman ever got." Simon laughed heartily while pulling his snow-white beard.

Matthew attached the cross ties to keep the horse calm and stationary while he finished the grooming. "*Ach,* I thought I'd charge Mr. Hartman twenty-five dollars."

"Twenty-five dollars?" Simon squawked. "You would work all summer long for that paltry sum?"

"I've seen his farm. It's real small. Besides, his wife is too old to sit by the roadside selling extra produce anymore. They probably don't have much spending cash." Matthew glanced up to catch Simon's astonished expression before it faded.

"That's real nice of you, and I'm proud to have a son with a generous heart. But I assure you Ben can afford to pay more than twenty-five dollars for training. Folk expect to pay a fair amount for a job well done. Don't give away your services for free or too cheap, or people will think this is just a hobby and not your vocation."

"I won't, *daed,* but I thought if I turn around Mr. Hartman's horse, and he's pleased with my work, he'll tell everybody in five districts. Then I'll get more work than I can handle."

Simon released a sound similar to an owl's hoot. "That's good thinking! You'll soon be saving money for those acres across the street."

"Yup, plus I've got a good-paying contract coming up in two weeks. The ranch that runs the all-day trail rides hired me for six weeks of work. They bought a group of young saddlebreds they want trained and not broken to the trails." Matt gently rubbed down the gelding's forelegs with a damp cloth.

"What's the difference?" asked Simon.

"With breaking you scare the horse into behaving submissively. With training you get to know the animal and learn its body language. You teach them signals and verbal commands; then they submit with their own will and not from fear. It makes for a better experience for the rider if the horse responds willingly. Nobody wants a mean, unhappy mount on a trail ride, especially inexperienced riders." Matthew smiled as he worked tangles from the horse's tail. "I'm going to bunk there during the week, but I'll come home on Friday night and have the whole weekend off. That way I won't miss anymore summer hayrides, volleyball parties, and cookouts like I have been."

Simon snorted. "I'm not so worried about your social life as I am your chores."

"Don't worry. I will pay Henry from my earnings for any chores he does. This ranch pays even better than Macintosh Farms. And on the weekends, I'll take many of his chores so he can go fishing or swimming."

Simon leaned over the stall gate. "You got your eye on some gal?"

Matthew laughed. "*Jah,* but it's too soon to tell if she can put up with me. Henry says I smell like a horse most days."

"Take a good scrub brush into the shower and maybe some of Leah's raspberry shampoo before the next singing. And make sure you don't whinny or neigh while you're talking to her."

"I'll try to keep that in mind, *danki.*" He applied salve to some old fly bites that had never healed properly and then released the horse from the cross ties. After latching the stall gate behind him, he stood with his *daed* in the main walkway. Simon stared up at the ceiling where doves cooed in their rafter nests. Matt turned his gaze upward too. Both men loved the evening barn sounds while critters were settling down to sleep and the flies flew off to wherever pesky creatures go at night.

"You've got plenty of time, son. You're still young."

Matthew shuffled his feet in dirt. "I'm nineteen. I'll be twenty soon. I'll probably take the classes and get baptized this fall. I have no reason to wait longer."

Father and son walked out into the warm evening air. The sun had dropped behind the western hills, casting long shadows across the lawn. Swifts headed for the loft door while purple martins soared and swooped into landing patterns toward the multiunit birdhouse.

"Not much of a *Rumschpringe,* then." Simon's words were more statement than question.

"Jeff Andrews taught me to drive his pickup during our lunch break at work, back in the days when we got along. I drove it around the farm roads and I got pretty good with the clutch and shifting gears." They had reached the porch but didn't enter the house. Matt sat down on the steps while Simon leaned his weary back on the porch post.

"Wha'cha think? About driving, I mean?"

"Oh, it was fun. I liked the heater and the AC and getting places quicker. But when Jeff had to buy gas in town, it would cost him fifty bucks to fill the tank." Matt shook his head. "Fifty bucks," he repeated.

Simon nodded sagely. "If you had to buy your hay, they charge five bucks a bale down at the elevator these days. And horses do love to eat, don't they?"

Matthew could feel his *daed*'s gaze—studying him, assessing his reactions.

"Then it's a good thing we raise our own hay and oats and have plenty of fine pastureland. That way we don't have to pay those prices." He stretched out his legs in the walkway gravel.

"Do you miss Macintosh Farms?"

Matthew thought before answering. "I do sometimes. That place was so beautiful, and everything was either brand new or at least top-notch. The stable ran like a clock too. And most of the time they did good by their horses. *Jah,* I miss it." He peered up into his father's eyes. "I know I'll never have a farm like that, no matter how hard I work or how good I get at training."

Simon lifted off Matt's straw hat, tossed it on the chair, and patted his head the way he had done when his boy was a child. "There are more important things than fancy ranches and expensive saddles and tack. And, you know, those horses you love don't care much one way or the other."

～

With the back of the buggy packed with baked goods, Leah headed to Winesburg to work. Feathery white clouds danced across the clearest, bluest sky...or so it seemed to Leah as her spirits soared this perfect July Wednesday. Did her upcoming outing with Jonah Byler have something to do with her exceptional good mood? Two weeks ago they had shared a wonderful holiday—listening to music, people-watching on the street, and finally enjoying the fireworks in the park. The six of them had found a hillside with an unobstructed view of the pyrotechnics for their lawn chairs. The deafening cacophony had reverberated up and down the valley.

Because horses didn't appreciate loud booms, Leah had never seen fireworks up close. After the first rocket launched into the night sky, Jonah had taken her hand and held it during the twenty-minute display. Somehow his dry skin and rough calluses felt soothing, especially since his large hand enveloped her smaller one. During the walk back to the van, he seemed to be studying her in the near darkness. On the ride home they had shared the backseat, but two *kinner* were wedged in between them, fast asleep. When Jonah walked her to the back door, he formally asked her for a second date.

Leah had said yes without a moment's hesitation. This Friday, a farm near Jonah's was hosting a hot dog roast and bonfire. Leah planned to ride there with the Hostetler sisters, but she hoped to come home with Jonah. And during the time in between, she wanted to hear about new calves or special batches of hot pepper cheese or any other topic, as long as he did the talking in his wonderful husky voice. She could think of little else yesterday while baking and washing clothes. Jonah had occupied her thoughts while weeding the garden, helping *mamm* clean windows, and cooking supper. At least with three days of work between now and then, time would pass quickly.

But as she pulled into the parking lot of Leah's Home Cooking, *daed*'s warning came to mind: *A gal has only one reputation; take good care of it.* As much as Jonah fascinated her, she wasn't sure about courting anybody seriously. Work was still exciting, and her newfound independence felt wonderful. She'd better enjoy Jonah's company within a group, so nobody would get premature notions.

Leah put her horse into the paddock and entered the diner through the back door. Packing crates were stacked beneath the window where she had perched to spy into the restaurant and then been discovered. That seemed so long ago but in truth, only five months had passed. Slipping on her full-length apron, she washed her hands and entered the kitchen, which was already fragrant with the scents of sizzling bacon and sausage.

April was chopping vegetables for omelets, and she glanced up with a smile. "Good morning," she greeted. "How was your weekend?"

"Very nice," Leah said. "We spent Sunday afternoon with Aunt Hannah and Uncle Seth. Their little boy is so smart for a three-and-a-half-year-old. He can name every plant in the garden. How about you? What did you do?"

"We drove to my in-laws on Sunday for a barbeque. It's nice when someone else does the cooking, no?"

"*Jah.* Aunt Hannah had a new recipe for stuffed peppers with rice and ground pork. She used green peppers along with sweet yellows and hot peppers too—something for everyone's taste. I cooked nothing but a pot of coffee, which I better get started here or customers will be banging their mugs on the counter." She plugged in the coffeemaker and the smaller decaf pot and took orange juice out to defrost.

"Coffee is something I sure need to get moving," said April.

Leah spotted dark circles under her partner's eyes and tiny red spider veins on her eyelids. Maybe the busy weekend hadn't allowed enough hours of sleep. If there was another reason for her exhausted appearance—an argument with her husband or maybe a sick child—Leah didn't wish to add to her woes. But on the other hand, it was time *this* half of the partnership knew what was going on.

Once the blueberries were washed and sugared and the creamer pitchers filled, Leah joined April at the griddle to pour the first batch of pancakes. "Say, April," Leah began. "I was wondering...is everything okay on the money end of things?" Her words sounded painfully childlike, as though asked by a nosy youngster. "Like the rent and utilities, and what about those picnic tables we ordered from the carpenter in Shreve? Have we paid him yet?"

For a moment anxiety flashed across the older woman's face, but it was soon replaced with confusion. "What brought this on? Yes, as a matter of fact Mr. Jenkins stopped in the diner a couple weeks ago and picked up his rent check. He saved me a stamp and a trip to the post office." She smiled indulgently before turning back to the sizzling bacon. "And I ran into that nice carpenter in town and wrote him a check then and there." She lifted the skillet to drain off grease into a large pickle jar. "Why do you ask?"

"Oh, no particular reason. I'm just a worrywart. That's what my *mamm* calls me, anyway."

"Well, you just worry about what the lunch special will be. It can't be egg salad—we don't have enough eggs. And it's too hot for sloppy joes, chili, or meatloaf." April breezed out of the kitchen into the dining car without a backward glance. The subject had been dropped and the matter was closed, as least as far as April was concerned.

But despite her boss' attempt to assure her that everything was fine, Leah didn't feel reassured. She'd seen the initial look of panic in her eyes. Although she believed April would not outright lie to her, sometimes withholding the whole truth could be just as bad. She remembered the desk drawer filled with bills and invoices, some stamped with "second notice," and they continued to trouble her. But how could she ask April directly about them? She would sound petty and insecure. Business partners needed to trust each other.

After lining up three types of bread next to the toaster, taking butter out to soften, and mixing another batch of pancake batter, Leah headed into the diner to greet their first customers. And by ten o'clock she felt much better. Regulars like her elderly *Englischer* and carloads of tourists down for an enjoyable day in the country had a way of doing that to a person. Business was brisk at both breakfast and lunch, and they managed to complete the shift without turning the kitchen into a disaster zone.

But the best news came later, right at closing time—better than paid-up rent or a tidy kitchen. The postman stuck his head in the door, hollered "Hello," and left a bundle of flyers, bills, and junk mail on the counter. April quickly ruffled through the stack and held up one yellow vellum envelope. "Miss Leah Miller," she read. "It's a letter for you, dear girl, delivered here to the diner instead of to your home. The return address is Pillsbury Corporation, Minneapolis, Minnesota. Do you suppose this is that contest you entered?" Her green eyes sparkled with delight.

Leah snatched the letter from April's fingers. *"Danki!"* she cried and ran down the back steps. Standing in the middle of the parking lot, she pulled the single sheet from the envelope. After skimming the addresses and salutation, her gaze fixed on the body of the letter. "We are pleased to announce that you have been selected as a finalist in this year's Bake-Off competition. Your recipe for Peach Parfait Supreme pie has been entered in the sweet treats category."

In her initial excitement over the good news, Leah didn't notice that the selection process involved an appearance with her pie before a panel of judges. Or that this year's final round would take place in Orlando, Florida. She ran back inside to hug her partner, and then the two women jumped up and down like puppies just released from their crates.

She barely remembered the drive home from work that day.

Perfectly uniform peach slices and softened cream cheese were dancing through her head like sugar plums on Christmas Eve.

THIRTEEN

Leah had little time to contemplate the letter from Pillsbury or her date with Jonah during the next few days. But each remained in the back of her mind like a secret cache of chocolate...a future pleasure to ease life's minor irritations. Once or twice she'd considered telling her mother about the contest. After all, she would have to now that she'd been named a finalist. But she decided to wait for the right moment. *Mamm* was up to her elbows in tomatoes to be cleaned, chopped, and canned. She wouldn't consider leaving the county, let alone the state, with so much garden produce to put up. But after the harvest, the idea might sound more appealing.

In their corner of the world early August was famous for low, heavy skies and thick, humid air, with the next thunderstorm just around the corner. But that Friday dawned sunny and clear, while a cool breeze blew from the south. Because many Amish went to Sugar Creek for the auction, few customers showed up at the diner. Leah appreciated the less hectic pace as it allowed time to plan her evening. Thoughts of what to wear, what to talk about, and what to eat that wouldn't be too messy filled her mind in between breakfast and lunch. April seemed quieter than usual, but Leah chose not to question her. Sometimes a woman needed to be alone with her thoughts.

After they closed for the day, Leah ran to the paddock to hitch up her horse. Fortunately, the mare didn't seem to mind the faster pace home. As a reward, Leah fed her several carrots before turning her out to the pasture. After her brother's instruction, she now allowed the horse to eat apples and carrots from her hand. In the past she would throw treats over the fence and retreat quickly. Considering the size of horse teeth, she still shivered with the feel of a wet muzzle in her palm. Leah patted the mare's neck once more and hurried to her chores.

Because *mamm* was busy in the garden, Leah had dinner to fix, sheets to take down and fold, and the bathroom to scrub, but she finished with enough time for a soak in the tub. Emma's old peach bubble bath and body lotion from her courting days soothed Leah's dry skin, but she had never developed a curiosity for cosmetics. Blushers and tinted lip gloss looked silly with Plain clothes. Besides, she had more natural color to her cheeks than her pale blond sister had. Emma had come to mind a dozen times this past week. Her turbulent *Rumschpringe* and heartache after falling in love with an *Englischer* didn't prod Leah to start courting, but Jonah wasn't like other boys, and that made her want to know him better. Still water ran deep, her grandmother used to say. She'd never understood what that meant until she met the cheese-maker from Wisconsin.

Martha and Sarah picked her up promptly at six o'clock, saving her a trip around by the snake-infested bog. Emma had loved it by the pond, often taking a book down there to read. How she wasn't eaten alive by mosquitoes remained a mystery.

Wearing her favorite dress and a big smile, Leah squeezed into the one-seat buggy.

"What did you make for the dessert table?" Rachel asked.

Leah laughed at her friend's question, bypassing a standard greeting. "Just my regular walnut brownies, a double batch." She patted her basket containing the pan. "I didn't want to show up the *nonprofessional* bakers and have you going home in tears," she said with a wink. Rachel pinched her arm and made a face.

Martha shook the reins lightly. "Do you suppose your *bruder* will be stopping by at the cookout?" she asked in barely a whisper.

Leah had no good news. "Probably not. He's working at that big stable in Sugar Creek that gives trail rides. He won't be home for a while, and it'll be too late to come out."

Martha didn't hide her disappointment. "Maybe he won't think it's too far."

Rachel and Leah exchanged glances. "I made mini strawberry cheesecakes in silver cupcake wrappers," Rachel said. "We'll just see who's taking home an empty baking pan at the end of the evening."

"Stop competing with one another, you two," Martha said irritably. "God's people shouldn't try to feel superior over anyone. Nothing good could be gained by that."

Leah's grin vanished and she remained quiet for the rest of the drive. She wondered what Martha would think of her entering the bake-off. For the first time, she wondered what the bishop's reaction might be, or that of the rest of her district. Her deacon father might not view this as quite the accomplishment, either.

But as they arrived at the cookout, her worries vanished. At least thirty young people milled around the picnic tables in the backyard. More were already roasting hot dogs using long willow sticks that had been soaked overnight. Some girls were playing a game of croquet; others had squared off over the badminton net, while a few couples strolled toward the slow-moving river. Leah recognized everyone, but the face of handsome, blue-eyed Jonah Byler wasn't among them. Just when she thought he might not have come, she spotted him walking toward her with the loose-limbed grace of someone accustomed to hard work.

"Hi, Leah," he said. "I've been watching and hoping you'd get here soon." He patted his washboard flat stomach.

"I gather you're hungry?" she asked, turning her face up to his.

"I was born hungry, and most likely I'll die that way. I already sharpened our hog dog sticks. Are you ready to try some of my cooking for a change?" He tipped up the brim of his hat.

"Sure. I like my hot dogs burned, but could you find a third stick?" She hooked her arm with Rachel's, out of friendship and to bolster her courage.

"No problem. Good to see ya, Rachel. I'll whittle another stick while you go find a log big enough for three. I'll meet you over there." He nodded toward the fire and headed toward the willows along the riverbank.

The two girls exchanged grins on the way to the fire pit. "I see why you haven't been thinking straight lately," Rachel said as soon as he was out of earshot.

"I have no idea what you're talking about."

Big rounds of tree trunks had been set in a circle around the blaze. Leah moved three of them close together and then perched daintily on the middle seat. Girls and boys leaned toward the heat to cook but retreated each time the wind shifted the flames. Before Jonah returned, Leah had to move her stump back twice.

"Here we are," he said, handing out sticks. Each stick had been loaded with two hot dogs. "You girls get them started, but I'll take over if it gets too hot. I believe I can manage all three." He winked at Leah.

"August is too early for a bonfire," Leah said, trying to get close enough to cook her hot dog. She began to perspire within moments. "I think I'd rather eat mine cold." She moved away from the blaze with watering eyes and a dress already sticking to her back.

Jonah pulled the stick from her hand and reached for Rachel's too. "Some of the roast corn is done. Why don't you girls shuck a few ears and find us a place in the shade to eat?"

"Okay, we'll get our side dishes. I know you love just about everything," Leah said with a sly grin.

"Good idea. I'll have these burned to perfection in no time."

At the food table, Leah and Rachel filled three plates from bowls of coleslaw and cucumber and potato salads. After quickly shucking four ears of corn, they found seats under an oak tree.

When Jonah arrived, he carried only four hot dogs. "Sorry," he said. "I dropped two into the fire. Apparently I'm not quite the chef I thought I was."

"Not so easy cooking for a crowd, is it? But don't worry, with the side dishes one will be enough for Rachel and me." She reached for the mustard bottle the same time as he and their fingers touched. She couldn't stop a blush, and if her red cheeks weren't bad enough, she realized she was sweating. Maybe it was from the fire, but more likely it was because Jonah kept watching her while they ate. Making eye contact while eating might be normal behavior, but it made her hands tremble. At least Rachel kept up a steady stream of chatter to help relieve Leah's anxiety. Jonah ate supper seemingly without a care in the world.

"This is the best-tasting corn all season," Leah declared after the first bite. She started to lick her buttery fingertips until she remembered her manners.

"I agree," said Jonah. "They soaked the cobs overnight so the corn would steam inside the husks. Then they roasted them beneath a layer of ash and coals. That way you can cook dozens for a big party without having to shuck the corn first."

"And they're more tender than boiling atop the stove." Leah bit down on the inside of her cheek. The last thing she wanted to talk about with Jonah was cooking. No man appreciated a steady stream of work stories.

Once they finished eating and clearing the table, Jonah gazed toward the stand of trees and the western hills beyond. "How about a stroll to work off supper? We need to make room for dessert." He lifted an eyebrow playfully.

"You two go ahead," said Rachel. "There's Sarah Mast, and I need to speak to her." Not waiting for a reply, she bounded toward a group of girls talking in the garden.

"Doesn't she ever walk?" asked Jonah, after Rachel departed.

"I can't remember her ever walking," Leah said. "She has the energy of five women." She didn't know what to do with her hands so she clasped them behind her back.

"Well, how about it? Want to take a stroll to the river?"

Leah blushed again, but she nodded. "You know, I think I would like to stick my feet in cool water for a while. I haven't done that yet this summer."

"You're kidding, right?" he asked. "You haven't been swimming or wading in the pond after a hard day of feeding hungry customers?"

"No, I'm not much of a hot weather person. I know it makes me an oddball, but summer is my least favorite season."

As they walked along the pasture fence, grasshoppers jumped before each footfall, while the tall weeds crackled with the sounds of a variety of insect life.

Jonah turned his cool blue gaze on her. "An oddball? I wouldn't say that, but I'd love to hear why you don't like summer." He took hold of her elbow, even though the lane was fairly rut free. "Don't you like nights with the windows open, listening to owls and tree frogs serenading you to sleep?"

His words, wafting on the summer breeze, sound like a serenade. "I guess so, but mosquitoes find their way in through the smallest tear in the screen. And the upstairs rooms get too hot for a good night's sleep. I toss and turn and wake up groggy the next morning," she said, while a red-tailed hawk studied them from a tree branch.

"But isn't it nice going places without first bundling in layers of wool, along with hats, scarves, and gloves?" Jonah asked.

"Maybe, but our Plain clothes get too warm on humid days, and I don't like to perspire."

"What about walking barefoot through the cool morning grass?"

"I've stepped on far too many bees as a child."

"How about the longer hours of daylight?"

"*Jah,* I suppose that's helpful for people coming home in the evening. But I love eating supper by lamplight. My sister still eats dinner by candlelight, even though her New Order district allows electricity. She says food tastes better that way."

Jonah laughed good-naturedly. "Your sister sounds like a newlywed."

"That has nothing to do with it," Leah protested, but she had to chuckle in spite of herself.

When they had reached a stand of willows growing along both sides of the river, they both spotted a log projecting over the rocky bank. It would provide a perfect foot-dangling place to sit.

Jonah jumped down to the creek bed and reached out to her. "So how about spring, when the world comes back to life after the long cold winter?"

Leah took his hand and stepped down as gracefully as possible. "Spring is pretty, I agree, especially the flowers and tree blossoms. But all that pollen makes my hay fever go crazy. And there's usually too much dust in the air from spring plowing."

Jonah shook his head. "Good grief. You've given this matter serious thought."

She felt embarrassed by her negativity, as though she were a hard-to-please fussbudget nobody invites to Sunday dinner. "I warned you I was an oddball," she murmured. Leah settled herself on the mossy log, refusing to contemplate what crawly things lurked beneath her skirt.

"Why do you like winter?" he asked. "Give me five good reasons, and maybe you can change my mind." He held up a hand and wiggled his five fingers. He ticked off each reason as Leah began her list.

"I love our woodstove with a pot of herbs simmering to scent the room, warm apple pie with mugs of hot chocolate, sleigh rides and making caramel apples, less tourist traffic on the roads, sleeping snugly under a warm quilt, no humidity to make my scalp itch, no bugs bites, no steamy kitchens from cooking, walks in the winter woods and following animal tracks through the snow." Leah paused and glanced up.

His expression was one of sheer amazement. "I've run out of fingers on both hands." He wiggled his ten digits.

Leah felt a surge of joy, as though finally somebody understood. "Everybody loves long summer days, but give me wintertime any day," she said. "Once I came upon a doe and fawn sleeping in the woods. The doe was as surprised to see me as I was to see her, but she didn't bolt as you would expect. She looked up with those big brown eyes and somehow knew I wasn't a threat. Then she laid her chin down on her fawn while I crept away. The fawn never woke up." Leah's heart swelled remembering the once-in-a-lifetime experience.

Jonah crossed his arms over his black *mutsfa*. "You're right. Deer wander closer to the house in winter; a person never gets to see them in summer. I do believe you have gained a convert to your side."

"I'm not even close to finished," she said. "But I'll skip ahead since I saved the best for last—Christmas. I love when relatives come to visit, and making gingerbread men, and hearing the story of the Savior's birth. When I was little, my *dawdi* carved me a wooden manger set that I wanted to keep out all year. But *mamm* said it wouldn't feel special if I saw it every day. So I take in out on December first and put it away in January."

Jonah took her hand and covered it with his larger one. "I could look at you every day and it would still feel special."

Leah almost fell off the log. She yanked her hand back as though touched by a toad. "You mustn't say things like that." Her expression turned cross.

"Even if it's the truth?" His soft voice caressed like a mythical siren's song.

"It's better to keep silly nonsense to yourself. I'm trying to overcome my fondness for flattery. My *daed* warned that I was becoming bigheaded, so please don't make things worse."

He opened his mouth to speak but closed it abruptly. He appeared to be pondering her request. "I'll not contribute to your weakness, Leah. I know just how hard it is to regain a sense of grace."

"Are you trying," she whispered, "to regain your faith?"

Crows above their heads stopped cackling as though they also waited for his answer.

"I've returned to preaching services, haven't I?"

"You could be figuring out your fall harvest schedule instead of paying attention, for all I know."

His smile revealed perfectly straight teeth. "I think I need to get up earlier in the morning to deal with you, Leah Miller. But in the meantime, what would you suggest?"

She thought to assemble her words carefully. "Every night before you blow out your lamp, open the Bible to a random spot, a different one each day. Read the chapter that you happened upon. It will contain something useful. Then ask God to guide you with His Word."

Jonah's eyes clouded over before he focused on the ground. "It's an idea, I suppose, but we had better head back to the fire. We don't want folk to talk."

The subject dropped like a hot potato as Jonah closed himself off. Leah jumped off the log and climbed the bank without his help. As they returned to the group, Jonah told her of the birth of twin Holsteins and the exceptional growing season for alfalfa. He spoke of a new cheddar cheese that they had been aging for two months. Leah listened with interest yet her heart remained troubled. To be separated from God was to be alone in this world, even if your house was full of people. She would do whatever necessary to help him.

"Look." Jonah pointed with an index finger. "Isn't that Matt talking to Martha?"

Leah craned her neck left and right to assess the young man with his back turned. One glance at his slouchy posture told her he was not Matthew. She felt a pang of sorrow for a *bruder* who worked too hard for his own good. Hopefully, Martha's companion was only a passing acquaintance or maybe a distant cousin. "I don't think so," she said, not wishing to stare at the pair. "Shall we try some dessert?"

"I thought you would never ask. I'm going to sample everything on the table."

She laughed, thinking that he was joking. Within minutes she realized he wasn't. Never before had she witnessed such an appetite in someone without an ounce of excess body fat. She could feel her own waistband grow tight just watching him eat poppy seed horns, pecan tarts, Apple Betty bars, and oatmeal cookies. Leah tried one of Rachel's mini cheesecakes and pronounced them delicious.

They carried cups of cider back to the fire, where a few couples sat holding hands. Many girls were singing songs they knew by heart, but Leah was content to watch night fall in the valley, turning the pastures deep violet with a thousand points of light from flickering fireflies. The air remained warm, the breeze cool, and surprisingly not one mosquito feasted on her arms or ankles.

Why can't this night go on forever? But knowing her workday started early, Leah perused the circle of familiar faces once more and reluctantly rose to her feet. "As much as I've enjoyed myself, I'd better head for home. I'll go look for Rachel."

Jonah scrambled up and grabbed her forearm. "May I take you home, Leah?"

"You live just down the road from here. Why would you go out of your way?"

He leaned close to her ear. "Oh, I don't know, maybe my mind has been addled by too much sugar."

"Okay," she said, feeling a rush of exhilaration. "But I need to tell Rachel and Martha while you hitch up the horse." She hurried off before she lost her confidence. *What would her girlfriends say about them going home together? What would her* daed?

Rachel and Martha were outside the barn when Leah found them. They barely lifted a brow when she told her news. The slouchy young man who had been hanging around Martha was nowhere around, and Martha seemed annoyed and eager to leave. However, Rachel was exuberant because her dessert pan was completely empty while Leah's still contained several brownies.

Leah hugged her friends goodbye, grabbed her baking pan, and headed for the buggies. When she found Jonah's at the end of a long line, a fluttery sensation began to build in her stomach. It felt similar to the time she rode in the backseat of Mr. Lee's van. She took his outstretched hand as she climbed inside while insecurities swirled through her mind. *Is this a mistake? What if I can't think of a single thing to say?*

Jonah remained quiet as he handed her the lap robe. The evening was still warm but she clutched it for security. "There are still four brownies left. Would you like them for tomorrow?"

"Sure, I'll take them off your hands." His lips formed the smallest smile possible.

As the buggy rolled down the driveway and turned onto the pavement, the silence between them grew unbearable.

"Tell me about yourself," she blurted. "You know plenty about me and my tastes. You've visited my restaurant and sampled my handiwork." She turned to face him on the bench. "What about you? What are you looking for in life?"

He leaned back and didn't reply right away. "I guess I'm content raising dairy cows. I'd like to build a bigger herd and sell more milk to the cheese producers. Maybe I'll build *mamm* a bigger facility on the farm for her specialty cheeses. Other than that, I'd like to get married and raise a family—six boys and six little girls would be just about perfect."

"A dozen *kinner?*" she asked with a voice rough and scratchy.

"*Jah,* a good round number, don't you think? The boys would help me around the farm while the gals could help...whoever is lucky enough to become my wife."

Leah couldn't see his expression in the darkness, but she distinctly heard him chuckle. She'd never given much thought to her future. She'd assumed she would marry some day and bear children, but this man's expectations unnerved her.

How would she work at Leah's Home Cooking once those *bopplin* started arriving? The obvious answer was she wouldn't. If she were to marry Jonah, her job would become a distant, pleasant memory. She knew she was getting way ahead of herself, but just the same...

Maybe she wasn't a good match for Jonah Byler after all. And that thought ruined an otherwise enjoyable ride home.

~

They don't call them the dog days of summer for nothing.

Emma swiped off her wide-brimmed bonnet to scratch her scalp for the third time that morning. She'd been picking tomatoes and peppers for hours and had plenty of mosquito and deerfly bites for her efforts. She didn't mind the hot sun, but the humidity sapped her energy and made her feel wilted. Straightening her spine, Emma shaded her eyes to scan the distant fields for a sign of Jamie.

The trouble with Hollyhock Farms was it was too big to keep track of one's spouse. Her *mamm* usually knew the whereabouts of *daed*—either in the hay, corn, or wheat fields, the cow pasture, or in the barn. But the Davis family owned frontage on eight different township or county roads. A network of gravel lanes might allow easy movement of farm equipment, logging trucks, or livestock haulers, but finding someone wasn't easy.

Sticking your head out an upstairs window and hollering was pointless.

Even their big iron farm bell was more for decoration than function with the pagers and cell phones of English agriculture. Her own cell phone sat in the pocket of her apron with a dead battery. Placing the device into the charger each night still wasn't second nature to her. Not that she often called Jamie anyway. The woodlot and high pastures had no service. Even reception near the house was spotty and unreliable.

Emma assessed her bushel baskets and declared them adequate for a morning's work. Carrying them one at a time to the back door, she planned what to fix for lunch. Maybe she would pack a hamper of cold chicken sandwiches and a thermos of iced tea. The foreman would know Jamie's location. She could hike to where he was working, spread her checkered cloth on a grassy hillside, and share the noon meal with him. Hollyhock offered spectacular vistas of the hills and valleys of southern Holmes County, especially on a day this sunny and clear.

However, her impromptu plan proved short lived. Barbara Davis was buzzing around the kitchen with twice the normal energy of a woman her age. "Ah, there you are, Emma. I was just going to look for you. I've got lunch all ready—tomato soup with toasted cheese sandwiches." Deep lines set off her blue eyes when she smiled.

"Isn't it a bit warm for a hot lunch?" Emma asked, walking to the sink to wash up. She swallowed down her frustration like a bitter pill.

"Do you think so? I enjoy a bowl of soup no matter what the weather is like. Come, sit, and start eating. I have plans for us for the afternoon." Mrs. Davis ladled soup into their bowls. Their sandwiches sat on paper plates, already garnished with bread-and-butter pickle chips.

Emma slipped into a kitchen chair feeling twelve years old. "Shouldn't we wait for Jamie and Mr. Davis?"

"Oh no, dear. They're cutting hay. With this stretch of hot weather, cut hay will dry quickly. The men won't stop until they finish all the eastern fields. But don't worry. We'll see them at suppertime." She sounded as cheery as one of those people on TV trying to sell you something.

Emma tried her soup, but burned her tongue with the first spoonful. "What are your plans for us?" she asked, picking up the sandwich instead.

"Today is my day to lead the Bible study group at the women's correctional facility in Canton." Her face shone with enthusiasm. "I would love it if you came to help out. It's a wonderful opportunity."

"What?" Emma croaked. The melted cheese stuck to the roof of her mouth and had made speech difficult. Her singed tongue didn't help much, either. "You want me to correct other women?" She put the sandwich back on the plate.

Barbara laughed wholeheartedly. "A correctional facility is just another name for a jail, dear. We have a Saturday Bible study group that's gaining in numbers each week."

Emma couldn't understand why *Englischers* insisted on changing the names of things, as though a "reclamation landfill" smelled any better than the "town dump." She tried the soup again. "Why do we have to read the Bible to these women? They can't read the Good Book for themselves?"

Her mother-in-law paused with the spoon midway to her mouth. "Well, almost all *can* read, but most of them don't. They've never been taught the habit or might not have their own Bible. Some of the women have never been inside a church in their lives." She returned the spoon to her bowl still full of soup.

Emma lifted an eyebrow. "Don't they have church services at this jail?"

"Yes, they hold Sunday services, but sitting around a table in small groups makes it easier for people to grasp the message. They can ask questions about words or ideas they don't understand."

Emma pushed away the plate with the sandwich. The melted cheese had cooled and turned rubbery. "Seems to me that if these gals are just starting to learn about God they should get their lessons from a preacher, not from the two of us."

Barbara stared at her and then spoke in a firm voice. "Jesus told His followers to go make disciples of all men."

"He was talking to His apostles."

"All Christians have the responsibility to spread the gosel."

"Old Order don't go around talking, talking, talking about religion to strangers. We're a whole lot quieter about our faith." Emma dragged out the word "whole" for emphasis.

"But you're not Old Order anymore, are you?" Barbara asked, lifting her chin. "You're New Order now, and I believe they do engage in Christian outreach to the poor, the sick, and those who don't know the Lord." She picked up her plate and bowl and carried them to the sink, leaving Emma at the table, fuming but silent. "If you don't want to come with me, you don't have to, but being quiet isn't going to help those young women find the right path when they leave prison and reenter society." She added her own inflection on the word "quiet."

Emma sat alone in the overly large kitchen feeling ashamed of her argumentativeness and also feeling cut adrift between two worlds.

How can they believe in him if they have never heard about him? And how can they hear about him unless someone tells them? She'd read those words from the book of Romans many times, and they now came back to haunt her.

~

After her morning and afternoon spent in the air-conditioned diner, the kitchen at home felt hot and airless. Leah opened every window on the first floor of the house as far as they would go and even brought down her battery-powered fan from her room. But no breeze stirred the white muslin curtains. Then she spotted the package of pork chops thawing on the counter and her heart sank. *Ninety-five degrees and* mamm *wants to fry chops for supper?* She wished she'd brought home the remaining chicken salad for a nice cold meal that wouldn't heat up the house anymore than it was. But she knew her mother wouldn't have any of that. "A hardworking man deserves a hot, home-cooked meal," had been Julia's reply the last time Leah suggested a meal of diner leftovers.

Tucking a damp lock of hair beneath her *kapp*, Leah poured oil in the frying pan to heat and went in search of recently picked produce on the porch. Buttered fresh green beans, carrots, and new potatoes would round out fried pork chops nicely. While she scrubbed and sliced the root vegetables, her thoughts focused on the best way to talk to her parents about the bake-off. Yet by the time Julia roused from her late afternoon nap, no great insight had come to mind.

"*Ach,* according to my joints, it's gonna rain later. Maybe it'll cool things off some," Julia said, lowering herself into a kitchen chair. "Good, you've started the chops; that'll give the kitchen a chance to cool off before we eat." Julia fanned herself with a paper fan she'd picked up at the dollar store.

After Leah turned the meat in the skillet, she sat down with her bowl of beans to snap and began without preamble. "*Mamm,* I got an idea a while back to enter my favorite pie recipe into a baking contest. You know, my Peach Parfait Supreme?"

Julia's attention drifted from what Leah was doing to what she was saying, but she remained silent.

"Everybody says my new recipe could be a contest winner, so, on a lark, I sent it in to the Pillsbury Company."

"On a lark?" asked Julia, frowning.

"*Jah,* I did it spur-of-the-moment, never thinking that I'd hear a word from the Pillsbury folk." She snapped the ends off her beans with expert precision.

"You thought it a wise decision to place yourself in competition with others...with *Englischers?*"

Leah didn't have to ask her mother's opinion; her tone of voice said it all. "It's just people sending in recipes. And then they put the winning ones in cookbooks and on the back of piecrust mixes." She chose her words carefully in an attempt to minimize the competitiveness.

"Plain folk don't enter contests. If you make up a good recipe, fine and dandy. Share it with those who ask for it or keep it your big secret, but don't set yourself up to crow about how special you are. God knows the worth of every one of His lambs, and you don't need to impress anybody other than Him." Julia moved the wastebasket underneath the edge of the table and swept the ends of the beans into it.

At that point Leah knew without a doubt what the final outcome would be, but she continued with stalwart determination. "I understand and agree with that, *mamm,* but I already entered the contest, and I just found out I'm a finalist in the Sweet Treats category. I received a letter inviting me to Orlando to bake my pie in their kitchen, and then the final judges will pick the grand prize winner." She stopped, knowing the nature of the grand prize wouldn't impress her mother in the least.

Julia moved slowly to the sink to fill a pot of water for the vegetables.

When she'd dumped in the colander of beans, she turned to face her daughter. "You shouldn't have entered, Leah. I don't think your *daed* will allow this to go any further. And you've just created a fuss for the Pillsbury folk because now they will have to pick someone else to take your spot as a finalist."

Leah tasted sour disappointment in her mouth. "Are you sure *daed* will say no? Maybe he won't see any harm in it."

Julia drummed her fingertips on the table. "Do you know how far away Orlando, Florida, is? You're starting to sound addled. Do you need to lie down for a while?"

"Couldn't we just ask him?" Leah's pleas rang harsh in the hot kitchen. Then in a childlike voice she added, "Couldn't you please ask him for me?"

Julia met her daughter's gaze and bit back whatever retort had initially come to mind. Perhaps it was because Leah had seldom asked for anything while growing up. Maybe the fact Leah worked so hard six days a week had something to do with it. But most likely, it was nothing more than the mother-daughter bond of love they shared. Julia shook her head and said, "All right, Leah. I'll ask your father when he comes in from the fields, but if I were you I wouldn't get my hopes up."

FOURTEEN

The following Tuesday Leah rose extra early to start her baking. She wanted her cakes, pies, and muffins finished by noon because April was picking her up for an afternoon of diner errands. April usually shopped for the meat, vegetables, and staples by herself. But their storage shed and pantry were depleted, so Leah assumed April needed her help. Leah thought she would enjoy visiting meat vendors and bulk food stores as a buyer rather than a seller of farm produce.

At one o'clock April drove up their lane and turned around. Leah grabbed her purse and flew out the door, climbing into the pickup before April could honk the horn.

"Good afternoon," April chimed. "You look bright eyed and bushy tailed today."

"I slept better last night since the heat finally broke with the rain. Where are we off to?"

"Let's pick up groceries first and meat last. I know an outlet that has canned goods and baking supplies on sale. We'll stock up your home pantry and then pick up eggs, milk, butter, and whatnot for the restaurant. I'm tired of berries, so let's go with pineapple topping on the breakfast special this week, something different."

Pineapple pancakes? Leah had never heard of such a thing. Wouldn't that be too tart early in the morning? But the mark of a good partnership was not questioning the other's decisions. April knew better the preferences of English tourists.

Inside the store they filled two carts with canned sweetened milk, bags of sugar and flour, solid shortening, coffee, tea, lemonade mix, and condiments. After they unloaded at the front register, April began to dig through her handbag frantically. "Dear me, I've left my checkbook at home. Do you have money with you?" she asked Leah. "Whatever the amount, I'll just tack it onto your next paycheck. Can you manage this?" April gazed with pleading blue eyes.

A ripple of apprehension snaked up Leah's spine. "I don't know if I have enough or not. How much do you think all this will be?"

"I don't know. Let's hope for the best." April appeared calm and relaxed while Leah began to perspire. The checkout girl passed item after item over the scanner as Leah's dress stuck uncomfortably to her back. She counted the bills in her wallet. "One hundred fifteen dollars," she said next to April's ear. Normally she wouldn't carry such a sum, but she'd planned to make a deposit at the bank while in town.

"One hundred nine dollars and seventy cents," the clerk announced.

"Oh, good. We have enough." April tugged the bills from Leah's fingers. "Don't worry. I'll jot this amount down the minute I get home to add to your paycheck."

"That'll be fine," Leah said, not mustering much enthusiasm.

The two women loaded the truck with their purchases and headed down the road with windows down and the radio tuned to a Christian music station. April sang along to a spirited gospel hymn and Leah soon started humming too. Her Old Order district didn't permit radio listening even if the song lyrics were inspirational, but at the moment Leah didn't want to think about the bishop's rules or her father or his refusal to accept the fact that she was an adult. She sang the words of the catchy tune's final chorus aloud.

"Here we are," April announced. "Stop number two."

Leah read the sign as they turned into the drive: "Free-range turkey, chicken, and duck, dressed rabbit and lamb, organic eggs, goat's milk and goat's milk cheese. I've passed by this place a million times but I've never stopped in."

"They're very popular since people have become interested in organic and no-cage poultry. This farm raises the best turkey I've ever tasted. The white meat is never dry and the thigh meat melts off the bone. No knife required."

"Sounds yummy," said Leah as they went inside to place their order. The bell over the door announced their arrival.

A young man working behind a computer screen left his desk and approached the counter. He glanced at Leah and then at April and his smile faded to an expression of unease. He leaned forward and whispered, "I'm very sorry, Mrs. Lambright, but my boss won't allow further additions to your account." He looked truly contrite.

"*What?*" April gasped. "There must be some mistake. I've been doing business here for years."

"Yes, ma'am, and we appreciate that, but we have been instructed to take only cash for your purchases."

April stared for several moments as though transfixed by blinding headlights, while Leah's stomach churned. She thought she might be sick. Then April murmured, "All right, young man. I'm sorry we placed you in this difficult position." She pivoted and hurried from the concrete block building, with Leah almost treading on her heels.

Once back in the truck April said with feigned gaiety, "Maybe frozen grocery store turkeys don't taste so bad after all."

Leah clenched her teeth while anger began to build. After they'd driven a few miles from the turkey farm, she asked, "What's going on, April? I'm your business partner. I have a right to know."

April released a weary sigh. "Oh, Leah, I'm ashamed to say that several months ago I got behind with paying bills. There's always so much to do at the diner between prep work and cleanup, and when I'm home my husband resents any time not spent with the family. Managing my time seems to be harder than keeping meringue from collapsing."

Leah didn't laugh at the joke. "So you got behind writing checks to pay folk?"

"Yes, but I have made amends. I paid a whole stack of bills and mailed them last week. I don't know why the poultry farmer hasn't received his yet, or maybe his bookkeeper isn't caught up with the accounts."

She looked so earnest and pitiful that Leah couldn't press the issue. This was April's first business endeavor too, and the adjustment would be harder with a family to care for.

"I'm glad you mailed the checks," Leah said. "Soon this will be behind us. Are we stopping anywhere else?"

"Not unless you have errands to run; otherwise we'll unload at the diner and I'll take you home. My heart's no longer in shopping, or I would treat you to lunch at the buffet."

Because Leah no longer had cash to deposit, her heart was no longer in the trip to the bank. "No other errands for me," she said and turned to watch the scenery beyond the window. She hoped to see hawks soaring, horses galloping, or children playing—anything that would take her mind off her growing money worries.

～

April gave Leah the day off because the Millers were hosting the Friday night singing. Leah had been looking forward to it for days. Jonah Byler had written a note saying he would be there. Though he regularly attended church services, somehow Leah knew his heart remained closed to God. Time and patience healed most ills, so she prayed that they would soften his stubbornness.

That morning she baked cheesecake bars and peanut butter cookies and then helped set up tables and benches. Because Matthew had come home for the weekend, her help wasn't necessary, but keeping busy kept her mind off the diner. During the long, drowsy afternoon, she couldn't seem to think about anything but Jonah. His soft voice floated through her mind like high summer clouds. *Does he really want a dozen children?* Some Amish families were blessed with that many, but could she manage such a brood? Or would she flounder like April at the diner, trying to juggle too many balls in the air?

As young people began to arrive for the singing, Leah set up the snack table and carried pitchers of drinks to the ice chest. Soon many more showed up than she'd expected, including Steven, Daniel, and John. All three had freshly washed hair, pressed dark shirts, and big smiles as they found seats on the other side of the long table. Though they belonged to another district, they had made the trip to her singing. Leah tried to tamp down a swell of exhilaration without success. She grinned brightly, tickled that so many had come.

The only person not smiling was Jonah Byler, who had quietly slipped into the barn. He leaned on a post, watching the socialization with indifference. While Leah bustled around the room, finding seats and passing out songbooks, she hadn't noticed him at first. And when she finally did, the seats close to her were filled. Jonah squeezed in at the end of the row and barely made eye contact with his hostess.

After the singing, the boys rushed to the table loaded with pastries and desserts. The girls followed behind with far more decorum. Leah stacked the songbooks into the trunk for the next event. When she finally headed toward the snacks, most folk had fixed a plate and moved outside to eat and chat. Only her three loyal diner customers still lingered around the dessert table.

"Did you make these cheesecake squares?" asked Steven. "I can't keep away from them. They're so good, I'm on my third helping."

"They can't be better than your peanut butter cookies. They're the best things here!" Both of John's hands held a stack of cookies. Telltale crumbs on his upper lip indicated he'd eaten several already.

"Don't pay any attention to them, Leah," said Daniel. "They're trying to turn your head with flattery. Come on outside to the picnic table. I've set two glasses of lemonade there so you can relax and take a load off. I know you were busy getting ready for tonight, and you did a right nice job."

Take a load off? She laughed at the odd English expression. "All right, Daniel. I can use something to drink. In fact, I might just drink both and leave you with none." She grasped his outstretched elbow so he wouldn't continue to stand there like a rooster with ruffled wings. When they reached the picnic table, she took one of the lemonades and drank it down in several long gulps. "*Danki,* Daniel. I was very thirsty."

Daniel handed her the other drink. "Go ahead, enjoy. I'll go get us more." He picked up the empty cup and disappeared into the crowd.

Outside in the cool evening air, she breathed deeply and gazed around at her guests. Everyone seemed to be enjoying themselves. Most chatted in small groups, while a few couples sat together on hay bales, speaking in low voices. Leah tried to imagine what things they talked about.

However, two people, both male, didn't appear to be enjoying the warm summer night. One was her *bruder,* who stood in the barn doorway. He was glaring toward the oak tree where a swing hung from a branch. Leah focused on what had captured his attention. Martha Hostetler grinned and giggled while being pushed on the swing like a child. Leah inched forward to see who was pushing, expecting to see Rachel. But the person wasn't female at all. Some boy Leah didn't recognize stood behind the swing.

"Oh, no," she murmured. She was about to approach the pair when she remembered the other unhappy face: Jonah Byler. She scanned the crowd for his tall, broad shoulders and glimpsed the back of his head as he walked down the driveway. Leah ran as fast as she could but didn't catch up with him until they were at the end of the row of buggies. "Jonah, wait a moment," she called. "Why are you hurrying off?" She was breathless from exertion.

Jonah stopped short and turned around. "Oh, hello, Leah. It's nice to know you still remember my name." His voice didn't sound quite so soft and dreamy now.

"Of course I know your name. Don't be a goose. I tried saving a spot for you but I couldn't be rude to my other guests." She dabbed a bead of perspiration with her handkerchief.

"No, I suppose not, but you could have shared dessert with me afterward. I went to get us glasses of iced tea and couldn't find you anywhere. Then I spotted you at the picnic table with Daniel...alone."

Leah blinked several times, trying to sort this out. "You sound angry, Jonah, and I don't like it. I drank the lemonade that Daniel brought because my mouth was parched dry. I don't know why you're making a fuss over this." A cool breeze caught the hem of her skirt, sending a chill up her spine. "I was glad you'd come tonight and had hoped to speak with you later."

He studied her face in the yellow light of a full moon, as though trying to memorize each detail. "You can't be so naive you thought Daniel only wanted to bring you something to drink."

A lock of hair blew across her face as she peered into his stony face. "What are you talking about?" The troublemaking lemonade churned in her belly.

He reached over to tuck the lock beneath her *kapp*. "He wishes to court you, Leah, same as me. He has no idea where your heart lies and, frankly, neither do I. You have to choose—either you want to court me or you want your ego stroked by all your male fans. You need to make up your mind."

Anger coursed through her veins like vinegar. "I think you're making a big deal out of a cup of lemonade." She sounded brittle and spiteful as she shifted her weight from one hip to the other.

"I don't think so, not this time. Good night, Leah." Jonah touched his hat brim and walked away, disappearing into the darkness.

Leah was left with flushed cheeks and a burning sensation in her throat. She glanced around. Did anyone hear the dressing down? She would die of embarrassment if someone had. As the first of many tears to come streamed down her face, she hurried toward the house, abandoning her guests.

Later, alone in her room, Leah tossed and turned as sleep refused to come. Finally, she got out of bed and padded to her desk. Lighting the kerosene lamp, she pulled pen and paper from the drawer and began an overdue letter to Emma. How she longed for her sister's shoulder to cry on. Once her annoyance with Jonah had passed, loneliness and melancholy seeped in to fill the void. Without Emma to offer perspective, Leah felt strange in her own skin.

Am I different from most Amish girls?

Do I possess the same willful streak that almost led to Emma's downfall?

With a shaky hand, she began to write:

Dear Emma,

How I miss you and wish you lived closer. I'm afraid that without your advice I've made a mess of my life. The only thing I'm sure of right now is that I love working. Going to the diner to cook and serve the community gives me more joy than I thought possible.

Why should I ever marry? Then I'd be forced to quit my job and cook for one man instead of dozens of friendly people each day. I fear keeping house for a family could never compare with running Leah's Home Cooking. I would go from taking orders from daed *to talking orders from an* ehemann. Daed *ordered me to withdraw my pie recipe from the baking competition. He refused to even discuss the matter with the bishop. He accused me of being vain and attention-seeking, and he demanded I write to Pillsbury to apologize for the confusion. Of course,* mamm *sided with him.*

I don't believe God frowns on baking contests.

If I never marry, I'll eventually grow old enough to live my life without so many people telling me what to do. I will pray for God's guidance and live only by His laws and no one else's.

Hurry home for a visit. I'm eager to hear about your wonderful life with Jamie.

Your loving sister,
Leah

~

Despite leaving the riding stable early, Matthew had rumbled up the driveway well after the time he'd hoped. His young standardbred had kept a fast pace, but many miles stretched between Sugar Creek and the outskirts of Winesburg. Fortunately, many buggies still remained in the yard after the singing. With any luck, one of those buggies belonged to Martha Hostetler. He'd thought of her pretty face all week and heard her soft voice in his head each night as he fell asleep.

Unfortunately, arriving home late didn't excuse him from chores. His gelding needed to be walked to cool down and then brushed and fed. With a sinking heart, Matthew noticed that the water buckets hadn't been cleaned and the feed stanchions were low. Henry must have anticipated his homecoming and started the weekend early. Matthew couldn't blame him, but tonight with the singing in his backyard, he'd hoped to join part of the festivities.

Matthew scrubbed the water buckets and refilled the troughs from the grain sack. After carrying in several bales to divide between the hayracks, he caught a sour smell coming from the sow's pen. *I'm not mucking stalls before I talk to Martha. Henry already says I smell like horses. I won't sink down to hog status.* He prodded the sow to her feet and then moved her and her seven piglets into an outdoor pen. Tomorrow would be soon enough to clean out her stall.

As Matthew exited the barn's back door, he spotted movement from the corner of his eye. Someone he couldn't see was pushing Martha Hostetler on the swing that hung from the oak tree. Matthew, hoping to avoid people in his present condition, decided to skirt around the house the other way. He hopped onto the front porch and slipped through the front door as stealthily as possible. His *mamm* sat in her rocking chair with her Bible open on her lap. Wrapped in a flowery robe, with her hair peeking from beneath her *kapp* and half-moon glasses perched on her nose, she looked like a storybook character.

"*Guder nacht,*" Julia said. "I'm afraid you've missed the singing."

"I got home as soon as I could. I'll take a quick shower and get out to the snack table." Better his mother thought him hungry than eager to see a girl.

He grabbed a set of clean clothes from the ironed pile and fled into the bathroom. Ten minutes later, he toweled his hair, combed it back from his face, and grabbed his best straw hat on his way out the door. Leaving the towel on the porch rail, Matt prowled the dwindling crowd looking for a blue-eyed gal with long eyelashes and the sweetest smile.

People hailed him with handshakes and slaps on the back. Many asked about his job at the riding stable. A few sought his advice about their problem horses. Matthew politely greeted his friends and promised to talk later. But right now he had only one thing on his mind—find Martha and ask to drive or walk her home. He'd dragged his feet for too long. Emma was right. Martha might fall for another guy while he was mustering his courage.

Like a hornet, he buzzed through every area where people talked and laughed, but she wasn't among them. Finally he spotted Rachel standing near the pasture fence with two other girls. "Rachel, do you know where your sister is?" he asked when he reached them.

"Hi, Matt. I was about to ask you the same question." Rachel leaned back against the rails.

Matthew stared with confusion. "What?"

"I can't find Leah. One minute she was talking to Jonah Byler, and the next both had disappeared into thin air." She cocked her head to the side. "He couldn't have asked to drive her home since she lives here." The three girls giggled ridiculously.

"Have you seen Martha? Where is *your* sister?" He didn't try to hide his irritation.

Rachel's silly grin disappeared. "Martha? John Yoder asked to drive her home and she said yes. I thought it was a stupid idea since we only live around the corner. Even if you take the road, you can be home in fifteen minutes."

Matthew barely heard Rachel's words. A stallion had once kicked him in the gut, and it didn't feel as bad as this. The air left his lungs while his shoulder muscles tightened into knots. "Are you sure?" he asked in a shaky voice.

"*Jah*, she told me she was leaving."

Matthew retreated a few steps and then turned and ran. Through the inky darkness he ran toward the cornfield, heedless of tree branches or other hidden obstacles. He didn't slow down even when he reached the long, uniform rows of corn. Down an endless row he ran, while cornstalks battered him from both sides. Twice he tripped and stumbled over rocks in the dirt, yet he kept going until he thought his heart would burst in his chest.

At the end of the row Matthew fell to his knees, gasping for air. Purple thistle had scratched his face and hands, while a dozen hungry mosquitoes sought the scent of fresh blood. But the tears filling his eyes and running down his cheeks had nothing to do with cuts or scratches. Everything he'd worked for and saved and prayed for was lost to him.

～

"Hi, Emma!" called Lily Davis. Her pickup stopped with a spin of driveway gravel.

Emma sat on the three-sided porch at Hollyhock Farms snapping beans into a bowl for supper. Surrounded by tasteful rattan furniture grouped into three separate areas, she watched for Jamie. "Hullo, Lily," called Emma. "Need a hand?"

"I sure do. I've brought tons of laundry. I had to come home—not a single clean thing to wear left in my closet or drawers." Lily set her purse, backpack, laptop, and tote bag of books on the steps, along with her water bottle, bag of pretzels, iPod, cell phone, and two empty soda cans.

English people never went anywhere without lots of stuff.

"Let me help you." Emma set down the bowl and hurried to the tailgate of her sister-in-law's truck. She liked the tall, robust woman with her thick blond ponytail, Buckeyes ball cap, and blue jeans tucked into high riding boots. How Lily could sit down with such tight pants mystified Emma, but she loved her boundless energy and generous heart.

"Thanks. Grab a bag but don't throw your back out. Each one weighs a ton."

Emma reached to grasp a garbage bag when Lily shouted, "Wait! Before you lift that, are you sure you don't have news you want to tell me?" Lily made an exaggerated motion of rocking something in her arms.

Emma blushed. Lily was always dropping hints about being ready for a niece or nephew. "Mercy, Lily, I said you'll be the second one I tell, so stop asking me that." She tried to sound cross without much luck. Flinging the bag over her shoulder, Emma headed to the back door as Lily grabbed two bags at a time.

The Davis home had a sunny laundry room off the kitchen with a long table for folding, an ironing board, and a clothesline for things not suited for the dryer. While Lily sorted clothes into piles of similar colors and fabrics, Emma perched on a tall stool. "How go your classes? I'll bet you're learning lots of interesting things."

Lily opened two cans of soda from the extra refrigerator and handed Emma one. "You'd be surprised how truly uninteresting most veterinary classes are. There is so much stuff to memorize about medications, treatment progressions, and infectious diseases. But soon I'll be doing a lot more hands-on work with furry creatures—the reason I got into this exhausting program in the first place." Lily hopped up on the wooden table. "Veterinary Orthopedics received the grant they've been waiting for to research degenerative hip diseases in dogs, mainly German shepherds and golden retrievers."

"What's a grant?" Emma asked, taking a sip of Coke.

"Basically it's a pile of money to pay for a particular research project. In this case, we got funding to implant a new kind of artificial hip in dogs."

Emma thought she must not have heard Lily correctly. "Did you say dogs? You want to put fake hip bones into dogs?"

Lily laughed as she shoved the first load of clothes in the washer. "Yeah, amazing, huh? We already have people getting replacement hips and knees with joint deterioration all the time. Pretty soon, when your dog needs a new body part, you can call up your vet and order a new hip." Her long ponytail swung wildly as she picked clothes off the floor.

"Amazing? I think it's the stupidest thing I've heard all week—no wait, all month," said Emma.

Lily paused for a moment with the cup of detergent aloft in one hand. Then she poured it in and closed the lid. She wiped her hands on a T-shirt and turned to face her brother's wife. "Why would you think it's stupid, Emma? Our research will extend the lives of dogs with hip dysplasia that would otherwise have to be put to sleep." She talked as though she were choosing her words carefully.

"You mentioned the key word—dogs. These are pets that you're planning to put fake hips into. How many people live in constant pain because they don't have good insurance or enough money to get these high-fallutin medical gizmos?"

"I see your point, but I'm training to become a vet, not an MD. This grant has nothing to do with clinical studies for humans or the limits of insurance policies or anything like that." She placed one hand on her own perfectly healthy hip bone.

"But that's just it—all the money that gets wasted on ridiculous research so that rich folk can indulge their fancy pedigreed dogs. I've seen tourists with dogs in baby carriers, dogs wearing knitted coats, and dogs getting expensive grooming and even spa treatments while the rest of the world doesn't get enough food to eat. Whole villages die of diseases that could be saved with one case of inexpensive antibiotics."

"Well, I can tell you've been attending Mom's missionary support group," Lily said, not hiding her tone of disdain. She chose not to mention that Amish ladies knitted those dog coats for tourists to buy.

"*Jah,* I have. I never realized how most of the world suffers while this country wastes millions of dollars on junk." Emma also took a defensive posture.

Lily sighed. "I know you like animals, Emma. I've seen you nurse sick sheep with poultices and injections and add supplements to their diets to improve their health."

"I do like animals. My family takes in every stray dog or cat dropped off in the neighborhood, but Amish folk know where to draw a sensible line. When a dog's hips wear out, he *should* be put to sleep." Emma was almost shouting.

The two women stared at each other as an uncomfortable silence spun out. Two different cultures clashed over the unlikely topic of animals.

Finally, Lily spoke. "Perhaps when I'm done with my expensive college education, I will have gained some of your innate common sense, but in the meantime I'm honored to have been chosen for this program, however *stupid* you think it is." Lily fled the laundry room in tears.

Emma was left standing on the tile floor as regret filled her. She had allowed her temper to flare in a hateful way and had made her bold, independent sister-in-law cry—something she wouldn't have thought possible.

If Emma could have found a hole big enough, she would have crawled inside it.

FIFTEEN

Leah wouldn't have thought that a person could experience so many emotions during a six-week period, yet she'd known the joy of new love, anger when Jonah stormed out of the singing, shame when forced to examine her behavior, and finally sorrow when Jonah didn't write or stop at the diner. He'd demanded that she make a choice between her bevy of fans or him.

She'd thought him obstinate and controlling, but he had been right. She had been using Steven, Daniel, and John's affections to stroke her ego in a vain and prideful fashion. How did a simple Amish girl turn into a competitive, attention-demanding woman? Each time she remembered how flattered she'd been by those boys she felt embarrassed all over again.

It had taken her only a few days to cool down, and when rational thought returned, the answer was clear—she wished to be courted by Jonah Byler. And she told her three admirers that the next time they came to the diner for breakfast.

Once they were seated with menus before them, she announced, "As much as we appreciate your business here, you three can stop all your foolishness...my heart resides elsewhere."

Not only had they not looked surprised, but Daniel slapped her on the back. "God bless you, Leah, and the lucky man," he said.

Steven added, "Can't blame a guy for trying, can ya?"

"I pretty much had that figured out a long time ago," had been John's reply. Apparently, she had been the only one wearing blinders.

For the next two weeks she planned her apology to Jonah and made sure she always had Peach Parfait Supreme pie on hand. But after she'd taken the second stale pie home to the sow, she began to think Jonah realized his folly in courting a vain, stubborn woman. He hadn't come to a singing, social event, or a preaching service since he'd left the Miller farm in a huff. Instead of helping to repair his fractured relationship with the Lord, she had made his alienation worse.

Leah didn't think anything could hurt as much as a broken heart. The wish that she'd written to Emma about—to spend the rest of her life cooking, baking, and serving meals—had come true. She would become a mere observer of couples and families, of those who had found true love. Yet Leah wasn't ready to add self-pity to her long list of character flaws. When the breakfast customers cleared out and her tables were clean, she wrote a note of apology to Jonah for her behavior and asked him to come to the hayride Friday night at the Hostetler farm. That is, if he was still speaking to her.

That night she prayed to be delivered from her selfishness and to be given another chance with the tenderhearted dairy farmer. And although she felt she was undeserving, God took pity on her. When she arrived at the Hostetlers, Jonah was sitting on the hitching rail.

"*Guder nacht,* Miss Miller."

"*Danki* for coming tonight…and for forgiving me," she said, forcing herself to look at him.

"*Danki* for inviting me…and extending the olive branch. I was hot tempered," he said.

"I was shallow and vain."

"I was jealous and impatient." The corners of his mouth turned up into a grin. "Perhaps we're not suited to anybody else but each other."

Leah's dimples deepened as she smiled. "Maybe we would be doing the rest of the district a favor if we court." She walked over to him. "Have you been waiting long?" she asked, seeing plenty of buggies already there.

"Since I first read your letter," he said, shrugging his shoulders.

It took Leah a moment before she grinned from ear to ear. "My, I hope Mrs. Hostetler took pity on you and brought out food and a blanket. You should have received my letter days ago."

"It was worth any physical discomfort. Ready to ride in the hay? They're loading up right now." He hooked a thumb toward the barn.

"I'm as ready as I ever will be." She didn't mention she'd taken two antihistamine pills. She would rather chance falling asleep than sneezing continuously. As they walked behind the barn where young people were climbing into the hay wagon, Leah didn't feel like the giddy teenager as before with Jonah. The past weeks of soul-searching had matured her. Hopefully, the changes would stick.

They found a bale to share near the back of the wagon. Because it was still daylight, no couples dared to hold hands or sit too close. Leah and Jonah joined in on a few songs, but when they ended, she contentedly watched the autumn landscape. Red, gold, and orange blazed across the distant hills while the pines remained a green contrast. Most of the corn had been harvested, with the stalks bundled together and tied upright to dry.

"I'm glad you're still speaking to me after how I behaved," she whispered.

"I'm glad you picked me over my worthy competition."

Leah peered at Jonah from the corner of her eye. "Truth is, I'm troubled about more than my vanity lately. I could use some advice about a problem at work."

He took hold of her hand, not caring who saw his boldness. "What's wrong?" he asked. "What happened?"

"That's just it. It's not one big event, but lots of little things that aren't quite right. April isn't being completely honest with me. She says we're caught up on bills, but late notices and second requests keep arriving in the mail. People that we do business with go into the kitchen to speak with her and come out frowning. And I see her take payment from customers and not ringing up the sale in the register." She stole a glance at him.

He was watching her closely. "Have you spoken to her about this?"

"No, not about the cash sales, but I have asked about late bills. Her explanations about the situation being temporary aren't very convincing. My *daed* will be furious if it turns out we owe money to everybody in the county. He once turned around and went back to the feed-n-seed after realizing he had been given five dollars too much in change."

"You're April's partner, right? You have a right to see the books."

"Books? More like one messy spiral notebook and dozens of papers jammed into a desk drawer. I know a restaurant should keep good records, but we're always so busy at the diner."

"She might be keeping accounts at home, updating them nightly. Maybe it only looks like total chaos."

"I hope that's the case, but she said her husband gets mad if she spends time at home on diner business. He wasn't big on her opening the restaurant in the first place. He's afraid their children will be neglected."

For a minute or two, both remained quiet while the hay wagon jostled along a potholed stretch of lane. Once or twice Leah was thrown against Jonah's solid shoulder and took comfort that the chasm between them had been spanned. A weight had been lifted since she'd confessed her troubles to him.

"Leah, it looks like you'll have to step up to the plate."

She tried not to scowl. "Please, no baseball analogies. My one trip to a game in Cleveland isn't my fondest memory."

"*Jah,* I heard about that from *mamm.*"

"From your *mamm?* How in the world—" Then Leah remembered her *daed*'s warning about how people loved to gossip. Despite not using telephones, pagers, or the Internet, word managed to travel around the Amish community with lightning speed. "Never mind about that. Just spell out your advice for me."

"You have to stop nansy-pansying around. If you're a business partner, demand to see the accounts payable and receivable—what money you owe and what money is owed to the restaurant. Does she ever keep tabs for people—allow them to pay later for meals eaten today?"

"Sure. Sometimes folk run short of cash in town or leave their wallets at home. Or they're plumb broke until payday."

Jonah shook is head back and forth. "You think the big buffet lets people do that?"

"No, but that's the difference between a restaurant catering to English tourists and the local diner serving regular folk."

Jonah laughed without humor. "But that could also be why the buffet has been in business for thirty years and has expanded three times. At least twenty people work for them now."

Leah leaned back against the wagon slats. This was their first time together in more than a month. Even though she'd brought the subject up, she didn't want to spend the entire hayride talking about problems at work. Especially not if she looked weak or irresponsible. "I agree with you, Jonah, but I'm nervous about causing trouble. She might think I don't trust her...which I guess is exactly how things are. She might lose her temper and dissolve the partnership. I'm not sure what that would mean regarding the money I invested." Her final admission had been so soft she wasn't sure if he'd heard.

"Leah, your investment could already be long gone. If you suspect April is mishandling the money, you must come forward and say something. Step forward in faith, even if it means losing your job. Wasn't that the advice you gave me a while back? Make a choice...is the diner worth more than your self-respect?"

He leaned back against the bales too, and pulled her head to his shoulder. "Enough about that. Let's just enjoy the hayride."

Silently they watched the landscape fade to purple and then total darkness. The evening star rose low on the horizon while the crickets and cicadas began their nightly chorus. The lively conversation and raucous laughter of the group diminished to hushed whispers. Couples snuggled, while single men talked in low voices and girls hummed hymns softly. The hoot of an owl, the cry of a coyote, the faraway blare of a car horn intruded only briefly on Leah and Jonah's time together.

Despite feeling safe tucked against Jonah's side, Leah's mind filled with new worries. Now that she had sought his advice, was she brave enough to take it? *Step forward in faith.* Leah believed those words with her whole heart. But like most things in life, it was much easier said than done.

～

Holmes County is especially beautiful in October when the hills are ablaze with yellow, gold, and red. Emma had loved walking to the pond on her family's farm, where it seemed that every tree imaginable grew. Not the farm pond that provided water for the livestock, but the beaver pond on the way to Aunt Hannah's. Few brave souls ventured down that path because snakes, insects, and even an occasional fox or coyote prowled the lowland bog. Emma, however, loved the peace and quiet and had gone there often.

Now that she lived at Hollyhock Farms, it was harder to find solitude when the constant activity of the house grew tiresome. Emma had found one such oasis the summer before and she headed in that direction after finishing the supper dishes. Jamie had hurried through the evening meal, not savoring the fresh herbs she'd added to the stew or her home-baked bread. He'd buzzed a kiss across her lips and ran out the door as though his pants were on fire. She'd hoped to linger over coffee and pie with him. Emma had a lot weighing on her heart, and only Jamie could lift her spirits...he and her Bible.

Because the former was gone, Emma headed to the stand of pine trees flanking the northern pastures. She carried her Bible, water bottle, bug spray, and a flashlight in case she stayed too long. Darkness fell this time of year soon after the sun slipped below the horizon. No more long periods of dusk while the land was bathed in wavering light and shadows.

Last summer Jamie had fashioned a bench from a wide plank set between two sawed-off stumps. The trunk of a gnarly cedar tree provided her backrest. As Emma hiked through the sheep pasture toward the pines, her mood vastly improved. Seeing the lambs frolicking or nursing always made her feel better. Lately, it seemed sheep were the only creatures she could get along with. First, she'd picked a nasty argument with Mrs. Davis. Although she'd tagged along to the outreach program at the ladies' jail, Emma's heart hadn't been in it. She'd remained meek and nearly mute—not much help with saving souls. To make amends, she participated in mission assistance for an afternoon, sewing up cloth diapers from cotton donated by the underwear plant.

Her hateful words to Lily hadn't been so easily remedied. Lily had finished her laundry at night and left before Emma came in from morning chores. Although Emma had sent a note of apology to her apartment on campus, she'd heard nary a word since. And she hadn't been able to relate the incident to Jamie, even though she thought he would know how to smooth his sister's ruffled feathers. Disagreements like this happened in families, especially when women possessed strong opinions. This argument was better off forgotten. But why did Lily think her view was superior to Emma's? Book learning and college lectures don't necessarily give a person common sense. Although Lily's compassion was commendable, Emma still thought dog replacement parts were an unnatural, foolish waste of money.

Once she reached her refuge, Emma stretched out on the log bench and stared skyward. Patches of blue sky peeked between the tall trees. Listening to the soothing sounds of birds and insects, she felt herself relax for the first time in weeks. Closing her eyes, Emma daydreamed of a small house sitting high on a ridge similar to the one she was on. Here she and Jamie could spend hours together at the end of the day, far from the Hollyhock commotion. She walked slowly through the rooms of her imaginary home, touching the delicate white curtains and smelling the bread baking in the oven, while a simmering pot of herb potpourri cast off a wonderful scent. She could hear the laughter of her children in the front room. Two, no, three little girls played on the rug with their faceless dolls and stuffed brown bears. Jamie came in after a hard day, tired but joyous to spend time with his little family. Oddly, droplets of water began to fall on her face as Emma was chopping vegetables for dinner. How could it be raining inside her kitchen?

Emma bolted upright as the few droplets turned into a steady drizzle. It only took her a moment to realize she'd fallen asleep in the tranquil forest. She glanced around in the thick gloom to orient herself. She might have her Bible, water bottle, and bug spray, but she had no umbrella. The woods were shrouded in near total darkness as she felt the ground for her flashlight. Forest sounds crept closer as inhabitants grew curious about the intruder. Once her hand touched hard metal among the pine needles, Emma grabbed the flashlight, switched it on, and scrambled to her feet. She feared no animal that roamed these woods but nevertheless ran pell-mell down the path with her Bible clutched to her chest.

Jamie must be sick with worry. No doubt he arrived home some time ago and had started looking for her. She'd told no one where she was going. She hoped the Davises hadn't formed a search party for a woman silly enough to fall asleep in the woods. As Emma crossed the sheep pasture, the drizzle escalated to a downpour. Spotting one of the many equipment barns, Emma remembered that umbrellas were often kept inside the door for occasions like this. Still far from the house, she headed toward the barn, hoping to prevent a total drenching. But as she slipped inside the side entrance the electric door clanged, rattled, and began to lift from one of those electronic devices.

"Oh, good," she whispered, wiping her face and hands on her apron. Whoever had borrowed Kevin Davis' truck could drive her up to the house. But no groom or horse trainer stepped out of the truck cab. Instead, it was the love of her life, James Davis Jr. He was dressed in Plain garb, including his black felt hat, but the keys to his former shiny pickup dangled from his fingers. As the electric door squeaked to a close, he walked toward the side entrance and almost ran into her in the dark.

"Emma! What are you doing in here?" he asked. Jamie reached for the light switch and soon fluorescent tubes illuminated her soggy state. "What happened?"

"I went to my favorite reading spot in the pines and fell asleep on the bench you made. Then the rain started or I might have..." She stomped her booted foot. "Never mind about me! Where have you been? Why were you driving your *bruder*'s truck? Have all the horses here at Hollyhock turned up lame?"

James' expression morphed from shock to concern to sheepish embarrassment. "Ah, Emma, my father sent me on an errand to Canton. Someone had to deliver bills of sale and get signatures tonight for six horses we sold. There was no one else to do it." He jammed his hands down into his back pockets and gazed at the floor.

Emma, quite uncomfortable in damp clothes, felt anger build like a brushfire. "You have a buggy and several *race* horses you could have hitched up."

James lifted his chin to meet her gaze. "I met the owner at his office downtown. I couldn't very well take my horse into the city. I promise you, there wasn't anyone else. Not anybody who could be trusted anyway. Please don't be angry with me."

"We both agreed to make changes, Jamie, hard changes. You know I'm not big on outreach work, yet I go with your *mamm*. And the first time life gets a bit hard to manage, you sneak off in Kevin's truck like you never made the commitment."

"The first time—" He stopped short and began again. "Emma, you're not being reasonable. You know my commitment to our new church is just as—"

But Emma was no longer listening. Her face had crumpled with misery and before he could stop her, she ran from the equipment barn, out into the dark night and pouring rain.

~

Late October

Leah refused to look at the calendar on the wall. It only served to remind her that several weeks had passed since her reconciliation hay-ride with Jonah. They had snuggled close during the ride back to the Hostetler barn and then enjoyed mugs of hot chocolate around the campfire. He'd found a bowl of tiny marshmallows that sweetened up the rich cocoa. They hadn't argued or even disagreed on a single topic. Wasn't that a sign they were meant for each other? Her mother had advised, "You surely don't want to spend a lifetime with some-one you can't be with for a few hours without arguing."

He'd taken her home afterward and talked of plans to expand his milking parlor during the winter. When he'd walked her to the back door, he brushed the lightest kiss across her lips. Not her cheek or her forehead or the top of her head, but right smack on her mouth. From that moment on her thoughts changed from Jonah-my-friend or Jo-nah-my-confidant to Jonah-the-man-I-will-marry. Although he never voiced promises or pledges of undying love, hadn't he asked to court her? Courting led to the end of *Rumschpringe,* preparations for baptism, and the announcement of an engagement unless someone discovered a past indiscretion or present personality trait they couldn't live with. As far as she knew she had no peculiarities a husband couldn't live with, except for the time Emma smacked her with a pillow for snoring.

And Leah did want to marry him. That realization had come over her slowly, like a head cold in the spring. She'd gone from wishing to work for the rest of her days to picturing herself surrounded by *kinner.* Maybe not ten or twelve, but as many as God thought her fit to raise.

Did all girls change their minds so quickly when love came knocking? Because Leah was certain this was love.

So why haven't I taken his advice? Days, even weeks had gone by, and she hadn't confronted April. Was she that weak or afraid?

After the hayride, Jonah had to travel to Wisconsin to help his uncle with the corn harvest. Leah had breathed a sigh of relief because this would allow her time to pick the perfect moment to approach her partner. But October brought tourists down from Cleveland and Columbus to view the foliage. Leah's Home Cooking had become twice as busy. Customers occupied every picnic table up until closing to savor the last warm days. No lull existed between breakfast and lunch. April and Leah had started coming to work half an hour early to finish preparations before unlocking the front door.

No opportunity for a heart-to-heart chat had presented itself, perfect or otherwise.

With a deep sense of shame, Leah realized three weeks had passed. According to his last letter, Jonah would soon be home and he was eager to hear her story. Today had to be the day, even if she had to block April's pickup with her buggy.

However when she arrived at the diner, April wasn't parked in her regular spot. An unfamiliar truck had parked cockeyed across two spaces near the entrance. Instead of releasing her horse into the paddock, Leah tied the reins to the signpost and marched toward the front door. A tall, thin man with a bushy mustache was peering through the diner window. He held papers in his hand while several others had already been attached to the front door.

"Excuse me, sir," Leah called from across the lot. "We don't open for another forty minutes. And we don't allow advertising flyers on the diner's exterior. We have a community bulletin board inside that you're welcome to use once we open for breakfast." She tried to keep her tone cordial, but people advertising free-to-good-home kittens, lost dogs, or cars for sale were often zealous with their postings.

The man turned and assessed her from head to toe. "You must

be Miz Lambright's Amish partner," he said without an ounce of warmth.

"Yes, I am Leah Miller. What can I do for you?" Uneasiness swelled in her belly. Something told her this man wasn't interested in selling used farm equipment from their bulletin board.

He moved away from the door so that she could read the posted flyer.

"Eviction Notice—the Sheriff's Department of Holmes County does hereby order said premises to be vacated by..." Leah stopped reading aloud as the words blurred before her eyes. She spotted a date, the diner's address, and "Leah's Home Cooking" all printed neatly in black permanent marker. But the more she studied the paper, the more confused she grew. She shook her head trying to clear the fog. "Who are you and what's this about—this eviction notice?" she asked, arching her back to appear taller.

"I'm Whip Jenkins, your landlord, in case you haven't figured that out. And I'm booting you ladies and your lit'l restaurant out of here." He glared down his thin nose with unbridled contempt. "That's what happens when you don't pay the rent. A man can only be patient for so long before he feels he's being taken for a fool by sweet-talkin' gals in long dresses."

Leah backed up a step. The smell of stale cigarette smoke on his clothes was overwhelming. "No one is taking advantage of you. There must be some mistake. April mailed you a check weeks ago to bring our account up to date."

"Yeah, and that check bounced higher than a kite." The landlord hooked his thumbs into his jeans pockets and tried to glare a hole through Leah's forehead.

It was more than the odor of smoke making Leah sick to her stomach. "The check bounced?" she asked weakly.

"Yeah, that's when you write a check and you ain't got money in the account to cover it." He moderated his tone slightly.

"*Jah,* I understand the concept. I just don't know how this happened.

Business has been good, very good. We sometimes have to turn customers away and send them up the road to the buffet." Leah wiped her damp palms down her skirt.

Jenkins rolled his eyes. "That's something you'll have to take up with Miz Lambright. I wash my hands of you women. You're not worth the trouble. Pay attention to them dates on the paper. You best have your stuff out by then or the sheriff will be putting it on the curb." He stomped down the steps and tried to go around her, but she blocked his path.

"Wait, please. What if I make good on whatever is owed you…in cash. Give me just one day and…" Her voice trailed off upon his vigorous head shaking.

"No, miss. I'm done here. And you don't need to throw away more money. Check out the other posted notice. This place has more problems than just back rent."

Releasing a sigh, his expression turned sympathetic. "You'd better save your cash, young lady, to hire yourself a good lawyer. It's your name up there on that sign, ain't it? It's not April's Home Cooking being shut down by the state." Without another word, Jenkins stepped around her and marched to his truck.

Leah stood staring at the other paper taped to the door. "Closed until further notice by the State of Ohio for failure to remit sales tax receipts and failure to complete local health department certification." There it was in big red letters: Leah's Home Cooking. She reached out to snatch the paper down before customers arrived to witness her shame. Then her focus landed on the small print, close to the bottom of the page: *Do not remove by court order.*

The only thing left to do was walk on wobbly legs to where she'd tied her horse, climb into the buggy, and go home, feeling more confused, embarrassed, and frightened than at any point in her life.

SIXTEEN

A cloud of tension hung above the heads of James and Emma. Following their argument in the equipment barn, he had apologized several times and brought her flowers and candy. But when Emma didn't open her heart and forgive without reservations, his mood soured. Both went about their business as though they were passing acquaintances instead of husband and wife.

Barbara Davis wrung her hands and allowed them as much private time as possible, but nothing worked. Emma noticed that Jamie was staying in the barns for most of the evening. He would mumble an excuse when he came inside, such as repairing harnesses or updating records in the computer. She too stayed downstairs in the living room later than usual, hoping James would be asleep when she came to bed. And he always was.

It wasn't that she was still angry with him. That had faded with the morning light. She was disappointed he'd broken a commitment to his faith and the Amish way of life. Did he still miss his old habits so much he was sneaking around behind her back? Maybe this hadn't been the only trip in his former truck. Did he regret taking the vow and becoming baptized in the New Order Church? Despite using modern technology, New Order was very conservative in other aspects when compared to the English world.

Did he regret marrying her? A lump rose in the back of her throat, one she couldn't swallow no matter how hard she tried. She regretted nothing. She would adjust to living in an *Englischer*'s home and change to New Order worldliness in terms of Christian outreach, but she couldn't live with a husband who resented her and privately yearned for the things he'd given up.

But as Emma's anger dissipated, loneliness soon replaced it. Too much time had lapsed, too many opportunities to say, "I forgive you. Let's not speak of the matter again," had slipped by.

Let she who is without sin cast the first stone kept flitting through her mind as she tried to distract herself with housework. Already she had washed the living room walls, and now Emma carried in a bucket and sponge to scrub the kitchen floor. But she wasn't down on hand and knees long when she felt a hand on her shoulder.

"Get up, Emma. I won't have you scrubbing when I own a machine that will make short work of this floor." When Emma didn't move, Barbara pulled her to her feet as though lifting a fifty-pound bag of seed corn.

"*Danki,* Mrs. Davis, but I want to do my share of work around here."

"Fine, *Mrs. Davis,*" her mother-in-law mimicked. "You can run the buffer over the floor later, but for right now sit down and tell me what's wrong. I know it's none of my business, but you and Jamie are going out of your way to avoid each other."

As the older woman voiced the obvious, Emma's eyes filled with tears. "We had a fight, a terrible fight," she sobbed.

"All couples fight, my dear. No marriage survives without an occasional disagreement."

"This one was awful. I caught him doing something he shouldn't have been."

Barbara looked surprised. "And it was something you cannot forgive him for?"

Emma shook her head. "I've already forgiven him. That's not the point." Tears streamed down her face as she reached for a napkin.

Barbara pushed the napkin holder closer. "Then what is the problem?"

Emma buried her face in a wad of paper. How could she tell Jamie's mother the truth? That maybe he had made a mistake by marrying her? That he was avoiding her because he didn't love her? And that she was tired of trying to make the marriage work while he climbed into his old truck whenever the spirit moved him?

"I can't talk about it, Mom Davis. I'm sorry." It was the first time she'd called her mother-in-law by the English word. It sounded strange to her ears.

Barbara patted her forearm. "Okay, that's understandable, I suppose. But you've got to talk to someone. If you keep this bottled up, it'll cause more harm than good. At the very least you'll get an ulcer."

Emma glanced up with a streaky face. "An ulcer would be the least of my problems." She forced a weak smile.

"Would you like me to drive you into Charm so you could talk to my pastor? He's young, like you and Jamie, and he might offer a fresh perspective."

Emma shook her head. No way could she bare her soul to a stranger.

"Well, then who? How about someone in your family? Shall I drive you home so you can talk to your mother?"

Emma thought for a moment. *Daed*...he would know what she should do. "*Jah*, I'll go pack a bag and you could drive me to Winesburg. My father will help me see things clearly."

Barbara's face paled. "Pack a bag? Why would you do that? I was suggesting a talk with a family member, not moving back home." She shifted uneasily in her chair.

"Just for the evening. You could pick me up tomorrow, maybe on your way home from work. I also want to spend a little time with my sister. Leah has written me letters seeking my advice on matters best discussed in person." Emma gazed out the window. "Not that I'm in any position to dispense advice."

"Nonsense," said Barbara. "Those who have never had problems or troubles are the ones who shouldn't give out advice." She rose to her feet. "Go pack your overnight bag, Emma, and I'll drive you on my way to the store. Let's take this bull by the horns."

Emma didn't know what a horned animal had to do with marital problems, but she flew up the stairs. She could be gone before Jamie finished work for the day. She wouldn't have to spend another sleepless night listening to him snore, wondering if he still loved her or not. Back home, she could pretend she was still a little girl without a care in the world, if only for one night.

But her return to childhood wasn't exactly what she expected. After Barbara dropped her off at the Miller driveway, Emma hiked toward the house hoping someone would spot her and come running. But she reached the porch steps without seeing a single human being. Even the cheery kitchen, smelling sweet from simmering potpourri, was empty.

"*Mamm*? Leah?" she called. "Is anybody home?" She listened as the wall clock marked the passage of time.

"Emma!" called a voice and then her mother's gray head appeared at the top of the cellar steps. She slowly walked up the rest of the way and into the kitchen. "What are you doing here?"

"I've come for a visit. Where is everybody?"

"Your *daed*'s sharpening cutting blades in the barn and Leah's at the diner. Matt's at the riding stable, Henry's cutting firewood, and I'm standing right in front of you. What's wrong?" She narrowed her gaze.

"Nothing is wrong." Emma hugged Julia tightly around the middle, laying her head on her mother's shoulder.

Julia drew her back and asked, "Emma, what's happened? You wouldn't show up unannounced in the middle of the week unless something was wrong." Her brows arched with alarm.

"I didn't think I needed an engraved invitation to come see my family." Emma mustered her most piteous expression.

"No, you don't, but you do need to tell me the truth. Did you and

James have a spat?" Julia set the jars she'd carried in her apron on the counter.

Emma perched a hand on her hip. "How did you know? Do you have spies in Charm?" she teased.

"Oh, Emma. I've been your *mamm* for quite some time now. Do you want to talk about it? I think I can clear my schedule." She grinned while Emma shook her head.

"Please don't be offended, but I think I need to talk to *daed*."

"No offense taken. He's out in the barn. Go on out and get it off your chest so you can put it behind you." Julia made a shooing gesture similar to the one she used with chickens.

Emma went in search of Simon and found him where expected— bent over cultivator blades with his long files. His beard was pure white while his hair seemed grayer than she remembered.

"Can I talk to you, *daed*? *Mamm* said I could find you here." The autumn sunlight didn't reach inside the barn so the interior felt cold and damp.

"Where else would I be?" He peered up without revealing much surprise. "What brings you home, daughter? You still need your pa's two-cents after two years of marriage?"

"Going on three and *jah,* I could use some advice. I've been butting heads with Jamie and most of his family lately."

Simon stopped working and pointed at an overturned bucket with his file. "Sit and talk to me. If I can help I will."

She did as she was told and poured out the story of her argument with her mother-in-law, followed by the spat with Lily. She tried her best to recount the stories as accurately as possible.

Simon leaned back on the stall wall and listened without interrupting. When she finished he asked, "And James. What about the argument with your *ehemann*?"

Emma couldn't relate the events during the rainstorm after falling asleep in the woods quite as objectively.

Afterward, Simon pulled on his beard as though wisdom could

be gleaned from there. "And his driving a truck...do you think he sneaks off often in this fashion?"

Emma paused to consider. "He says no, that this was his first time." Her words were shaded by skepticism.

"Regarding his observance to the other rules of your New Order district, do you think his adherence has been only halfhearted?"

"No, in other ways he has tried very hard." She didn't like where the conversation was headed.

"Seems to me, daughter, that you blew this way out of proportion."

"Are you condoning his sneaking around behind my back?"

"Of course not, but this might have been the only time he used the truck. Every man and woman makes mistakes, backslides if you will, but that doesn't mean their commitment, their dedication is false. Unfortunately, we all fall short of the Master's example." Simon turned his attention back to the cutting blade.

Emma gritted her teeth and folded her hands into a tight knot.

"Your admission that you've been arguing with two other people beside James leads me to think the problem rests with you."

Emma scrambled to her feet. "*Daed,* I have tried—"

Simon held up a hand. "Stop and listen to me. I know you've tried, but this time when you return to your husband's family, try without your willfulness getting in the way. Put aside your pride and forgive your husband his error. And apologize to Mrs. Davis for your obstinacy."

"But she treats me like a child!"

"Maybe that's because you've been acting like one."

Emma sat back down clumsily as Simon came to stand beside her. "Trust her to guide you," he said softly. "And pray, Emma, for God's guidance. We never grow too old for that."

Emma barely heard his final directive. With her head buried in her hands, the truth of his words hit home. What a mess she'd made of her life. She didn't wait until bedtime to start her prayers. Sitting on a feed bucket in a cold, damp barn, she prayed for forgiveness and to be delivered from herself.

"I'll leave you now, but I'll see you inside the house. Don't stay too long out here." His hand lightly grazed her shoulder. "I know you can forgive James. Just make sure you can forgive yourself too."

∼

Matt sat rocking on the porch like an old man. If there were some kind of get-together tonight, he hadn't heard about it. Leah had stayed up in her room all day complaining of a headache, so he couldn't rely on her to let him know about bonfires, hayrides, or marshmallow roasts.

Not that it would make much difference. He'd seen Martha talking and laughing with John Yoder with his own eyes. Then Rachel said she had accepted a ride home with him. Any interest Martha had had in Matthew must have existed only in his own mind.

Why did I even come home for the weekend? If he'd stayed in Sugar Creek and kept working, he wouldn't have passed her farm and been reminded of lost chances. As he stared off at the darkening fields where tied cornstalks stood like sentinels, he heard the sound of a diesel truck engine winding down. A double-axle pickup turned into their driveway and slowly approached the house. The decal on the driver's door read Macintosh Farms. Matt couldn't fathom who would stop for a visit; his list of former work friends was short. When the door opened, a distinguished-looking gentleman stepped out wearing a fancy wool blazer.

"Hello, Matthew. How have you been?"

"Mr. Mac," stuttered Matt, "what are you doin' here?" He scrambled to his feet, flabbergasted.

"You probably wouldn't believe me if I said I was in the neighborhood," he chuckled. "So I'll be straight with you. Mind if I come onto the porch and sit a spell?"

"Sure, come on up. You want some coffee or something?"

"Nah, I'm good. Thanks." Mr. Mac took the rocker just vacated, so Matt pulled a green lawn chair close to his former boss.

"I won't beat around the bush, son. I fired Jeff Andrews—what I should've done long ago. When you came to see me to explain what Andrews was doing, I thought it was an isolated incident. I chose to look the other way and that was wrong. Since then two other owners pulled their horses from my training facility after more of Andrews' shenanigans. And if word gets around, others might follow suit. My reputation's at stake, and I have no one to blame but myself." He paused to study Matt's face.

Matthew had no idea what kind of response Mr. Mac expected as he wrung his hands nervously. "*Jah,* Andrews was a bad sort," he said.

"Yeah, he was. I should have kept him on a tight leash, but I didn't come here just to talk about him. I came to talk about you. One owner asked which stable you went to work for. I said you worked out of your home, mainly for the Amish."

Matthew nodded, choosing to remain silent.

"I'm asking you to come back to work for me. I'll pay you what I paid that bum Andrews. I know you folk don't use insurance, but if you want medical benefits I'll pay those too, along with three weeks vacation and all the normal holidays."

Neither man spoke for several moments as moths batted their wings around the porch light. Finally Mr. Macintosh asked, "What do you say?"

"I'm curious—what was Jeff earning?"

The figure quoted made the hairs on Matt's neck stand on end. He whistled through his teeth, trying to imagine what he would do with so much money. The bank would surely give him a loan for the Lee acreage with that kind of salary. Not that he had any pressing need to build himself a house with Martha courting somebody else. He met the man's gaze. "That's more than I thought. A lot more."

"So you'll take the job? I think you'll like the place now that—"

"No," Matthew interrupted before he changed his mind. The love of money could skew a man's good judgment. "Don't think I don't appreciate the offer, sir, but I'm contracted to work several months down in Sugar Creek. Once that's done, I'll need to catch up on local work. Plus I like not being tied to a job in case my pa needs me." He glanced inside the kitchen, where his parents sat drinking their evening cups of tea.

"I don't suppose there's something I can add to sweeten the pot?"

"No, sir, can't think of anything, but I'm honored you made the offer. Thanks for stopping by." He stood and extended his hand.

"Hold on there a minute." Macintosh held up his palms instead of shaking. "Didn't you say you're doing contract work?" He rose to his feet too.

"I did, at a riding academy."

"Why don't you contract with me...say six months out of the year. Three months in the summer after the planting's done, and the three winter months after the harvest is in. That way you'll be home when your father needs you, and I'll have the extra help when I need it most." He looked at Matt with anticipation.

Matt scratched his stubbly chin. "That sounds good, but I first have to see this contract through, plus I'll want to talk to my pa. Can I call you from our neighbors' with my answer?"

"That'll be fine," his former boss agreed as he stuck out his hand.

Matt pumped it eagerly. "Thanks. I'll be in touch."

Mr. Macintosh bent to look inside the kitchen window. "Your place is real nice. You're a lucky man, son." He nodded and walked down the steps to his truck, leaving Matthew pondering his lucrative but lonely future.

~

Leah had planned to tell her parents anyway. After all, she couldn't hide for the rest of her life up in her room. Today was Saturday—formerly the diner's busiest day. Her parents knew it would take something far worse than a headache to keep her home. Dressing in her shabbiest clothes, Leah went downstairs feeling guilty, despite the fact *she* had never forgotten to ring up a sale.

Her parents sat at the kitchen table with mugs of coffee untouched and cooling before them. An open newspaper had been spread out and they pored over a story. Leah walked straight to the coffeepot. *"Guder mariye,"* she greeted. "Something interesting in the newspaper?"

Two pairs of dark eyes turned toward her. Her *mamm* and *daed* stared as though she'd turned unrecognizable while asleep.

"What's wrong?" she asked with growing anxiety.

"This!" Simon stabbed the paper with his finger.

Leah leaned over his shoulder to read aloud. "Local diner closed. Owner arrested on suspicion of fraud." Her eyes quickly scanned the story and locked on April Lambright's name and "Leah's Home Cooking." She stopped reading and slumped into a chair. "This is worse than I thought," she moaned.

Simon shook the edge of the newspaper. "Mr. Lee walked over at dawn after picking this paper up yesterday in Wooster. He was real upset. This says that your partner wrote at least a dozen checks from an already overdrawn checking account. Folk who got these checks deposited them in their bank accounts and paid bills, thinking the money was there. Mrs. Lambright caused an avalanche of problems for these people, one right after another." Simon glared at her while Julia wrung her hands as if she were doing arthritis exercises.

"I didn't pay any bills. April took care of all that."

"No, Leah, it looks like *no one* took care of that!" Simon stormed. "And that kind of behavior is called fraud."

Julia spoke in a gentler voice. "Didn't you know this was going on? Couldn't you have stopped her? Lots of folk are hoppin' mad, and she's sitting in the county jail right now."

"Mamm, I asked her if we were current with bills and she said yes. She lied to me."

"That's not all, young lady," Simon blustered. "The paper says the landlord has evicted you two and that the state might be bringing charges. If your restaurant was collecting sales tax on restaurant meals, nobody sent a dime of it into the state treasury. They're not real happy about that."

With trembling fingers Leah reached for her coffee and drank down half.

"How much did you know about this, Leah?" Julia asked. "I take it this is the source of yesterday's migraine."

"You could say that," she murmured.

"You'd better be saying a lot more than you are, daughter." Simon's face had turned the color of mulled cider.

Leah refilled her mug and began the saga of her short history as a restaurant partner. She told about the drawer of late notices, the unhappy vendors speaking to April behind closed doors, and the embarrassing trip to the poultry farm. She culminated with the visit from the nasty Mr. Jenkins two days earlier. When she placed a harsh inflection on the landlord's behavior, her father interrupted.

"Don't be taking that attitude, Leah. That landlord deserves to be paid the rent fully and on time. He's not the bad guy here."

Leah relaxed her tense shoulders. "I know, but April spent a lot of money remodeling the train cars to turn them into a diner—some of it her own, some borrowed from her father."

"All the more reason she needed to pay the rent, to protect her investment as well as her good name…and yours, I might add!"

Leah sipped her coffee, wishing she'd never seen that rundown train.

"Did she really get turned away at the organic turkey farm?" Julia asked.

Leah could only nod her head.

Simon leaned toward her. "People coming to the diner to demand payment…that's not good. How many people in Holmes County does she owe money to?"

A shrug of the shoulders was Leah's second nonverbal reply as she concentrated on not weeping. This was an adult mess. She wouldn't respond like a little girl. Tension in her back and shoulders returned with a vengeance.

Simon wouldn't let the matter drop. "Local folk showing up at the diner for a meal and finding the place padlocked...do you understand how bad this looks? It reflects on your character too, not just Mrs. Lambright's." He stared, waiting for an answer she didn't have.

Leah downed her coffee, feeling the burn in the back of her throat. She might as well get everything out in the open, not leaving out a single detail. She couldn't endure another conversation with her parents if more sordid information reached their ears. "It wasn't just her father and husband she borrowed money from to get started," she said.

Her parents gazed at her with utter disbelief as she revealed where most of her savings account had gone.

～

Helping *mamm* in the house and Henry with farm chores kept Leah busy and her mind off the fact she no longer had a job to go to. She also no longer had a paycheck to help with household expenses. With the first frost just around the corner she couldn't plant extra vegetables to sell. Any apples or pears left on the trees would be bird pecked by now. She couldn't work for Aunt Hannah because spinning and weaving wool made her allergies unbearable. Mrs. Lee already employed a girl for housecleaning once a week. That only left her pie making. April hadn't reimbursed her for the last baking supplies. She would have to spend some of her decimated savings to stock up.

"Leah!" Julia's voice finally pierced her daydreaming. "I've been calling you for ten minutes." Her head appeared in the henhouse doorway. "What are you doing?"

"Changing straw in the chicken cages and washing water bowls."

"With your allergies? Come out of there. Henry will finish that. You need to go take a shower."

"Why?" Leah patted the straw down and closed the cage door. One hen offered an appreciative cluck.

"Because you're going with me to quilting today. And don't even think of arguing. You can't hide from people. You're guilty of being naive and nonconfrontational, that's all. I know you are nineteen now, but most young people your age are naive. By the time you're my age you won't be so trusting."

Leah looked into Julia's warm brown eyes and felt that she might just survive this nightmare. "All right, I'll come to quilting. It's been a long while since I've done anything like that. And I can't wait to put this behind me."

Mother and daughter walked to the house with linked arms. Autumn leaves swirled at their feet while migrating ducks flew in formation overhead toward sunnier states. Leah found a sense of peace on the buggy ride over to the house hosting the bee. But her serenity didn't last five minutes once inside the door.

Their hostess greeted them in the kitchen. Mrs. Walters hugged Julia and offered Leah a shy smile. They added their pie to the plates of cookies brought by the ladies for snack time. But when they entered the living room with their sewing baskets, welcoming smiles were few. Most ladies stared at Leah with blank faces devoid of emotion, while a few younger gals stared with open hostility.

A thin, dark-haired girl was first to speak. "You dare to show your face, Leah Miller? But then again I suppose you've got no place else to go since the sheriff shut down your little scam!" Her words stung Leah like wasp bites.

"Anna Boyer, you keep silent if you're gonna talk like that," said Mrs. Walters. "This is my home, and all are welcome here."

Anna looked chastised but added, "My Aaron is still owed six hundred dollars for those picnic tables he made for you. He needs the money to pay the lumberyard. Pressure-treated wood ain't cheap." Her lips thinned to an angry line.

Julia sat down heavily in one chair and pointed at another to Leah.

Because running out the back door apparently wasn't an option, Leah sat down and addressed Anna. "I'm sorry that Aaron still hasn't been paid. Upon my word, I had no idea this mess was brewing behind my back. I'll see that he is paid back if I have to sell pies until I'm ninety-five years old."

Anna bobbed her head in acceptance while Julia smiled at Leah. However, another young woman at the end of the table didn't want the matter dropped so easily.

She cleared her throat, drawing everyone's attention. "Maybe, Leah, you might have noticed what was going on in the restaurant if you hadn't been so busy flirting with every young man in Winesburg—Amish or English."

SEVENTEEN

L eah crept out of bed as quietly as possible. It had been several years since she had to share a bedroom, but her sister had come home unexpectedly. Emma explained that she had a fight with Jamie but didn't wish to discuss the matter. She was only going to stay one night, but then she decided to spend a few days at home to help *mamm* finish the fall canning. Seeing Emma's pale, wan face filled Leah with sadness, adding to her own pile of woes.

Looks like both Miller girls are plagued with trouble.

She had pictured Emma and Jamie as happy as clams, living in Charm with a tractor for him and a dishwasher for her. How naive she'd been in this matter too. It took far more than modern appliances to make a marriage work. Leah had prayed long and hard that her sister and brother-in-law wouldn't allow their grievances to separate them for long. She'd never seen anything so romantic as the way James Davis looked at Emma during their courtship, especially while she was mending after her accident.

Will any man ever gaze on me with such devotion?

The likelihood of that diminished with each passing day. Jonah should have returned by now, and he had probably heard the news of the diner's demise. Leah hoped he hadn't stopped by there on his way home and seen firsthand the posted notices telling the world of their failure.

Leah tucked the quilt under Emma's chin before heading down-stairs to start breakfast, finding comfort in her soft snore. As much as she would like to, this was no time to hide her head under the covers. She wouldn't be in this mess if she hadn't been such a wilting violet.

In the kitchen her spirits improved by doing what she did best—cooking. While sausage sizzled in the pan, she heated her flat skillet to make thin, sweet pancakes called crepes by the *Englischers*. She would roll them around strawberry, peach, or apple preserves, and a few around cottage cheese—her personal favorite. She mixed a pitcher of orange juice and started oatmeal for Henry. That boy ate more than anybody she knew...except for Jonah.

Melancholy swept over her like a sudden chill. *Jonah.* Maybe, just maybe, he would understand the disaster had been impossible to pre-vent.

"Guder mariye," Julia said upon entering the room. "Looks like I timed things right this morning. There is a hidden blessing in you not having a job—at least for me." Julia poured coffee and lowered herself into a chair.

"At least you now have a trained professional taking over breakfast duties," Leah said with a smile. "How would you like your rolled pan-cakes this morning—with strawberry, peach, or apple preserves?"

"Surprise me, or better yet, one of each." She turned toward the win-dow, as did Leah to the sound of gravel crunching in the driveway.

Leah pulled back the curtain and spotted April Lambright climb-ing out of her pickup. "Oh, no. I don't know if I'm ready for this."

Julia was out of her chair and by Leah's side in an instant, despite her arthritic stiffness. "Go, Leah. Be brave. And ask her in to break-fast if she cares to eat. Have courage and compassion in your heart. I'll fry up the pancakes for you."

Leah walked out to the porch feeling like Daniel headed into the lion's den. "Hullo, April," she said without emotion.

"Hi, Leah." April approached the steps slowly, looking as though she hadn't slept in days. "I came here as soon as I could, as soon as things calmed down at home." She crossed her arms over her chest, hugging herself as though cold.

"I'm sure you're in hot water with your husband." Leah crossed her arms too while she walked down the steps to be on level ground with her former partner.

"That's the understatement of the century."

"I heard you were you in jail."

April's features tightened. "Yes, for one night, and then my sister and her husband posted bail."

"Your sister, not your husband?"

April looked at the ground, but not before Leah saw two big tears slip from her lashes. "No, he tried to…but our bank had frozen our checking and savings accounts due to this…trouble I've caused. My husband said it was okay with him if I cooled my heels in jail for a while to give me some thinkin' time."

"He sounds quite put out…just like I am." Leah straightened her spine. "Why, April? How could you do such a thing? Our customers and vendors were also our friends."

April lifted her chin to meet her gaze. "I didn't mean to. I hadn't *planned* to not pay folk. But when the money first started coming in, I started thinking about all the things my kids have done without since Tom's hours were cut back at the plant. My son has never had a decent bicycle like other kids, and my girl has wanted horseback riding lessons for years."

"You stiffed people who have their own bills to pay for *riding lessons and toys?*" Leah's voice rose to reflect utter disbelief.

April shrugged. "I never planned to stiff anybody. I thought I'd get a few things for my kids and pay the bills with the next few weeks of profits. But then the pump broke on our septic system, and it turned out we needed a whole new system. Ours no longer met codes. I had already sunk every dime of our savings into the remodeling, so

I had to use the diner income to pay for it. The man insisted on payment in full before he installed the new system."

"Smart man."

April winced as though she'd been slapped. "I know I deserved that. I put you in a tight spot and you're stuck sharing the embarrassment. I surely didn't mean things to turn out this way." She gazed toward the road for a moment. "I like you, Leah. I think you're a fabulous cook and baker, and I've loved working at the diner with you. I'm sorry my mishandling finances has caused so much pain for you, my family, and for our town." Tears ran freely down her face. "My dad warned me that running a business and keeping accounts were harder than it looked, but I wouldn't listen. I had stars in my eyes... and dollar signs. Budgeting has never been my strong suit, but I was too proud to ask someone as young as you for help. If I had, maybe we wouldn't have lost our money."

The reality that Leah's investment was truly gone hadn't hit home until then, yet still her anger and indignation evaporated. She felt only pity for a woman whose pride had caused so much heartache. Especially as she was in no position to cast stones, considering her own past behavior. "What's to be done now, April? How can you put this behind you?"

April looked up with a spark of hope. "My lawyer said that if I make restitution to the people I defrauded, and if they sign affidavits that they have been paid and don't want to press charges, she might be able to convince the district attorney to drop the charges against me before my trial date. I'll have to appear before the judge and explain I'm a bad manager but not a thief. And that is the honest-to-goodness truth. I didn't mean to cheat anybody."

The solution didn't sound quite so simple to Leah. "How do you plan to accomplish that?"

April withdrew two pieces of paper from her handbag. "My lawyer took a look at the stack of IOUs and invoices I had in the drawer and compiled a list. Then she split the list in two—one for me to pay off and obtain affidavits and the other half for you." Without a moment's hesitation, she handed a sheet to Leah.

"Me? Why would I have to pay these folk? I didn't handle the money!" Indignation came roaring back.

April said quietly, "No, but you were my partner, and the attorney said it would look better to the judge if we both bore responsibility."

Leah's eyes swelled to the size of a barn owl's. "This is not fair!"

"Maybe not, but I did always pay your wages regularly and reimburse you for baking supplies, except for when things had snowballed out of control." She stood anxiously like a child waiting for a birthday present.

Leah fought the urge to mention those reimbursements never came close to the total Miller family outlay for expenses and supplies. "This isn't fair," she repeated in barely a whisper.

"I know it isn't, but I can't possibly pay everybody back before my trial date, no matter how I beg, borrow, or sell everything I own. I'm desperate, and I'm begging you to help me." She held out the sheet of paper in her long thin fingers.

Leah stared at it as though it were a snake in the henhouse, but she saw little alternative. No way would she let her foolish business partner be sent to jail if it could be prevented. Without speaking, because her throat had grown painfully tight, she plucked the list from April's hand.

April impulsively threw her arms around Leah's neck and hugged. "Oh, thank you so much. God bless you, Leah. I will be forever in your debt."

Just don't try to convert that debt to dollars and cents. "You want to come inside for breakfast? My *mamm* has crepes ready to go with your choice of filling." For a second it felt as though she was back in her beloved diner talking about the daily specials with enthusiasm.

April looked stricken. "Oh, no. I couldn't face your parents. I'm not that brave, but thanks just the same." She kissed Leah's cheek with sisterly affection and then hurried to her truck. Leah watched April's pickup reach the end of the driveway as her words "I never planned to stiff anybody" ran through her head. Somehow that knowledge didn't lift an ounce of the burden she clutched in her hand. When her former partner disappeared from view, she looked down at the onerous paper and gasped.

The kitchen door opened with its familiar squeak. "Breakfast is ready. Come inside and eat, daughter." Julia stood with her hands on her hips, looking sympathetic. "Things will improve with a full belly." Leah trudged up the steps feeling almost faint. Not only was the list of names longer and the amounts greater than she'd feared, but close to the bottom she spotted a name particularly unnerving: Joanna Byler—cheese-maker, $285.00.

As her mother had predicted, Leah did feel somewhat better after breakfast, though not from the peach-filled pancakes but from having a plan. She would withdraw her remaining savings from the bank and pay as many people on the list as possible, starting with the smallest debt and working upward. More people paid off would mean fewer wagging tongues in town. She would then visit the others, or if they lived too far away, write a letter and promise to pay every dime owed. If they were expecting interest, that would be a concern for another day. Having a plan helped; having the courage to see it through would be her concern for today.

After chores and a quick bath, Leah walked to the neighbors' with her purse and bankbook. She bargained fall cleaning in exchange for Mrs. Lee driving her around the county. She had read the news about the diner in the Wooster paper and wished to help without bartering. But Leah insisted, remembering Romans 13:8: "Owe nothing to anyone, except your obligation to love one another."

Because Mrs. Lee's schedule was open today but busy later in the week, Leah's day of reckoning came sooner than expected. *Might as well get this over with—nights spent tossing and turning in sleepless anguish will only magnify the task.*

The Byler farm on County Road 535 became their first stop after the Winesburg Savings and Loan. Joanna Byler answered after a few moments and a second knock on the door. "Leah," she said. "How are you? Come inside." To say she looked surprised would be a gross understatement.

"*Guder mariye,* Mrs. Byler. I'll just step in for a minute. My neighbor is waiting in her van for me."

Joanna's expression turned anxious as Leah stepped past her into the kitchen. The room smelled faintly of cinnamon. "Jonah isn't here, dear. His uncle had plenty of work for him to do—maintenance projects after the harvest. There was too much for one man to tackle alone. His sons are still young."

"I'm not here to talk to Jonah. I'm here to see you." Leah set her purse on the table and dug inside. She took out an envelope and carefully counted two hundred eighty-five dollars. "I believe this is what the diner owes you, Mrs. Byler. If your records indicate differently, please let me know." She held out the stack of bills.

Joanna shook her head. "I can wait to be paid back. It won't cause any hardship." The money remained motionlessly suspended in the warm, fragrant air.

Leah placed the bills on the table. "*Danki,* but I'm paying off my share of the debt in a certain order, and I wish to take care of yours today." She glanced up into the woman's face. "I'm really sorry how things turned out. I didn't know about the money turmoil, but that's no excuse—I should've known. I'm owning up to that." Feeling emotion began to creep insidiously up her throat, she blurted out the rest of her words...ones she knew she would repeat many times that day. "I'm sorry for the inconvenience and hard feelings my partner and I have caused."

Joanna chewed on her lower lip. "I know you're sorry and not responsible for the shell game April Lambright was playing. But folk are mad, and they're lumping you in the same boat with her. Because April is Mennonite and lives near Wooster, the gossip and finger-pointing won't affect her nearly as much..." Her voice trailed off.

As it will me, Leah thought, finishing her sentence. "That's why I'm paying off as many people as I can so this will blow over as soon as possible."

Mrs. Byler offered a half smile. "Maybe you could write to Jonah in Wisconsin. He should hear what has happened from you instead of hearing the story at the auction house." She walked to the drawer for her address book while Leah gripped the edge of the kitchen table.

Write to Jonah? What would I say? Hey, Jonah, everything I worried about came true, plus much more, while I was busy baking pies and flirting with customers. She didn't think so.

Joanna jotted an address on a slip of paper and held it out to her. "He might be there for a while, but mail service to Wisconsin is only three days. I'm sure he'd like a letter from you."

"*Danki,* Mrs. Byler, especially for believing in me." Leah tucked the address into her purse and hurried from the house. Mrs. Lee and the other names on her list were waiting. She had no time to stand around in a cozy kitchen thinking about a blue-eyed man with big hands and a gentle voice.

~

By the time the two women ran out of energy and daylight, two-thirds of the names on Leah's list had been crossed off. Her financial resources were similarly depleted. After buying Mrs. Lee lunch at the buffet restaurant, she had less than forty dollars to her name after years of building up her savings. Endless summer hours spent selling eggs at a roadside stand and then hours and hours creating recipes and baking pies had been wiped out by her misguided belief that a diner would be a fun place to work. But being broke didn't trouble her nearly as much as the gossip and community criticism that would surely linger. *Will the district elders shun me? Will Jonah retract his request to court me, considering my new reputation as a thief and charlatan?* Plenty weighed on her mind as Mrs. Lee's cell phone rang on the way home, jarring Leah back to the present.

It was James Davis calling Mrs. Lee for the second time that day. He wanted Emma to call him that night or he was coming in person to Winesburg. When they arrived home, Leah delivered the news to Emma while Mrs. Lee waited in the van once again.

Emma's face became a sea of conflicting emotions upon hearing about Jamie's calls. She borrowed Mrs. Lee's phone and walked to the swing for a private conversation. *The Miller girls will owe Mrs. Lee free peach pies and wool scarves for many years to come,* Leah thought. After Emma returned the phone to Mrs. Lee, Leah thanked and hugged their dear English neighbor. Twice Mrs. Lee had offered to pay off the remaining debts and allow Leah to pay her back over time, but Leah politely declined. She knew her father would never permit such an imposition on their friendship.

That night, unbeknownst to each other, the Miller sisters said their prayers and slept soundly for the first time in many days. In the shared bedroom of their childhoods, both women possessed a glimmer of hope.

They had turned their problems over to the One who knows our needs even before we do.

~

"You're up awfully early," Leah said, "for a man on his first weekday home in some time."

Matthew smiled at his sister, who was cooking up a fancy breakfast. Having her home instead of at the diner had benefits for the rest of the family. "*Jah,* today's the auction in Sugar Creek. My Mennonite friend is picking me up in twenty minutes. He wants to buy a new trail horse, and I want to see if any bargains are for sale."

"You're going back to Sugar Creek the first day you don't have to?" asked his younger brother. He'd walked in from the back hall with a nose pink from early milking.

Henry's arrival at breakfast meant that *daed* would soon be in too. Matthew had wanted to be gone before his father came inside.

He needed one more day of freedom before resuming his fair share of farm chores. With a knife and fork in each hand, he waited for the first platter of food to be set down.

"Matthew Miller! Get your elbows off the table and stop acting like a barbarian," scolded Emma. Her tone indicated she wasn't someone to be challenged this morning...like a large snake in the path that you know is harmless but you skirt around it anyway. "This is not the bunkhouse at the riding academy." Bad-tempered Emma poured herself coffee and then peeked over Leah's shoulder at the skillet.

Having this sister home didn't have quite so many advantages.

"You going to the Sugar Creek auction?" asked Henry, still waiting for his answer.

"*Jah,* as soon as I eat. I want to buy a few yearlings if they are cheap enough, ones other folk don't think are worth the trouble of training. If I can turn them around, I'll sell them in the spring as riding stock for *Englischers* or buggy horses for Amish...or barrel racers for either—whatever suits the particular horse."

Leah set the first platter of French toast on the table. They were decorated with strawberry preserves and dusted with powdered sugar, touches his *mamm* usually dispensed with. Matthew speared two slices with his fork and reached for the maple syrup.

Henry duplicated his action. "Can I ride along to the auction?" he asked.

"Nah, I don't know how much room will be in the truck cab and I don't know this guy, Bob, well enough to be a hassle for him." Matt started eating Leah's cuisine with gusto. "Besides, Pa needs you around the farm today."

"Seems to me that your *bruder* has been doing more than his share *around the farm* lately." Simon mimicked his son's words from the doorway. "If there's only room in the truck cab for one, maybe Henry should go buy the horses." He settled himself at the table while Emma hurried to bring him coffee.

Matthew's first bites of breakfast hit his belly like rocks. "Pa,

Henry doesn't know anything about buying horses. He doesn't know which traits to look for." Matthew spoke very softly, not displaying an ounce of impatience. He'd learned the hard way what didn't work with his father.

"All the more reason he should go too. You could teach him a few things, and he needs a break from chores."

Matthew stopped shoveling food into his mouth and wiped his chin. "Are you saying you can spare us *both* away from the farm?"

Simon took a long swallow of coffee. "I'm not ready for the porch rocker yet, young man. I can manage just fine for one day. After all, both my girls are home in case I get a sudden urge to scrub out the henhouse or mix chemicals into the manure compost pile."

Leah looked as though she might faint while Emma frowned as though she'd swallowed half a lemon. Julia held up her apron to hide her grin.

Simon chortled. "Henry, eat hearty. Matthew will walk your legs off, I'm sure." He dug into his own stack of French toast.

The two young men finished eating, set their plates in the sink, and hurried down to the road to wait for their ride. They wanted to avoid both women before one of them tried to wheedle a favor. Matthew had little luck refusing either sister, and Henry had no luck whatsoever. But as neither Emma nor Leah appeared, it seemed they had accepted their fate valiantly.

"How will you pay for any horses you might buy?" Henry asked.

Matt pulled his checkbook from a back pocket. An image of a horse's head had been stamped into the leatherette cover. "I had my paycheck direct-deposited while I worked at Mac Farms and at the riding stable." He showed his name imprinted on the pad of checks. "This register helps me keep track of expenses and income, plus I keep a ledger book at home. I want my horse-training business to get off on the right foot."

Henry inspected the checks and nodded, duly impressed. But his excitement soon escalated when they arrived in Sugar Creek. Buyers, sellers, vendors, and tourists mingled in loud, frenetic chaos. Henry had attended auctions in Mount Hope and Kidron, but with no interest in buying he had concentrated on what to eat next or hanging out with friends. As Matthew took him from stall to stall and pointed out certain horse characteristics, Henry proved to be an eager student.

"We're looking to buy yearlings that are spirited but not mean tempered," Matthew explained. "If the filly or colt backs away from a slow hand, beware. Watch their eyes—they will reveal whether a horse is simply skittish or has a nasty disposition. We can handle the former, but we don't want to tangle with the latter even if the price is dirt cheap."

Henry nodded, asked appropriate questions, and showed genuine enthusiasm. Matt pulled out a small spiral notebook and pencil. "I brought an extra one of these along for you. As you wander around, jot down the number of any horses that catch your eye, along with good and bad traits. You can use three stars or four, or whatever method you prefer to indicate your favorites. Just don't rely on memory. And most of all, don't get too excited when you question the owners because then everybody else will know you're interested. Suddenly, plenty of bidders show up at auction time and the price will climb beyond our range."

Henry slipped the notebook into his pocket. "*Danki* for bringing me along."

"Glad to see you're interested. When things get busy, I could hire you as my first employee. Why don't you wander around the stalls and check out the holding pens outside. More horses are out there. Bob wants to introduce me to a Wooster breeder that he knows." Matthew watched his brother hurry off with surprising animation. The shy boy had always preferred reading under a shady tree or collecting bugs in a jar to anything equine. It would be nice to have help so close at hand.

Matthew joined his friend and the two headed to the coffee shop to talk while tack and equipment were being sold. It wasn't until some time later that Henry found his *bruder* sitting in the auction barn just as the auction was winding down. Matthew had bid unsuccessfully on three different colts, but the price had soared beyond what he wished to pay.

"Matty! Matty! You've got to come see this. I can't believe it." Henry looked white as a bedsheet and more agitated than Matt could ever remember.

"What's wrong? Did somebody get hurt?"

He shook his head. "Please, just come with me." Henry grabbed his arm and started pulling.

Matt handed his auction card to Bob with a dollar limit on his final bidding attempt and followed Henry outside.

Around the back of the barn Matthew discovered the cause of Henry's distress. "It's called the kill pen," Henry moaned. "Any horse that gets no bidders is put in here, and if no one buys them, they are killed." He kept his voice low, but there was no hiding his shock and revulsion. There were tears in his gentle blue eyes.

Matthew jammed his hands into his pockets and felt awful. He had heard about the pen but had never seen it firsthand. He'd purposely avoided doing so.

"We've got to do something," Henry whispered next to Matthew's ear. At least he'd learned the lesson about keeping his intentions a secret.

Matt gazed into the pen of sad-eyed beasts and felt a lump the size of a goose egg rise up his throat. "What exactly do you want me to do?" he asked hoarsely.

Henry Miller, who seldom asked anyone for anything, wiped his nose with his handkerchief and looked him in the eye. He didn't need to say a word. Matthew knew.

That afternoon, after bidding on the final horse concluded, Matthew pulled out his checkbook, embossed with the likeness of these same creatures during better days, and bought all eleven horses in the kill pen. The checkbook came out several more times as he lined up men with trailers to transport his purchases back to Winesburg.

Bob's initial reaction when they met up to ride home was disbelief, as though Matt and Henry were teasing him, and then disbelief morphed into astonishment. His reaction would pale in comparison to *daed*'s later that night.

But the bond of love forged and strengthened that day between two brothers was worth every hard-earned penny spent.

EIGHTEEN

Leah awoke with a start in the cool bedroom. Emma had left the window open an inch overnight. Because it was almost November, that wasn't a good idea. Loud talking in the driveway drew her to the window. One, two, three...she counted four horse trailers pulling up close to the barn.

How many horses did Matthew buy yesterday?

Leah glanced at Emma's neatly made bed. Another sleepless night had taken her sister downstairs early. Now that Leah's financial troubles had abated, only the consequences to her reputation remained. Because her parents had agreed to pay off the rest of the names on her list, Leah could concentrate on helping Emma. Last night Emma had talked to James, yet her overnight bag remained empty in the corner of the room.

Downstairs in the kitchen, Leah found her hollow-eyed sister sitting at the table. "Is Jamie coming to take you home?" she asked on her way to the refrigerator.

"No. I'm staying another day." Emma sipped her coffee.

"Why? Your place is with your *ehemann*. It's time to swallow your pride and patch things up."

Emma lifted an eyebrow. "Are you tired of me already—anxious to have the room to yourself again?"

"Not at all. I love having you home, but it makes me sad seeing you so unhappy. Jamie loves you and you love him."

Emma smiled and patted Leah's hand. "He and Kevin will pick me up tomorrow. I told him that *mamm* needs my help with canning."

Leah's expression turned doubtful.

"It's true. *Mamm* bought ten bushels of Bartlett pears from the produce stand in Wilmot. They were going bad, so she got them for a song."

"Not ten bushels!" Leah was aghast. "Good grief, it'll take the three of us forever to trim, core, and can that many pears."

"But they were so cheap, I couldn't pass them up." Emma exactly mimicked her mother's voice.

Both girls laughed with relaxed familiarity. "You'll be lucky to see Jamie by Thanksgiving."

"Then we better get the breakfast show on the road. Oatmeal and fruit for today—no fuss, no muss."

The sisters had everything ready by the time the rest of the family sat down. But if the sisters had served pretzels for breakfast, the menfolk wouldn't have noticed. Matthew, Henry, and even Simon excitedly talked horses, horses, horses for the entire meal. Julia filled a thermos of coffee and then shooed them out the door. Emma washed the dishes and Julia set out the canning equipment while Leah carried in six bushels of pears from the porch. Once they'd settled into the peeling and slicing stage of the operation, Leah assumed *mamm*'s conversation would focus on Emma's mysterious estrangement from her husband, but she was wrong.

"Now that you've helped Mrs. Lambright avoid jail for writing bad checks, what do you plan to do next?" Julia asked.

Leah stared blankly. "I...I don't know what you mean. I know there are more problems at the diner other than debts, but until April clues me in, I'm not sure how to proceed." She peeled her pear in one continuous strand.

Julia peered over her half-moon glasses. "There's more to worry about than your empty savings account, young lady. Your reputation is sullied, same as Mrs. Lambright's. But she's not concerned with courting anymore. She has a husband and children."

Leah swallowed hard. With the diner padlocked, her opportunity to spend her life cooking for other people looked grim. And any thoughts of Jonah Byler filled her heart with unbearable sorrow. "What can I do? I'm open to suggestions." She glanced at Emma, who lifted her shoulders in a shrug.

"You saw how the women acted toward you at quilting, especially those your age. You need to appear at every social event and explain that you're doing everything possible to right the situation. Your *daed* will talk to the bishop and ministerial brethren too." She tossed one particularly withered piece of fruit into the slop bucket. "This is no time to hide your head. If folk think *you* tried to cheat people, no man will choose you for his wife."

Leah concentrated on cutting a small wormhole from her pear. "There's only one man whose opinion I care about."

"Who?" Emma asked, her paring knife stalled in midair. "Is my little sister *en lieb*?"

"I was in love with Jonah Byler, the grandson of Amos Burkholder. He moved here almost a year ago from Wisconsin. He asked to court me but then this happened."

Emma looked at her mother while Julia stared at Leah. "What has he said about all this? I saw Joanna Byler's name on your list already crossed off, so I know you stopped there."

"I need to put water up to boil." Leah filled two huge Dutch ovens and set them on the stove. When she returned, the other Miller women were waiting for her answer. "*Jah*, I stopped at his farm to pay Mrs. Byler, but he wasn't home. He's helping an uncle in Wisconsin bring in the harvest. Joanna wasn't sure when he would come back to Ohio."

"Have you written to explain what has happened?" Julia asked. "I shouldn't be butting in, but you're so naive, Leah. I don't think you understand the seriousness of this."

That got Leah's goat. "I understand just fine. I know that Jonah told me to come forward and confront April a while ago, but instead I dawdled and made excuses. Maybe I couldn't have changed the outcome, but at least I would have acted. Now he'll think I'm irresponsible, unreliable, and too stubborn to accept advice. He just started getting to know members of our district, and he tangles up with a headless chicken."

Emma frowned at the unpleasant mental picture. "At least you discussed your suspicions with him. I think you should write him tonight…or tomorrow…or at least within the week—whenever we finish canning all these pears."

Leah managed a smile.

"Write to him, *jah,* but keep your letter focused on the diner fiasco," said Julia. "Don't talk about your courtship. This kind of scandal gives him the option to court someone else. It's up to him from here on out."

Leah didn't need that to be pointed out so succinctly. She'd already come to the same conclusion. She would write to Jonah tonight and bring him up to date on the demise of Leah's Home Cooking. She had such high hopes and had enjoyed both the work and the attention she'd received. But the praise for her culinary creations had gone to her head. That girl at quilting had been right—if she hadn't been lapping up the attention, she might have noticed April's tricks. Jonah had seen her for what she was. Only time will tell if he saw any *positive* characteristics worth suffering turmoil for.

After a sandwich break at lunchtime, the Miller women processed pears all afternoon. At least the kitchen didn't grow oppressively hot in October as it did when canning at the height of summer. Conversation around the table centered mainly on Emma's amusing tales of adjustment to her New Order district. Leah started a kettle of beef vegetable soup for supper. The kitchen smelled wonderful from the variety of cooking scents. Leah began to relax as they cleared off the table and rang the farm bell to call the men.

Simon entered the house wearing a scowl. His sons followed on his heels looking only marginally less dismal. "Matthew's friend from Wooster stopped over to see the new horses," said Simon, "and he brought some pretty disturbing stories, daughter." He focused on Leah as he and the boys took seats at the table.

Leah remained rooted to her square of linoleum. "What did he say?" she asked.

"Oh, Simon, can't this wait until after supper?" asked Julia. "Let's have a quiet meal."

"*Ach,* all right." Simon grunted in agreement.

Once everyone was seated, they bowed their heads in silent prayer. Emma served the soup, ladling each bowl to the brim while Leah sliced and passed fresh-baked bread. During the meal no one spoke as the gloom of bad news hung over the meal like a dark cloud. Finally, as bowls were scraped with crusts of bread, Leah blurted, "Please, *daed,* tell me what was said. I can't wait another moment."

Simon's spoon clattered into his bowl. "Bob heard that Mrs. Lambright is putting the blame for the fraud squarely on your shoulders. She's saying you were the one in charge of Leah's Home Cooking—that it was *your* restaurant. Why did you let her put your name up there on the sign?" His cheeks flushed as his blood pressure rose.

Leah pushed away her remaining soup, her appetite gone. "It seemed like a good idea at the time because my pies were so popular."

"Does it seem that way now, Leah?"

She tried to hold back her tears. "It truly does not." One tear fell on the smooth oak tabletop.

"Plain folk will know it's not true," Julia interjected. "A single Amish woman would never enter into leases and business contracts as Mrs. Lambright had."

"I thought of that," said Simon, "but why would she say such things?"

Leah remembered April's fear of her husband and thought she knew the answer. But too many suppositions were being tossed around as truths, so she didn't add hers. "I don't really know." She dabbed at her nose with her handkerchief.

Simon shook his head. "Let's get back to work, sons. We have more temporary pens to put up before dark."

With the men gone, work resumed on the pears with a subdued mood in the chaotic kitchen. More fruit was carried in, additional jars sterilized, and pears seemed to be everywhere. Even the window-sills became lined with jars set to cool. One Starlight peppermint was placed into each jar of pears before sealing. It added extra sweetness and a hint of mint. Because two bushels yielded twenty-seven quarts, by the time they finished for the night, every surface downstairs was covered with quarts of pears. They would be used in cobblers, stru-dels, and pies, as a side dish with pork roasts, and as a topping for pancakes and waffles. Jars would become gifts to new brides, new mothers, and new neighbors. Jars would be given to visiting friends and relatives to take home, as well as the milkman, propane deliv-eryman, and every shopkeeper in town. Emma planned to take sev-eral jars to the mission outreach, the ladies' jail, and to the women in her Bible study group.

Leah had far fewer ideas on how to spread the bounty. In fact, she had no thoughts about anything other than her former beau, Jonah Byler. After she and Emma showered and slipped on flannel nightgowns, sleep refused to come despite their exhaustion. Both lay awake staring at the ceiling.

"Thinking about Jamie?" asked Leah.

"*Jah*," Emma replied. After half a minute, she asked, "Thinking about what *daed* said?"

"Can't think about anything else. I have disgraced my family. Now Jonah will no longer want to court me."

Emma sat up and lit a candle. In the thin wavering light, she turned to face her sister. "You listen to me—you've done nothing but cook, bake wonderful pies, and try to make customers happy. One would think you had no faith by how easily you've given up. April's words are untrue and will soon die on the vine the way all lies eventually do. Pray to God for guidance and for His will to be done. And in the meantime, tell the truth when asked and hold your head up high. Things will work out, Leah. Now stop worrying and go to sleep." For a minute, the sisters watched the flickering light and shadows dance across the bedroom ceiling.

Then Leah whispered, "*Danki,* Emma. I love you."

Emma blew out the candle. "I love you too."

∼

It wasn't Emma's habit to look out the window the moment she awoke, but she did so the next morning. A shiny green truck stood parked in the turnaround. "Oh, good grief," she muttered under her breath. "Jamie and Kevin must have left the house before dawn to be here already." After washing and dressing, she threw her things into her overnight bag as quickly as possible and hurried downstairs. Her stomach churned, not from hunger but from nervous apprehension. Her one-day visit had turned into three. What if Jamie was angry with her for fleeing their home without explanation? She loved him so much and had thought about little other than her marriage since she arrived in Winesburg.

Emma inhaled a deep breath and walked into the kitchen. Jamie sat at the table drinking coffee. "Hello, *fraa,* did you miss me? I sure have missed you." His sea-blue eyes sparkled to match his brilliant smile.

"*Jah,* I have." Emma ran and threw herself into his lap.

"Hey, Em, what's new?" asked Kevin, in between bites of bacon and scrambled eggs.

"Hi, Kevin," Emma managed to say.

"Does this mean you're not staying for day two with the pears?" Julia asked from her position at the stove.

Jamie tried to turn in his chair to gaze around the room. "Don't you ladies think you've canned enough yet?"

Julia set a plate of food in front of her son-in-law. "Oh, no. We have four more bushels of fruit to go."

"Can you manage without Emma? I can't live another day without my wife."

Emma, whose face was buried in his neck, thought her heart would burst.

"It'll be a struggle, but Leah and I will manage." Julia smacked Emma's head with her pot holder. "Sit in your own chair, daughter, and let this man eat his breakfast before it gets cold. And I want you to eat too so you don't get carsick. How about more sausage, Kevin?"

"Yes, ma'am." Kevin held up his plate with both hands like a character in a Charles Dickens novel.

"We're starving," called Henry and Matthew, stomping in from the back hall. Simon followed on their heels. With their ruckus Emma was able to extricate herself, fetch more chairs, and sit down to her own breakfast without anyone noticing her reddened eyes.

She and Jamie left soon after the meal. Leah still hadn't come downstairs yet. Emma wrote Leah a quick note to say goodbye, kissed everybody else, and then climbed in Kevin's truck. Wedged in between the two brothers, she chewed on her lower lip. With Kevin driving, they couldn't very well air their marital laundry.

After a few silent miles, James had his own ideas. "Speak your mind, Em. Tell me what's bothering you. I know you stayed to help your mother with canning, but that's not why you left in the first place. My mom said you were homesick and needed a day with your family. Is there more than that?"

"Shouldn't we wait to have this conversation?" She angled her head toward Kevin, who seemed amazed by the passing scenery out the window.

"No," Jamie said. "My brother thinks you're practically an angel sent from heaven. He'll have a hard time finding a wife and will be doomed with unrealistic expectations if we don't disabuse him of that notion."

"*Disabuse* him? You're no longer on the campus of OSU," she said and they all laughed.

"Just tell me what's wrong." He slipped his arm around her shoulders to offer encouragement.

Heartened by his touch, Emma forged ahead. She realized they would find little more privacy at the Davis home. "It's me, Jamie. I get really out of sorts with your family. I wasn't exactly a model of cooperation with your *mamm,* and I picked an argument with Lily over what she does for a living, of all things. I can't seem to get along with anybody."

"You haven't fought with me yet," Kevin said quietly.

"Only because you're almost never home. Just stick around a while and see what happens."

The Davis brothers laughed, but Emma folded her hands in her lap. "It's true. I'm a crabby old woman."

When the snickering died down, Jamie said, "Why do you suppose that is, Em?"

She didn't answer right away but thought carefully and chose her words, "I'm frustrated. We have so little time alone. We rarely share a quiet dinner, and at lunch it's hard to track you down for a picnic. Your farm is so large I never know where you are. Even when your *mamm*'s at work the kitchen is never without people—friends, relatives, workmen, horse buyers, trainers, church folk, vets, deliverymen. Once I was in the Akron train station and it wasn't as busy."

With that much off her chest she relaxed against his shoulder. "I hope I don't sound like a spoiled little girl, because I'm not. I was raised in a family of six with one bathroom, but somehow we weren't always in each other's way. I feel like I'm always in your mother's way... and I don't like it."

There it was—the honest truth. Maybe Jamie would regret that he didn't postpone the conversation.

Kevin looked over at her with sympathy. After another moment, Jamie said, "That's it? That's what's making you unhappy?"

Emma peered at him suspiciously. "*Jah...*"

"You aren't sick of my snoring, or the way I smell like farm animals most of the day? Or tired of my habit of lateness, or the way I wolf down food like I haven't eaten in days?"

She smiled. "No, none of the above. I'm used to my *bruders*."

"Well, *fraa*, your days of misery are numbered. That's all I have to say." He stared out the window until Emma slapped his knee.

"What are you talking about? Please tell me."

"I wanted this to be a secret, a surprise for you, but with you running away from me, I'd better not wait another day."

She choked back the taste of guilt in her mouth. "Go on."

"My father had a surveyor stake out a nice eight-acre homesite for us. When you drive up Hollyhock Lane, you'll turn down a road on the right and drive up close to that pinewoods you're so fond of. We'll start building our new home next week. The foundation walls have already been poured; the well and septic are in. We should have it framed, exterior walls and windows in, and the roof on by December first, unless we get an early blizzard. My dad hired two farmworkers who know carpentry to help me all winter until spring planting. What do ya think?"

Emma had to swallow twice. "You were going to surprise me? But then your spoiled brat of a wife threw a fit and ruined everything?" she asked, burying her face with her hands.

James gently pulled her hands down. "I prefer to phrase it as my dear wife couldn't wait another day to have me all to herself."

"Oh, Jamie." She blushed as joy surged through every blood vessel down to her toes.

"Oh, Emma!" He tugged one *kapp* string.

"Well, you two haven't exactly disabused me of any notions. You're still tops in my book, Em."

"Just stick around a while longer," they both said together.

～

From the moment the eleven new horses marched down the trailer ramps at the Miller farm, Matt had his hands full. Simon insisted they be kept separate from his horses until checked out by the vet. Then Simon had begun to suggest potential diseases no one had heard of in twenty years. Not only did the new arrivals have to be segregated from Simon's stock, they didn't seem to care much for each other, either. To prevent confrontations, Matthew and Henry erected temporary pens within the paddock until temperaments could be assessed. That would have to wait until they were groomed, had their hooves trimmed, sores salved, tails clipped, infected eyes and ears medicated, and in most cases, fed plenty of quality grain to fill out bony frames.

But Henry's enthusiasm knew no bounds. At first Matthew couldn't leave Henry alone with them or he would have been knocked down, bitten, or gut-kicked. But once Henry learned how to approach wary beasts, how to read body language, and employ some basic safety rules, he proved to be a natural. His sensitivity and gentleness seemed to be recognized by the neglected horses. Matthew knew he'd found the perfect partner when the horses began to respond as well to Henry as to himself.

Even Simon warmed up to the forsaken lot—once the initial shock of Matthew's impetuous purchase wore off. Up until then he walked around muttering, "I would've expected such a stunt from your Aunt Hannah, but not from my two practical sons" at least half a dozen times.

Henry didn't think much about practicality.

And by the following week Matt no longer viewed his action as the sentimental whim of a spoiled *Englischer*. He began to see potential in every one of his acquisitions. With patience, some could be retrained as buggy horses, while others would make acceptable riding stock for those not interested in looks or blood lines. Others could become pets to a family who couldn't afford worthier horses, while the three elderly mares could live out their days in the company of old Belle.

But in the meantime the Miller brothers worked from before dawn until well after dusk. They still had their regular chores, such as mucking stalls, milking cows, feeding chickens, and harvesting the last of the garden. Their father needed help with the repair of buildings and equipment, besides fertilizing the fields to prepare for winter. So when Saturday dawned clear and bright, Matthew and Henry marched out of the house early with buckets, scrub brushes, and the garden hose. The newcomers would get baths in the warm sunshine. Nobody would refer to them as smelly old nags ever again. With their concentration fully on the skittish horses, neither young man heard the sound of footsteps.

"Say, I'm looking for the Matthew Miller Horse Rescue Society. Have I found the right place?"

Matt dropped his brush into the bucket of sudsy water and pivoted around. He recognized immediately the grinning face of the local veterinarian. "Dr. Longo, what are you doing here? Did my pa call you?"

"Nah, I heard about what you did in Sugar Creek and thought you might need some help." Longo rested one boot heel on the fence rail.

Matt tried not to let his face give away his disappointment. Farm calls by veterinarians didn't come cheap, and as vets were concerned, Longo was the best. Buying the herd had already crimped his budget, so he couldn't afford treatments and therapies. Especially as they didn't exactly own Kentucky Derby bloodlines. "That's mighty nice of you to stop by, but I'm in no position..."

"I cleared my schedule for today and brought everything we might need, including boxes of pharmaceutical samples that those salesmen keep dropping off at my office. The only payment I will accept is a sandwich at lunchtime and, if I'm still here, maybe supper with your family. Nothing else." He held up both palms.

Matthew pulled off his hat and ran a hand through his untamable hair. "Shucks, I couldn't let you do that. You haven't even seen the state some of these critters are in. I've got cracked hooves, mange, and infected fly bites. And that's just what we can see."

"In that case, I better get started if we plan to turn any of them around by winter. You're not the only horse lover in this county, Matt. It would be my pleasure to support your project."

"Then it's time you know who's responsible. Henry, come on up here."

Henry had been pretending he wasn't listening while working knots out of a mare's mane. He shuffled over to the fence, looking shy and somewhat nervous.

"Henry is my new partner in equine rehabilitation. Buying these eleven challenges was his idea." Matthew slapped Henry on the back. "*Danki* for coming out to help us today."

Longo gazed skyward at a crystalline blue sky dotted with lacework clouds and then looked from one Miller to the other. "On a day as gorgeous as this? I couldn't imagine a better way to spend it."

NINETEEN

November had a bad reputation for cold, damp, rainy weather. Even a snow flurry wasn't out of the question. And overnight frost was practically assured. So when Leah received the subpoena to appear in district court, she wasn't surprised when the weather turned dismal to reflect her mood.

She had had three weeks to consult an attorney. Or prepare financial statements to support her innocence in the crime of tax fraud. Or at least discuss the matter with her former business partner, April Lambright. Yet she had done none of those things. She had no money for lawyers and neither did her parents after they had generously paid off the remaining names on her list. She had no financial records to assemble because the books for Leah's Home Cooking had never been available to her. And she wasn't about to call April from the neighbor's phone and voice her grievances where she might be overheard.

If the rumors flying around Holmes County were true, and April meant to dump the legal matter of sales tax evasion into her lap, she had no documentation to support her side. She had only the truth. And it would have to be enough. She would attempt to convince the court she had no culpability in April's crimes. But if the judge saw things differently, she would face the consequences.

Since she'd received the subpoena, her parents spent their days casting her sidelong glances with exaggerated sighs. They didn't understand the legal system any better than she. Their questions haunted her for days: *What if Mrs. Lambright doesn't tell the truth? What if you're sent to jail? What if the state demands immediate payment in full for tax money owed?*

What if...what if...what if?

Leah had had enough of suppositions and fear. She would leave the matter up to God. He who had the power to create heaven and earth, to right every wrong, had this matter under control. Leah wasn't blameless. If she deserved to go to jail for being irresponsible, then so be it, but she wouldn't spend another day fretting as though she had no faith. So when the day of her court hearing dawned sunny and bright, reminiscent of September's pleasant weather, her spirits lifted. Dressing in her Sunday best, she waited down by the road for Mrs. Lee to pick her up. She'd insisted that her parents not come along. Her father would be mortified with shame, while her mother would wring her hands with worry throughout the ordeal. She hadn't been a child when she entered into the partnership, and she wasn't a child today when she would face the music.

During the drive to Millersburg, she felt only mild car sickness from an empty stomach. Somehow *mamm*'s lumpy oatmeal hadn't appealed to her at six o'clock in the morning. As Mrs. Lee fiddled with the radio buttons, Leah tried to distract herself from queasiness by thinking about something else. Memories of Jonah Byler returned— unbidden and unwarranted. *Jonah.* She'd neither seen nor heard from the blue-eyed dairy farmer whom she'd once considered her future husband. He certainly wasn't in Wisconsin anymore. And he'd surely heard about the unfortunate turn of events by now.

She really couldn't blame him. How many Amish fellows wanted a fiancée on her way to prison? *Let's plan for a wedding next winter, Jonah...before spring planting and right after I'm released on parole...*

Leah laughed at her absurd thoughts.

Mrs. Lee glanced over. "I'm glad you thought of something humorous, my dear. Other than prayer, keeping your chin up is sometimes all you can do."

"You're right. If there ever was a time for a stiff upper lip, this is it."

The neighbor reached over and squeezed her hand. "At least it will soon be over. Are you sure you don't want me to wait with you until your case is called?"

"No, the hearing is more than an hour away. You can run your errands and still be back in time. I'm not sure if you'll be able to testify on my character or not, but I'm glad you'll be in the courtroom."

"I'll find a way to get my two cents in. I've watched every Perry Mason rerun at least five times."

Leah didn't know who Perry Mason was, but she doubted he would be much help today. After Mrs. Lee dropped her off in front of the district courthouse, some of Leah's confidence evaporated. The one hundred-thirty-year-old structure with patina copper dome and soaring white columns seemed far too imposing for a simple Amish girl. With the directions on where to appear clutched in her hand, she climbed the steps to face her future. Upstairs at the end of the hall, she saw the one person she hadn't considered facing today...April Lambright.

Looking very thin, April's eyes seemed to grow larger in her pale face. "Oh, Leah!" she exclaimed. Within seconds she had crossed the polished wood floor and thrown her arms around Leah's neck. She hugged and squeezed so tightly Leah couldn't draw breath. Over April's shoulder, she saw a middle-aged woman in a gray wool suit and high heels sitting on a bench. When Leah met the woman's gaze, she rose to her feet. "Hello, Miss Miller. I'm Mrs. Daws, April's attorney."

Leah couldn't reply since April was squeezing her neck so hard speech was impossible. When April released the hug, Leah murmured to the lawyer, "How do you do?"

Then April grabbed her hand. "Please come with me. I want to talk to you. There's a room we can use before we go into the hearing."

April pulled Leah into a small chamber with four plastic chairs and a wooden table. The lawyer returned to the bench and didn't follow them in. Once they sat down, Leah extracted her hand from her former partner's and cleared her throat. "Why, April?" she asked. "How could you tell people that Leah's Home Cooking was *my* restaurant? That I was responsible for all the shenanigans?"

April's face turned paper white as she stared down at the table. "I'm so ashamed. I have no excuse other than I panicked when my husband confronted me. I was afraid he would divorce me and take away my children, so I blamed you. And once my pack of lies began I didn't know how to stop. I was ashamed to admit to my parents and sister that they were right all along—that I had no business running a restaurant without previous experience."

Leah sat so stiffly in her chair her back muscles began to spasm, but she remained silent.

"Once the story—my web of lies—began to circulate I despised myself. I had broken the ninth commandment: Thou shalt not bear false witness." When she lifted her face, the toll of guilt and anguish was evident. "So I told my husband and family the truth and begged to be forgiven. I called my lawyer and told her what I'd done. She said it wasn't too late to make things right." April once again reached for Leah's hand. "Please forgive me, Leah. I beg you. I will clear your name in court and eventually pay back everything I owe."

"It's too late. The damage is done." She had allowed her hand to be enveloped, but felt no warmth, no mercy for the deceitful woman.

"I will testify that you only cooked and that I handled all financial matters. My lawyer says this is a preliminary hearing to determine if there was intent to defraud the state. If the judge feels I had no intent to avoid taxes, they may drop the charges. Then an independent accountant will determine how much is owed, and I would pay that amount along with penalties and fines." A ghost of a smile lifted the corners of her mouth.

"How in the world do you plan to do that? Give *me* another list with my half of the debt? I have no more money." Leah felt an un-charitable surge of anger.

"No, of course not. My sister and her husband have come forward to help. She said she'd never thought I would work so hard or that the diner would do so well. She felt proud of us, and she wants to keep the restaurant open. She has paid Mr. Jenkins for the back rent. Once we have straightened out the tax issue, she intends to buy out your investment and become my new partner. My brother-in-law will handle the books, and I'll get a very small salary for a long time to come." April's moist eyes glowed with hope and promise. "Even my husband supports this idea. He says it's my chance to fix the mess I caused. I'm just so glad he's talking to me again!" Tears slipped from her lashes and trailed down her face. She made no effort to wipe them away.

"I'm happy for you about the new developments," said Leah, only she didn't feel happy. She felt smug and judgmental and mean spir-ited. Why should April's woes melt like butter on a hot griddle while Leah's life had been ruined? April wouldn't even lose the diner after all because her family had rallied to her aid.

Leah's cynical tone of voice hadn't been lost on April. "I'm sorry for what I have done. I hope you believe that, and you will one day find it in your heart to forgive me."

Leah stared out the window's wavy glass where sunlight streamed through into refracted prisms. Then in a soft voice she chose to open her heart. "It's not that I don't forgive you; I do. I believe you're sorry and that you hadn't meant things to turn out like this. But please excuse me if I don't clap my hands with joy that you'll still be able to save the diner. My problems aren't so easily fixed." After the truthful admission, Leah felt her anger dissipate.

"But my lawyer prepared a statement that I have signed and will be submitted in court. I take full responsibility and release you of any culpability. Although you must appear with me in court, most likely you won't be asked to testify. When I'm called before the judge I will accept the consequences for my actions." April inhaled deeply and then released her breath with a whoosh.

"It's not money nor my future obligations that worry me. I wasn't even afraid to go to jail. April, my name and reputation have been ruined. Despite what you say today in court, many people will choose to believe ill of me. I will be shunned, if not by the ministerial brethren, at least in people's hearts. My Jonah...the man I'd hoped to marry...has already forgotten me." Tears she'd held at bay for so long began to fall. Leah laid her head down on her forearm and allowed misery to wash over her.

"I wouldn't be so sure about that, Leah. I wouldn't be so sure." April wrapped her arm around Leah's shoulders in a tender embrace and stroked the back of her head.

Leah was too weary to resist comforting or to remain angry or even to care much about her future. When the attorney knocked and entered with several pieces of paper, she signed her statement with only a cursory read-through. Soon after that, the bailiff arrived and announced it was time for the two former partners and Mrs. Daws to enter the courtroom. Other cases had been heard, settled out of court, or continued to another day. Leah uttered a silent prayer for strength and forgiveness as she walked in at April's side.

To her amazement, the courtroom was filled with people while others stood along the back wall. She spotted Mrs. Lee sitting directly behind the carved polished banister that separated onlookers from participants. Mrs. Lee lifted her hand in a friendly salute, as though greeting someone at the mailbox. Emma's bright grin caught Leah's attention next. Her sister was sitting next to her husband and his brother Kevin. James Davis smiled and winked at her. His suntan was long gone now that he wore a hat whenever he was outdoors. With a gasp, Leah noticed that Plain folk had crowded into the last four rows of seats. They nodded and offered smiles of encouragement. She even spotted Anna Boyer from the quilting bee with her beau, Aaron, the picnic table craftsman. Anna waved like a tourist while Aaron held both thumbs high. With the debt paid, all seemed to have been forgiven.

Leah felt weak in the knees, as though her legs might buckle. Her district had come not to condemn but to support her. Mrs. Daws steadied her arm and led her to the defendants' table. As Leah took her place behind her chair, a man in the last row rose to his feet. He was tall and held his black felt hat between very large hands. With an olive complexion and the brightest blue eyes she'd ever seen, Leah stared into the face of Jonah Byler—the love of her life. Her heart swelled inside her chest until her ribs began to hurt.

When an elderly, gentle-faced judge entered the courtroom, the bailiff called the room to order. As Leah took her seat, she knew she could handle any outcome, any punishment. For the next fifteen minutes, Mrs. Daws read both April's and Leah's statements and presented the signed affidavits from those who had been paid back and no longer wished to press charges. Surprisingly, even Whip Jenkins had signed a document that all back rent had been paid in full. April was called to the stand and kept her word about taking the blame. Leah did not have to testify, although she wouldn't have minded doing so. Jonah was no longer in Wisconsin or at home, but in Millersburg where she needed him. With Jonah in the courtroom, sitting only a few rows away, she had the courage to handle anything God placed in her path.

She could barely sit still as the judge reviewed the documents in evidence and then called April to the bench. He read a lengthy list of terms and conditions, but all charges would be dismissed in six months if April fulfilled her obligations to the Sales Tax Division for the state. He then suggested she change the name of the restaurant to April's Home Cooking and that she hire a good accountant. He also mentioned he'd eaten at the diner once and hoped pineapple pancakes would become a permanent item on the breakfast menu.

Pineapple pancakes! Leah thought. *It takes all kinds, doesn't it?*

Leah had been absolved of any culpability. Her name had been cleared. The clapping and shouts from the back of the courtroom, highly unusual for Amish folk, attested to their support. After thanking Mrs. Daws and hugging April with every ounce of strength she had, Leah walked from the courtroom to the crowd waiting in the hallway. Their trust lifted her heart. She thanked each person for making the trip to Millersburg...and for believing in her.

Finally it was over, and she hurried outside with Emma, Jamie, Kevin, and Mrs. Lee. The members of her district had gone out the back to where their horses and buggies were tethered. Only one Amish man remained on the courthouse steps. He sat leaning against a tall white pillar as though he was just another tourist taking in the Millersburg sights.

"I'll wait for you in the parking lot, dear," said Mrs. Lee. "It looks like someone wants to speak with you." She leaned over to kiss Leah's forehead.

"We'll wait there too," said Emma, "but something tells me you won't need a ride home."

After thanking them, Leah went down the steps with legs that had turned to jelly. "Jonah Byler, what brings you to town today?" she asked with feigned casualness. "How were things in Wisconsin?" She tucked her skirt beneath her and sat down on the concrete steps. Below them on sidewalk and streets, pedestrians and vehicles went about their business unaware her heart was slamming against her ribcage.

Jonah sat down beside her and slipped an arm around her shoulders as though mere hours instead on several weeks had separated them. "Wisconsin was just fine. My uncle and I got the farm shipshape after we brought in the harvest. He should be able to manage for the winter while his back finishes healing. By spring, his sons will be that much older and able to help more with planting." His eyes sparkled with animation.

"How long have you been home?" she asked, focusing on two pigeons fighting over a piece of popcorn.

"Almost a week now. My *dawdi* had plenty of chores for me when

I got back. I thought I'd never get caught up." He gently squeezed her shoulders and then released her. "Didn't you get my letters?" he asked with a curious expression. "I was hoping you would have written back. I was mighty lonesome in Wisconsin. All my old friends have gotten hitched and forgotten about me."

The squabbling birds no longer held her interest. "You wrote to me, Jonah? I never received any letters."

"Twice. I sent them to Leah Miller, Route 585, Winesburg, Ohio." He turned on the steps to face her. One lock of dark hair fell forward into his eyes.

Leah felt the seed of hope take root. "I know it's confusing, but everyone on our end of the township road has Wilmot addresses, and considering how many Millers there are in the county, I'm not surprised they never found me."

"That explains why you didn't get my letters, and I suppose why you didn't write."

Her cheeks flushed to bright pink. "Your *mamm* gave me your address and I wrote three different times." She glanced up to catch his expression of confusion. "But I never mailed any of them. I chickened out." She shifted her focus to the steps where the pigeons had eaten the popcorn and now pecked at seedpods.

Jonah released a perfect imitation of a clucking hen.

She rolled her eyes. "I deserved that, but I was afraid to tell you how badly things had spun out of control. I should've confronted April sooner."

He covered her small hand with his. "It might not have changed a thing. Let's forget about the past. It's finally over for you."

His touch warmed her to her toes. "I was so happy to see you in the courtroom. Did you come to hear the testimony—to find out if what folk said was true?" She glanced at his handsome face.

"Nope. I didn't hitch up my buggy and leave before dawn to hear what Mrs. Lambright had to say. And I have no need for gossip to know what's going on. I know *you*, Leah Miller, and you would no more cheat somebody or the State of Ohio than you'd take up bare-back barrel-racing." He tightened his grip on her hand.

She pondered that mental picture and grinned. But when she opened her mouth to reply, no words came out. A knot had formed in her throat as her emotions boiled to the surface.

"How about if I drive you home? Then you can tell me your plans as you don't have a job anymore. Maybe you could open another diner. I think I spotted a rundown, abandoned gristmill on my way into town. At least three sides are still standing."

Leah stood and pulled Jonah to his feet. "Let's go tell Mrs. Lee and Emma they can start for home since I've got a ride. But we are not looking at any gristmills on the way back—even if I have to put on a pair of blinders."

~

"I am so glad that ordeal is over!" said Emma, watching the passing scenery. "Now my little sister can get a decent night's sleep."

The drive back to Charm from Millersburg took the three Davises through some of the prettiest countryside in the state. Everywhere you looked Amish farmers were preparing their fields for a long winter rest. The upright tied bundles of cornstalks reminded her of her *daed*'s old-fashioned ways.

"You have no idea how that gal tossed and turned and punched her pillow," Emma continued. "I couldn't sleep a wink those three nights at *mamm*'s." She had stopped referring to her parents' farm as home. She was part of her husband's family now.

"Maybe she couldn't sleep from all your snoring, dear one," James said, not taking his eyes off the twisty road.

Emma angled a glare. "Don't make up tall tales in front of your brother. We both know I don't snore."

James patted her knee. "Well, I think you'll sleep good tonight." He leaned forward to wink at Kevin.

She looked from one brother to the other. "If you don't mind, I'd like to go straight home. All that courtroom drama has worn me out. I'd love to rest before making dinner."

James laughed. "Straight home is where we're headed, but catching a nap in the sunroom is out of the question."

Emma turned suspicious. "What are you two cooking up?"

"Words would only spoil the surprise, *fraa*. Wait and see. I'll not say another word." When he set his jaw with that determined pose, she knew she wouldn't get another word on the subject.

Fortunately, Emma didn't have long to ponder the mystery. And words couldn't describe the scene they encountered as they drove up Hollyhock Lane. Three flatbed lumber trucks, in various stages of being unloaded, sat along the gravel road leading to James and Emma's plot of land. Cars, pickup trucks, and at least forty buggies were lined up in the recently mown meadow. A billowing white tent had been set up with tables and chairs, just like the one used for barn raisings. And people seemed to be everywhere—carrying stacks of lumber, ladders, scaffolds, buckets of tools, containers of water, or plates of food. Kevin pulled the truck to the side to view the panorama. A beehive in spring was no more frenetic with activity.

In her heart, Emma knew what she was seeing but was too bashful to believe her eyes. "What's going on, James Davis?"

"I thought you wanted me all to yourself. If you've changed your mind, I'll just tell these folk to go on home." He opened the truck door and stepped out for a better view.

She scrambled out right on his heels. "These people are here to build our new house?" she squeaked.

"Every single one of them. And I sure hope they know what they're doing. I'd hate to end up with stairways going nowhere or doors that open up into solid walls." He wiggled his eyebrows.

Emma punched his arm playfully. "Oh, Jamie! Why didn't you tell me about today? I could've helped your *mamm* get ready. I'll bet she's been cooking up a storm."

James brushed a kiss across the top of her head. "That would have ruined the whole concept of surprise."

She peered up at him. "But on the same day as Leah's hearing? We could've been stuck in that courtroom all afternoon."

"That was the tricky part. The pastor organized our district to come out today and tomorrow. Some folk took vacation days. Dad and I compiled lists of material and scheduled deliveries for early morning. The farm foreman divided the men into work teams, and I hired a group of professional carpenters to run the show. All that would have been hard to change after you mentioned your sister's hearing, so I hoped and prayed for the best. The foundation and basement were put in weeks ago so they would set up in time. I can't believe you hadn't noticed when you took one of your afternoon walks."

Emma remembered the night she'd fallen asleep in the pinewoods, was rained on, and run into Jamie in the barn. She shuddered inwardly for the self-righteous way she had behaved. "I haven't taken that path in a while. I confined my walks to the river and back."

"You'll soon be able to see your favorite forest from our back porch." He encircled her waist with both arms and hugged. "Are you happy, Mrs. Davis? Or should I tell everybody to pack up and go home and we'll just live with Mom and Dad forever?"

She turned within his embrace. "You are impossible! I hope your *mamm* knows how much I appreciate…" Emma's voice broke with emotion. The past years spent in the Davis household with Jamie's family had been loving and kind. She didn't deserve what was happening before her eyes.

James kissed her forehead, her nose, and then her lips. "She knows, Em, and she loves you too. But the time has come for this Davis family to be on their own."

Kevin crept up to stand beside them and for a minute, the three just watched the work happening down below. "I hate to break up this lovey-dovey scene, but you can't wait up here until the house is finished. Let's go, you two. There's plenty to be done if we want the roof on and windows in before the first snow." He grabbed Emma's sleeve and James' arm and pulled them back to the truck.

Emma went eagerly. She couldn't wait to greet her friends and neighbors who had taken time off to build them a house. She couldn't wait to help feed the hungry workers who were laboring on their behalf. And she couldn't wait to move into the little house high on the ridge near her beloved pine forest.

God had shone His mercy on Leah today, and He still had some left over for her too. The Miller girls were blessed after all. And she would never forget this day or cease being grateful for the rest of her life.

TWENTY

December, second Sunday of Advent

Matthew loved December. Workloads grew lighter as hours of daylight waned. He enjoyed walking in fields touched with frost on crisp mornings. Before long the deep cold would set in, covering the world in a thick layer of white. With the preaching service at the Miller home today, he'd risen early to set out the long benches in the barn and build a fire in Emma's old woodstove. Hymnals still needed to be passed out and tables put up for lunch, but for a few moments he looked over the rolling hills of Holmes County. Nothing could compare with the peace and silence of a Sunday morning in winter.

He, Henry, and Leah had helped *mamm* clean house all week. If any ladies chose to drag a gloved finger along their windowsills, they would find no dust for their efforts. Not that any of them would do such a thing. Matthew thought women fretted too much over inconsequential things like dust, streaky windows, or whether the raisins in the oatmeal cookies hardened during baking—Leah's pet peeve that morning.

A man tended to worry about the important things in life—whether he was living in a way pleasing to God, to his family, and to his community; whether he enjoyed his work and if it could sustain him for a lifetime; and if he had somebody who could tolerate him enough to share that life. Matthew felt fairly confident about the first two, but he had made no progress on the third since Martha Hostetler accepted a ride home with John Yoder. *Were they courting? Had he proposed?* Matt didn't know and was too shy to ask Rachel or Leah. He'd also been too shy to return to district social events. What was the point? No gal wanted a beau with red hair and an untamable cowlick, whose own sister had called a barbarian. Perhaps it was his fate to be admired by females solely of the equine persuasion. Mares and fillies didn't seem to mind his lack of conversation skills or the way he wolfed down a meal.

As the first buggy rumbled up their driveway, he scrambled to finish preparations and then hurried into the house to don his Sunday clothes. Without much inclination to greet neighbors as they arrived, and with a strong desire not to see any of the Hostetlers, Matthew waited until the church service was ready to start before slipping into the last row. But try as he might, he couldn't keep the sweet face of Martha off his mind.

"Pay attention," warned Henry. "The service has begun and you seem to be a million miles away." He jabbed his elbow into his *bruder*'s side.

Matthew shook off his daydream and concentrated on the first Scripture reading and then the hymns, followed by the initial sermon delivered by his *daed*. He willed himself not to look in the direction of Mrs. Hostetler or her daughter Rachel. Because he knew if he craned his head left or right, Martha would be somewhere in the vicinity. And seeing her soft green eyes and peaches-and-cream complexion wasn't something he needed today. His heart ached enough the way it was.

The three-hour service seemed longer than six hours that morning, but finally it was over. Matthew fled the barn without stopping to talk to his friends. He hadn't seen some of his pals since finishing the contract work in Sugar Creek, but catching up would have to wait for when there was no chance of running into the girl who had broken his heart. He headed straight for the horse pens, where the new acquisitions were still separated from the main stock. He had time to kill before the women brought out lunch to the long tables. And he would just as soon spend that time right there.

One or two of the rescues from the kill pen stood out from the rest. Although he'd been pleased with the progress he and Henry had made with the lot, a haflinger filly had captured his heart. She'd been weak and emaciated when he'd bought her, with more than one digestive woe. Dr. Longo had saved her life and accepted no compensation for his hard work. She'd been steadily gaining weight and thriving ever since. Matthew fed her a handful of dandelion heads every day as a digestive aid. His Aunt Hannah called dandelions antacids for horses, and she'd picked several burlap bagfuls before the first frost killed the plants to the roots. She'd spread them out to dry on her worktable and then presented them bow-tied as though a special gift. Aunt Hannah had taken a shine to Sam. As did her son, Ben, and just about everyone else who laid eyes on her. Several had offered to purchase her when rehabilitation was complete, but this was one horse Matthew would be hard pressed to part with.

When he reached the paddock and whistled through his teeth, Sam came running. With her dark eyes flashing and silky blond mane flying in the breeze she looked impressive, if still on the lean side. He reached through the rails to scratch her nose and received a soft whinny for his efforts.

"Matthew Miller, I hope you're not doing any training over there, this being the Lord's day and all."

The cherished voice of Martha Hostetler rang in his ears, causing the hairs on his neck to stand straight up. He wheeled around and almost knocked her down in the tall grass. How she'd crept up without his knowledge was a mystery. "No, ma'am. I was just having a private conversation with my favorite student, no work involved."

Martha leaned up against the paddock rails to stroke the horse's flank. Surprisingly, Sam didn't shy away from the unfamiliar hand.

"Well, I must say you picked a beauty to chitchat with. I guess I can't blame you for running out the moment the service was over. What's her name?"

"Miss Hostetler, this is Sam. Sam, I'd like you to meet Miss Martha Hostetler."

Both species of females peered at him oddly. Martha ducked her head low to assess the animal's underbelly. "I do believe this is a *girl* horse."

"Sam is short for Samantha."

"Have you lost your mind?" she asked, fighting back a smile. She reached up to scratch an ear.

Matthew blushed nearly to the color of his hair. "It's possible. I guess I spend too much time with horses since you took up with John Yoder."

She stopped stroking the beast and turned to face him. "Took up with John Yoder? Is that what you think?" She squinted in the sunlight.

"*Jah,* I saw him taking you home from a singing a couple months ago." Matthew steeled his resolve and met her gaze. "I assumed you two were courting."

She clucked her tongue. "That was some very serious jumping to conclusions, I'd say. He took me home, *jah,* but I nearly dozed off along the way. All he talked about was baseball. Since he began *Rumschpringe* he listens to Cleveland Indians games on a transistor radio. I can't see the big deal about hitting a ball with a stick and then running around a bunch of sandbags."

He smirked. "I'm not much of a fan either. So...you two aren't courting?"

"No, and you would know that if you bothered to come to a social outing now and then."

He scuffed his shiny black Sunday shoes in the dirt. "That's very interesting," he mumbled, feeling like an idiot.

Martha turned her attention back to Sam. "Say, is this one of the horses you and Henry rescued?" she asked. "I need to stop by on a day other than the Sabbath to take one off your hands. I appreciate what you did, and I'd like to buy one for my open buggy, if any are suitable." Her smile revealed perfectly straight teeth and her generous heart.

"This one is the best of the lot. Her problems were strictly medical. Once Dr. Longo cleared up bad digestion, she's been the easiest horse to train. She responds to verbal commands, besides the reins. She would make a great buggy horse."

Martha patted Sam's neck. "I don't recognize the breed."

"She's a haflinger from Austria, bred originally to work in the mountains for farming and as a pack horse. They're good for light draft work, harness, driving, even saddle riding, if you want to follow in Rachel's footsteps." He clamped his jaw closed before he landed in the same category as John Yoder with baseball.

"I have no intention of climbing onto her back, but she is a beauty."

"She's not the only one." Matthew spoke the words so softly they may not have been heard.

But Martha's blushing cheeks indicated otherwise. "Don't change the subject. I believe I want this horse when you're done training…if, of course, you set a fair price." She winked at him without an ounce of shyness. "But right now my stomach is growling for food. Do you think there'll be anything left for us?"

"I'm sure there will be, and you'll find my price for the horse quite reasonable," he said, deciding to make Sam a Christmas gift if things went well between them. He stuck out his arm. "Why not grab hold on our way to lunch? You never know when a gopher hole lurks beneath the leaves to trip you."

She rolled her eyes but took his elbow just the same. "I brought my lemon bars for the dessert table. If memory serves correctly, you were fond of them."

Matthew couldn't stop grinning, and it had nothing to do with lemon bars. Martha was walking by his side, and she actually seemed to like him.

He would probably be smiling up until New Year's.

～

"Git up there, Bo," Emma called. She grabbed at the reins in Jamie's hands. "Can't you make this former *race horse* go any faster?" She tugged the wool blanket up to her chin.

"Easy, *fraa*. It's a long way to Winesburg with plenty of hills in between. Let's not tire him. We'll get there by and by." Just the same, Jamie clucked his tongue and Bo marginally picked up the pace.

"You seem awfully calm for a man who yesterday was jumping up and down and shouting to the hills at the top of his lungs." Emma snuggled close to his side.

Jamie put an arm around her shoulders. "The news that you're pregnant did make my day, and I thought the people living in Canton might like to hear about it"

"It is a blessing, *jah,* but don't use that term for me—say 'with child' or 'expecting a *bopplin*.' My old-fashioned *daed* thinks only horses, cows, or hogs should be described as pregnant."

James laughed. "How do you think your parents will react? Has Simon finally accepted the fact I'm not going to shave off my beard and run off with a pack of English motorcycle riders?"

Emma tried to pinch his arm, but too many layers of wool made it impossible. "*Daed* likes you just fine. He grunts and groans a lot around everybody."

"We'll have to see if his reaction can match that of my parents. Dad just stared dumbfounded for a while, and then he blushed and hugged me, something he never does. And my mom? She crossed her arms and said, 'Right after moving into your new house? I would've gotten this project going sooner if I'd known that's all it would take.'"

Emma giggled. "Mom Davis sounds happy to no longer have me underfoot in her kitchen."

"Nope. She's just happy to finally become a grandma. She's been jealous of some of her friends. You might see her at our new house so often, it'll seem like we never moved."

"*Danki,* Jamie," she murmured.

"For what, dear one?"

"For taking me home today to tell my family. I just couldn't wait for Christmas. My *mamm*'s eager for grandchildren too. And I can't wait to find out how things are between Leah and Jonah. It's not too late for them to take the classes and get baptized this winter."

"Whoa. Settle down, Emma. If they are courting, you don't want to scare the guy off, do you? Let him get to know the unusual Miller girls at a snail's pace."

Emma glared from beneath her lashes. "If I didn't know you better, James Davis, I'd say you were trying to rile me. But it's not going to work. I've made up my mind to be joyous today…and tomorrow and for many days to come." Emma filled her lungs with the crisp cold air and decided to count houses until they reached her parents' home. Before she reached triple digits, James pulled up the long Miller driveway, still lined on both sides with buggies. Many had stayed for an afternoon of socializing after church.

"We're here and it's still daylight," he announced.

"Oh, Jamie, look!" Emma exclaimed, pointing at two people under a tree.

Beneath the bare branches of a huge oak stood Leah and a tall, dark-haired man that had to be Jonah Byler. And if the way they were looking at each other was any indication, Emma's *other* prayer had just been answered.

～

"You have to talk to me some time, Leah," Jonah said. "I'm not going home until you do. And it will look mighty suspicious to your *daed* come Tuesday when I'm still hanging around the backyard."

Leah stopped in her tracks and turned around. "I'm not avoiding you, Jonah, but when you're the hosting family you're expected to do the lion's share of running back and forth from house to barn. I can't very well let my *mamm* overdo." Carrying a tray of bowls and platters to be washed, she walked back to where he stood.

"Looks like you've been chatting up a storm with everybody but me. I'm starting to think you don't like me." He cocked his head and winked, not looking at all as though his feelings were hurt.

"I'm trying to make sure no one harbors ill will from the problems at the diner."

"Why don't you let me help? Then you'll get done faster and we can spend some time together. Just tell me what to do."

"Carry these to the house and I'll get another load. As soon as they are washed, I can take a break." She handed him her tray and hurried back to the barn. The buffet table had been picked down to broken cookies, dried out casseroles, and wilted salads.

Jonah delivered the dirty dishes and was shoed out of the kitchen by the women. Leah found him rocking in the porch swing when she climbed the steps with another armload. "I'll wait for you right here," he said. "And look, there's room for one more." He patted the seat beside him and winked again boldly.

She blushed to her hair roots. "Let me wash these and then I'll be back."

But inside the overheated kitchen, Julia had other ideas. When Leah set the stack of bowls in the sink and reached for the scrubbing pad, Julia said, "Go back outside, daughter. You have someone waiting for you."

"No, I won't have you doing my work." Leah gently nudged her mother aside so she could reach the dishwashing liquid.

Julia bumped Leah with her hip so hard that Leah had to grab the counter for balance. She stared at her mother gape mouthed as the other women giggled like schoolgirls.

"Can't you see I already have plenty of helpers?" Julia asked. "Do as I say before I go cut a switch."

"You've never switched me in my life," Leah muttered, drying her hands on a towel.

"It's not too late to start." Julia's eyes twinkled with more mischief than anger as she pointed at the back door. "Now go."

Leah tossed the towel on the counter and walked out to meet her fate. She *had* been avoiding Jonah. She had secretly dreaded asking some questions—ones she'd steered clear of on the drive home from the courthouse. But she needed answers before her heart became hopelessly entangled again.

Jonah jumped up the moment she appeared in the doorway. "My goodness, you're fast. Must have been all that practice at the diner."

"Let's take a walk instead of swinging," she said, glancing back toward the kitchen window. Someone had parted the curtains just a tad.

"Do you miss it?" he asked as they started down the steps.

"Miss the diner? *Jah,* I guess so, but I've been so busy I don't know how I managed working four days a week, plus one day of baking." She turned to face him. "Where are we headed? I don't want to wander too far. I still have plenty of cleaning up yet to do."

Jonah settled an arm around her waist. "Let's head to the pond. I want to see if your ducks have flown south yet. Ours just left two days ago."

Leah had no desire to discuss ducks or the diner, so she asked the first of many questions still troubling her. "How come you didn't ask for the full story of my legal troubles? I thought you would on the way home from Millersburg, but you didn't."

He shrugged his shoulders. "No need to. I knew you hadn't broken the law, cheated people or the state, or anything else people were accusing you of."

"How did you know, considering all the lies flying around?"

"I know you, Leah Miller. I know your heart. The people who believed the tall tales must not."

His answer bolstered her courage. "Is that why you didn't come see me when you came back from Wisconsin? I thought for sure you would either come for an explanation or to bawl me out, or at least to say I told you so."

As they reached the pond, he tipped back his hat and gazed out over the water. "Would you look at that? Your ducks are still here, swimming around as though they have all the time in the world." The breeze ruffling the surface created small waves that rolled gently onto the bank. But somehow the water didn't tempt a person to dip in a toe the way it did during the summer. "I wouldn't have had any pleasure from gloating, Leah. It ate me up inside when I watched you walk into the courtroom with Mrs. Lambright. I was sorry you had to go through that."

She sat down on the edge of the dock. "It served me right. I felt better when I saw that so many district members had come out, and my sister...and you. I had just about given up on you, Jonah Byler."

"What? Aren't you the one who taught me to believe the best will happen, not the worst—to pray for what you want and then step out in faith?" As he sat down beside her, the rickety dock creaked and groaned. It tilted that much closer to joining the deep dark mud on the bottom.

"*Jah*, that was me."

"That's what I thought, and so that's what I did. My *mamm* wrote to say there was trouble at the diner and that you had been subpoenaed. She said I should come home as soon as possible. Well, I couldn't leave right away, so I started praying for guidance and for God to be near you since I couldn't be. Then I prayed to be able to come home in time for your hearing, to be there when you needed me."

"Sounds like you found your faith again." She spoke in a near whisper as the milling half dozen ducks swam closer.

"I had plenty of time to think up north. And I read a little Scripture during the evenings when sleep wouldn't come. The first night I opened my Bible I found Psalm 130:5: 'I wait for the Lord, my soul waits, and in his word I put my hope.' I memorized that verse so that every time I found myself growing impatient I would say the words to myself. My *mamm* says that when God says no to our prayers, it's because He's got something better in mind for us. And sometimes it's better than we could imagine. I sure didn't believe that after my *daed* died, but I believe it now."

"What changed your mind?" she asked, hoping today wasn't the day the dock crumbled beneath them.

"You, Leah. If we hadn't lost my father, we never would have sold the farm and moved to Ohio."

"I recall you didn't want to make the move. You were all set to spend the rest of your life in Wisconsin." She couldn't stop smiling.

"That was before I met you and tasted your Chocolate Mousse Cream pie." He picked up her hand and kissed the backs of her fingers.

Shivers ran down her spine to pool deep in her belly. She didn't pull her hand back but allowed him to press it to the side of his face. "Are you saying you prefer the Chocolate Mousse Cream to the Peach Parfait Supreme?" she asked breathlessly.

He leaned over and kissed her, not on the cheek or the forehead, but squarely on the lips. "Ask me again in twenty years. By then I'll have made up my mind."

"Jonah, stop," she said and scooted away until the dock creaked ominously. "I'm just recovering my reputation." Leah glanced over her shoulder but nobody was paying any attention. "Is there anything else you prayed about?"

"Hmm, let's see. I prayed for us...that you would come to love me and be willing to marry me."

She was afraid to look at him or even draw breath. He had spoken the words with no more difficulty than inquiring about the soup of the day. She glanced up to find him grinning from ear to ear.

"What do you say? Do you think you can make the change from cooking for dozens of adoring fans who sit with forks in hand to just one dairy farmer who happens to love you? Will you marry me, Leah Miller?"

She sat very still, letting his words soak into her soul like syrup on waffles. These were the words she'd longed to hear from practically the time she'd met him in his *dawdi*'s barn. Yet no snappy reply came to mind, no memorable answer that she could repeat to daughters and granddaughters in the years to come.

Her Aunt Hannah would have said something like "It's about time you got around to asking me that!"

Emma would have had the perfect romantic reply planned out months in advance, while her long eyelashes fluttered above her blue eyes.

But Leah's response was direct and to the point. "*Jah*," she said. "I would love to."

Jonah leaned over and kissed her again. "That's my girl. And now my *last* prayer has been answered."

He'd whispered his admission low, but Leah heard him clearly.

Apparently, so did the mallards swimming around in the frigid water. As though on cue they rose into the air and with a rapid beating of wings, circled the pond twice and flew off toward the road.

"Looks like they have been hanging around to hear your answer," he said.

Leah felt an odd shiver snake up her spine. "Do you think they are gone for good, on their way south for the winter? They should have started out earlier in the day than this."

Jonah rose to his feet and pulled her up to his side under the spreading branches of the oak tree. "Don't worry. Even if they are officially gone till spring, they won't fly down to the Carolinas all at once. They'll probably get as far as Charm and settle down for the night. Tell your sister to watch for them on the Hollyhock Lake."

"Speaking of whom...isn't that Emma and James standing in the driveway?" Leah arched up on tiptoes to see but people had crowded around the pair, obscuring her view. "I didn't know they were coming today. I can't wait to tell her my...our good news." She smiled up him.

"After we make our announcement, you can get caught up with

your sister while I look for the bishop," said Jonah. "I want to see if we can still get into a class to prepare for baptism and joining the church."

"Do you mean it? You're prepared to take your vows?" Her wide-eyed expression revealed her shock.

"Why not? We can't marry until we join the church. I don't have any doubts about you, Leah. Are you getting cold feet already? It's not even been ten minutes."

"No, silly, no cold feet here." She lifted her skirt to show off her best black boots. "But are you sure you're ready to pledge yourself to God? You were pretty mad at Him not too long ago."

He lifted her chin with one finger. "I'm ready to trust again. I've given up trying to figure everything out on my own. I wasn't having much luck anyway. I'd prayed for a sign that He had forgiven me, and I believe you're it. God would never let a fine woman like you marry me if He didn't have high hopes for my spiritual future."

No bolt of lightning struck the earth. Not even a timely parting of clouds revealed rays of sunshine, but Leah and Jonah felt the earth move beneath their feet just the same.

"Now let's go tell your family I'm about to steal away the best cook and baker in Holmes County."

She felt giddy as they approached the knot of people surrounding Emma and James. *Mamm* and *daed* were there along with Henry. Matthew and Martha Hostetler had pushed up to the front of the group. *Aren't those two standing awfully close together?*

Aunt Hannah, Uncle Seth, Phoebe, and little Ben had come and were smiling about some unknown good news. Leah spotted Rachel toward the back, and as she was about to call out her name the crowd parted. Emma Davis came marching toward her as though on a mission.

"It looks like you'll be last to hear our announcement instead of the first." Emma kept glancing over at Jonah as he joined Leah's side. A grin filled her entire face.

Leah felt Jonah's steadying arm on her back. "I have news too, sister, that I...we were just coming to share." She barely recognized her own voice. Joy seemed to have tied her vocal cords into knots.

Emma closed the distance between them in a few short steps. Her pretty blue eyes were filled with tears, while Leah's honey brown ones weren't exactly dry, either. They met each other's gaze for a moment and then opened their arms to embrace.

Neither sister had to explain a thing.

Somehow they both just knew. Upcoming marriages and on-the-way babies couldn't remain secrets for long in a small town on a sunny day in December when a family loved one another as much as the Millers did.

Peach Parfait Supreme Pie
Rosanna Coblentz

Pie Crust (makes 2 crusts)

2 cups flour
1 teaspoon salt
⅔ cup Butter Flavor Crisco
Cold water

Use a fork to mix the salt with flour and then work in the shortening until the mixture resembles coarse crumbs. Add 4 to 6 tablespoons cold water and mix well. Divide the dough and roll out both pieces to fit two 9-inch pie pans. Place a crust in each pan, crimp the edges, and prick the dough with a fork. Bake at 350 degrees or until slightly brown. Crusts should seem loose inside the pans.

Rosie's secret: To prevent the crusts from shrinking, place them under the broiler for a few seconds before baking.

Filling

1 small box vanilla instant pudding
1 cup milk
1 8-ounce package cream cheese, softened
1 cup sour cream

Mix the pudding and milk according to package instructions and set aside. Cream together the cream cheese and sour cream and then stir in the pudding. Pour into the cooled piecrusts and let set.

Topping

1 cup sugar
2 cups water
1 tablespoon light Karo syrup
1 tablespoon lemon juice
Pinch of salt
3 tablespoons unflavored gelatine
2 tablespoons Peach Jell-O
2 tablespoons Orange Jell-O
Peach slices from six ripe peaches (canned peaches may be used as well)

In a medium-sized saucepan, bring the sugar, water, Karo syrup, lemon juice, and salt to a boil. In a separate bowl mix 2 to 3 tablespoons of gelatine with enough water to moisten. Slowly stir the gelatin into heated syrup until it reaches desired thickness. Remove from heat and add the Peach Jell-O and Orange Jell-O (more Jell-O may be added to taste). Cool the topping mixture and then add peach slices. Top pies over the filling and refrigerate until well chilled. Serve with Cool Whip or whipped cream.

Chocolate Mousse Cream Pie
Rosanna Coblentz

Pie Crust

1 box chocolate cake mix (your favorite)
¾ cup melted butter

Mix the cake mix and butter and divide mixture into two pie pans. Press dough evenly up the sides and in the bottom of the pan and bake at 350 degrees for 15 minutes. Cool.

Rosie's secret: Use 9-inch glass pie pans and spray with cooking spray.

Filling

1 8-ounce package cream cheese, softened
1 cup powdered sugar
1½ cups Cool Whip or whipped cream

Fold ingredients together and divide between the 2 pies. Spread the cream cheese mixture in the bottom of the chocolate pie shells.

Topping

1 cup sugar
2 tablespoons cornstarch
2 tablespoons cocoa
Pinch of salt
2 egg yolks
2 cups milk
1 tablespoon butter
1 teaspoon vanilla

In a medium-sized saucepan, mix together the sugar, cornstarch, cocoa, salt, egg yolks, and milk and cook over medium heat while stirring with a wire whip. After the mixture thickens, remove from heat and add the butter and vanilla. Cool the mixture and then pour over the cream cheese layer in the pie pans. Chill and top with Cool Whip or whipped cream. Shaved chocolate or chocolate sprinkles may be added on top.

Rosie's Secret: Whip egg yolks and milk together before mixing with other ingredients—this makes a really smooth mix.

Spellbinder Cookies
Esther Miller

Cookies

1 cup sugar
1 teaspoon baking soda
1½ teaspoons baking powder
1½ cups all-purpose flour
1 cup rolled oats
1 cup salted peanuts
1 cup chocolate chips
2 sticks butter or margarine, softened
1 egg
½ cup corn flakes, crumbled

Glaze

1 tablespoon water
1 cup powdered sugar
1 teaspoon vanilla

Mix all the dry ingredients together. Add butter or margarine and egg and mix well. Drop the cookies onto a baking sheet and flatten with a glass. Bake 15 to 20 minutes at 350 degrees. Drizzle on the glaze while still warm.

Simply Delicious Cinnamon Rolls
From Simple Pleasures Bed-and-Breakfast
Carol Lee Shevlin

⅓ cup natural sugar (may substitute with white)
½ teaspoon salt
1 stick butter, melted
1 cup milk
2 eggs, beaten
1 package yeast
½ cup warm water
3½ cups all-purpose flour
Melted butter for brushing on dough
Cinnamon sugar
Raisins, optional
Pecans, optional

Mix together the sugar, salt, and melted butter in a large bowl. In a small saucepan scald the milk (but do not let it boil) and pour over the sugar-and-butter mixture and mix. Add the eggs. Dissolve the yeast in warm water and add to the mix and stir. Add in the flour, a little at a time, until the dough reaches a good consistency. It should be firm and not "wet" looking. Refrigerate dough overnight.

The next morning roll out the dough and brush with melted butter. Then sprinkle generously with cinnamon sugar (raisins and chopped pecans may also be sprinkled on). Roll up the dough and cut into 1½-inch slices. Place cut-end up into a round cake pan that has been sprayed with cooking spray or lightly coated with oil. Let rise for 1 to 2 hours. Bake at 350 degrees for approximately 20 minutes or until slightly brown. Cool for a few minutes and then ice with your favorite icing.

Carol's secrets: I use real butter, not margarine, and I also use Robin Hood Flour.

Blackberry Cheesecake Pie
Mary Ellis

1 8-ounce package cream cheese, softened
½ cup sugar
2 cups blackberries (washed and drained), reserve some for garnish (fresh fruit is best, but canned also works if out of season)
1 10-ounce tub Cool Whip
1 graham cracker piecrust (you can use storebought or prepare one yourself)

Cream together sugar and cream cheese. Stir in berries. Fold in Cool Whip. Use a spatula to scrape the cheesecake filling into graham cracker piecrust and refrigerate for three hours. (Eat any leftover with a spoon.) Garnish with the prettiest berries of the bunch!

DISCUSSION QUESTIONS

1. Why would working at a local diner be especially appealing to Old Order Leah?

2. Members of the Amish community usually steer clear of conflicts in the English world. Why is it so hard for Matthew to stay removed from the problems at the horse farm where he works?

3. Jamie's devotion to his bride, Emma, has changed his life in profound ways. How do the "little changes" threaten to undermine their relationship more than the major ones when he became New Order Amish?

4. With the runaway success of the diner, what particularly female character flaw rears its head in Leah's personality? Why would this be especially onerous for an Amish woman?

5. What is it about Jonah Byler that makes him irresistible to Leah? Why does human nature cause us to seek the apple beyond our reach, while surrounded with prime fruit ready to be picked?

6. How does Matthew's God-given gifts serve him well as a horse trainer, but doom him to a lonely future with humankind? How would becoming an independent trainer be hampered by the *Ordnung?*

7. Why would Leah enter a baking competition, knowing her parents wouldn't approve? What about the contest becomes problematic for someone Amish?

8. Leah long suspects something isn't right with her business partner at the diner. Why does she wait so long to confront her, and what is it about April's personality that allows this to snowball in the first place?

9. Why does Leah believe the diner's closing has ruined her chances with Jonah, even though she wasn't culpable in the mismanagement?

10. Why wouldn't Matthew return to his beloved horse-training job after the owner fires his former boss?

11. How does Emma's frequent disagreements with Jamie's family members help her to mature in her marriage and grow as a Christian?

12. What had caused Jonah's lapse of faith, and how does Leah help him restore his relationship with God?

ABOUT THE AUTHOR

~

Mary Ellis grew up close to the eastern Ohio Amish Community, Geauga County, where her parents often took her to farmers' markets and woodworking fairs. She and her husband now live in Medina County, close to the largest population of Amish families, and enjoy the simple way of life.

The Way to a Man's Heart is Mary's third novel with Harvest House, following up on her bestselling first and second books in The Miller Family series, *A Widow's Hope* and *Never Far from Home*.

www.maryeellis.wordpress.com